THE
JUMBEE

THE
JUMBEE
by Pamela Keyes

Dial Books · New York
an imprint of Penguin Group (USA) Inc.

DIAL BOOKS
An imprint of Penguin Group (USA) Inc.
Published by The Penguin Group
Penguin Group (USA) Inc., 375 Hudson Street, New York, NY 10014, U.S.A.

Penguin Group (Canada), 90 Eglinton Avenue East, Suite 700, Toronto, Ontario, Canada M4P 2Y3 (a division of Pearson Penguin Canada Inc.) • Penguin Books Ltd, 80 Strand, London WC2R 0RL, England • Penguin Ireland, 25 St. Stephen's Green, Dublin 2, Ireland (a division of Penguin Books Ltd) • Penguin Group (Australia), 250 Camberwell Road, Camberwell, Victoria 3124, Australia (a division of Pearson Australia Group Pty Ltd) • Penguin Books India Pvt Ltd, 11 Community Centre, Panchsheel Park, New Delhi - 110 017, India • Penguin Group (NZ), 67 Apollo Drive, Rosedale, North Shore 0632, New Zealand (a division of Pearson New Zealand Ltd) • Penguin Books (South Africa) (Pty) Ltd, 24 Sturdee Avenue, Rosebank, Johannesburg 2196, South Africa • Penguin Books Ltd, Registered Offices: 80 Strand, London WC2R 0RL, England

Designed by Nancy R. Leo-Kelly
Text set in Requiem
Printed in the U.S.A.
1 3 5 7 9 10 8 6 4 2

Library of Congress Cataloging-in-Publication Data
Keyes, Pamela.
The jumbee / by Pamela Keyes.
p.   cm.
Summary: Devastated by the death of her Shakespearean-actor father,
Esti Legard moves to a tropical island for her senior year in high school, where she
finds herself torn between a mysterious, masked mentor and a seductive island boy,
as she tries to escape the overpowering shadow of her famous father.
ISBN 978-0-8037-3313-8 (hardcover)
[1. Theater—Fiction. 2. Fathers—Fiction. 3. Shakespeare, William, 1564–1616—Fiction.
4. Actors and actresses—Fiction. 5. Superstition—Fiction. 6. Caribbean Area—Fiction.]
I. Title.
PZ7.K5262Ju 2010   [Fic]   dc22   2009040048

To Walt, the love of my life. I see you.

Acknowledgments

First and foremost, I would like to thank Rebecca Sherman for being the most patient and encouraging agent I ever could have hoped for, and Alisha Niehaus for being the best editor on the entire planet (and that's an understatement). Rebecca and Alisha, thank you both from the bottom of my heart! Thanks to my son and daughter, Zachary and Zia, who always keep my priorities in perspective. I cherish the support of my mom, Betty, and my sisters, Deb and Julie, who have been with me every step of the way. I can't possibly include all the friends who helped me, but I would especially like to thank Maaike Schotborgh, Susan Leader, and Ed Hoornaert, for your endless reading and critiquing and re-reading. Thanks to Dawn, Rose, Sandi, Frances, Kerri, Tiina, Gretchen, Sammy, and Doug for always believing in me. Thanks to Tracy and Carolyn for introducing me to *The Phantom,* and to Cassie and her parents Sally and Bob, for giving me personal insight into a Caribbean high school theater department. And finally . . . Walt, thank you for everything. ❧

THE
JUMBEE

Prologue

"Paul is dead!"

Esti's head jerked up at the wail from the old theater building. She jammed her books into her backpack and leaped to her feet. Heart pounding, she raced across the grassy courtyard, fumbling to close the zipper of her pack. In front of her, a girl stumbled from the building, catching herself against a palm tree.

Esti grabbed the main door before it could close. Two teachers knelt beside a boy on the stage, speaking in urgent voices. Other students shoved into the theater behind Esti, jostling her to get closer. As people crowded around, she fought a rising sense of panic. She recognized the clothes and the colorful knitted cap on the boy's head. Outside, someone yelled for an ambulance.

"I think he broke his neck," the theater teacher said in a shaky voice. "He must have fallen from the catwalk."

Esti clutched her pack against her chest and backed into the corner, following the teacher's gaze to the narrow metal bridge above the stage. It didn't look like enough of a fall to kill someone.

Not an omen, not an omen, she chanted desperately to herself. Asking to move to the Caribbean for her senior year surely wasn't a giant mistake; it was the most independent choice she'd ever made. Her father would have been proud of her. As a ceiling fan creaked in the shocked silence, relentlessly stirring the humid air, Esti felt the sharp coral pattern of the wall digging into her shoulders.

So what if Paul was the first boy she'd met at Manchicay High School? Half an hour ago he had appeared on the stage from nowhere, scaring the living daylights out of her. She was still trying to shrug it off as a silly "new girl" moment, but it no longer mattered. He was dead.

"Miss Legard, I understand you was the last one who speak with Paul."

Esti looked up at the strong West Indian dialect, startled by the deep brown eyes of a policeman. The police had shown up right away, then an ambulance. They had asked Esti not to leave the scene, although they moved her to the other side of the lush green courtyard. Now she sat on a carved stone bench at the edge of the school grounds as they stretched yellow tape across the theater entrance. She hadn't been able to watch when they carried Paul's body away on a gurney.

"I had try to call your mother," the policeman said, "but no one answer the phone. I need to ask you a few question."

"I don't know what happened." Esti picked at the belt loop of her faded jeans. She had called home several times, more frantic with each try, but Aurora wasn't answering. "I don't know anyone at Manchicay. It's my first day here."

"Yeah, miss." Although the officer's dark forehead dripped with sweat, his expression seemed kind enough. He sat down beside her, his arm remarkably black next to her pale freckled skin. "I ain't accusin' you." He spoke slowly, making sure she understood his words. "You teacher say you was in class today, and I know you come to Cariba Island just a week ago. But you was in the theater before he fall."

Esti didn't know if the sweat trickling down her neck was from the heat, or from the anxiety churning inside her. Tucking a stray wisp of brown hair back into her long ponytail, she managed a quick nod.

"Paul Wilmuth was my nephew." The policeman's eyes became sad. "My brother son. You's the last one talk to he, and I had like to know what he say."

Esti slumped on the bench, wishing she could disappear into the tranquil sea. As a distant splash sent ripples surging, however, she couldn't suppress a matching shiver. Sharks were probably hiding beneath the calm surface out there. She should tell Officer Wilmuth the truth, even if it wasn't what he wanted to hear.

After her classes she had gone into the empty theater to get a feel for the stage layout, determined to start the year off right. She'd been reciting Juliet's lines for almost twenty minutes, working herself into an unexpected reverie as the theater welcomed her with its nice acoustics. The knowledge of starting from scratch—making her own name in a new theater with a blank slate—filled her with a growing sense of joy. The very air around her seemed to radiate delight.

Then a boy appeared from behind one of the sets, laughing at her involuntary scream. "Scare ya, gal?"

He spoke with an accent so thick, she strained to understand him, his dreadlocks bundled beneath a tall, brightly knitted cap. Esti wasn't particularly short, but the cap made the boy look huge. Her heart thudded as he approached in his flamboyant island clothing, and she forced herself to stay calm. She was going to make friends with the other theater students this year. *This* time she wasn't going to blow it.

Before she could speak, however, he laughed again. "You got no chance at Juliet."

She felt her face turn red. How could six words, spoken by a boy she'd never met before, hurt so much?

"For true," he continued. "You best try something else."

She should have told him he had no right to cut her down. *You're the one in control, Esti,* her dad had always said. *No one but you.* The problem was, she'd never been as good at clever comebacks as her dad was. Not even onstage, where she could think the fastest. So she had shrugged and turned away, blinking back tears as the boy sauntered over to a long metal ladder. She knew he'd seen her slink away, his shoes ringing against the high metal floor of the catwalk as he moved above the stage. When she reached the main entrance, she could barely drag open the heavy door, muttering the words that now tied her stomach in a knot. "I hope you fall."

Esti forced herself to meet his uncle's eyes. "I didn't really talk to Paul. I hardly understood what he said."

The policeman nodded. "He had say something? Anything?"

Esti took a deep breath. "He told me I didn't have a chance of getting a part in the school play."

Officer Wilmuth frowned. "That don't sound like Paul."

She chewed on her lower lip, trying to calm the heat in her cheeks. Officer Wilmuth looked so forlorn. "Paul probably wasn't trying to be mean," she whispered. "My dad died a few months ago too. I'm so sorry for your loss. . . ." She clamped her mouth shut, knowing from experience the inadequacy of those words.

"All right, miss." Officer Wilmuth sighed and rose to his feet. "Good afternoon." A white-skinned policeman across the round courtyard was speaking to a slender black girl with solemn eyes. They both glanced at Esti for a moment, then resumed talking.

Esti turned away, staring bleakly over the low stone wall that surrounded the grassy hills of Manchicay School. Bougainvillea and honeysuckle framed a breathtaking view of islands and turquoise water fanning out from the beach below.

For a few minutes in the theater she'd been happy again. She was certain she hadn't imagined that part. It still crept around somewhere deep within her. She had to believe in the tiny flash of hope that sparked when her mom agreed to move to Cariba Island for Esti's last year of high school. At her dad's funeral, an old family friend had reminded them that he owned a house here. It was empty at the moment, Rodney Solomon said, within walking distance of Manchicay School.

Esti had jumped at the idea, but she'd felt cursed from the moment they arrived a week ago. She hadn't left her painful memories behind at all. The airlines had lost her luggage, including a big box packed with a bunch of clothes and her dad's last Shakespeare treatise, the one he had lovingly signed to her just before he died. Then she was sick for three days from something she'd eaten on the plane.

"Paul, he was wrong." The girl with the solemn eyes stood several feet away, her expression hard to read. "I had tell Paul's uncle you was the last one talk to he."

"You?" Esti asked, startled. She sat up straight, studying the girl's yellow T-shirt and matching head-wrap. "Do I know you?"

"Lucia. I come in with Ma while she clean this morning. We watch you practice."

"I didn't see anyone."

"You had not look."

Esti locked eyes with her. "Did you see Paul fall?"

"Nah, we was in the back when it happen." Lucia scowled, then gave Esti a piercing look. "You gotta try out for Juliet. 'Tis a good thing you do."

"A good thing?" Paul's last words still filled Esti with anxiety. She'd been through countless auditions in her life, each one overprepared, but this one was different. Her dad was no longer here to hold her hand. "A good thing," she repeated.

Lucia's lip curled with a cynical expression that seemed too old for her. "I will try out, also. Sometime Mr. Niles does let in freshmen. The jandam had tell Headmaster Fleming he close Manchicay School this week to respect Paul, since he pass. Next Monday you do Juliet, eh?"

Lucia waited until Esti nodded, then she turned and walked away.

Who was the jandam? Esti doubted she would ever understand the local customs, or why half the school had apparently been hiding in the theater this morning, watching her. All she'd wanted to do was to get a fresh feel for Juliet, to bring her favorite character alive again in this new place. Instead, she had left the building too embarrassed to even look at Paul, desperately longing—as usual—for her dad's reassurance.

With a pensive shake of her head, she started across the parking lot. Had she imagined the rich murmur as the theater door thudded to a close behind her? A ghost of Shakespeare emanating from the stone walls. *And right perfection wrongfully disgrac'd. . . .*

She had definitely imagined it. Maybe she was pulling a Hamlet and finally going crazy after her dad's death. Strangely enough, the idea brought a brief smile to her face.

Act One

Act One. Scene One.

Esti stood outside the screen door for a minute, letting the breeze dry her damp tank top as she recovered from the hot, muggy climb up Bayrum Hill. Sandalwood incense wafted out the door, her mom's chirpy voice singing *"what a long, strange trip it's been"* along with the Grateful Dead.

"Hey, sweetie." Aurora sat cross-legged on the floor, her hair pulled into a disheveled braid, while she finished unpacking. She was twenty years older than Esti, but she still looked like a hippie, with her bare feet, her swirling skirts, and dangling earrings. Esti couldn't remember ever really calling her "Mom."

"One of the airline guys found your suitcases in the freight area," Aurora said without looking up, "so I got them this morning. The only thing still missing is your box, but the woman I talked to promised they should have it by the end of the week. How was your day?"

Esti suppressed a fleeting urge to crawl into her mom's lap for reassurance. "I tried calling you all afternoon."

"I just got home a few minutes ago." Aurora finally looked at her. "What's the matter?"

As the story of Paul Wilmuth unfolded, Aurora slowly

rose to her feet, then led Esti out to the balcony with a glass of mango juice. When Esti finished talking, they both stared in silence at the nearest small island, lush green hills smoothing into long white stretches of sand. A single, rocky cliff reared up from the island on the northeast side, reaching toward Cariba. From the corner of her eye, Esti saw a lizard scramble up the wall beyond the balcony railing.

"That poor boy," Aurora finally said. "I wish the police had called me before talking to you. Are they sure it was an accident?"

"What else would it be?" Esti wiped her eyes.

"Your dad told me this might not be the best place for us to live."

Frowning at the lizard, intent on its single-minded pursuit of food, Esti wished her own needs were that simple. Her dad had discussed Manchicay School with Rodney several times, of course, finally concluding that Esti was better off in Ashland. *Safely hidden behind his overpowering presence,* she thought with a touch of resentment.

"I love Cariba," she said firmly to her mom, although she wasn't yet sure about that. "The police did call you, but you weren't here. I tried calling too." Hiding a sigh, she swirled mango juice around the inside of her glass. "I guess the answering machine isn't unpacked yet. We need cell phones that work here."

"You're right, we do. And I'll hook up the answering machine tonight." Aurora's fingers twitched, almost like she wanted to reach for Esti's hand. Instead she took a sip of her wine. "Did you say they're closing school for a whole week?"

Esti's eyes lingered on her mom's short-bitten fingernails. "That's what a girl—Lucia, I think—told me."

"I'm glad they respect the death of a student so much. I don't know if they would do that back in Ashland. Look, I'll give the police a call right now, then maybe we can go down to the beach for a while."

As her mom picked up her wineglass and went back in the house, a wave of sadness swept through Esti. She watched the dark strands of a distant rain column reach down to the sea from a puffball of white clouds. The sweet soprano of Sarah Brightman drifted across the balcony, muting Aurora's request to speak to Officer Wilmuth.

Esti turned to study her mom through the sliding screen door. Despite her strong facade, a hint of puffiness around her eyes suggested she'd been crying again.

"Inside? Anyone home?"

Esti jumped to her feet at the unfamiliar voice, hurrying in from the balcony as her mom looked toward the front door.

"I'll get it," she whispered, gesturing for her mom to take the phone in the other room.

A pretty girl in a white sundress stood on the step, her blond hair swept up into a precisely tousled knot, her fingernails and toenails perfectly lavender. She leaned against a dark-haired boy with deep brown eyes, his arms and legs as nicely tanned as hers.

"Esti Legard?" the girl asked.

"Yes?" Esti pushed away her sudden shyness. "Please, come in."

"I'm Danielle Graaf. You know, Gabrielle Simpson-Graaf's daughter? And this is Greg *Timmons*." Danielle's eyes swept Esti from top to bottom as she entered the house, taking in Esti's long tangled ponytail and sweaty tank top, the faded jeans and rubber flip-flops. "We didn't get a chance to meet after class today."

Esti kept the smile on her face, unsure how to react to the name-dropping. "I saw you in history this morning," she said, "but I had to run back to the office to find my science class."

"History is a freak show," Greg said with a chuckle. "Miss Rupert spent half the class talking about ghosts."

"On Cariba, that's all history seems to be sometimes," Danielle's smooth voice almost purred, in stark contrast to the interest in her blue eyes as she glanced around the living room. "Rodney Solomon told my mom you would be living here." She peeked through one of the two bedroom doors, then quickly turned back when she saw Aurora on the phone. "Everyone's talking about The Great Legard's daughter, of course."

"Uh—can I get you something to drink?" Shoving down a burst of confused emotions, Esti slipped into the perfect hostess role she had so often played for her dad. Danielle couldn't possibly know how her casual words sliced through Esti's hopes to separate herself from her past.

Esti followed them out to the balcony with a pitcher of mango juice and chilled glasses. Ice cubes rattled against each other as she set the pitcher on the glass-topped rattan table, and she firmly told herself she was happy they were here, no matter what their reasons. Her issues weren't their fault. She wanted to have friends on Cariba.

"Where are you guys from?" she asked.

"Greg's from New York," Danielle answered before Greg could speak. "His family's all over Broadway."

Greg gave Danielle a cynical smile, then turned so she wouldn't see the quick wink he shot at Esti. Esti pretended not to see as she carefully poured juice for each of them, wondering if Greg liked having a famous family.

"My mom met my dad on a movie set in Puerto Rico," Danielle continued, her eyes not missing a detail as Esti wiped a drop of spilled juice from the glass tabletop with the hem of her tank top. "He was born on Cariba, though, and so was I. I'm a local," she said pointedly.

"Hey," Greg interrupted, "did you hear what happened to Paul Wilmuth? I saw jandam everywhere when I left school."

"It was awful." Esti sank into the weathered cushion of her rattan chair. "Um . . . does jandam mean police?"

"Yeah. A butchered version of the French *gendarme*."

"It's not butchered," Danielle said. "The West Indian patois is a whole different language."

"What do you bet Miss Rupert thinks he'll be haunting the theater now?" Greg added. "Cariba's newest jumbee."

Esti tried to hide her dismay at Greg's cynicism.

17

"Don't disrespect Paul," Danielle said sharply. "You know that's not done around here."

"Sorry." Greg shrugged. "I'm not saying he's another Somand. Just trying to give Esti some of the local flavor. Some *useful* information."

Esti wrapped her hands around her icy glass, keeping her voice neutral. "I don't understand."

"Ghosts are called jumbees." Greg pointed out to the nearby island. "And that place is haunted by Manchicay's final slave owner, Elon Somand. Be very afraid."

"I'm changing the subject now," Danielle snapped before Esti could reply. "Esti, I assume you'll be at the auditions?"

"They're postponed for a week," Greg added, "in honor of Paul's jumbee." He shrugged at Danielle's expression. "Are you still worried about a Legard stealing your fame?"

"No." As Danielle's eyes narrowed, Esti abruptly understood the purpose of today's visit. Danielle was checking out the competition.

Suppressing her ever-present pang of anxiety, Esti took a deep breath. She understood about competition. She'd almost always gotten the lead back home, but she knew too well how much it had to do with her dad. She hadn't performed in over a year, and no one—not even Aurora—understood how urgently Esti needed to shine at next week's audition. Danielle's dismissal was unnerving, to say the least.

"I'm trying out for Juliet," she said. "I guess you are too."

Danielle leaned back in her chair. "It'll be interesting to see who Mr. Niles chooses."

Esti slowly nodded at the implicit battle line drawn between them. "Good luck," she said softly. "It might not be either one of us."

"Ha," Danielle actually laughed. "Right."

When the screen door rasped open, Esti spun around in relief. "Danielle and Greg," she said, "this is my mom, Aurora."

They both studied Aurora in surprise, apparently not expecting bare feet and a tie-dyed skirt. "Aurora and I are about to head down to the beach," Esti continued. "I want to learn how to swim."

"You don't know how to swim?" Danielle raised her perfectly shaped eyebrows. "Well, at least you're in the right place for *that*. The Solomons own a scuba diving shop. Maybe you can get lessons."

"Rodney said that Rafe might work there when he comes to visit at Christmas," Aurora said. "He could probably teach you."

Danielle gave Esti a piercing look. "I'm sure Rafe would *love* to give you lessons."

"I hope so." Esti lit up at the thought. She and Rodney's son had been best friends in elementary school, and she was looking forward to seeing him again. Startled by the growing scorn in Danielle's eyes, however, Esti turned away to look out at the nearby cay. "I was ten the last time I saw him," she added uncomfortably. "We might not even recognize each other now."

Act One. Scene Two.

Several people were already onstage when Esti walked into the theater a week later. Flat wooden panels on the exterior stone walls had been opened to let in a whispery breeze and outdoor light; ceiling fans stirred the humid air. She sat down in the back row, ignoring the catwalk over the stage. Her heart gave a nervous thud as she saw Danielle stride across the stage in crisp slacks and high heels.

"You trying out?"

Esti spun around.

A curvy Hispanic girl met her eyes, her hair braided into a thick rope down her back. "I'm Carmen," she said, flopping down in the seat beside Esti. "Who are you? I've never seen you here before."

"I'm Esti." Esti returned her smile, pleased that Carmen didn't already know.

"Misti?"

"*Esti.* Like the initials S.T."

Carmen grinned. "That's a cool name." She glanced up at the stage. "Can you believe what happened to Paul last week?"

Esti shook her head, wondering if Carmen had known Paul very well.

"I got back from Puerto Rico in time for his funeral yesterday," Carmen said morosely, "but I'm glad Niles is holding

20

the student memorial tomorrow. Paul had bit parts in all the plays since ninth grade. He was a nice guy." She continued as though she didn't expect a response. "And now Danielle's going first, as usual. Niles is so predictable."

The West Indian teacher sat in the middle of the front row, his curly black hair shaved close. Esti studied the back of his head as Danielle took center stage. Although she knew he'd been in some minor movies during the years he lived in the States, she didn't know anything about his teaching.

"Danielle is a good actress," Carmen added, "but talk about an ego. Even her own sister can't stand her."

Esti watched Danielle open her script, cradling the pages in her perfectly manicured fingers. They had gone from lavender to bloodred.

"I'm going to read the balcony monologue." Danielle's words reached into the far corners of the room, and Esti sat up straight, trying to ignore Carmen's soft chatter. Danielle projected beautifully.

"O Romeo, Romeo! Wherefore art thou Romeo?"

Esti whispered the words along with her. *Romeo and Juliet* had been the first play Esti ever memorized with her dad. Danielle apparently hadn't even learned her short part for the audition, but maybe Mr. Niles didn't require the same vigorous preparation that Alan Legard had always demanded.

"What part are you trying out for?" Carmen asked, breaking her concentration.

Esti felt her cheeks heat up.

"Juliet?" Carmen grinned in delight. "That's great. Too bad you don't stand a chance, because you sure have the right looks."

Esti was startled to hear Paul's words repeated by Carmen. "Why would you say that?"

"What I mean is," Carmen said, "your face is pretty and kind of pointy and serious-looking, like I always pictured Juliet. Well, except for your freckles. But Danielle rules this place. Honestly, give Lady Capulet a try. Lucia wants Lady Capulet, but we all know Niles won't give any real parts to a freshman."

With a shudder, Esti's eyes flew to the catwalk for a moment. Her self-esteem had been so touchy in the past couple of years—maybe Paul *hadn't* been making fun of her.

Mr. Niles shuffled some papers as Danielle came to the end of her soliloquy. "Who's next for Juliet? Esti Legard?" He glanced at the sign-up sheet, pronouncing her last name "Leg-guard."

LeGAR, Esti almost blurted out. *Don't tell me* you *haven't heard of him.* Then she hunched in her seat, ashamed. If Mr. Niles didn't recognize her dad's name, she might finally be judged on her own merits. Instead of the powerful thrill she'd always imagined, however, she felt only terror. Had she really believed she stood a chance on her own at a school like this, against someone as good as Danielle Graaf?

A low voice interrupted the silence. "Esti will try Juliet."

Lucia stood by the stage, her skinny arms folded over her chest. She gave Esti a brief, curious look.

"Come on, then," Mr. Niles said. "Esti—" He broke off and searched the theater with his eyes. When he finally found her at the back, he stared at her for a moment. "Legard." This time he pronounced the name right.

Still onstage, Danielle studied her with an inscrutable expression.

"Let's hear the balcony scene," Mr. Niles said.

When Carmen nudged her, Esti lurched to her feet. She tried to project confidence, but her sneakers boomed awkwardly against the hollow wooden steps.

Danielle sauntered into the wings beside a stocky redheaded boy. "Doesn't matter who she is," the boy whispered in an overly loud voice. "You already got the part."

Esti spun away from them and forced herself to center stage.

"Did you forget your script?" Mr. Niles asked.

"I know the scene." Esti focused on projecting without becoming shrill. "O Romeo, Romeo!"

She closed her eyes, pretending she stood in front of her dad in his comfortable mahogany office. That was a scene she had played a million times. "Wherefore art thou Romeo? Deny thy father and refuse thy name. Or, if thou wilt not, be but sworn my love and I'll no longer be a Capulet."

"Shall I hear more," a deep voice questioned softly into the air around her, "or shall I speak at this?"

Goose bumps traveled up Esti's arms, and her eyes flew

open. She couldn't see who had said Romeo's words so beautifully, but it didn't matter. She felt her tension twist and change into the hopeless frustration of Juliet. The rows of seats in front of her became a cluster of fruit trees on the Capulet estate.

"'Tis but thy name that is my enemy." She leaned against an imaginary wall, looking out in longing over the moonlit orchard. "Thou art thyself, though not a Montague. What's Montague? It is nor hand, nor foot, nor arm, nor face, nor any other part belonging to a man."

She had fully immersed herself in Juliet, eagerly offering her very soul to Romeo in exchange for his name, when Danielle shoved her back into reality.

"There you are, Greg," the blond girl cried out. "Steve tried to convince me you weren't coming today."

Esti looked around blankly, trying to remember where she was.

"Esti, your mouth is open." Danielle gave her an exaggerated look of apology, hurrying offstage with the redheaded boy. "Oops, sorry, Mr. Niles. I didn't mean to interrupt. I thought Esti was finished."

"Esti," Mr. Niles said thoughtfully, "please ignore Danielle and Steve. I'd like you to continue."

"I'm done," Esti said, a sense of disorientation warring with her frustration. She felt like she'd banged her head against the stone wall.

"You're trying out for Lady Capulet too, aren't you?" Carmen called up from the back.

Mr. Niles raised his eyebrows. "Lady Capulet?"

Esti slowly nodded.

He studied her for another moment. "Danielle," he called. "Get back up on the stage. Carmen, you might as well audition for Nurse right now, so come on. Let's start at the beginning of Act One, Scene Two, where Juliet's mother tells her to marry her cousin."

Carmen raced up the steps, clutching her tattered script. Behind her, Danielle sauntered back, looking pleased.

"Go ahead, Esti," Mr. Niles said.

As Carmen held out the script to her, Esti shook her head. "Thanks, but I know it."

She cringed at Carmen's expression, hoping they didn't think she was showing off. Mr. Niles now looked somewhat as if Esti had arrived from a different planet.

With a deep breath, Esti charged into the scene. "Nurse, where's my daughter? Call her forth to me." She spoke with as much maternal dignity as she could manage, but the magic of a moment ago had disappeared. She didn't want to play Lady Capulet. She *needed* Juliet, to find her passion for acting again. She could almost hear the thud of her flat dialogue dropping to the stage, underscored by a jaunty Nurse and desperate Juliet on either side of her.

When they finished, Danielle smiled sweetly at Esti. "Nice job. You know all the words."

Esti hid her embarrassment behind a stiff smile, giving Mr. Niles a brief nod. "Thank you for the opportunity to audition," she said automatically. Then, forcing herself to walk as regally as she could from the stage, she fled outside, wishing she had never heard of Manchicay School.

❧

"Are you okay?" Carmen asked in a cautious voice.

They sat on the stone bench at the edge of the courtyard. Esti gazed out over the sea, taking deep, calming breaths of the sweet-smelling spider lilies blooming beside her. She felt almost serene, now that it was over.

"I'm fine," Esti said. "Thanks for finding me. I shouldn't have run out of the auditions like that."

"I wondered what was going on. I mean, your Juliet floored all of us, even Danielle." She shook her head in amazement. "Then what happened?"

Esti had to smile at Carmen's expression. "Stage fright."

"No kidding! You're funny, Esti. Do you want me to tell you the cast list before we even see it?" Carmen's voice became a deep, mysterious drone. "I will now look into the future."

Esti laughed.

"Danielle is Juliet." Carmen gave her an apologetic glance. "Unfortunately, Niles is on a mission to launch a local Cariban—that would be Danielle, even if her skin is white as snow—to the stars. He's friends with her parents, you know, and he would be raked over the coals if he bumped her now. You'll get Lady Capulet, though, I guarantee it." She sighed.

"Greg is Romeo," she continued. "He moved here last year from New York, and he's awesome. He *is* kind of a jerk, but he'll land an agent, easy. Steve is Lord Capulet, I'm Nurse, and Chaz is Mercutio. We're all pretty good, if I do say so myself, even though all the boys are wrapped tight around Danielle's fingers. Too bad," she added mournfully, "'cause Chaz is awfully cute. But even if Danielle dominates, the scouts notice everyone."

"The scouts." Esti kicked her foot against the stone bench. The Late Great Legard's daughter was red-hot property. Mention his name, and—bing—Esti had any talent agent she wanted. The scouts were the reason she had come to Manchicay School, but if she couldn't get an agent on her own, she didn't want one.

"Don't tell me you don't know about the scouts!" Carmen studied her in amazement. "Seriously, you are such a rookie. Have you heard of Rodney Solomon?"

"Well, yes." Esti was suddenly embarrassed again. "I know Rodney."

"You *know* Rodney?" Carmen raised her eyebrows with a touch of sarcasm. "So you know he's a big-name talent broker. Every year he wines and dines a handful of talent scouts, and in exchange, they promise to sign on at least two of Manchicay's graduating seniors to select agencies in New York or Hollywood. That, my dear Lady Capulet, is why I'm in school here, instead of San Juan. I'm not going back to Puerto Rico when I graduate next year. I'm moving to Hollywood, and I'm going to be a movie star."

Esti couldn't help responding to Carmen's enthusiasm. She was a refreshing change from most of the theater people

Esti had known in Ashland. "I like you, Carmen. I think you're going to be good for me."

"We'll be good for each other," Carmen declared. "No negative thoughts allowed."

"Right." Esti sat up straight. "It's time for me to get over myself already. Your audition was great, and you'll get an agent, for sure."

Carmen grinned. "You have the whole play memorized, don't you? You must have played Juliet before."

Esti nodded reluctantly, knowing what was coming. "My dad started reading Shakespeare to me the day I was born."

"Really? Where are you from?"

"Oregon. I mean, Ashland, Oregon, is where I did a lot of acting with my dad. I was born in Los Angeles."

"So, your dad's an actor?"

"He died a few months ago." Esti still found it difficult to say the words. "He had cancer."

"I'm sorry." Carmen paused, her eyes suddenly wide. She spun on the bench, facing Esti with an incredulous look. "Alan Legard. Oh, my God. Your dad was Alan *Legard*."

Esti shrugged. It was inevitable.

"Esti Legard!" Carmen whooped. "I can't believe I'm such a slowpoke. I watched you play Juliet on public television a couple of years ago, when your dad played Lord Capulet. No *wonder* you're the Shakespeare queen."

Esti squirmed. All of the reviews, including every single comment about her own performance, had focused on her dad.

"What other roles did you have with him?" Carmen said eagerly. "It must have been incredible to be around The Great Legard all the time."

"It was." Esti nodded, unable to deny that her dad was incredible. "I acted with him a lot, but always in small theaters. *Romeo and Juliet* was my only major production." She paused. "It was kind of intense."

"I bet." Carmen studied her thoughtfully. "You're pretty low-key for such a hotshot name fame diva. Why aren't you hanging out with Danielle and Greg?"

"You said it yourself." Esti sighed, thinking about her classmates back in Ashland. Aurora had thought they were all so intimidated by The Great Legard that they never reached out to Esti, but no one ever seemed to consider the possibility that Esti might be overwhelmed by her dad, too. She'd always told herself it was easier to keep her distance from everyone. "Boo-hoo, poor Esti is too famous," she muttered. "Can I ask you a favor?"

"Sure." Carmen gave her an uncertain look.

"I'm so tired of being a—whatever you called it—name diva. I'm just a normal person, trying to be a good actress. Can you pretend my name is Jane Doe and you've never heard of my dad? I wish I'd thought of that before I moved here. It sounds awful, but it would make my life so much easier."

"I'll try." Carmen nodded. "That was rude of me, wasn't it? I didn't mean to insult you, and I'm sorry about your dad." She paused with an awkward smile. "Are you going to the student memorial for Paul?"

Esti slowly relaxed. "I think so." She flinched at the memory of being onstage with Paul, then abruptly remembered something else. "Does Mr. Niles use a sound system for prompting?"

"Not that I know of. Did you have that in Oregon?"

"No, it's just that Romeo sounded like he was right beside me during my Juliet audition."

"Romeo?"

"That deep voice during my balcony scene."

"I have no clue what you're talking about. Greg's the only guy I know with a sexy voice, and he wasn't anywhere near you." Carmen raised her eyebrows. "Do you usually hear voices when you're acting?"

Esti had to giggle. "Sure, all the time. Don't you?"

"Yeah, gal." Carmen smiled, rather sadly. "I heard that Paul's haunting the theater now, and his voice was pretty deep. Maybe his ghost was talking to you."

Esti thought about Paul's last words to her, trying to picture him as the rich voice of Romeo. Not a chance. When she shook her head, Carmen gave her an abashed look.

"Sorry, I'm being rude again. Just don't tell me you got the gift, like Lucia."

"The gift?"

"Second sight. Everyone's afraid of Lucia, because her mom talks to jumbees. Since her mom's the janitor here at Manchicay, Lucia gets free tuition." As Carmen crossed her forefingers to ward off evil, her voice took on an exaggerated West Indian accent. "You be careful, mon, or de jumbee come get you in de night. No one ever see you again."

"I've heard about jumbees." Esti laughed and shook her head. "But I don't believe in ghosts. Do you?"

"I don't think so. But you'd be surprised how many people do around here."

Esti was pretty certain she hadn't imagined Romeo's reply, or—she straightened in surprise—the murmured sonnet on her first day in the theater. The memory filled her with unexpected warmth. With a quick, startled smile, she moved the subject away from jumbees. "You're sure I'm Lady Capulet this semester?"

"Let's go see. Niles always posts it beside the stage."

"Won't the theater be locked by now?"

Carmen grinned. "No one on Cariba ever locks their doors."

Esti followed her new friend across the grass, suddenly hoping for the tiny part of Juliet's mother. It might be a nice change of pace. For once in her life, she could focus on being a real girl, and maybe she would even find a boyfriend. Yeah, Carmen was definitely good for her.

"I got everyone right!" Carmen heaved herself up to sit on the stage. "Evening rehearsals, as usual. I promise it will be the very last time I say this, but I can't believe I'll be acting with The Great Legard's daughter this year. I'm so excited."

She studied Esti's face, then shook her head. "Didn't you like your dad?"

"He was perfect." Esti perched on the edge of the stage,

pulling her legs up until she could wrap her arms tightly around them. "Absolutely, totally perfect. I miss him so much that sometimes I think part of me died too." Resting her chin on her knees, she contemplated the cast list above the stage. "But I'll never live up to his reputation."

"Don't talk like that." Carmen gave Esti a quick, unexpected hug. "We're both going to rock the talent scouts this year, Jane Doe. You just wait and see."

Act One. Scene Three.

"How did it go today?" Aurora came out through the sliding doors, juggling a wineglass and two boxes of takeout Chinese.

Esti jumped up to help her arrange things on the tiny balcony table. "I got the part of Lady Capulet, and I met a very cool Puerto Rican girl named Carmen. She's playing Nurse."

"Lady Capulet?" Aurora didn't hide her indignation. "Who got Juliet, then?"

"Danielle, the blond girl who was here the other day. I always suspected that Shakespeare didn't really envision my straight brown hair and flat chest."

"You know the actors were all men back then." Aurora sat down and took a sip of wine. "Juliet probably had to shave every morning."

Esti tried to laugh.

"I was so sure you'd be Juliet again," her mom said with a frown. "I can't believe they're making you play Juliet's mother."

"It's okay, Aurora. The other kids are really good."

"They'd better be."

Esti squirmed on her rattan chair, pretty sure the words were meant as a compliment. Aurora still seemed to harbor some reservations about Cariba, and Esti wasn't entirely certain what her mom expected from her.

Her dad had always expected perfection, of course. When Esti was younger, she'd always been eager to comply. She thought about how she had worshipped his private office in the middle of their house, warm and regal, with full-length windows overlooking Lithia Park. She hadn't been allowed in at all until she turned ten, but by the time she was a teenager, she spent most of her time there. The day she turned thirteen, she had devoted her entire birthday to making a collage of pictures for an upcoming acting seminar he had planned.

They worked side by side, she remembered, surrounded by cheerful lute music and the tap-tap-tap of the computer keyboard. Occasional bursts of cinnamon and honey swirled through the air, promising a yummy birthday *tarte* to follow Aurora's annual Elizabethan birthday dinner of *artichoak pye* and *spinnedge fritters.*

"Why don't you use the same handout you used last time?" Esti had asked her dad, stealing glances across the room as she arranged her ideas into words and images. His unruly black hair had needed a haircut, she remembered, his hazel eyes twinkling beneath the signature bushy eyebrows.

"Each seminar is different." He reached over to tousle her long hair. "This class is for kids your age, so they'll relate to your ideas. In fact, I'd like for you to come with me, if Aurora lets you miss a couple of days of school. I can't think of a better teacher than a girl who already knows what she's doing."

Esti barely remembered the pride she'd felt around her dad before she decided to jump headfirst into his world. Before he proved to her the brilliant, devastating perfection of his acting. Since the television performance, all Esti had accomplished was a lot of self-doubt. And after today, she was pretty sure Aurora must doubt her abilities as well.

"You know what Dad would say," she said, glancing back at her mom. "*It's fine that you didn't get Juliet this time; this is a chance to prove yourself in a different way.* He could always steal the show, even when he played a small role."

Aurora smiled. "You can too, sweetie. You know that."

"Thanks." Esti picked up a spoonful of fried rice, then put it back down again. She couldn't eat with this feeling of knives in her stomach. Only her dad had been honest with her—both supportive and ruthless—in a way she never doubted.

"Listen," she said, "after dinner I want to walk back down to the school. I'd like to see the theater again, without so many people around."

"That's a good idea. Do you mind if I stay here?" At Esti's nod, Aurora lifted her glass of wine. "I'm in the mood to feel sorry for myself."

"I'm feeling the same way." Esti's eyes were drawn to the nearby island, beautiful despite the eerie rumors. It was so hard to let go sometimes; no wonder people believed in ghosts.

❧

The high school campus had been renovated from a centuries-old sugarcane plantation. The theater was the biggest and most ornate building, with conch shells and coral worked into mosaics of rock and red brick. As she approached the old stone structures, Esti thought about the school brochures Rodney Solomon had given them before they moved here. While the glossy photos were stunning, they didn't capture the exquisite reality of seashell patterns fading in the twilight. Its peacefulness lifted her spirits until she recognized the two people sitting on the grass.

"Hi, Danielle," she said awkwardly. "Hi, Greg."

"Hey, Leg-guard."

Greg smiled at her just as Danielle demanded, "What are you doing here?"

"I wanted to come down and look around." Esti glanced at the fading silhouettes of islands in the sea. "It's pretty."

Danielle shrugged suspiciously. "Yeah, the campus is nice."

"Built on misery." Greg leaned back, his hands propped on the grass behind him. "Elon Somand was a brutal slave master."

"Don't even get started." Danielle whacked him on the shoulder.

"Danielle comes from slave owners, but her dad's ancestors were the *nice* kind, right? Not the ones who worked their slaves to death." Greg grinned. "It does get kind of spooky around here after dark. If you listen hard enough, you can hear the jumbees wailing."

Esti wondered if Greg was trying to scare her, or if this was some sort of subtle flirting. All she wanted was a few minutes of quiet meditation in the theater building, and maybe—she suppressed a sheepish smile—the unlikely chance to hear Romeo's voice again. Before she could think of an excuse to go inside, however, the theater door swung open.

A tall West Indian man walked out with Mr. Niles, breaking into a movie-star smile as he saw her. "Esti! How are you doing?"

"Hi, Rodney." She returned Rodney Solomon's hug. "Hi, Mr. Niles."

"Good evening, Mr. Solomon," Danielle said formally. "My mom didn't tell me you were back on the island."

He laughed. "I've had a lot of catching up to do. Esti, could you tell your mom I'll stop by tomorrow? Jayna wants me to make sure there are no problems with your house."

"The house is great," Esti assured him. "But I'll tell Aurora you're coming."

As the two men walked away, Danielle gracefully rose to her feet. "Come on, Greg," she said in an irritated voice. "My parents hate it when we're late for dinner."

With a sigh, Esti walked to the front of the theater. Although the wooden panels along the side walls were firmly shut, she was relieved to see that Mr. Niles had left the main doors unlocked. She groped along the rough wall for a minute, trying to remember where she'd seen rows of light switches. Finally she gave up and carefully made her way into the room, her peripheral vision slowly discerning the faint path of an aisle.

As her footsteps echoed in the room, she inhaled deeply, tasting the scent of damp stone and old wood, a hint of mothballed costumes and greasepaint lingering in the air. The smell of the dark theater reminded her of the old playhouse in Los Angeles, and she smiled.

No one in the world had existed in that playhouse except little Serene memorizing lines with her dad. He loved to recite Shakespeare with all the lights off, testing her memory and praising her efforts. Darkness was the best way to rehearse, he often said as she grew older, as it kept an actor honest. It also made sure she would never be afraid of the dark.

She sat on the edge of the stage, tapping her heels against the wood. She rarely thought of Serene Terra unless she was filling out official paperwork. Rafe Solomon had actually been the one who started calling her by her initials when she was in kindergarten. Even though she liked the hippy-chick name her mom had given her, it had been thrilling to have a different identity around Rafe.

With a sigh, she leaned back. Rafe had been so shy when he first moved to Los Angeles, she remembered; a lot of kids avoided him because he had a West Indian accent and the darkest skin in her high-priced neighborhood. Since Rodney worked with her dad, however, Esti and Rafe soon became friends. He would help with her math homework, then watch while she practiced her Shakespeare skits, cracking her up with silly comments, like *"What pencil have Hamlet use, mon? 2B or not 2B?"*

With his accent, he made the name Esti sound mysterious and grown-up, like one of Shakespeare's characters. Although he was a year older than she was, they quickly became inseparable. When her family moved away to Oregon a few years later, she decided to stop introducing herself as Serene. Esti had become her name.

"Serene, doff thy name," Esti said to the empty theater. Sighing again, she added wistfully, "And for that name which is no part of thee, take all myself."

"I take thee at thy word." Romeo's rich voice filled the stage.

Esti leaped to her feet, instantly forgetting about Rafe. "Who's there?"

"Call me but love, and I'll be new baptized." A hint of a smile colored his reply. "Henceforth I never will be Romeo."

His voice sent a delightful thrill along her spine. "What man art thou," she said before she could stop herself, "that thus bescreen'd in night so stumblest on my counsel?"

"By a name I know not how to tell thee who I am. But I'd like to know what Niles is thinking, to have Danielle play Juliet when he has such a rare opportunity in you."

She couldn't help the smile playing on her lips. "Okay, where are you?"

"On the stage, of course."

She twisted around, surprised at her difficulty in pinpointing his voice. She knew she should feel uneasy talking to a strange guy in the dark, but the warmth in his tone made the thought of fear seem ridiculous. "What are you doing here?"

"I watched the auditions today. I've rarely seen such a convincing Juliet as yours."

She cringed, knowing he must have seen the entire thing. "Uh . . . thanks for your help."

"Did I help?" he asked in bemusement, an intriguing accent touching his words.

"You helped with Juliet," she said, embarrassed. "My Lady Capulet was awful."

To her surprise, he burst into laughter. "Not many actresses are so honest. I admire what I'm seeing."

"It's pitch-black." Esti forced a light note into her voice, hoping she didn't sound as flustered as she felt. "You can't see a thing."

"Talent doesn't require visual cues, especially when speaking Shakespeare."

Suddenly shy at the unexpected compliments, Esti wrapped a long strand of hair around her finger. "That sounds like something my dad would say." *Except*, she thought, *my dad wouldn't have let Lady Capulet off so easily.* "He liked rehearsing in the dark because he could focus better."

"And what about you? Does the darkness help Esti Legard focus better?"

"It helped a lot when I practiced with him." She drew her brows together. "So, you know who I am. But who are you?"

"My name"—the voice hesitated—"is Alan."

"Like my dad?" Chaotic longing surged through her, and she wished she had turned on the lights when she walked in.

"Yes. I studied Legard's theories in school."

"Did you go to his acting seminars? He taught at a lot of different schools during his theater tours."

"Acting seminars," Alan repeated softly. "Yes."

"I usually helped him prepare for those." As Esti's heart gave an odd thump, she wondered if Alan had ever gotten any of the handouts she'd made. She barely controlled an urge to tell him every last detail about honeyed birthday tartes and lute music. *This is crazy,* she thought. *I have no idea who this guy is. Why would he care about lutes?* "So you met my dad?"

"I did have that great fortune," Alan said. "Shakespearean actors have rarely influenced American culture, but your father certainly did. His film presence was amazing."

"Mmm hmm." Esti instantly grew wary. Just one more fan, enthralled by the Great Legard's *presence*. She couldn't escape it.

But Alan's next words surprised her.

"I imagine it was difficult around your father," he added. "You're an exceptional actress in your own right, you know."

Esti sank back against the edge of the stage, her knees trembling as Alan drew out one of her deepest fears and effortlessly smoothed it away. Where *was* this guy who practically read her mind? His voice seemed close enough for her to touch him, but she could swear she was the only one on the dark stage. "Thou know'st the mask of night is on my face," she managed with a deep breath, "else would a maiden blush bepaint my cheek."

He burst into another delighted laugh. "I like you, Esti. I'm surprised you don't have a string of movies under your belt."

Her knees grew even weaker, and she took a deep breath. "My dad made sure I could audition for parts all over the Oregon Shakespeare Festival. And in my high school theater. Not to mention the occasional Renaissance Faire. He wanted me to have lots of acting opportunities."

"Mmm hmm." As Alan repeated her generic reply, she realized how spoiled she sounded.

"It's not like I didn't have a blast doing it," she quickly added. "People loved it when we showed up in theaters all over the country with very little warning. I just haven't done any acting since . . ." She shoved away the memories of her last performance with her dad. "Since before he died."

"His death was a terrible blow." She barely heard Alan's soft words.

Relief swept through her at the chance to really talk about the loss of her father—a topic she still didn't dare bring up with Aurora—followed by unexpected fury at yet another stranger pretending to understand. "Yes, it was," she muttered. "I've got an entire notebook of tabloid memorials from people who barely knew him."

For a moment Alan didn't speak. "I'm sorry," he finally whispered. "No one could imagine what it must be like for you."

"No, I'm sorry." She took a slow, controlled breath at his genuine sorrow. "Thank you for saying that."

"I wish I could help." She almost didn't hear him.

"You are helping." As she said the words, she was surprised to realize how true they were. She stared into the darkness, feeling like she could pour out all her anger and hopes and fears, and this stranger *would* somehow understand. "I'm glad so many people respected my dad."

"Yes." Alan paused. "And I'm glad you're here."

A weird, tingling sense of hope began to grow inside her at his uncanny ability to follow her mood.

"Who are you?" She casually kicked her foot against the stage. "Are you in the play?"

"I'm not a student," he said.

"So you teach with Mr. Niles?" she continued.

"I'm not a teacher here either. I am merely an actor, like you."

"Oh, I wouldn't use the word *merely*." Esti suppressed a laugh. She felt a sudden giddy empathy for Juliet on the balcony, falling so quickly for a voice in the dark. "I don't remember my dad talking about any young actors named Alan. What's your last name?"

"What's in a name? That which we call a rose, by any other name would smell as sweet."

This time she couldn't help giggling. "Don't distract me,

Romeo. Tell me you're not one of those jumbees I've been hearing about."

Soft laughter brushed her like the caress of a silk scarf, and her skin jumped in response. For the first time since she was a child, her easy comfort in the darkness wavered. Rubbing her arms, she rose to her feet.

"I'd better turn on the lights."

"As you wish."

"I don't believe in jumbees." She felt her way back along the aisle with a calm, measured stride. She *knew* she'd seen light switches somewhere beside the main doors.

"Wise of you."

Despite her unease, she couldn't help smiling again as his amused voice followed her up the aisle. Even her dad would have been impressed by Alan's perfect projection.

"What I want to know," she said, "is how I heard you this afternoon, when no one else seemed to."

"Magic."

She snorted. "You're enjoying this, aren't you?"

"Immensely."

"How old are you?"

"Twenty-five."

Esti felt an odd satisfaction at his answer. Boys her own age seemed unable to see past the fact that she was The Great Legard's daughter, but Alan didn't seem intimidated. "What does Mr. Niles think about your prompting work?"

This time, however, Alan didn't answer.

Esti half turned to face the dark stage, her smile fading. "Did Mr. Niles know you were here?"

"This evening has been my greatest pleasure, but I must leave." Alan's formality suddenly returned. "Please don't mention me to anyone."

"I . . . why not?" She quickly swept her hand along the rough wall beside her.

"I wish . . ." He trailed off, his voice wavering. "I think it was a mistake to talk to you."

"No, it wasn't." She felt the truth of her reply all the way down to her toes. As she finally found the switch, light enveloped the theater in a comforting glow.

She studied the empty stage for a moment. "Alan?" she said uncertainly.

A chill crept over her as the silence lengthened, not broken by even the sound of departing footsteps. Although Alan's voice still played in her head like fine music, she was very clearly alone.

Act One. Scene Four.

"Trade winds have always been a dominant influence in the West Indies"—Mr. Larsen drew another chalk line on the board—"blowing northeast from the coast of Africa. They are the driving force behind our hurricanes, which are typically born far away in the Sahara desert."

Ignoring the rhythmic thump of a foot against the back of her chair, Esti scribbled a couple of notes. She wasn't about to turn around and look, even though Danielle's friend Steve seemed to have a new focus in life: making Esti Legard miserable. In the three weeks since classes started, he was doing a pretty good job.

"It's easy to think of a hurricane as a kind of monster," Mr. Larsen said. "A tropical storm requires food in the form of warm, moist air, and optimal wind. If it finds enough of this food, it will build energy and grow as it moves across the ocean. Trade winds form these optimal conditions, occasionally turning the tempest into a giant monster within a couple of days, or sometimes even a few hours."

A monster tempest? Cariba Island seemed to be a haven for strange Shakespearean creatures. With a sigh, Esti studied the blackboard. She wished Mr. Niles had chosen *The Tempest* instead of *Romeo and Juliet.* No matter how she tried, she just couldn't immerse herself in Lady Capulet. She'd been counting on some kind of magical Manchicay motivation to bring her passion back. If not Juliet, then—perhaps—a voice named Alan. But he hadn't returned since the night of her audition. A mythical creature indeed.

When class was over, she headed to the parking lot to wait for Carmen. They were walking downtown together for some magic chocolate chip cookie ingredients that would absolutely, Carmen insisted, help Aurora feel better about life.

"Jane Doe," Carmen called out. "Don't you have any jeans without holes in the knees?"

"More ventilation this way. It's hot here in the tropics." Reaching up, Esti twisted her hair into a knot, jamming a pencil through it to keep it in place on top of her head. "I'm even ready to cut my hair, but Aurora would kill me."

"Wear shorts like the rest of us," Carmen said. "You need a tan. How were your classes?"

Esti rolled her eyes. "I'll never be a science major. I like history, but psychology is a waste of time. Did you ace your math quiz?"

"Failing algebra," Carmen said with a sigh. "No question about it."

As they walked down the steep road from Manchicay School to Manchicay Bay, Carmen happily complained about math and language arts. They had just reached the grocery store when she paused and pointed down a nearby street.

"Danielle's mom," she whispered, "over at that restaurant balcony beside Mr. Niles. That's Danielle's younger sister with them."

Esti knew what Gabrielle Simpson-Graaf looked like from the movies, but this was the first time she had seen Danielle's mother on Cariba. The glamorous actress laughed and chatted with Mr. Niles. Beside them, a morose girl hid behind a curtain of black hair, sipping a soda and scowling at an incoming ferry.

"I can't imagine having Danielle for a sister," Carmen

said. "That has to be why Marielle got tangled up with a boy like Rafe."

"Rafe Solomon?" Esti straightened in surprise.

Carmen snickered. "You've already heard of him?"

"Kind of." Esti shook her head, remembering Danielle's scorn. "Tell me."

"Just that he's been embarrassing the Solomon family since he was old enough to talk back to the jandam. That's why his mom sent him to school in L.A." Carmen abruptly stopped, her mouth open. "Your dads probably knew each other. Don't tell me you're friends with him."

"When I was little." Esti shrugged uncomfortably. "I haven't seen him since fourth grade."

"Oh, that's rich!" Carmen burst into laughter. "I love discovering these little things about Jane Doe. No wonder Danielle is so jealous of you."

"Danielle likes Rafe?" Esti glanced back up at Danielle's sister.

"All the girls *like* him. He's gorgeous, and he knows all the right things to say. That's the problem. My mama would kill me if she ever caught me alone with him, although I gotta admit I've thought about it." Carmen grinned. "I mean, who hasn't? He caused a big scandal last Christmas when Marielle's dad came home and found him and Marielle . . . well, you know. I mean, she wasn't even sixteen at the time. If he finds out you're not dating anyone, I can guarantee he'll be all over you as soon as he gets here."

"Yikes." Esti watched the dark-haired girl with a mixture

of interest and disappointment. She'd been looking forward to seeing Rafe again, but now she wasn't so sure. If he was just another cocksure guy, she didn't want anything to do with him. But she couldn't imagine shy, devoted Rafe turning into someone like Greg.

"I've never met Marielle," Esti said. "I haven't even talked to Danielle since the day of auditions. Apparently I'm invisible now."

"Huh." Carmen snorted. "It's all a bunch of stupid theater politics. What do you bet Mr. Niles promised the Graafs that Danielle will outshine the star-studded competition, no matter what?"

"Whatever." Esti studied the trio on the balcony, still thinking about Rafe. "Nurse does a much better job than Juliet. It won't be Danielle who scoops up the agents this year; it will be you."

"Ooh, pile it on." Carmen's dark eyes sparkled. "Don't tell Aurora, but I'm giving you the biggest cookie this afternoon."

❧

"It's weird," Esti whispered that evening, staring at the stage. "Danielle keeps overacting, and Greg seems totally bored. Am I right?"

"The thing is, I've seen them both do better. I guess Greg is taking his cues from Danielle." Carmen shook her head. "She wasn't so self-conscious last year. I honestly think you make her nervous."

Esti sensed more than a grain of truth in Carmen's words,

but she knew Danielle had nothing to worry about. For a single sweet moment during auditions, Esti had almost believed it could happen, that a wisp of true talent still lived inside of her. If she had gotten Juliet, perhaps her passion for acting would have returned. Maybe Alan would have been interested enough to return as well.

She rubbed her temples. What good was an actress who couldn't mold herself to any role required of her? Esti had stayed after practice almost every night to work on Lady Capulet, but she was completely unmotivated. She couldn't blame her mysterious Romeo voice for not coming back. Alan Legard had loved cameos, effortlessly ruling the stage with a mere handful of lines. *A Legard by any other name,* Esti thought, *might as well give up.*

Onstage, Romeo and the Montagues were talking about crashing Juliet's party, and Esti took a determined breath. She had to concentrate on the play. Analyze the plot. Bring the characters to life. Find a reason to care about Lady Capulet.

"Romeo was a gang member," she said to Carmen. "He needed to act bored and cynical around his friends, right?"

"Yeah, and Juliet was always on her period."

"Shhhh!" Esti tried not to laugh.

"What would The Great Legard say?"

"The Great Legard." A whiny voice repeated Carmen's words. "Wherefore art thou, oh Great Legard?"

Carmen glared at the redheaded boy sauntering past them. "I sure hope one of the teachers catches Steve smoking his *ganja*," she muttered as soon as he was gone. "All he's done is cause trouble since he got here last semester, and he is *so* replaceable as Lord Capulet."

Esti couldn't answer. The Great Legard would be watching his own daughter in bewilderment right now, so easily replaceable as Lord Capulet's wife.

"Chaz," Mr. Niles called up to the stage, "roll your eyes while Greg is talking. Mercutio never takes his friends seriously, not even when Romeo predicts his own death. Okay, Romeo, go ahead."

"My mind misgives some consequence, yet hanging in the stars," Greg began, following his friends to Juliet's fateful party.

"I get why Niles has to focus on key scenes," Carmen said. "But I wish he'd give the whole cast more time. The Christmas show isn't that far away and you've had—what—a total of thirty seconds on stage? And I've only been up there twice. Maybe Danielle will break her leg on opening night."

"Carmen!"

"I mean that completely as a good luck thing, of course."

Esti hid a grin behind her hands. "Romeo is such a shallow character, I'm not surprised by Greg's apathy. Romeo *needs* a great Juliet in order to shine."

"Romeo's the hottest guy Shakespeare ever invented." Carmen sounded indignant.

"Romeo's a fickle poet who happens to look hot." Esti thought about what her dad had always said. "He goes suicidal over every pretty girl he sees. The minute Juliet smiles at him, he forgets his last girl and does everything he can to get into Juliet's pants."

Carmen's snort of laughter was so loud that Mr. Niles turned and raised his eyebrows. As he turned away again, she closed her eyes and placed a hand over her heart. "You've ruined Romeo for me," she whispered in a broken voice. "I'll never fall in love again."

Esti smiled, swinging her leg back and forth under her chair. Her dad had delved tirelessly into Shakespeare and his characters. They would spend hours at the dinner table discussing the tragic childhood of Richard III, the witty strength of Rosalind, Shakespeare's own scandalous love life. Esti had treasured those times with her dad, even at the very end. Especially at the end.

"Besides," Carmen continued, "Juliet didn't wear pants. She was a naive idiot."

"Juliet starts out naive, but she's smart." Esti was still smiling, remembering the expression on her dad's face as she worked this one out for herself when she was ten. "She sees through Romeo's beautiful words and makes him do the right thing. Romeo is the idealist, but Juliet's the brain, which is even more tragic by the end."

"Speaking of tragic, remember that Romeo voice you told me about?"

Esti forced herself to keep smiling, even though she'd almost decided that Alan had to be a Freudian figment of her poor-little-Esti imagination. *Please don't mention me to anyone.* Right. A girl losing it was just that—a girl losing it.

"No," she heard herself say to Carmen. "What voice?"

"You know!" Carmen gave her an impatient look. "You told me you heard a sexy voice prompting you during your audition."

"Oh." Esti gave a dismissive wave. "I'd forgotten about it."

"Well, rumors are flying about a real jumbee in the theater. Chaz overheard Mr. Niles talking to Headmaster Fleming about finding some furniture rearranged, then Chaz said that *he* actually heard strange noises from inside the walls. I dare you to stay with me after rehearsal tonight to try and hear the voice again." Carmen raised her eyebrows with a devious grin. "We can pull a Hamlet and see if the ghost comes back. I still have some chocolate chip cookies we could use as a lure."

Before Esti could respond, Steve's head appeared between Esti's and Carmen's.

"Esti talks to sexy jumbees?" He grinned widely.

"Get away from us, Stoner," Carmen snapped. "Sexy is a concept totally beyond you."

Steve laughed, flopping back into the seat behind them. With a huff, Carmen stood up, motioning for Esti to follow.

Of course Steve would play up the gossip for all it was worth, Esti thought morosely. Now Alan would never come back.

After rehearsal, Carmen walked Esti to the bottom of Bayrum Hill, still joking about Hamlet. Esti stood in indecision as she watched her friend disappear in the direction of her own house. Sea-scented trade winds gently rustled the palm trees, tickling Esti's hair against her face and muting the faint sound of waves on the beach below.

She didn't want to go back up Bayrum Hill yet. As soon as she reached the house, her mom would know something was wrong. Esti was afraid to explain her delusions of Romeo, her lame rehearsals, or her difficult classmates. What if Aurora decided that Cariba had been a big mistake all along?

Imagining a sudden low moan in the breeze, Esti spun around and strode back to the old building. She quickly felt her way down the dark aisle and perched on the edge of the stage, hoping she wouldn't lose her nerve. Her pathetic acting obviously hadn't brought Alan back out of the shadows, so it was time to be more direct.

"Alan, are you here?" she said loudly. "I need you."

"You *need* me?"

She jumped at Alan's astonished reply, a bizarre range of emotions flooding her. She wanted to laugh and cry and scream while simultaneously leaping to her feet and demanding to know where he—or to be precise, his voice—had been all this time.

Instead, she dug her fingernails into her knees, overcome with shyness. She willed her heart to slow down enough that she might at least *sound* somewhat calm and rational.

"I'm thinking about quitting the play," she said, "and moving back to Oregon."

"No!" He cleared his throat as if his own spontaneous

outburst embarrassed him, then added more softly, "Why in the world would you do that?"

His reaction warmed her all the way to her core. After a moment, however, she shook her head. "Now that my dad's gone, the whole thing seems pointless. Would you tell me something?"

"What?" He sounded cautious.

"Am I wasting my time? I want you to be honest with me. Tell me I should just quit."

"Esti, you can't quit." The shock in his voice turned into determination. "Not when you've come so far, and you have so much potential."

"What potential?" Esti threw her hands up in the air. "That sounds lovely, but Mr. Niles has let me on stage exactly once."

"Has it occurred to you that Danielle needs more help than you do? That she has a tendency to overact when she's nervous?"

Esti opened her mouth in surprise, goose bumps covering her skin. "Were you eavesdropping?"

"Not really." He sounded embarrassed. "It's just that some seats are in the right place. . . ."

Esti wondered where he'd been hiding. Beneath the stage, or behind one of the walls? Maybe floating in the air, invisible to all mortal beings?

"Never mind," she said. "The thing is, I thought Manchicay would be good for me, but my so-called potential has shriveled up and blown away."

"It hasn't. I've been listening to you practice here in the evenings."

"You were here all along." She rubbed her hands together, embarrassed. "Why didn't you say anything. Is it because my Lady Capulet stinks?"

"I wanted to speak, believe me. I thought about it, but . . ." He took a long, deep breath. "I never knew you might bring me cookies."

"You *were* eavesdropping." Oddly, his tone actually made her wish she'd swiped one of the cookies for him. "Carmen thinks cookies are the cure for all the world's problems. Even . . ." Esti hesitated. "Even to lure a ghost from the darkness."

A long silence followed her words. "There is no darkness but ignorance," he finally said.

She drew her brows together, wondering if she was imagining his sadness. "My dad insisted that rehearsing in the dark kept him honest."

"Did he say that?" Alan sounded startled. After a moment, he added, "To seek the light of truth, while truth the while doth falsely blind the eyesight of his look."

A thrill of exuberance stabbed through Esti. "Light, seeking light," she replied, "doth light of light beguile; So ere you find where light in darkness lies."

Alan burst into laughter. "Beautiful."

She closed her eyes, overwhelmed by a deep contentment she hadn't felt in a long time. "I could get used to this."

"Yes." Alan sounded happy too. "I *am* curious why you never turn on the lights when you're here alone."

"Practicing in the dark is what I did when I was younger." She picked at the frayed hole in the knee of her jeans, still smiling. "My dad told me his movies made him lazy on the stage. Theater needs perfect delivery, since you can't rely on a close-up to create the mood. Gestures aren't any good if your words don't hold the audience. He always said that darkness would teach me to control my voice better."

"You have wonderful control over your voice."

"Well, thank you," Esti said, suddenly glum again. "Or maybe I used to. I just can't find the enthusiasm for it any more. What's to control, with Lady Capulet?"

"Since Juliet is one of Shakespeare's most capable female characters," Alan said, "the role of her mother is vital. Lady Capulet is totally subservient to her husband, yet she produced a daughter with Juliet's strength. How?"

Esti almost smiled. This was the kind of question no one had asked since her dad died. "It wasn't because of a strong mother-daughter relationship, that's for sure."

"Could you use that?"

"Maybe." Esti felt a stirring of interest. "Maybe I could build on Lady Capulet's lack of interest in her daughter, and how she forces Juliet into impossible decisions. She'll be mean and scary, instead of indifferent and shallow."

"Exactly!" Alan laughed. "I knew I was right about you. If anyone can turn Lady Capulet into a complex character, it's Esti Legard."

"You keep flattering me." She stared into the darkness, overwhelmed. "But I like it," she added softly.

He was quiet for a moment. "Esti, I want to know more about you. What is it about acting that you love so much? Are you hoping for fame?"

Esti felt a tremble deep inside her body as she realized that no one had ever asked *why* she wanted to be an actress. Everyone, even her father, had just assumed she would follow in The Great Legard's footsteps.

"I already have fame through my dad." Her words felt tentative, like she was exploring a new side of herself. "Quite honestly, I hate that part. What I love is hearing the magical prose, and the escape in being a different person in a different time. Right now," she added shyly, "what I love is talking to you. You remind me how important it is to *feel* the words."

"Mmm." Alan sounded pleased. "Is that why you called to me this evening?"

"I have forgot why I did call thee back." Juliet's words left her mouth before she could stop them.

"Let me stand here till thou remember it." Romeo's soft reply sent shivers through her body.

"I shall forget," she whispered, "to have thee still stand there, remembering how I love thy company."

"And I'll still stay, to have thee still forget—" He abruptly broke off.

Esti was glad he couldn't see the blush heating her face in the darkness. "It helps," she said rapidly, "talking to someone who understands."

"Yes, it does."

The pause that settled between them held a raw comfort. Esti yearned to nestle in it, to deepen her ties to this mysterious Romeo.

Alan spoke again before she could ask, his voice growing formal. "Might you be interested in occasionally getting together after rehearsals? Perhaps early next week?"

"Of course." She shoved down a flash of joy, forcing herself to sound casual. "I would love that."

"I would, also." His quiet words betrayed a happiness so like her own that Esti couldn't stop herself.

"Please," she said, reaching out in the darkness. "Tell me you aren't just a voice."

"Parting is such sweet sorrow." His words fell through the humid air with a painful thud, and she suddenly knew he was gone.

"Alan, wait!" She pressed her trembling fingers together to keep them steady. Only silence wafted across the stage in reply, Alan's strange presence as fleeting as a tropical breeze.

Act One. Scene Five.

"The Caribbean has always been a difficult part of the world."

Esti wrote as fast as she could, trying to keep up with the history teacher's brisk voice while she tuned out Steve's low chatter. She couldn't concentrate after last night, and seeing Danielle from the corner of her eye did nothing to calm her nerves.

"Despite the ferocity and cannibalism of the native Caribs, they were destroyed by Spanish explorers," Miss Rupert continued. "After Denmark conquered the island, Cariba became a patchwork of sugarcane fields worked by African slaves. The slaves had to provide their own food, often eating raw crabs or lizards for protein."

"Wherefore art thou, raw crab?" Steve's voice whispered.

Esti tightened her jaw.

"Slave ships brought nearly ten million of my ancestors to the West Indies. Most of them died a brutal death on the sugar plantations." Miss Rupert's dark eyes flicked around the room. "Do you think that's funny, Mr. Jackson?"

"No, it's horrible." Steve straightened so quickly that his pen clattered to the floor.

Danielle choked back a snicker.

With a deep sigh, Miss Rupert glanced at her watch. "Who can tell me about Elon Somand?"

"He was the last owner of Manchicay Plantation before it was abandoned," Greg said. "His own slaves killed him on the day slavery was abolished."

"See, that's what I'm talking about," Steve chimed in. "He was barely older than we are, yet he brutally murdered most of his slaves before they finally took him down. The infamous Manchicay Massacre. Horrible, I tell you. Horrible."

"His jumbee lives on Manchineel Cay." Greg glanced at Esti

in amusement. "That's where those weird drumbeats come from, and the eerie screams in the middle of the night."

Esti was certain she had never heard drumbeats from Manchineel Cay. Maybe an occasional odd whisper in the wind, but screams?

"Yes," Danielle broke in, "and I've heard he's haunting the theater building now." She smiled at Esti. "He has a very, um . . . compelling voice."

Esti forced herself to smile back as the bell rang, praying the others didn't know anything beyond Steve's stupid taunting. Perhaps after Esti had practiced with Alan for a few weeks, Danielle would have an actual reason to feel threatened. *If* Alan showed up again. Forcing the doubts from her mind, Esti shoved her notebook into her backpack and rose to her feet along with the rest of the class.

"Is that why Manchineel Cay's beaches are covered in warning signs?" Steve asked as he followed Greg and Danielle out of the classroom. "I've been wondering ever since I got here."

"That's right," Danielle's voice answered briskly from outside. "No one has ever lived on Manchineel Cay. Set foot on the island, and you're never seen again."

"Why doesn't the jandam go out there and do something?"

Danielle laughed. "Are you kidding? The jandam won't touch anything having to do with jumbees."

"And here we have Miss Talks-to-Jumbees herself," Steve announced.

Esti braced herself as she stepped outside. To her surprise, however, Steve was walking beside Lucia Harris, matching her skinny, long-legged stride with an exaggerated gait of his own.

"Leave her alone," Esti snapped without thinking. "She's a freshman." She stopped beside Lucia, her head throbbing at the sneer on Steve's face. For a moment she and Lucia stood side by side, staring at him.

"Ooh," he finally said, "jumbee girls stick together, huh?"

Esti had no idea how to answer, and beside her, Lucia remained silent. When Steve finally rolled his eyes, Esti forced herself away, feeling her classmates' eyes boring into the back of her tank top. Lucia immediately fell into step beside her.

"Steve he is a pot head," Lucia said quietly. "And Danielle a spoil bitch."

Esti let out a soft burst of laughter. Although she'd noticed Lucia in the wings each night at rehearsal, everyone usually forgot about her. She rarely spoke to anyone as she studied the script and sketched out designs for the sets.

Esti wasn't sure what to say, but after a moment she cleared her throat. "I'm sorry I took the part of Lady Capulet away from you. I know you wanted—I mean, Carmen told me you wanted it."

Lucia shrugged. "You had try a good Juliet. 'Tis not you fault when Mr. Niles do a favor for he friend them." The tone of her voice told Esti that they both must accept the inevitable.

"Uh . . .Thank you." Esti watched Lucia from the corner of her eye as they silently walked to the parking lot. A single dreadlock escaped from the neck of the blue denim head-wrap that matched her baggy jeans. She was already taller than Esti, with the skinny awkwardness Esti remembered from her own freshman year. Yet, somehow Lucia almost seemed older than most seniors. Before Esti could figure out what else to say, she heard her mom's voice.

"Esti!" Aurora waved from the car.

Lucia walked away as if she and Esti had never spoken, climbing into the back of a rusty blue pickup without looking around. Frowning uncertainly, Esti watched the truck drive away.

Her frown deepened as she sprinted across the parking lot toward her mom. She always walked home, so her mom had no reason to be here. As Esti drew closer to the car, she skidded to a stop. "Aurora," she gasped, "are you okay?"

The sedan's right front was deeply dented, its crumpled bumper pressing against the partially buckled hood.

"I'm fine." Her mom gave her a wry look. "I forgot to drive on the left side of the road, coming home from my interview. Fortunately, the car still runs."

Whistling softly, Esti studied the damage. "Did someone hit you?"

"Head-on with a safari cab. I didn't swerve fast enough. The cops acted like I killed someone, even though the taxi barely got a scratch. I was only going about five miles an hour when we hit. But I need to get some groceries, so I thought I might as well pick you up."

Esti got into the passenger side, studying her mom in concern. "What about the job?"

"They didn't hire me." Aurora pulled out of the parking lot, carefully keeping left.

Esti looked out the window, hiding her concern. All Aurora talked about lately was finding something to get herself out of the house, but it had taken days for her to work up the motivation to get this job interview. "Do you have any other interviews coming up?"

"I don't really want to work in a tourist shop," Aurora said flatly. "It's not like we need the money; I just need a life."

At the bottom of the hill, she turned into a one-way street lined with restaurants and shops. Smoke wafted along the street, filling the air with the scent of barbeque as a group of laughing tourists stumbled out of a restaurant carrying drinks.

"Maybe I'll try my hand at waitressing," she said. "I know you had a good time at practice last night. How was school for you today?"

"History is good," Esti said, watching a rooster strut across the road in front of them. The cocky bird reminded her of Steve. "Some of the kids are jerks, but I like Miss Rupert." She had felt so much better after talking to Alan last night that she hadn't told her mom she was spending most of her time in rehearsals twiddling her thumbs. Esti didn't want Aurora worrying about something she had no control over, like a disappointing theater teacher.

Or—Esti suppressed a wave of anticipation—a secret new friend.

"I'll bet local history *is* interesting." Aurora's earring caught the sunlight as she glanced at Esti. "It might be fun for me to see your rehearsals now and then, if it's not an intrusion."

"You never intrude." Despite her words, Esti's fingers tightened around the seat belt. "Uh, the problem is that Mr. Niles isn't working on any of my scenes right now."

"Later in the semester, then." Aurora almost sounded relieved that the pressure was off. "Or I can just wait for the Christmas show. Let me know, okay? I'm a little worried about you."

"I'm fine. Things at school are great." Esti leaned back into her seat, contemplating her own relief mixed with guilt. What was she supposed to tell her borderline-depressed mom anyway? *Don't worry about me. Starting next Monday, I'll be spending my extra time alone with an awesome guy I've never seen. Apparently in the dark.*

❧

"Leg-guard, c'mere."

Esti heaved her backpack over her sweaty shoulder, ignoring Greg as she walked toward the theater building. It had been less than a week since Alan promised he would practice with her this evening, but it seemed like years ago. It was all she could think about.

"What's the rush?" He stepped in front of her, blocking her way.

"Niles is looking for you." Danielle came around from

behind, twining her arm through Greg's. "You're busted for missing rehearsal on Friday without permission."

Esti shrugged and kept walking. Carmen had left school early last Friday to spend a long weekend with her family in Puerto Rico, and Esti had decided she couldn't face the others by herself at rehearsal, even if Alan *was* watching from somewhere in the wings. Instead, she had gone down to the beach that evening, longing for her dad's advice as she paced back and forth in the warm October breeze.

She'd stared out at the dark sea with aching eyes, almost hearing a wail in the trade winds to match her mood. The Great Legard had been a prodigy at eighteen, studying and touring with the Royal Shakespeare Company on a full scholarship. Had he ever been picked on?

He had seemed so impervious, she thought enviously. He could brush off any irritation, any distraction—like swatting at a fly—without losing control. When he was home, he would get up long before the sun, checking his detailed calendar and making phone calls all over the world, before pulling out his latest script and getting to work. Esti would creep into his office, still in her pajamas, to huddle on his leather couch and do her homework while she watched him.

As long as she stayed quiet and didn't bother him, he would let her stay until Aurora came in to insist on breakfast. During the weeks and months that he traveled, Esti would use his office as her own, reading his books and counting off the days until he returned. Even after she started pretending she no longer cared, she would often fall asleep on his couch when he was gone.

She sighed.

If he were here on Cariba, she knew he wouldn't jump in and rescue her. That wasn't his way. Instead, he would insist that she come up with her own method to overcome Danielle and ignore Steve. *You're the one in control, Esti, not me.*

But would he understand how difficult that was for other people? He was so good at becoming any character he read in a script, but had he ever really been able to put himself in the shoes of another real, live human?

Shaking her head, Esti walked into the theater, preparing to face Mr. Niles. With a sigh, she glanced through the open door of his empty office, then walked down to the brightly lit stage to wait. Although rehearsal didn't start for another hour, she knew he would show up before the rest of the cast got here. She wanted to get his lecture over with, hopefully alone.

"Esti."

She gasped, then quickly twisted around to study the bright stage. Peering into the wings, she sat back with a wry smile. "Okay, where are you?"

"On the stage, of course," Alan said in amusement, his voice practically on top of her.

"How do you *do* that?"

He chuckled. "Does it bother you?"

She closed her eyes, letting his delicious, subtle accent wash over her. "Not at all. But what if Mr. Niles walks in?"

"Precisely what I was thinking." He hesitated. "Are you still sure you wish to . . ."

"To work with you? Absolutely." She raised her chin. "I couldn't even face rehearsal on Friday night."

"Yes," he said softly. "I'm aware of that. And you truly don't mind the darkness?"

Esti opened her eyes again to look around the stage. "Does it matter? You seem pretty good at hiding, even with the lights on."

When he didn't answer, she managed a half-teasing smile. "I'm used to working in the dark."

"Please walk to the back of the stage," he said. "Quickly, before Niles returns. There's a small door hidden behind the stage curtain."

"A secret room?" She almost clapped in delight.

"I'll probably regret this," he said faintly. "But I can't seem to help myself."

As Esti followed Alan's voice through a pitch-black passage a moment later, she hoped *she* wouldn't end up regretting it. She thought she heard the faint beat of footsteps as she followed his voice down a tiny hallway, and she suddenly, desperately, wanted to see him.

Determinedly trailing her fingers along the wall, she closed her eyes and created the role of a blind girl falling in love with an exotic, brilliant boy. The girl refused to fear this stranger, and since she would never see his face, she could invent anything she wanted. With his intelligence and sophisticated voice, he had to be descended from European nobility, or British aristocracy. Very good-looking, of course, with blue eyes and a thoughtful, crooked smile she would die for. She suppressed a giggle, and by the time they reached a dark room at the bottom of a steep staircase, she'd worked herself into a giddy sense of anticipation.

She carefully eased herself onto a wooden chair, reaching into the darkness with a smile. "Will you let me see you now?"

"No," he said. "And you won't try to look for me either."

Taken aback, she let her hand drop.

"If you're afraid of me," he added stiffly, "I'll take you back upstairs."

"I'm not afraid." Despite her frustration, she managed to keep her voice calm. "Am I going to work on Lady Capulet or what?"

"Yes, let's do that." Alan seemed to relax. "Think of a feeling you can summon at will; something you can sustain onstage. An intense memory is best. Perhaps a painful or frustrating moment with your father?"

An unexpected ache squeezed her heart like a giant fist. Alan couldn't possibly know about Esti's deep frustration with her dad; she'd never talked about it with anyone, not even Aurora. She wondered if she could somehow put the complex confusion of her father's death into the shallow Lady Capulet.

"Tell me what you're feeling," Alan said. "Quick—don't analyze it, just tell me."

"Sadness and confusion." She closed her eyes. "Panic. Anger."

"Show me. You are now Lady Capulet. 'I swear it shall be Romeo,' Juliet says to her mother, 'whom you know I hate, rather than Paris.'"

Esti rubbed her temples. "Here comes your father," she said to Juliet, picturing Lord Capulet entering the bedchamber. "Tell him so yourself, and see how he will take it at your hands."

"When the sun sets," Alan began in a commanding voice.

As Lord Capulet began chastising Juliet, every inch the controlling patriarch, Esti found herself back in Oregon. When she had played The Great Legard's daughter on television, she'd been reduced to literal tears by Lord Capulet as he raked Juliet over the coals. Her dad had made it so real, so devastating. He had controlled every aspect of the scene, playing her emotions like he owned them.

"How now, wife!" Alan said haughtily. "Have you deliver'd to her our decree?"

"Ay, sir," Esti replied, shaken by her memories. "But she will none, she gives you thanks. I would the fool were married to her grave."

She felt herself shrinking from Alan as his voice filled the room again, his righteous wrath growing stronger with every word of Lord Capulet's monologue.

"Go with Paris to Saint Peter's church," he finally raged, "or I will drag thee on a hurdle thither. Out, you green-sickness carrion! Out, you baggage, you tallow face!"

Her stomach churned at his hateful words. "Fie, fie," Lady Capulet cried. "What, are you mad?"

"Hang thee, young baggage," he said to Juliet. "Disobedient wretch!"

Lady Capulet listened to her husband, appalled and confused by her own chaotic thoughts. Maybe they were wrong to judge their daughter so strictly? Didn't he realize she had her own life to live, away from her father's ironclad control? *Control,* The Great Legard had said, *is nothing more than attitude. If you believe you're in control, then people will believe you.* He controlled everything, even his own daughter's identity. When she wasn't reflected in the mirror of his vast presence, she became invisible.

Esti had pushed her father away after that performance, avoiding his award ceremonies and his parties, dropping her friends when they dared compare her to him. She knew it hurt him, but how could she tell him that he was just *too* good? Even at the end, when he breathed through his tubes and clutched her hand, she'd been too intimidated to tell him the truth. A coward, that's all his daughter was. A coward who didn't deserve what she'd been given.

"Talk not to me," she spat at Juliet, "for I'll not speak a word. Do as thou wilt, for I have done with thee."

"Incredible," Alan said. "You did it."

Stunned, Esti took a deep breath, trying not to cry.

"You're shaking, aren't you?" His voice touched her soul like a gentle hand.

Esti felt the rage and confusion drain out of her as if Alan had pulled a plug. "Ouch," she whispered. "That hurt." The words sounded ridiculous as soon as she said them.

"Acting is not supposed to be easy." To her relief, Alan's reply held only respect. "And that's why very few people are good at it."

She leaned against the rough wooden table in front of her, cool in the humid darkness of the basement. "You're good at it."

Silence followed her words, slowly replaced by singing voices drifting through the air in lilting harmony. The utter absurdity of listening to an ancient madrigal in a spooky old basement after a mind-blowing rehearsal in the dark made her smile. Especially because it felt . . . *right*. "Where's the music coming from?" she asked.

"My iPod," Alan said dryly. "Did you think it was magic?"

"You're crazy." Esti laughed and closed her eyes. "Or I've gone over the edge."

"Maybe we both have."

They listened to the cheerful music in silence for a few minutes, then Esti smiled again. "This is perfect."

"Yes," he said in contentment.

She opened her mouth to ask if she could please see him— *please, for just a single minute?*—but he suddenly inhaled sharply.

"Niles is back," he said.

"That figures." Esti tried to hide her disappointment. "How do you know?"

"I always know." He sighed. "I'll show you a different way out, but first I have something for you."

Squinting at the brightness outside a few minutes later, Esti let the back door swing shut behind her. Clutching a small package, she made her way up the hill through a tangled path in the wild tamarind, as Alan had described to her. She couldn't see the back door at all from here, and she raised her eyebrows. Even though it *was* perfectly camouflaged, she wasn't sure she believed that no one knew about it but him.

She stealthily emerged from behind the building, checking to make sure she was alone. Suppressing a smile, she half skipped across the round courtyard before sinking down on the stone bench to look out over the water.

From here, she saw no warning signs on Manchineel Cay. The island was beautiful, with its picturesque cliff rising from silky white beaches. A dark rain column drifted along the water beyond the cay, its edge sharply outlined in silver where the rain hit the sea. Thick white clouds piled up around it, fluffy and stunning against the blue sky. Esti had never seen a place less likely to be haunted.

Her eyes wide in anticipation, she opened Alan's gift. A local specialty called *roti*, he had explained when her fingers found it on the dark table. With a growing smile, she studied the unexpected dinner. A curry smell wafted up from tortilla-wrapped chicken, and a flower lay to one side, sweetly fragrant even over the curry.

A perfect white flower.

Esti let her eyes trace the blossom, enveloped in its warm scent as she touched her fingertip to a velvety petal. She already knew she was totally falling for Alan, despite his odd quirks. Could he possibly feel the same way about her?

She felt a tremble growing inside of her. Lady Capulet

might actually steal the show for a few moments; Esti now knew it was possible. Starting with the Christmas performance, she might finally face the critics on *her* terms. Esti Legard, creating her own legacy at Manchicay School, without her father. Accompanied by her . . . her boyfriend instead. It wasn't an impossible idea. He'd told her he wouldn't be back until next Monday, though, and she didn't know how she could wait another endless week before she talked to him again.

For the first time, she allowed herself to imagine the feel of his fingers on hers, his lips touching her face. Her smile grew dreamy as she leaned back to eat her roti, savoring the blossom's sweet fragrance, the taste of curry, and a soft, moaning whisper beneath the breeze brushing her skin.

Act One. Scene Six.

"Rumor has it," Carmen said, "Steve was set up."

"Set up for what?" Barely listening, Esti studied the stage. She had strolled past the secret opening a dozen times during the horribly long week, casually brushing aside the curtain to reassure herself that the small door existed. She couldn't help wondering if Alan had other secret passages as well; openings he could speak through, and strategic locations from which he watched and listened.

"Drug bust."

"What?" Esti straightened, suddenly interested. "They caught Steve smoking?"

"Even better." Carmen snickered. "A stash in his locker, confiscated by Headmaster Fleming over the weekend. Steve is history."

"He was dumb enough to keep drugs in his locker?" Esti asked in amazement. "They can kick him out for that?"

"They have to kick him out." Carmen almost sang the words. "School policy. Stupid Steve is gone."

Esti looked around the theater as she realized the entire cast was buzzing with the news. "But who's going to play Lord Capulet?"

Carmen burst into laughter. "You *would* worry about that! Hmm, I'll use my own gift to read the future." Her voice dropped an octave. "I now predict Lance as Lord Capulet. Want to put money on it?"

"I'll take your word." Esti had been wired with pent-up anticipation all day; this was icing on the cake.

Onstage, Mr. Niles's expression was stony as he talked the boys through some fighting techniques for the Capulet-Montague brawl.

"I heard Danielle tell Niles that someone planted the stuff," Carmen added in a softer voice. "Niles told her to shut up, which is the first time *anyone's* ever told her off that I know about. You are making some good changes at this school, Esti girl."

"What's that supposed to mean?" Esti asked, startled. "I didn't have anything to do with this."

"Don' vex." They both whirled around at the unexpected whisper. Lucia sat down behind them, leaning forward so they could hear her. "Niles he talk like some freshwater Yankee, but he is West Indian, for true. Maybe 'tis someone he fear."

"Who would he be afraid of?" Carmen glanced at Esti. "A jumbee?"

Lucia met Esti's astonished expression with a steady, jet-black gaze. When Esti finally looked away, the overhead lights flickered, then dimmed. A spotlight swept the room, stopping briefly on Danielle sitting at the edge of the stage. She looked up with a tight, amused smile.

Carmen shot an impatient look behind them. "Lance keeps messing with the lights. I swear, he's almost as bad as Steve. He deserves to inherit Lord Capulet."

The spotlight made its way around the theater, gathering interest from the cast as it moved from seat to seat. Just as it fixed her in its piercing beam, Esti felt a tickle on the top of her head. With a disgusted sound, Carmen yanked something away from Esti and flung it toward the back. "Steve, what are *you* doing here?" she snapped. "Is this one of Danielle's tricks?"

Esti spun around in time to see an evil-looking carnival mask land on the ground, made of black foam and glitter. As Steve ducked behind a row of seats, the main lights came on again, and the spotlight went dead. Onstage, Danielle didn't bother to hide her growing laughter.

A sharp cracking sound cut the laughter short. One of the

thin plywood sets was slowly tipping over, and with a shriek, Danielle scrabbled away from it on her hands and knees. She rolled off the edge of the stage, falling to the floor as the wall landed with a heavy thump where she'd been sitting an instant before.

"Who put these sets together?" she exploded, rising to her knees.

"Check Esti's locker," Steve yelled from his hiding place. "She's got voodoo dolls in there. Who's next on her list?"

Stunned, Esti felt her mouth drop open as Carmen jumped to her feet.

"Where's Steve?" Carmen ground out. Striding to the aisle behind them, she stopped with her hands on her hips, glaring down between the seats. "Get off the floor, Stoner. I can't believe you would dare accuse Esti."

The shocked silence was broken by Mr. Niles's steely voice. "Steve, I want you out of here, *now*. My theater department is not Carnival, and if the rest of you can't keep your private lives off the stage, you will follow Steve out the door." His eyes moved back and forth between Esti and Danielle. "No matter who you are."

As whispers from the cast accompanied Steve's sauntering exit, Lucia's quiet voice startled Esti. "Don' worry, gal."

Esti spun around to look at her.

"Even if the jumbee he don' like Danielle," Lucia said softly, "he take care of you, mon."

A chill crawled down Esti's spine.

"Danielle, she have live on Cariba all her life." Lucia didn't bother hiding her amusement. "She need more respect for the West Indian way."

"I want to see Act Three, Scene Five," Mr. Niles snapped, "starting the moment Romeo leaves Juliet's bedroom. Lance will play Lord Capulet, now that Steve is gone."

"See?" Carmen crowed softly.

The sound of shuffling paper filled the theater, Lance studying his script more frantically than the others. As Danielle led the way, Esti followed Carmen toward the stage, wondering if her life could become any more surreal.

"You're the one in control, Esti," a deep voice murmured. "No one else."

She stopped in shock, halfway up the first step. Alan sounded like he was right beside her, whispering her dad's famous mantra into her ear.

"If you believe you're in control," he added, "people will believe you."

It took every ounce of control she had to keep from spinning around to see if anyone else had heard him.

"Esti," Mr. Niles said. "We're waiting for you."

Esti forced her legs to move, raising one knee, then the other, until she reached the level of the stage. Her eyes searched the steps as she climbed. Alan wouldn't do this to her, she thought, if she didn't already know he had hiding places. He obviously had the theater rigged so she could hear his voice. But why did no one else notice anything?

Her shivering grew stronger.

"Let your emotions build," Alan said softly as she crossed

the stage. "Work up the confusion and the anger. Use that frustration you've stored for so long. And stop walking before you come so close that the others might hear me."

She came to an abrupt halt ten feet away from Danielle, relief sweeping over her in huge waves at his warning. If there was a chance that others could hear him, then maybe Esti wasn't going insane.

"Look at Juliet," Alan whispered. "Does she look smug? Think about Lady Capulet's purpose now, as you show Niles some *real* acting."

"Esti," Mr. Niles said in growing annoyance, "do you know your lines?"

"Ho, daughter! are you up?" she forced out.

"Who is it that calls?" Danielle replied. "Is it my lady mother?"

"Let Shakespeare's words use your voice to become real." Alan's whisper wove seamlessly through Danielle's response.

"Why, how now, Juliet!" The words burst from Esti's mouth.

"That's good." Alan's compliment sent goose bumps up her arms. "I see your confusion. Once again, you are creating Lady Capulet's reality."

Whose reality? she wondered wildly. Not just Alan's voice, but his dead-on perfect advice following her through thin air across the stage. As the scene progressed with Juliet, then with Nurse and Lord Capulet, Esti felt herself getting worked up in a way very different from this afternoon. Confusion about Alan, anger at Danielle and Steve, agitation and bewilderment at herself as she tumbled headlong through the scene, dragged along by Lady Capulet's lines.

By the time Lance haltingly finished his new role, demolishing Juliet as convincingly as he could, emotions crashed through Esti's mind and body like a fierce, cascading waterfall. Fury and confusion filled her, leaving room for nothing else as she spat her final words at Danielle. "Do as thou wilt, for I have done with thee."

Raising her chin, Esti strode from the stage and flung herself into a seat at the edge of the third row, as far as possible from the others.

"O God!" Danielle flung herself to the floor with a wavering cry. "O Nurse! how shall this be prevented?"

"You've rattled her." Alan's voice tickled Esti's ear again. "She will never play an audience the way you can."

Esti shivered and spun around, searching the theater with her eyes. She sat alone beside the coral-studded wall of the building, but Alan's voice still seemed as close as it had been onstage. A speaker in the wall or the seat, perhaps?

"What sayst thou?" Danielle shrilly begged Carmen forward. "Some comfort, Nurse?"

Esti looked up to see Mr. Niles staring back at her from beside the stage. His face reflected a mixture of uncertainty and admiration. Esti met his eyes, unable to hold back her own astonished smile.

After rehearsal, she listened to Carmen's excited chatter as they walked outside together.

"That was good," Carmen said. "I mean, *really* good. Wow, Esti. I always thought of Lady Capulet as kind of a non-character. Boy, was I wrong."

"Thank you." Esti hoped her expression didn't look as foolish as it felt, as her memory replayed Alan's glowing words.

"Nice job, Leg-guard," Greg said, Danielle pausing beside him. For a moment he looked like he wanted to say more, then he actually smiled instead of the usual wink. He turned and walked away, his arm around Danielle's shoulders.

"Lady Capulet is one mean mother," another voice said from behind them. "No wonder she married Lord Capulet."

Esti couldn't help laughing in surprise. "Thanks, Lance."

"You scared the hell out of him, Esti," Chaz teased, ducking to avoid Lance's fist. "It was supposed to be the other way around."

"Ooh, do you wish it was you?" Carmen said to Chaz. "Don't tell me you like girls who intimidate you? Can I try?"

"Peace, you mumbling fool." Chaz grinned at her. "Hold your tongue."

Carmen stuck out her tongue at him, shrieking when he reached up to grab it.

"Careful, or I'll hold it for you." He abruptly glanced around at a honk from one of the cars in the parking lot. "My own mean mother is waiting. Come on, Lance. Carmen, I'll see you later."

Esti watched them sprint away. "I think Chaz has a crush on you."

"Maybe he'll finally admit it." Carmen's eyes gleamed. "Especially if Danielle's stranglehold is crumbling."

"What do you mean?"

"Oh, come on. Steve is gone; check. Greg's got his eye on you; check. Juliet was totally outperformed by her mama; big check. Go, Jane Doe, go." Carmen laughed as they reached the edge of the parking lot. "See you tomorrow."

"See you tomorrow," Esti replied in bemusement.

Leaning against a palm tree, she looked out at the sea and waited as the last cast members trailed out of the building, laughing and talking. Manchineel Cay had become a delicate silhouette in black, surrounded by a ring of pale sand and silver glints of moonlight on the water. Esti stretched her arms over her head, tingling with anticipation. A fragrant breeze whispered across the courtyard, as sweet as the flower Alan had given her last week.

"Esti."

She spun around at Lucia's voice.

"I thought you had maybe sneak back to the theater." Lucia flashed a rare smile.

Esti studied her, unsure how to respond

"You come to my house soon," Lucia said.

"Why?" Esti demanded, then immediately softened her tone. "I mean, of course I would love that." She smiled, even though this seemed more like a command than a casual invitation.

"We go on the boat." Lucia handed Esti a scrap of paper with a carefully drawn map. "This show you to find my house. Ma, she want to meet you."

"Why does your mom want to meet me?"

"You gon find out." With a piercing look, Lucia turned and walked away

Act One. Scene Seven.

Despite her eagerness, Esti found herself hesitating at the main door of the theater after everyone finally left. "Are you here?" she tried softly when she reached the stage. Her fingers twitched nervously, and she hoped Alan hadn't spooked himself away after rehearsal.

Please, she thought, *I need to know who you are. Please be waiting for me in the basement.* Reaching for the backstage curtain, her fingers instantly found the heavy cloth in the darkness. Without dwelling on what she was actually doing—Aurora would kill her, if she knew—Esti hurried through the pitch-black corridor.

"You were wonderful." Alan's voice filled the tiny room as she sat down.

She hoped her sigh of relief didn't sound as explosive as it felt. "No, *you* were."

"They all loved Lady Capulet."

"Because of your help." Esti hesitated again, her heart pounding. "Are you going to tell me how I heard you, when no one else could?"

After a predictable silence, she finally heard his soft,

indrawn breath. "I probably owe you an explanation." He sounded subdued.

"You don't . . ." Esti trailed off. "You don't owe me anything. But I would like to know."

"Have you studied the old sugar mills in your history class?"

His stiff question startled her. "Not yet. I'm supposed to research them for a term paper, though."

"Not too many plantations had sugar factories with two levels, but Manchicay did. Slaves in the stifling cellar fed bonfires for the boiling cane juice above."

She leaned back, wondering if this was supposed to be her answer.

"When the place was renovated into a school," Alan continued, "they made the main factory structurally sound, then sealed off the lower level for safety purposes and money."

"This theater?" A swarm of emotions buzzed through her body, like restless bees.

"Yes. The basement has too many low ceilings and corridors that would have cost a fortune to enlarge. The main floor also has several long ventilation chambers, which Niles either dismissed or never knew about." Alan's voice became slightly more relaxed. "I'm sure you've realized that these spaces are essential for what I do."

"And what do you do?" Esti held her breath.

"I'm trying to help Rodney Solomon root out the best talent at Manchicay."

"You work for Rodney?" Her relief almost paralyzed her. That simple bit of knowledge was almost as comforting as turning on a light.

"You will attract plenty of interest during the Christmas performance this semester, Esti, and it won't merely be because of your name." As Alan's voice came close to her, she felt an unexpected flicker of warmth from his breath. To her amazement he smelled warm and nice, like an island flower blooming in full sunlight. She couldn't move, stunned by the heat spreading through her body, but he drifted away again as if unaware of his effect on her.

"It is essential that I be hidden from prying eyes and foolish questions."

"Of . . . of course," Esti stammered, flustered by his formality and his nearness.

"And you inspire me, Esti," Alan continued. "I'm amazed at how rude most people are, with no idea what it's like to *work* for something, to truly suffer. Yet you gracefully ignore Danielle and her clique each day at school. You've shunned the status of your father's name, nourishing instead your friendship with a talented nobody like Carmen."

His voice became soft. "You accept unusual . . . conditions . . . that most people would find disturbing."

"I love working with you," Esti said uncomfortably, wondering if he truly believed that her motivations were so selfless. "I'm not sure I deserve all that, but thank you. You—you seem to have some suffering in your past."

"Certain things are better left unknown." The words came

out in a harsh whisper. "Ignorance is bliss, in the true island way."

"What is the island way?" she asked, half reaching into the empty darkness to comfort him.

"The simple life." His voice abruptly grew rich and mocking. "The seductive dream that brings people to Cariba, then sends them packing a few months later, tails between their legs."

Esti sat back, dazed by his roller-coaster emotions.

"Now it's your turn," he said crisply. "Why are you here?"

"At Manchicay School, you mean? Or here in the basement?"

He chuckled. "*Touché*. With your talent and your name, you could have anything you want. Why did you choose a haven for shiny scouts wanting a paid vacation in the tropics?"

"That's harsh," Esti said. "I thought you were Rodney's friend."

"Forgive me." Alan sounded contrite. "Yes, Rodney Solomon is building Manchicay into a premier acting school to showcase the best young—if already wealthy—talent. If he wants to give scholarships to those without money, his success depends on launching his discoveries into the real world." His voice grew cynical. "I have no problem with that, but Mr. Niles tries my patience."

Esti couldn't help laughing. "Yeah, he tries my patience too."

"Back to my question." Alan now sounded amused. "What brought you here?"

"Rodney Solomon, at least partly." Esti shrugged. "After my dad died, Aurora and I thought it would be nice to go somewhere new. My dad had told us about Manchicay School, of course."

"What did your father tell you about Manchicay School?" Alan asked sharply.

Esti raised her eyebrows at his tone. "That it was a haven for shiny scouts wanting a paid vacation in the tropics."

"I deserved that." He chuckled. "Somehow, you can always make me laugh. How would you like to work on comedy? It might be interesting to try the part of Rosalind."

"*As You Like It.*" Esti felt like leaping into the air. "I love Rosalind!"

"I thought you might." He laughed again. "Her strength has always reminded me of you. I would like playing Orlando to your Rosalind."

Esti savored the delicious sound of his laughter. If she could keep Alan laughing, maybe he would reveal more about himself. "*I* would like playing Juliet to your Romeo," she said coyly. "Nurse said that you're an honest gentleman, and a courteous, and a kind, and a handsome—"

"Stop."

In the silence following his barked interruption, Esti barely discerned his breathing, harsh and controlled, like a wounded boy searching for strength. She felt a sudden overwhelming need to see his face—his expressions—so that she might know what he was thinking.

Her heart thudded painfully. "I want to see you, Alan."

"That is not possible," he ground out. "I'm not who you think I am."

"And who do you think," she asked evenly, "that I think you are?"

He didn't answer.

"Tell me something else, then." She didn't let herself hesitate. "Why did Lucia think you knocked over that plywood tonight?"

"Lucia said that?" he asked.

"Not exactly." Esti shrugged. "But she seemed to know *something*. And her mom wants to meet me."

"I have never talked to Lucia Harris." Alan cleared his throat. "I imagine Ma Harris will tell you to avoid me."

"Why?" Esti carefully tucked one leg beneath the other, torn between her longing for Alan's company and the increasing spookiness she couldn't deny.

"She is quite superstitious," Alan said. "Many West Indians on Cariba are, and they generally have little to do with Continentals."

"Continentals?"

"People like you, who come here from the States."

"Alan." Esti paused. "I don't care what people say."

A very long silence followed.

"You, O you," he finally said. "So perfect and so peerless, are created of every creature's best."

Warmth swept through her body as his voice deepened into a caress. "But I'm intimidated by my dad and by Danielle, and I can't even—"

"Shhh." She heard his smile. "Both truth and beauty on my love depends. So dost thou too, and therein dignified." The words of the sonnet touched her like an exquisite, unexpected kiss.

"Alan," she whispered. "I'm not making you up, right?" She reached futilely into the darkness again. "Right?"

She tried not to betray her frustration at the growing silence in the tiny room. "I thought we were working on Rosalind and Orlando tonight." After a moment, she snorted and leaned back against her chair. "This disappearing routine is getting old," she muttered.

❧

The lights were off when she slipped through the front door of the house. Candles burned on the coffee table, and the place smelled strongly of incense. Esti tiptoed across the small living room to peek in the door of Aurora's bedroom. Her mom wasn't in there.

Sighing, Esti continued past the kitchen to the balcony. As she suspected, Aurora had fallen asleep in her patio chair, a book on her lap and a bottle of wine on the table. The wine had become quite a habit lately, Esti thought uneasily.

"Aurora." She placed her hand on her mom's shoulder. "Wake up."

"What?" Aurora heaved herself upright. "What's the matter?"

"I'm worried about you. You fell asleep outside again."

"Oh, dear." Her mom frowned at the wine bottle. "I'm probably covered with mosquito bites."

Esti gave her a sympathetic nod. "Do you need help getting back inside?"

"Of course not. I'm fine." Aurora stood up, clutching the book. "How was rehearsal?"

"The best one so far. Steve got expelled after they found drugs in his locker over the weekend." Esti followed Aurora into the living room and pulled the balcony door closed. "And I finally had a chance to bring some real life to Lady Capulet. Even though it's a tiny part, I think Dad might have been impressed."

"Of course he would have been impressed. He was always impressed with you."

Esti and her mother shared their first real smile in a long time. "What are you reading?" Esti asked after a pause.

"Caribbean history. I'd like to know this place better. This book is about their spiritual beliefs." Aurora gave Esti a weak smile as she sank down to the couch. "I've been looking for insight into life and death, but we'll see. Obeah. Voodoo. Jumbees. I know, it's silly."

"What have you heard about jumbees?"

"Some type of evil spirit." Aurora thumbed through a couple of pages, then dropped the book into her lap.

"I've heard about them too." Esti tried to laugh. "Manchicay School is supposed to be haunted. The other kids tease me whenever I practice by myself, and Carmen says I must be talking to a jumbee."

"Carmen would say that." Aurora smiled, and Esti nodded in relief.

"You know how Rodney brings in talent scouts for our performance at the end of each year?" Esti asked, casually sitting on the couch beside her mom.

"Mmm hmm." Aurora stared at the flickering candles.

"Did you ever wonder if the scouts look for more than just that final performance? If someone were hired to root out hidden talent at Manchicay, beyond the leading roles?"

"Your father would approve of that." Aurora closed her eyes. "He was a great champion of the underdog." Then her voice broke. "Oh, Esti, I miss your father. I miss dancing with him and talking to him. I miss my life in Ashland. It's so lonely here." She dropped her head into her hands.

It was the most Aurora had said about Esti's dad since his death, and a wave of guilt swept through Esti as her mom began crying. She had no right to feel this bizarre happiness tonight, when her mom still ached so deeply, and it was Esti's needs that had brought them to Cariba.

She put an awkward arm around Aurora's shoulders. She had often walked in on her parents dancing. They loved weird music, like rock and roll played on Celtic harps, or strange Elizabethan electric guitar solos. They had met at a Renaissance Faire, her dad instantly falling for the pretty girl who sang Bob Dylan lyrics to the sound of a lute and ate French fries with her honey mead. The girl who was more hippie than groupie, not letting anyone tell her who she should be. As her mom's shoulder bone pressed sharply into her neck, Esti's remorse grew stronger. She hadn't even noticed that Aurora had lost weight.

"Do you remember when your dad hosted that monologue-othon last year?" Aurora finally said. "Before the diagnosis?"

The diagnosis. The day the world stopped. "Monologue what?"

"Reciting monologues nonstop on television to create a national fund for disabled actors. I think he lasted fifty-seven hours before he fell asleep in the middle of a sentence."

Esti honestly had no such recollection. "Oh, yeah," she said uncertainly.

"He raised over a million dollars in less than three days," Aurora muttered, without looking up. "By himself. He wanted everyone to have a chance."

Esti felt the knives stabbing into her stomach again. She couldn't remember anything at all about television monologues. What else had her dad done before he died? How many things had she ignored, she wondered, between the time of her performance with him as Juliet, and *the diagnosis?*

She pulled her mom even tighter in a hug. The airlines never had found the box she'd brought with her, the one with her dad's last autographed treatise in it. Now it was lost forever, along with so many other things.

"Oh, sweetie," her mom whispered, lifting her head to look at Esti with red eyes. "I'm the mom; I've been trying so hard not to fall apart on you like this. I need to find a job, something to distract myself so I'm not alone all day. Rodney and Jayna come by every once in a while, but I know it's not enough. I should go out there and get to know people, I just can't make myself do it. I'm the one who's supposed to be strong, and I've all but abandoned you lately."

"Aurora, you haven't," Esti said. "I—I think I'd like to talk about Dad sometimes, but I'm *fine*. If you're sad, though, maybe we should go back to Ash . . ." She couldn't bring herself to finish the word.

"Nonsense." Aurora blew her nose. "Your only job is finishing school and making a name for yourself. We have enough money from your dad, and we're not going back to Ashland yet, not if things are finally getting better for you here. If Manchicay launches your career, I'll have done everything your dad wanted for you." She wiped her eyes, then leaned back against the couch. "Now, what were you saying about Rodney's talent scouts?"

Esti looked out the open window, avoiding Aurora's eyes. "Just that it would be interesting if they had someone working behind the scenes for them. Like private tutoring or something."

Aurora rubbed her temples, giving Esti a tired smile with a hint of her old impishness. "The talent scouts I've met don't know how to act, they just recognize good acting when they see it. People like that are accustomed to getting any pretty young thing they want. That kind of private tutor might not be such a good idea."

Esti spun away so that Aurora wouldn't see her blush.

When she went to bed a few minutes later, Esti knew she wouldn't be able to sleep. Pulling out her history book, she began scribbling notes about sugarcane, then finally tossed her notebook on the floor.

Depressing, that's what it was. Lucia's family had survived slavery, and so had Rodney Solomon's. It was impossible for her to picture Manchicay School as a treeless plantation with naked, starving Africans toiling on the terraced hills. She didn't want to know about the European nobles who couldn't care less about millions of lives lost for the teaspoon of sugar they put in their tea. She didn't want to think about the legends the locals had created to survive.

Esti turned off her light. Even worse than her studies of Cariba was the nagging knowledge that she'd completely missed the final year of her dad's life. Those memories were as fleeting as the sunset, even less real than an invisible boy who spoke to her in sonnets. Alan certainly didn't seem like the type who was used to getting all the pretty young things he wanted. He was as ethereal as Romeo, his existence seeming to revolve around her alone. And what was Esti giving in return—to him, to her mom, to anyone?

She pressed her aching forehead against the cool steel window frame to look out at the moonlit sea, as tiny coqui frogs filled the humid air with their endless chirping music. Manchineel Cay's silhouette rose darkly from the sparkling waves, and Esti straightened in surprise. She had never seen a light on the little island before. Had some poor tourist missed the warning signs in the dark? Or maybe it was a local teenager acting on a dare.

She watched as the light wavered and appeared again.

When it finally blinked out for good, she couldn't help thinking that it might actually be possible to disappear out there, never to be found again. On Cariba, Esti was beginning to believe, almost anything was possible.

Act One. Scene Eight.

Esti studied the plantation diagram on the blackboard, leisurely stretching her legs under the table in an attempt to pay attention. As much as she liked her history class, she was having a hard time concentrating on anything but Alan. After his abrupt departure on the night of the tipped plywood set, something had changed. He'd relaxed somehow, and since that night they'd been together almost a dozen times. Esti was beginning to understand the dumb cliché about walking on clouds.

"First," Miss Rupert said, "ripe sugarcane was cut short and fed into the grinders, powered by trade winds. Manchicay's massive windmill stood in the round grass courtyard beyond the theater building. Since Elon Somand was known to force his own slaves into the grinders on occasion, the hateful windmill was destroyed by Cariban slaves after abolition. Cane juice was collected from the ground-up sugarcane into a large vessel."

Miss Rupert swept her arm across the diagram. "The juice then ran along a great trough to the sugar factory, which is now Manchicay's famous—if perhaps haunted—theater building."

Esti barely heard the mutters sweeping the classroom as she let her eyes dreamily trace the route of the cane juice. Alan was the opposite of everything Somand represented. Besides his intelligence, he had the intriguing shyness of a boy who'd never had a girlfriend. If anything, it was Alan who was haunted—from the inside. Something kept him in hiding, and Esti had just about decided that this afternoon she'd finally make him tell her what it was.

"Manchicay could process more than a thousand gallons at a time," Miss Rupert continued. "Slaves tended huge fires underneath the clarifying vessels to boil the juice and collect impurities on top. The juice was then transferred to enormous copper kettles, where slaves constantly fed fires to further clarify and evaporate the juice, continuing the process in smaller and smaller kettles until it became thick enough to crystallize. As it cooled, the resulting molasses was strained into large cisterns, leaving *muscovado* to be shipped either as brown sugar, or treated with clay to make white sugar."

Squinting at the sugar production diagram, Esti was surprised to see no basements in the drawing.

"And, as you all know," Miss Rupert added wryly, "you can't produce sugar without making rum. Cariba has long been known for two things—our jumbees, and our rum."

"How about a science experiment?" Lance suggested over the class snickers. "We could build a distiller."

Miss Rupert raised one eyebrow, her accent growing stronger with her amusement. "You chat with Mr. Larson, eh? Let me know what he say. Don't forget we have a long weekend for Hurricane Thanksgiving. I see you all next Monday."

Esti waved back at Lance on the way out of class. He'd been much friendlier in the past month, since inheriting the role of Lord Capulet. Lucia had become friendlier too, and Esti was finally going to her house this weekend. Esti hummed as she approached the theater, happy that her luck was changing. Sometimes it was all she could do lately to keep herself from dancing with joy.

♣

"I pray you, what is't o'clock?" Rosalind asked.

"You should ask me," Orlando said glumly, "what time o'day. There's no clock in the forest."

"Then there is no true lover in the forest," she countered, "else *sighing* every minute and *groaning* every hour would detect the lazy foot of time as well as a clock."

Alan chuckled. "The cadence of your voice is the rhythm of a clock. Very nice. And," he continued in Orlando's voice, "why not the swift foot of time?"

Esti loved that Rosalind was so funny and intelligent, dressing up as a boy to get away with things a girl could never do. Alan did Orlando perfectly, of course, his voice softening in distress as he wondered how to deal with his eternal love for the eccentric girl.

"I would not be cured, youth," he finally concluded in dismay.

"I would cure you," Rosalind said. "If you would but call me Rosalind, and come every day to my cote, and woo me." In her own voice, Esti added, "Not that your basement *cote* is boring, but I've been coming here ever since we met."

He laughed. "You slip in and out of Rosalind like a glove."

"Better than my Juliet?" Esti took up Rosalind's teasing note again.

"Shakespeare hasn't written a character you couldn't do, if you set your mind to it," Alan said. "How about *Richard the Third*?"

"Now is the winter of our discontent," she began in a deep, scornful voice.

"Nice." He sounded impressed. "You manage to bring a hint of Irish and a touch of Cornwall into your pronunciation, just as your father did."

"Thanks. But we were talking about your *cote*"—she smiled at Alan's chuckle—"and I can't help wondering about this basement. In my history class, it's not even hinted at. How did you discover it?"

He hesitated. "I have my ways."

"Stop evading me!" She couldn't hide her frustration. "Look, I clearly have a high tolerance for—how did you put it?—conditions most people would find disturbing, but this is making me crazy. Do you *have* to keep hiding from me?"

His answering silence seemed more unbearable than usual, the darkness as heavy and thick as a blanket.

Refusing to let herself falter, Esti continued. "Is it because you work for Rodney? Does he make you stay so secretive?"

"I never said that I worked for Rodney Solomon," Alan said stiffly.

Esti's eyes widened, and she took a long, shaky breath. "Does anyone besides me even know that you're here?"

He didn't answer.

"Pretend you're a jumbee, then." She tried not to be frightened. "Can't you at least tell me where you learned Shakespeare so well?"

"No, I can't."

Although she expected his blunt rebuttal, it still hurt. "Will you tell me where you grew up?"

"No."

"Where do you live, then?"

"This conversation is getting out of hand," Alan whispered.

"No, it's not! I *like* you, Alan."

His groan was almost inaudible. "I can't do this."

"Fine." Impatience swept through Esti. "Aurora wants to move back to Oregon anyway. I'll tell her to get plane tickets."

"Esti, you can't quit."

"Why not? If *you* quit, *I'm* quitting."

"That's not fair."

"You're not being fair."

As the silence lengthened into a minute, then five minutes, Esti began reaching around the tiny room to make sure he wasn't hiding in the darkness. She finally rested her forehead on the edge of the table.

"I'm sorry, Alan," she whispered. "Please talk to me. I'll stop asking questions."

"Come back here Sunday morning," he said in a voice as thin as hers, and then he really was gone. Esti wasn't sure how she knew, but she knew. Digging the palms of her hands into her eyes, she slowly rose to her feet.

❧

Esti paused for a minute while she tried to catch her breath, glancing back down the steep hill she'd just climbed. She hadn't seen any white faces in the shabby apartments along the road, but several people had waved at her with an unusual local gesture. She knew Lucia wouldn't have invited her to this neighborhood if it were dangerous for her.

She stepped up to the porch, where red paint peeled away from the weathered wood in ragged strips. Taking a deep breath, she tapped on the door. She heard voices inside, so she knew someone was home. After a moment, she knocked again, louder this time.

The door burst open.

"I forget." Lucia gestured for Esti to come inside. "Continentals, you always knock on the door. Be careful," she added, grabbing Esti before she could step in a pan of water next to the door.

"Sorry," Esti mumbled in embarrassment. "I didn't see it."

"To keep out the jumbee them," Lucia said.

Esti studied the crossed pair of shoes and open scissors arranged next to the pan. Perhaps they were part of the anti-jumbee regimen too, but she decided she'd better not ask.

"If I didn't knock on the door," she said awkwardly, "how would you know I was here?"

Lucia raised her eyebrows. "You stand at the front and you call for me, instead of sneaking up on the house. 'Inside,' you yell, 'Lucia, is Esti.' I have keep the window open to hear you."

Esti's face grew warm. "I didn't mean to sneak up on the house."

"No problem, mon. I forget, is all. Hey, you take off you shoes before you go in, okay?"

Blushing more deeply, Esti returned to the door and pulled off her shoes. She'd been wanting to know more about Lucia, but now she wondered if today would merely be one long string of social gaffes. Hopefully she wouldn't say anything insulting, or—she winced—something to inflame their superstition even further.

"Come," Lucia ordered. "Uncle Domino is almost finish with breakfast."

Esti followed her into the living room, looking around in fascination. Bright rugs and blankets hung on the walls and over the furniture, interspersed with frightening tribal masks and strange warrior statues.

"You like it?" Lucia asked. "Ma she got family travel around with Carnival; they bring the mask them. The black one is a true Cariba Island mask, without color. Cariba jumbee mask is always black, you know."

Esti nodded uncomfortably.

"Lucia!"

A shout from the other room made Esti jump, but Lucia didn't even blink.

"You ready or what, child?"

"We ready, Uncle Domino."

A very dark man came into the room, wiping his mouth. He was followed by a woman Esti recognized from school.

"I is Ma Harris," the woman said, "and dis my brudda, Domino."

Esti smiled shyly. "I'm Esti."

"I hear so much ting about you," Ma Harris added with a significant look.

"Come," Domino said. "Lucia promise she friend we go on de boat, and a storm gon come dis afternoon. It have plenty time for chit-chat while we catch fish dem."

"We talk on de boat," Ma Harris agreed.

Esti peered nervously over the edge of the boat, watching the coral reefs fly past them. She and Lucia sat at the rear, wedged between a smelly bait bucket and the noisy outboard engine. A ragged tarp provided some shade, and they moved over the turquoise water with exhilarating speed.

The faded old life vest she wore didn't seem substantial enough to save her life in such a huge expanse of water, she suddenly thought. She should talk to Rodney pretty soon about learning to swim. Clutching the straps of her life vest, she impulsively leaned toward Lucia.

"Do you know Rafe Solomon?" she yelled.

With a startled look, Lucia nodded. "Yeah, mon. Everyone know Rafe."

"Is he nice?"

Lucia shrugged. "Ma, she like Rafe, for true. He ain't afraid of she."

Esti pondered Lucia's words, not sure if that really answered her question.

"He keep you sweet and warm." Lucia grinned. "Ain't nothin' wrong with a warm boyfriend, long as he know who is boss."

"Have you dated him?" she asked before she could stop herself.

Lucia let out a burst of laughter. "Nah, mon. I already got a boy, he nice-nice. Quintin, he ain't afraid of Ma, but he let me call the shot. 'Tis Manchineel Cay," she added, pointing in front of them.

Esti straightened, forcing Rafe out of her mind as her eyes wandered over brilliant white sand. She couldn't see this side of the cay from Cariba. Gorgeous beaches surrounded the island, broken only by the single rocky cliff plunging into the water on its northeast tip. Beyond the narrow strip of sand, heavily forested land rose in a gentle slope.

As they approached, the boat began slowing down. Although Domino had brought them the long way around, the cay sat very close to the west end of Cariba. Esti knew it was near enough to swim from Manchicay Beach, if a person knew *how* to swim, of course, and wasn't afraid of the legends.

Now she could clearly see the police signs Steve had mentioned. *Extreme Danger,* they read. *Private Property. Keep Off.*

"Are we getting out of the boat?" she asked in surprise as Domino brought them closer and turned off the engine. Despite the danger signs, her feet longed to bury themselves in the silky white sand.

"No! 'Tis cursed." Lucia's voice seemed very loud in the sudden silence. She looked at Esti with a shocked expression. "The cay is cover with manchineel tree also."

Esti studied the lush trees growing along the beach. They weren't very tall, only about twenty feet high, with apple-like fruits hanging from their branches. She thought the trees looked pretty. "What's wrong with manchineel trees?"

"Death," Ma Harris said, sitting down in front of Esti. She spoke slowly, her voice solemn. "Taste dey fruit, you die from you stomach. Burn dey wood, dey smoke kill you lung. Sit under dey branch, dey sap eat you skin. Dey be poison, dem."

Esti looked back at the cay with a startled shudder. Now that Domino had silenced the engine, she heard disturbing noises from the island, a faint drumming interspersed with eerie, whispery wails. The rumors couldn't possibly be true, she thought firmly. There was no such thing as a ghost.

"When people set dey foot to Manchineel Cay," Ma Harris continued, "dey always meet dey maker. Is death, for true. Jumbee haunt dis cay, an' some jumbee dem cause dey sour mischief on Cariba. Now . . ." Her eyes pierced Esti. "I know you does talk to a jumbee."

Esti felt her face heat up. "I don't believe in jumbees," she finally said.

Ma Harris stared at her. "You don' believe in zombie dem?"

Zombies? Wide-eyed, Esti shook her head.

"I tell you someting," Ma Harris said softly. "*Zumbi* fetish from old Congo is bad magic, use by vex slave. Yeah, I tell you someting about Cariba Island. Slave work to death by dey owner, cast many evil curse. De jumbee is powerful danger—angry dead spirit who haunt Manchineel Cay and suck away you soul with dey voice." She narrowed her eyes. "Zombie dem."

Esti squirmed as Ma Harris's expression grew even more solemn.

"I ain't tink you some bazadee child. You ain't crazy. But you have *de gift*. We come to Manchineel Cay today, so you hear pain and understand you full danger. I tell you someting, and you mus' believe what I say. Even a moko jumbee, he can hurt you also. He is powerful danger when he have power over you, child."

"Moko jumbee?" Esti asked weakly, unable to ignore the desperate moans drifting through the air.

"A good jumbee does push away evil spirit them." Lucia's

eyes flashed. "Moko jumbee he scare people who want to do bad. Like he scare Danielle on the stage, mon."

"You don' know," Ma Harris said. "Moko jumbee can protect you, but he fool you, also. De jumbee is always unpredictable, and can control you thought, if you let he. He does appear in many confusing shape and size and sometime he possess people, for true. If," she added grimly, "he let you see he at all."

Ma Harris turned to her brother. "Domino, take we away from Manchineel Cay. Esti have see danger now, but I not gon have jumbee hear all my chat."

"You say jump, sister, I ask how high." Domino's face was impassive. "Where we go now?"

"You gon catch tuna before de storm come, or what?"

Domino grinned. He powered up the engine again, and Ma Harris returned to her seat near the front of the boat.

Lucia nodded at Esti. "Don' worry," she yelled as they began speeding over the water. "Ma she teach you how to keep jumbee them out of you house. And I have like to rehearse the play with you some, if you want. The big Christmas show does come in just a few week, and Mr. Niles he put the pressure on we." She lowered her voice and glanced at the front, making sure her mother wasn't watching them. "I know you practice Shakespeare with you jumbee. *Sighing* every minute and *groaning* every hour. . . ."

She grinned at Esti's horrified expression. "You's good, for true, and I like to see if you think I got talent."

Act One. Scene Nine.

"I caught fish for dinner," Esti announced, closing the front door behind her.

"I was hoping you would say that." Aurora put aside her book as she looked up from the couch. "My mouth is watering."

"Blackfin tuna." Esti took her plastic bag to the kitchen side of the little living room, barely keeping herself from slamming it into the sink. She didn't want her mom to know how upset she was. "Lucia's uncle cleaned it for me. He unloads cargo at the airport during the week, but on the weekends he catches fish and sells it to the restaurants."

"Did you have fun?"

"Sure." Esti forced herself to nod. "I'll tell you about it while we eat, but I *have* to take a shower first. Have you seen the lightning? Apparently some hurricane east of here, which is unusual for November." She hurried out of the room before Aurora could ask any more questions.

Her mom hummed happily in the kitchen as Esti tried to wash away the reek of fish and sweat and gasoline fumes. The pleasant sound was such a nice change from the usual silence that Esti managed to calm down by the time she came back out, combing tangles from her wet hair.

She grimaced at the smell of broiling tuna, however. All she wanted to do was crawl into bed and bury herself under the covers until morning, so she could race down to the theater. She wanted to throw herself at Alan, demanding to know more—she sighed—so that . . . so that he could tell her to go away. Maybe she *needed* a hot boyfriend like the Rafe that Carmen warned her about, if only to snap her out of this growing desire for cold rejection.

Sighing again, she stared at her mom's glass of wine. The lightning had gotten closer now, accompanied by growing rumbles of thunder.

"Tell me what you did today," Aurora said. "I can't wait to hear about it."

Esti stabbed a bite of the fish with her fork. "Well, I found out that Lucia is a good actress."

Aurora raised her eyebrows.

"I mean, Carmen said she was, but I've never seen her act. Lucia planned to try out for Lady Capulet, then Mr. Niles gave that to me. She has a bit part in the chorus and mostly works on sets. She comes to every rehearsal, though, and she has big chunks of dialogue memorized with an accent she learned from a British radio station. She and I worked on the boat this afternoon with her doing Lady Capulet, and me doing Juliet. Apparently"—Esti kept her face expressionless—"she's been listening to me practice all semester after rehearsals."

"Very good," Aurora said in approval.

"Yeah."

"Did you go to Manchineel Cay?" Aurora asked as the lights flickered. "It looks so pretty from here."

"We stopped to see it, but we didn't get out of the boat. The cay is cursed. Drumbeats and eerie wails and everything."

"Really!" Aurora leaned back in her chair, taking a sip of wine. "Tell me more."

Carefully choosing her words, Esti began to explain about zumbi magic and the infamous massacre of Elon Somand. "Since Manchineel Cay is so close," she ended, "that's why the jumbees come to Cariba. We're supposed to bar up our windows at night and keep a pan of water by the front door, and a hundred grains of rice by the back door. That distracts jumbees if they try to sneak inside. Potted herbs work as repellents too, like rosemary."

"Jumbee repellent." Aurora chuckled. "That's good."

"Of course," Esti added dryly, "*moko* jumbees also live on Manchineel Cay. Those are the good spirits who fight evil and protect people."

"Hmm." Aurora looked intrigued. "Does Lucia believe all that too?"

Esti studied her tuna, wondering if she could change the subject now. "Lucia's whole family is afraid of Manchineel Cay. They were nice to me, though. Lucia said none of her friends hold grudges against white people who were born on Cariba, even if their ancestors used to own slaves. They go to all the same big island parties as Lucia's family, like Rodney's upcoming Christmas feast."

"Really? That surprises me."

"It's the Continentals they turn their noses up at. Manchicay School has brought in a lot of rich outsiders, and I think they resent us."

"It seems quite a privilege that Lucia is friends with you, then."

Esti nodded, although she still wasn't exactly sure why. At least this was a safer topic of conversation than jumbees.

"And," Aurora continued thoughtfully, "Mr. Niles probably teaches theater here because he's a local. I know you don't think he's all that good, but it might be necessary to keep the peace."

"Probably," Esti said. "Carmen thinks the theater department is all about politics. Mr. Niles has been putting a lot of pressure on Danielle, with the show coming up so soon. I guess he plans to spotlight Danielle to a few select scouts from Hollywood and New York."

"Your dad was a master at avoiding theater politics." Aurora's expression grew distant. "Especially after your television performance, he . . ." She stopped, her eyes snapping back into focus.

"He what?"

Aurora gave her a sympathetic look. "He just didn't want to hurt you, sweetie."

"But what did he do? You started to say something."

Taking a sip of wine, Aurora slowly shook her head. "I don't remember what I was going to say."

"You don't *remember*?" Esti's unsettled mood coalesced into a sudden stab of fury. "How can you forget what you were saying three seconds ago? Too much wine?"

Lightning flashed very close, followed by a deafening crack of thunder. Esti's heart pounded in shame as the lights and music went out completely. She gave her mom a mortified look in the candlelight. "I'm so sorry, Aurora. You didn't deserve that."

"No, you're right." Aurora closed her eyes, pushing her empty wineglass away. "Maybe we need a few moko jumbees around here, to get our lives under control."

"Control." Esti closed her own eyes. Her dad's favorite word suddenly felt awkward on her tongue, like an ungainly attempt at a foreign language. "What a strange concept."

❧

Although the sky still flashed with lightning, the rain briefly let up enough for Esti to hurry down Bayrum Hill the next morning without getting thoroughly soaked. Thousands of coqui frogs, delirious with the warm moisture, serenaded her progress with chirps and trills. Judging from the rain columns scattered among the nearby islands, Esti knew the lull wouldn't last.

Ma Harris's warnings pounded through Esti's brain like the uneven drumbeats from Manchineel Cay, but all she could think about was Alan's voice. Sexy, *yes*; scary, *no*. Brilliant, *yes*; dangerous, *no*. Actor, *absolutely*; zombie, *not a chance*. Boyfriend, *yes, oh yes, oh please!*

Unzipping her jacket as she walked into the theater, she shook her damp hair out of her face, listening to make sure the building was empty. Not that she would have any clue, apparently, if Ma Harris or Lucia were here.

The unmoving ceiling fans seemed unnaturally silent in the humid air, and Esti still heard the frog chorus from outside, singing endless praises to Carmen's favorite hobby. *CooKIE, cooKIE, cooKIE.* Esti wanted to tell Carmen about Alan, especially since Lucia already seemed to know, but she wasn't sure Carmen would be able to keep such an irresistible piece of gossip to herself.

Esti quickly made her way to Alan's secret door, the cookie refrain tinkling through her mind as she navigated the tiny passage. To her astonishment, she saw a flicker of light as she approached the little room downstairs. As the air began dancing with soft lute music, she stopped in the doorway. A small wooden table took up most of the tiny room, lit by a single candle. Creamy white blossoms were scattered across the table, filling the air with wonderful sweetness.

"Alan?" She felt her own heartbeat vibrating through his name, hope making her dizzy. "Pardon me, I pray you," she added breathlessly, "I thought that all things had been savage here."

"I couldn't find Shakespearean rose or lily for you," he replied, "so the frangipani is tropical. No doubt by any other name it would smell as sweet."

She smiled, trying not to be too obvious as she searched the dim room for some physical sign of him. Neat rows of red brick and white mortar rose from the floor to above her head, the arched ceiling barely high enough for her to stand. The doorway was arched as well, and she strained to see some movement in the pitch-black hallway she'd just left.

She would give almost anything for Alan to walk through that opening. *Sweep me into your arms,* she thought. *Please please please, no matter how lame that sounds.*

She sat down, raising one of the blossoms to her nose. "What's the occasion?"

"This morning I will answer your questions." She heard a deep sigh. "It was the only time I could be sure we are alone."

"Without Ma Harris and Lucia, you mean?" Esti wondered if he'd always known about the eavesdropping.

"On Sunday mornings"—his voice held a hint of amusement—"they are at church."

"They don't seem like the church type." Esti leaned back in the hard wooden chair, pretending to be calm.

"Oh, they are; very much so. Most West Indians have a complex belief system comprised of ancient Obeah traditions, centuries of slavery survival, and a powerful dose of Christianity. It's fascinating, and they are generally quite devout."

"You're trying to distract me with all of this."

"No," he said softly. "I'm ready. On your mark, get set, go."

Esti smiled again, her mind racing with the questions he'd already rebuffed, as well as a million others she hadn't had a chance to ask yet. "Where do you live? Why do you hide? You're not *really* a ghost! Who taught you Shakespeare? What do you look like? Who *are* you? How do I hear your voice? Are you ever afraid of the dark?"

He burst into laughter. "One at a time, please."

She gripped the chair. "Okay, where were you born?"

"On a sailboat."

"Here?"

"Essentially, yes."

She could barely sit still. "Did you grow up here?"

"No."

"Please," she said when he didn't continue. "Are we going to be so literal?"

"Yes." She heard his smile. "We are."

"Where did you grow up?"

"I lived on my parents' sailboat until a hurricane killed them."

"I'm sorry," she said, startled that she had no better response than a platitude she'd always resented from others. "How old were you?"

"A baby."

"You weren't on the boat, then?"

"I washed up on a nearby island."

She traced the edge of the table with her thumb. "Alan, come on."

"I'm utterly serious."

"Discovered in the wreckage?"

"Of course."

"How suspiciously Shakespeare." She shook her head. "Were you rescued by a passing king?"

"Possibly," Alan said, amused. "I don't remember."

"Hmm." Esti forced a smile, backtracking to an earlier question. "Where did you say you grew up?"

"I didn't say."

She gave her chair a not-quite-playful kick. "Alan, where did you grow up?"

"Around. A Danish uncle took me in for several years when I was little."

"And when you got big?"

"As soon as I was old enough, he sent me to boarding school."

"In Denmark?"

"London."

"Ah," she said in satisfaction. "Is that where you learned Shakespeare?"

"Yes."

"You must have loved it there."

"I despised the place," he said flatly.

"Why?" She kept her voice neutral.

"That would be far too complicated to explain." Esti heard a familiar tightness in his voice. "Let's stick with single-word answers."

"You're too complicated to be explained away in single words," she said.

"To be sure." He was silent for a long moment. "I've answered enough for today."

Her heart began pounding again as she realized her tiny window of opportunity had slammed shut. "Alan, I haven't even begun to ask!"

"I can't do it, Esti," he forced out. "I thought I could, but I was wrong. Perhaps I should answer a question you haven't precisely asked. The answer is no, I can't give you what you're looking for."

"You don't know what I'm looking for." She barely kept herself from slamming her hand on the table. "Alan, I can't see you. I can't touch you. You're a voice telling me things you think I want to hear. I mean, *no one* washes up on an island in real life. So here's a question that only needs one word. Are you a jumbee?"

He didn't answer.

"Here's one I'll answer for you. Do you have power over me?" She took a deep breath. "Yes, you do."

Silence.

"Will I *ever* see you?"

Nothing.

"Why are you doing this?" Her heart pounded so loud in the silence now, she could almost feel it rattling the door. Clutching the edge of the table, she resorted to a quote from *Hamlet*. "Be thou a spirit of health or goblin damned? Be thy intents wicked or charitable?"

"Oh, Esti." She heard a soft, reluctant chuckle. "You are the one with power. I can't run away from you, no matter how hard I try." He sighed. "My intents are charitable, but I am not a spirit of health."

"You're a goblin damned?"

"I like you, Esti. I like you far too much." His voice grew so soft she could barely hear him. "And you terrify me." The whisper brushed her ears, floating like a wisp of cloud in the flickering darkness of their practice room.

Esti knew she hadn't heard him right. "What did you say?"

"Act One, Scene Two." This time he spoke clearly, even if he sounded a bit strangled. "Rosalind, be merry."

Act One. Scene Ten.

"What do you mean, Danielle won't be here tonight?" Esti stared in disbelief at Carmen's reflection in the mirror. The dressing room had become a madhouse as the cast raced to get their costumes and makeup perfect. Esti couldn't have possibly heard her right over the chaos.

Carmen was laughing so hard, she couldn't talk. Wiping tears from her eyes, she leaned against the wall and slid to the floor, pulling Nurse's brown robe around her drawn-up legs.

Esti replaced the lid on the jar of makeup and carefully turned to look at her friend. "You're kidding."

"She has dysentery."

"What's that?"

"A tropical disease of the intestines. I looked it up." Carmen couldn't keep a straight face, and she started laughing again. "She has *the runs*, Esti. Is that the most perfect thing you've ever heard? For four years Danielle managed to convince Niles she didn't need an understudy. Now Manchicay's Christmas performance starts in an hour, and Juliet is stuck on a toilet for the next three days. If this doesn't prove she's full of crap, I don't know what would." Carmen almost howled. "I just overheard Niles talking to Rodney Solomon. Boy, is Niles furious."

Esti couldn't quite bring herself to laugh. "What's he going to do?"

"Niles need someone who have Juliet memorize." Lucia emerged from behind the heavy curtain surrounding the girls' private changing area. As she casually picked up Lady Capulet's satin gown, holding it against her for size, a chill ran down Esti's spine. Lucia had been practicing for the part of Lady Capulet all semester.

"You knew this was going to happen."

"Nah, mon." Lucia shrugged. "I had tell you a long time ago, you got a moko jumbee take care of you. 'Tis always good to be prepare."

Esti shook her head. Alan couldn't possibly have made Danielle sick.

"Esti!"

She shrank back as Mr. Niles strode through the door.

"You played Juliet before," he said. "Is there any chance you still know the part?"

The dressing room fell silent. Esti swallowed and nodded.

"And I have Lady Capulet memorize," Lucia said softly.

Niles glanced at Lucia, then turned back to Esti. The confusion and fear in his eyes hit her like a slap in the face. "I'll see you on stage in forty-five minutes."

As Niles raced back out, Greg leaned against the far mirror, his expression suspicious.

"Don't look at me like that," Esti said, trying to suppress her rising panic.

"It's not her fault, you idiot!" Carmen shoved herself back up to her feet and glared at Greg. "You spent all day with Danielle. I bet *you* knew she was getting sick, didn't you? You didn't warn Niles, so don't you dare blame this on Esti."

Greg had opened his mouth, but now he closed it and turned away, muttering to Chaz.

Oh, God. Esti wasn't sure if she said the words aloud. When nobody turned to look at her, she decided she'd managed to keep her panic inside. Even more astonishing, nobody seemed to hear the wild thudding of her heart. *I can't do it.*

"You need a costume," Carmen whooped. "We've got forty-five minutes to turn you into a hot Capulet *chiquita.*"

"Two households, both alike in dignity, in fair Verona, where we lay our scene."

Esti realized she'd bitten her fingernails down to the quick as she listened to the opening lines of the prologue. Carmen applied her makeup for her, since her fingers shook too much to do it for herself. Lucia had tracked down Ma Harris to get the janitor keys, and in the costume closet behind the stage, they found an old green velvet gown, musty and three sizes too big.

"A pair of star-cross'd lovers take their life," the chorus continued on stage.

Esti had been certain she was ready to face the critics again, but she knew now that she wasn't. Juliet would crumble during the scene with Lord Capulet, and no one would ever pick up the pieces again. She would limp through the rest of the play like she had last time, desperately hoping they wouldn't notice she was a fake. They would notice, of course. She was certain they'd all been waiting for this moment, when they could tear apart the imitation Legard like hungry piranhas.

I can't do it.

"The clothes don't matter *so* much," Carmen insisted. "This will be good enough for tonight. All we need are a couple of safety pins, and you're set."

It took the whole box of safety pins, but Carmen finally managed to drape the green velvet around Esti, pulling the gown tight above her waist in a way that almost looked authentic. Esti barely noticed the reek of mothballs; she just hoped the pins would hold.

She had been fooling herself. What had made her think that Manchicay School would be different? Had she really thought she would be far enough from her dad's perfect presence, just because he was dead and Ashland was thousands of miles away? They would seize the Legard name with both hands, wringing her performance dry.

I can't do it.

"Act One is about to start," Carmen said. "I have to get out there, so you need to finish the rest of this by yourself. All you've got to do is pull back all that hair and pin your cap on. Don't worry, Jane Doe, you'll be great."

"Thank you," Esti managed as Carmen rushed out the

door. Only Lance still remained on the far side of the dressing room, pretending to ignore her as he put the finishing touches on his Lord Capulet costume.

❧

"Oh, God," she whispered. She wasn't worried about her lines; she'd had the dialogue memorized since she was ten. Of all the characters she'd ever practiced with Alan, however, he had avoided playing Romeo to her Juliet. She had never practiced blocking Juliet's actions with anyone here, and she dreaded the love scenes with Greg. Worst of all, Lance was about to rip her heart into tiny shreds, although he didn't even know it.

"I'm in control," she murmured. "If I believe that, I can make everyone else believe it too."

"Of course you're in control."

"Alan!" She fought to keep her voice down so that Lance might think she was rehearsing her lines.

"You'll bring down the house tonight, you know you will." His voice wrapped around her with surprising warmth. "You're going to show them a Juliet the island will talk about for years."

Although Esti felt a surge of strength at his confidence, she hesitated. "You didn't have anything to do with this, did you?"

"Your Juliet will be impeccable." Alan laughed. "And how could I have known Danielle would choose today to get sick? For the first time since I've known her, her timing is perfect."

"Perfect?" Esti shook her head, searching for some humor. "Do you see what I'm wearing?"

She saw Lance look over as her joke fell flat. With an uncertain smile of encouragement, he walked out the door.

"Stay calm." Alan sounded amused. "You could walk out there in your blue jeans, and nobody would notice after the first thirty seconds. Juliet will be clothed in the words Shakespeare has written for her. You'll hold that audience with your voice and with your passion, Esti. Everyone in the theater will be in tears tonight, you take my word for it."

His eloquent reassurance sounded eerily like her dad, and she rubbed the goose bumps on her arms. "But Greg . . ."

"You're an *actress.* Fortunately, Greg is worthy of a much better counterpart than Danielle. By the end of the evening, Romeo will be completely yours."

"And the scene with Lord Capulet?" she whispered. "I can't do it, Alan."

"Use that emotion," he whispered. "You are in control, and you are going to bring the stage alive."

Esti dropped her head into her hands.

"In a few moments you will *be* Juliet. The cast will fly on your energy."

Staring into the mirror, Esti made herself nod. Carmen had done a nice job with her makeup, and Esti had been feeling a lot like a star-crossed lover lately. Maybe she could pull this off after all.

"That's better, gentle Esti. Now, close your eyes. Promise you'll keep them closed for a moment."

"Okay." She took another deep breath and let her eyelids drop.

"Wear this for me," he murmured Rosalind's words, "one out of suits with fortune. As you feel it against your skin, remember what we've been doing all semester. Don't be afraid to dig deeply into your own emotions. When the lights come up, everyone in this building will be stunned to realize they are not in Verona."

As Esti became aware of a warm scent—an island flower in sunlight—she felt a feathery tickle against her shoulders that instantly drove all other thoughts from her mind. Alan had touched her. He wasn't just in her mind, some cruel voodoo trick of a haunted island. He was real, and he was *here*.

"Esti, your hair!" Carmen's voice filled the dressing room.

Esti's eyes flew open as Carmen pulled her hair back into a barrette and jammed a cap on her head. A frangipani blossom lay on the table before her, and in the mirror she saw a delicate chain necklace, like the one Rosalind had given Orlando to prove her devotion. Esti's fingers flew to her throat, grasping for proof that she wasn't imagining the flower captured in a tiny golden pendant.

"Come on!" Carmen dragged her away from the dressing table. "Scene Two is almost over. Lucia's waiting for us in the wings."

Esti was grateful that Juliet only had a few short lines in Scene Three. She let Carmen beckon her out on stage, aware of the necklace around her neck, but forcing her twitching fingers to remain at her sides. Juliet wouldn't be fiddling with a golden chain.

She listened in growing wonder as Carmen and Lucia bantered the words of Nurse and Lady Capulet like they'd been rehearsing together all semester. As the audience began chuckling partway through Nurse's monologue, Esti caught a glimpse of Aurora near the front of the packed theater. Focusing on the necklace against her skin, she closed her eyes and pretended she was in Italy.

By the time Lucia led her off the stage, Esti could almost hear vendors hawking their wares on the streets of Verona as Romeo discussed romance with his friends. And when she returned a few minutes later for the masquerade ball, she was ready.

She gave Greg a polite, questioning look, as Juliet would do when approached by a friend in disguise. Esti was gone, she thought, from this moment on to be Juliet. Her emotions were Juliet's emotions.

Control.

Juliet will be clothed in the words Shakespeare has written. Alan was right; she controlled Romeo and the rest of the cast—perhaps the entire audience—with the emotion and attitude of Shakespeare's words.

"If I profane with my unworthiest hand this holy shrine," Greg began, a hint of sarcasm in his voice, "the gentle sin is this: My lips, two blushing pilgrims ready stand, to smooth that rough touch with a tender kiss."

Esti allowed the audience to watch her study Greg.

After a moment, she turned away from him, pleasure in her voice. "Good pilgrim, you do wrong your hand too much, which mannerly devotion shows in this." She shyly bit her lip and glanced at him again. "For saints have hands that pilgrims' hands do touch, and palm to palm is holy palmers' kiss."

He straightened, his eyes showing real interest. Esti felt a stab of satisfaction. Or was the satisfaction coming from Juliet? Gazing into his eyes as they continued, she watched him slowly melt. The farthest row in the theater heard her subtle invitation for Romeo's kiss, yet the words felt like a whisper. By the time his lips brushed hers, the entire theater shimmered with anticipation.

Esti closed her eyes, her body consumed by the warm delight of Juliet. "Then have my lips the sin that they have took."

"Sin from my lips?" Greg's voice had precisely the right amount of distress. "O trespass sweetly urg'd! Give me my sin again."

She giggled, already in love with the charming poet who stood in front of her.

❧

Esti had forgotten the audience existed by the time she laid Romeo's dagger to rest in its final deadly sheath. She lay motionless on the stage with her arm draped over Greg's chest, aware of the sounds of sniffs and nose-blowing. As she listened to the Capulets and Montagues make grieving amends with one another, she abruptly realized that she had succeeded.

"For never was a story of more woe," the prince concluded somberly, "than this of Juliet and her Romeo."

As Juliet slipped away from her, Esti blinked back tears. Alan's necklace tickled her throat, and she knew without a doubt that this was the best performance she'd ever given. If only her dad could have seen her.

Esti followed the cast onstage three times for curtain calls. Emotions churned beneath the veneer of her smile, threatening to explode before she could safely tuck them away. Incredulous joy, overwhelming gratitude, aching sadness. Although she enjoyed the standing ovation, she wished everyone would quit clapping. Her head pounded in time with the applause, and she wanted to go home and collapse.

As soon as the house lights came on, however, the stage was mobbed. Trapped beside Greg, Esti forced herself to smile and nod at people marveling at Manchicay's excellent production. She heard Carmen exclaiming *she* knew all along that Esti was better than Danielle, and hadn't the whole cast been great?

Even Mr. Niles congratulated Esti with a pat on her shoulder, although his smile seemed a little forced. With a sigh, she watched him until he disappeared on the far side of the stage. He was obviously disappointed by Danielle's lost chance, but the hard-earned praise made her smile.

As she began planning her exit, Greg suddenly draped his arm around her shoulders and drew her close. "I always knew you could act," he whispered into her ear. "You're incredible. Let's go out and celebrate."

"Right." Trying not to laugh, she gave him a wink. "Don't you need Danielle's permission for that?"

To her relief, Aurora appeared in front of her with a knowing look. "Ready to go home?"

Esti ignored Greg's protests. With an excuse about being exhausted, she followed her mom out of the theater. As soon as they got to the courtyard outside, she sagged with relief in the cool night air.

"Thanks. Oh, my God."

Her mom laughed. "You looked floored in there. I am so proud of you, sweetie. I was thrilled to see you come onstage as Juliet. What happened to Danielle?"

"She got sick," Esti said. "I found out just before the show started."

Aurora smiled. "I feel sorry for her, but I can't deny that she kind of deserved it. You did a great job tonight. The entire cast was wonderful."

"Thanks." Esti couldn't help smiling too. "I sure wish Dad had seen it."

"Oh, sweetie." Her mom suddenly gave her a hug. "I do too. If he'd seen you tonight, I *know* he would have approved of us coming to Cariba. Do you want me to pull out your old Juliet costumes, in case you need them tomorrow?"

"Yes, please." Esti closed her eyes as a puff of warm wind whispered across the parking lot. "That would be great. I dropped safety pins all over the stage tonight."

"You drop-kicked the whole audience, mon. Juliet was a knockout."

They both looked up in surprise. A West Indian boy leaned against a Jeep in front of them, his black hair braided in tight cornrows. His eyes reflected the building lights as he grinned at their astonished expressions.

"Fourth grade. Los Angeles."

"Rafe Solomon," Aurora exclaimed.

"For true." He laughed.

"How did you get so tall?"

"It happens." He flashed an easy smile at Esti.

Speechless, she stared up at him, her heart giving an extra thump. His eyes sparkled as they met hers, his teeth white and perfect against smooth dark skin. She'd had no idea that cornrows could look so good in a boy's hair. No wonder Carmen had warned her, she thought. Rafe was gorgeous.

"What's with the program tonight saying you were Lady Capulet?" he asked. "And why did I used to think your name was Serene?"

Act Two

Act Two. Scene One.

"You're visiting your parents for Christmas?" Esti traced her fingers along the necklace Alan had given her, determined not to let herself be taken in by Rafe's charm. The tiny golden pendant followed her touch.

Rafe had offered to drive them up Bayrum Hill in his dad's Jeep, and Aurora happily invited him into the house. Her mom must not have heard about his reputation, Esti thought, or she wouldn't have left them alone so soon on the balcony. As Rafe grinned at her behind his glass of juice, however, Esti couldn't help wondering why they had never reconnected after she moved to Oregon. He was a walking dream; even his eyelashes were long and perfect.

"I start at UCLA next fall," Rafe said. "I've been working in Los Angeles since I got out of high school last year, until I quit my job a couple of days ago. I can make better money at my uncle's restaurant, and I don't have to pay rent at my parents' house. You want to go snorkeling in the morning?"

"I can't swim." Taking a sip of juice, she smiled at him.

"You haven't seen the reefs yet?" Rafe didn't hesitate. "You gotta come with me, then. We can stay in the shallows until you get the hang of it."

Private lessons from Rafe Solomon. Tomorrow morning she would drown, never again to play Juliet. All because of a good-looking boy she'd known in fourth grade. What would Alan think of that? She studied Rafe for a moment longer, trying to decide whether he was flirting or treating her like a long-lost friend. The hopeful look in his eyes gave it away.

"No, but thank you," she said.

"You sure?" Rafe said in disappointment. "Well, think about it anyway. The water's super warm this year, and I got plenty of snorkeling gear." Undeterred, his face quickly lit up again. "So, what are you doing on Cariba? When my dad told me you had a bit part in the school play, I didn't believe him. Of course, Juliet isn't any bit part. I thought Danielle had that all wrapped up for herself. And what's with the name Esti?"

"Don't you remember? You called me S.T., for Serene Terra." She briefly glanced up at a whispery wail in the breeze, not sure what to make of Rafe's barrage of questions. Although Manchineel Cay wasn't visible in the darkness, she could barely discern an uneven drumbeat. *The island doth protest too much,* she thought absurdly.

Ignoring the sounds, she turned back to Rafe. "I always liked the name, so now everyone calls me Esti."

"You changed your name because of *me?*" Studying her face, he slowly smiled again.

With a deep breath, she looked back out at the sea again, twisting the necklace around her fingers. Despite Carmen's warnings, Rafe's smile did something disturbing to her heartbeat. A warm boyfriend would be awfully nice.

"I thought about you sometimes," he said. "No, a lot, actually. Especially whenever your dad had a new movie coming out. And I saw you a couple of years ago on TV. I bragged to my buddies that you were my girlfriend in fourth grade." Before she could answer, he gave her a rueful grin. "I was too embarrassed to try and track you down. I didn't think you'd remember me, but then my dad told me you're staying here in the Bayrum house."

Esti seriously doubted that he'd been too embarrassed to find her. More likely he was too busy chasing girls. "I remember you doing my math homework for me," she said.

"You know what I remember," he said earnestly, "is you speaking in Shakespeare, like some foreign language. You were always in total control, and I couldn't understand a word you said."

"Control?" Was that really how he remembered her? "Not even close. It was all an act."

"So to speak."

Esti laughed. "Honestly, I didn't understand much Shakespeare either, when I first started. I just memorized the sounds."

"That makes me feel better." He gave an exaggerated sigh. "You're still so good, I'm surprised you'll even talk to me now. After watching Juliet tonight, I don't know if I have the nerve to ask you out."

As Esti raised her eyebrows, the corner of his mouth slowly turned up in another smile. When her body responded with a delightful tingle, she shook her head. He was very good at this game, but she wouldn't go out with him. She had no reason to doubt Carmen's list of troubles behind that stunning smile, and her heart was focused on Alan.

Rafe's eyes became serious, intently searching hers. "Please tell me you're not dating Greg Timmons."

"Of course not." She shook her head again. "He's a jerk."

He leaned forward. "Are you seeing someone else?"

"Yes." Her skin tightened over her scalp as she thought about the delicate necklace resting against her throat. She had never *seen* Alan.

"Of course you got a boyfriend." Rafe scowled. "How dumb can I be?"

"Well, he's . . ." Another tingle swept through Esti as Rafe's eyes again grew hopeful. When he nudged his chair closer, she quickly turned away. "I'm not available."

They were both quiet for a moment, the silence only broken by trade winds swirling around them. Finally Rafe cleared his throat. "Let me know if that ever changes."

Although his words left the future open, the resigned tone of his voice seemed real, for the first time all evening.

Esti looked at him again, unable to resist a teasing smile. "I'm sorry."

"Me too." He met her eyes with an abashed grin. "You sure you don't want to go swimming tomorrow? For what it's worth, I'm a certified instructor. I *am* capable of being completely professional."

"Promise?"

He sighed. "If I have to."

"Because a girl can't live on a Caribbean island without knowing how to swim. Right?"

"Still in control." Shaking his head, he began to laugh. "You haven't changed at all."

❧

As Esti stood in waist-deep water the next morning, she wondered what she had been thinking.

"My uncle owns a dive shop, so I actually know what I'm doing." Rafe adjusted the face mask to fit her head.

Although the warm water felt nice, the ocean looked huge from this far out in the shallows. Esti had never been in past her knees before, except from the safety of a boat. She couldn't imagine anything beneath the surface worth risking her life for, and she felt vulnerable in her skimpy black swimsuit, reeking of coconut sunscreen.

"You'll be fine," Rafe added. "The best thing about snorkeling is how you can just let go and stop worrying. Let the sea take control, while you relax and enjoy the show."

Esti slowly draped the mask over her head. "You're telling me it's all about being out of control."

"It'll be good for you, honest." He gave her a mischievous look. "So, here's how you work the snorkel."

Clamping down on her fear, Esti copied Rafe's movements, wrapping her lips around the mouthpiece and biting. It felt as absurd as it looked, and she tried not to hyperventilate at the concept of breathing underwater. The idea of deliberately not being in control was as scary as it was compelling.

"The best reefs are out by the cays," Rafe said, spitting out his mouthpiece to talk, "but Manchicay Bay is a great place to see fish. Put your face down until you're under the water, and the top of your snorkel will stay in the air so you can breathe. I'll be right beside you if you need help."

She felt his hands on her shoulder and her waist, light and restrained. Clutching the mouthpiece in her teeth, she lifted her feet and sank into the water with deep, sucking breaths. She was about to drown, for the privilege of seeing a few fish.

To her surprise, the fish were beautiful. A large yellow and black striped angelfish hovered beside her, long fins and tail streaming gracefully from its body. As it darted away, she saw hundreds of bright blue fish dancing and turning in perfect harmony; the slanting rays of the morning sun caught them like iridescent sequins sparkling in the water. The nearby rocks rose from the sea floor like underwater mountains, covered with swaying seaweed and bright coral in alien shapes.

She was flying, she thought in astonishment, magically suspended on the undulating surface of the sea. When Rafe's face appeared beside her, she laughed out loud. Water immediately filled the mask as her smiling cheeks broke the airtight seal. Lurching upward in panic, she tried to speak, and the sea rushed into her mouth as well. Rafe yanked her out of the water, pulling the mask and tube away from her face.

"It's okay," he said. "The bottom's right here, just put your feet down. Nothing to be afraid of."

Esti grabbed him, spitting salty water and choking for air. He wrapped his fingers firmly around her waist, holding her steady as she became aware of the heat from his hands. As electricity raced through her body, she instantly pulled herself away. Although the water barely came above her hips, she hoped he would think her rapid breathing was due to nearly drowning, rather than the breathtaking proximity of their bodies.

"Sorry about that," she said without looking at him. It had occurred to her that the biggest danger today might have nothing to do with the sea.

"You're doing great!" he said enthusiastically. "Most beginners glue their feet to the bottom, but you were floating on the first try."

"It felt like flying." She gave him a quick glance as she brought her breathing under control. "Flying in the sea, while watching an alien ballet."

"Yeah, mon," Rafe said with a smile. "That's *exactly* how I feel."

When her body tingled again, she lifted her chin in determination. "I'm ready to start over." Rafe had promised to stay professional, and Esti would make sure of it. "I had no idea how pretty it was down there."

"Yeah." His eyes hadn't left hers. "Makes me wonder what else is hiding beneath the surface." He looked away before she could, untangling the masks he had draped over his arm. "Keep the mask tight against your face once you're underwater. No smiling this time. But we'll only float for a few more minutes. As soon as you're ready, I *am* going to teach you how to swim."

She readjusted the snorkel against her face, fiddling with her mask until her heartbeat returned to normal.

First he showed her how to relax, letting her body float while she watched the fish. Then he swam circles around her while she kicked with rubber fins. Best of all, he taught her how to move her arms and legs in deeper water so she stayed up even without a snorkel and fins. "You're swimming," he pointed out as she tried to get used to the idea of keeping her head above the water. "I knew it wouldn't take long."

When they finally flopped onto their beach towels, Esti was exhausted. "Thank you," she said, studying a pretty seashell Rafe had plucked from the ocean floor for her. "If this is being out of control, maybe I like it."

Rafe laughed, rolling onto his side and propping his head on his hand to look down at her. "That's the thing," he said. "When you swim, the sea takes over. Nothing in the water gives a rip about you and your problems. Not that *you* have any problems, but it sure keeps my head on straight."

Esti smiled at the bizarre notion of having no problems.

"If you want more lessons," Rafe added, "let me know. By the end of Christmas break you could be racing me across the bay. I need someone to go diving with."

"Scuba diving?" She raised her eyebrows. "You mean, in deep water?"

"We'd start easy and hang out near the cays. Their corals aren't as damaged as the reefs close to Cariba."

"Not that cay, though."

Rafe snorted as she gestured toward Manchineel Cay. "Of course you've heard the legends."

She attempted a poor imitation of Ma Harris's voice. "I hear so much ting about jumbee dem."

"Dey jumbee dem stay away from you when I's around, babe," Rafe shot back. "You sweet too bad, an' I ain't gon stand for no jumbee threaten you and thing."

She burst into laughter. "That's right. You used to have an accent. You sound just like a California boy these days."

"I learned how to turn it off in L.A." He grinned. "Most of us turn it back on when we talk to each other. West Indian dialect has a great rhythm, and it's a sign of respect when we talk *real* to each other. If you heard me and my parents talking, you wouldn't understand a word. Just like when you used to hit me with your Shakespeare."

"I always liked the way you talked." The memory made her strangely happy. "How often do you come to Cariba?"

"Every Christmas." Rafe stared out at the water, his expression content. "And most summers. My family's been here forever. The Solomons and Harrises—you know Lucia—were slaves on the old Manchicay plantation. Now my uncle owns three restaurants and a dive shop, and my cousin's a senator. This time I'm staying for a few months, like I told you. I gotta save up some money for college next year, and I'm hoping . . ." He paused, then gave her a quick sideways look. ". . . you might decide to learn how to scuba dive. I'm a certified instructor for that too."

Esti thought about the beautiful secret world hiding within the sea. "I can't believe I'm saying this, but it sounds appealing."

"Very appealing." He clearly wasn't speaking about scuba diving, and the flirting words played her like a light switch, the charge pulsing all the way to the tips of her toes.

She instantly looked away, rolling over to sit up on her towel.

"Completely professional," Rafe added dryly. "I promise."

I could talk you out of that, Esti thought in confusion, disturbed by how easily he was able to turn her on. "Do you teach scuba diving at your uncle's shop?" she asked.

"Nah, I make better money bartending. Continentals are annoying unless they're throwing big tips at me while they're drunk." He gave her his irrepressible grin. "When I'm flying in the water, I'd rather do it with someone I like."

It was all Esti could do to keep from reaching out to stroke her fingertips along the smooth black cornrows braided over his head. She wanted to touch him and feel his hands on her again, and it was unsettling. Very deliberately, she dropped his seashell into her beach bag, then lifted her fingers to touch Alan's necklace. "I'm a Continental."

"Not really. You already got a reputation on Cariba, you know."

"*I* have a reputation?" she asked flippantly.

"Even you." Rafe managed to keep a straight face. "'Tis a small island, babe."

She tried to imagine the things Danielle might have said about her. "And what would my reputation be?"

"Everyone says you got *de gift*. Most West Indians never met a white girl who talks to jumbees."

"That's ridiculous." Of all the gossip she might have worried about, it had never occurred to Esti that the crazy jumbee rumors were spreading beyond Danielle's little clique. "I don't know anything about jumbees, except what Ma Harris told me."

He laughed. "Ma Harris has her own ideas. Everyone on Cariba is afraid of her."

"Great." Tightness crawled up Esti's spine and along her scalp, like a keening wail from Manchineel Cay. Alan couldn't have touched her if he weren't real. Zombies didn't go around giving girls necklaces. And he wouldn't have done it unless it meant . . . something.

As Rafe leaned back down on his towel, still smiling, her restlessness grew. She scooped her fingers into the sand, wondering what exactly she had with Alan. He'd finally admitted that he liked her, even if his weird paranoia kept him in hiding. Her time with him was sheer magic; their minds seemed to meet perfectly when they were together.

But she clearly needed someone she could see and touch. She wanted a face to look at; she craved warm hands holding her waist. And she couldn't help wondering what it felt like to kiss a boy—not a rehearsed moment in front of an audience, but for real.

Aware of Rafe's eyes on her, she scraped her fingers

through the sand, wondering if she really *was* going crazy. What normal, sane girl would fall in love with a disembodied voice in the dark anyway? When Aurora finally heard the wild rumors—which she would, even in her seclusion—Esti was going to have a lot of explaining to do.

No. It was Alan who had some explaining to do.

Esti abruptly wiped the sand smooth. It was time for him to prove the rumors wrong. She *did* want to be with him, and if he could give her a necklace, he could give her more. This time she wouldn't back down.

She looked up at Rafe. "We should go. I need to start getting ready for tonight."

"Okay." He seemed amused, undoubtedly aware of the turmoil he'd been wreaking in her body all day. He'd probably been through the same thing dozens of times. When he held out his hand to help her up, she shook her head, scrambling to her feet by herself.

Undeterred, he scooped up her beach towel and flung it over his shoulder to carry for her. "Can I give you a ride to school?"

Esti nodded, suddenly impatient with herself. Whatever his intentions, Rafe was being very nice. She had no right to jump to conclusions, especially since part of her secretly wished he *would* try for a kiss.

"Sure," she said with a smile. "I appreciate it."

Act Two. Scene Two.

The parking lot was already half full, locals chatting and gesturing toward the theater as Rafe parked the Jeep.

"Check this out," he said. "Everyone's here early to see what the hype is about."

"Because the play was so good last night?" Esti told herself it was no big deal; in Ashland she had performed before bigger crowds than this.

"My dad got the word around. Hey, thanks for going snorkeling with me today."

"Thanks for teaching me how not to drown." She glanced around the parking lot again. People were staring at her, many of them whispering animatedly as their eyes moved between her and Rafe.

"A lot of them just want to see Esti Legard, jumbee whisperer," Rafe continued casually. "They're fascinated by you."

"Huh?" She turned to him in disbelief.

"Huh?" he teased. "See, I'm not the only one. I'm just the lucky one."

"What do you mean?"

"I mean I had a great time today."

As he flashed his million-dollar smile, Esti realized Rafe was playing up his audience. She wondered if Alan knew the jumbee gossip had been spreading like wildfire.

"How old were we when we met?" Rafe added. "I feel like I've known you forever. That sounds dumb, though, doesn't it?"

"Dumb as a doornail," she said absently. After a moment, she focused back on Rafe, softening the sarcastic words with a repentant smile. She couldn't get mad, even if he was using the moment to his advantage. She'd honestly had a wonderful day. "I was five."

"And you split when I was eleven. How could I have wasted all these years? I'm an idiot, obviously."

"Obviously," she quipped. *And you're not the only one.*

"My dad has front row tickets," he said. "I'll see you later tonight, even if you don't see me."

She nodded, her mind on Alan again. Trying to pretend the crowds of people weren't watching, she reached behind her seat for the big plastic bag of Juliet costumes. "Thanks, Rafe. I had fun today too."

Carmen stood at the doors of the theater, her expression incredulous as Esti approached the building with her costumes. "That *was* Rafe Solomon, wasn't it? Lucia said she saw you leave together last night, but I wasn't sure I believed her."

Esti blushed as her eyes met Carmen's. "I told you we were old friends."

"Esti!"

She winced at Carmen's shriek. If anyone had somehow missed her arrival with Rafe, they certainly knew Esti Legard was here now.

"Did you spend the night with him?"

144

"No, I didn't spend the night with him." Dragging her friend into the theater, Esti slammed the door shut behind them. "We went swimming today."

"I thought you didn't know how to swim."

"I do now. He's a certified instructor."

"Right." Carmen sounded impatient. "He's certified, all right. You know he's slept with half the girls on Cariba?"

"You already told me that." Esti strode down the long aisle, wondering if Alan was listening.

"And I can practically guarantee he'll tangle with the jandam before Christmas break is over. He attacked a cop last summer after they busted up one of his fights."

"Your point is?"

"My point is, you're smarter than that. Do you know that when the rest of us went out after the play last night, the only thing Greg could talk about was you? He never realized what a truly superb actress you are, and wasn't it good Danielle got sick so you had a chance to prove yourself. I mean, like it never occurred to him before that you're going to be this famous actress we can all say we went to high school with."

Esti came to a dismayed stop. "Carmen . . ."

"I was thrilled, thinking how Danielle's had this coming to her and you deserved glory more than anyone after being picked on so much. And here I bet you were fooling around with Rafe Solomon all night, weren't you?"

Now Esti *really* hoped Alan wasn't listening. "I was not fooling around with Rafe."

"Carmen, you leave she alone." Lucia's dark eyes flashed as

she approached. She stopped in front of them, jamming her fists on her hips. "Esti she does need to be perfect tonight, and so do we. You maybe just shut up now and get you costume together."

Carmen frowned at Lucia, taken aback. "Well, sure," she said. "Don't get all worked up. I'm coming."

As soon as Carmen and Lucia were occupied with their costumes, Esti slipped away. Although she appreciated Carmen's concern, the drama seemed a bit overblown. Could Carmen be jealous? Quietly creeping into the back hallway maze, Esti felt her way to the staircase. She was grateful that Lucia had come to her defense, except, she thought uneasily, maybe it was because Lucia knew something she didn't. It wouldn't be the first time.

The air pressed against her skin, stifling and humid as she made her way down the narrow steps. Beads of sweat trickled down the side of her face as she wondered how much Alan had heard. She didn't want him assuming she had jumped into the arms of a cute boy the minute she had a chance.

"Alan?" She swept her hand over her forehead as soon as she reached the bottom, hoping he wasn't upset with her. "Where are you?"

Despite the cooler air in the basement, the silence felt thick and heavy as muffled voices filtered in from above. She'd been sure Alan would be here somewhere, and she wondered if he just wasn't answering. After calling for him one more time, Esti finally gave up and hurried back upstairs.

As she ducked behind the curtain of the girls' changing area to get into Juliet's first gown, she uneasily touched her necklace.

"Guess what?" Carmen drawled from the dressing room doorway after Esti sat down in front of the mirror to put on her makeup. "Danielle's here. Chaz saw her. He said the theater's packed, and people are even sitting in the aisles and standing in the back."

Esti was glad Danielle felt better, but she wanted to play Juliet again, to prove herself to the talent scouts—and to Alan.

"Don't vex," Lucia said, stopping in the doorway beside Carmen. She gave Esti a reassuring look in the mirror. "Danielle, she ain't gon get onstage tonight."

"She's in the back row by the door, so she can make a run for the bathroom." Carmen laughed at Esti's expression. "And Rafe is in the front row, panting."

"Stop it." Esti's head began to throb. Whether Alan was listening or not, everyone else in the crowded dressing room was soaking up every word. "Why are you telling me this?"

"Carmen," Lucia snapped, "you worse than Danielle, or what?"

"I'm sorry." Carmen glanced at Lucia, then sighed. "I'm acting like a witch, aren't I?"

"For true." Meeting Carmen's eyes without expression, Lucia turned and disappeared into the girls' changing area.

"Maybe I'm a little miffed." Carmen looked at Esti in the mirror. "It just that you've been ignoring me because of your homework lately, and I guess I feel a little left out. Especially now that you're really a shooting star. But that's selfish of me, and I'm thrilled for you, truly I am."

Esti grimaced, smearing her lipstick. It was true; ever since she and Alan started meeting more, she'd frequently put off Carmen with the excuse of too much schoolwork. But where was Alan tonight?

"I'm sorry, Carmen," she said lamely. "I've been the selfish one lately. You know you're my best friend."

"That's okay." To her relief, Carmen grinned. "Here, I'll help you with your makeup, like I did before. You're looking nervous again, and you just messed up your mouth." She started toward Esti. "I guess it's not your fault that every talent scout on Cariba wants to sign you up now; we all knew it was coming. And I just can't help it," she snickered, "but after looking at Danielle and at Rafe, I do think the theater's going to implode when Romeo kisses Juliet." She stopped. "Where did I put the greasepaint?"

"Greg won't give Danielle a passing thought." As the smooth murmur tickled Esti's ear, she gasped. Alan sounded like he stood right beside her.

Carmen gave Esti an apologetic look before turning back to the girls' changing area. "Your costume looks great, you know. That's what you wore on television, isn't it?"

"You were stunning last night," Alan whispered. "Better than I dreamed you could be."

Carmen was far enough away, Esti thought, that she hadn't heard him. No one in the room had heard him. How did he do that? She stared into the mirror, swept by guilt and relief, and an unexpected pang of worry that maybe no one had *ever* heard his voice except for her. She touched the solid necklace for reassurance.

"Thank you," she said.

"You're welcome," Carmen called out.

"Tonight no one will exist for Romeo on that stage but his Juliet," Alan added. "She won't be distracted by anyone. Not by Danielle, and not by Rafe . . ." He paused for an instant, his voice tightening. ". . . Solomon."

"You okay?" Carmen sounded concerned as she peered out from the girls' changing area. "You're white as a ghost."

Esti could barely nod.

"Juliet has only one Romeo." The longing in Alan's words made it clear that he'd heard everything since Esti walked into the theater.

"Of course," Esti breathed.

When Carmen raised her eyebrows, Esti bit down on her words, closing her eyes as Carmen smoothed on the heavy makeup.

"I'm done," Carmen finally said. "I didn't mean to get on your case so hard. I'm sorry."

"No problem," she managed. "I'm . . ." She trailed off helplessly, forgetting what she'd been about to say.

"Who would ever think someone like you could get stage fright so bad?" Carmen pinned the cap on Esti's hair and patted her shoulder. "I'm glad I saw you go through it before, or I'd be worried. Lucia, can you get her some water? I've got to get out there." She jumped to her feet.

"Yeah, mon." From the doorway, Lucia studied Esti's face as Carmen hurried out of the room.

"You hold the house in the palm of your hand." Alan's words stroked Esti, soft as a kiss. "Thou doth teach the torches to burn bright."

"Esti, you drink this." Lucia held out a small paper cup, her expression clearly worried as she approached. Esti automatically took the cup from her, choking as something hot and powerful sluiced down her throat. She shuddered, then felt herself relax from the warmth spreading into her arms and legs. She wanted so badly to see him and touch him.

"Rum," Lucia explained over her shoulder, taking the cup to the trash can. "Ma had watch you getting bazadee, gal. You can't get crazy now. She say a shot of Cruzan calm you down."

"Tonight you are Juliet . . ." Alan's yearning melted into the warmth of the rum as Lucia walked away, until his voice was the only thing holding Esti up. ". . . for me."

"You ready, or what?" Lucia's dark face tightened with concern as she came back. "We had better go to the stage."

"Yes," Esti whispered. Desire and hope raging through her body, she forced herself to stand and follow Lucia out of the dressing room.

❦

"Give her some air." Aurora sounded angry. "No, she's fine, Officer Wilmuth, thank you. Look, here's the dagger. It's just as plastic as it's always been. She didn't kill herself with it."

Juliet struggled to sit up, confused by the noisy blur of

faces in front of her. She remembered killing herself, but something must have gone wrong. Where was Romeo?

"Rafe, you sure managed to get up on the stage fast. Help her over here, then."

Rafe? She shook her head as strong hands helped her to her feet, pulling her away from the noise.

"That's okay, Officer. Rafe can stay up here, but if everyone else would just leave us alone for a few minutes, she'll be fine. Yes, the play was great and she was incredible, that's why she's all wrung out now. Esti is her father's daughter, you know."

Esti, she thought numbly, oh yeah. Juliet, doff thy name.

"Esti, you all right?" Rafe sounded upset.

She couldn't help leaning into him, trying to shake off Juliet's overwhelming despair. "I think so."

As they reached relative privacy behind a set, Aurora unpinned the sweaty cap from Esti's hair and held a cup of water in front of her.

Rafe let go of her. Startled, she watched his dark hands draw back from the pale skin of her arms. Compared to the chaos inside of her, the simple image was beautifully, intensely *real.* Impulsively, she reached out and touched her fingers to his before he could move away.

He squeezed her hand, giving her a piercing stare. "I never saw anything like what you just did," he finally said. "I thought you killed yourself with that knife."

Esti took the cup from Aurora, trying to steady her shaky hands. "Yeah. Me too."

Aurora smiled at Rafe. "Amazing, isn't she?"

"Scary," Rafe corrected. "My adrenaline's going, mon."

Aurora laughed. "You know, her father would get light-headed after some of his performances too. It was like his own soul had to find him again."

Esti wondered if her dad had ever fainted when the curtains went down. The thought seemed absurd.

"They were all incredible tonight, weren't they?" Aurora continued. "What a talented group of kids."

Someone peered around the edge of the set.

"Are you up to a quick appearance?" Aurora sounded concerned. "We'd better let them know you've recovered. Rafe, can you let Mr. Niles know we're coming right out?"

"No problem."

Esti finished the water as Rafe darted back around the set. As she started to follow him, however, she felt the blood drain from her face. A frangipani blossom rested on the floor, its sweet scent drifting up from where Rafe had crushed it with his shoe.

"A toast to Juliet."

Esti leaned back against her chair, forcing a smile as Rafe held up his glass beside her. Although she had let herself be talked into joining the cast party, she could barely speak over the huge knot growing inside of her.

"We won't be out long," Carmen had assured her, "since we have our closing performance tomorrow. But we *have* to celebrate tonight, after that awesome show. Did I tell you

Chaz asked if I would sit by him?" Her eyes sparkled. "Rafe might as well come too. I mean, everyone already knows him."

The theater would be empty by now. Esti itched to run back and fling herself at Alan, demanding that he become the Romeo he'd promised, but it had been impossible to disappear without attracting attention. He must have seen Rafe's arms around her after she passed out, watching as she grabbed Rafe's hand when he tried to pull away. Why hadn't it been Alan rushing to the stage? Where was *he* when she needed someone to hold on to? Surely he knew that her mind-wrenching Juliet existed only because of him.

Swallowing her agitation, Esti lifted her glass. "And a toast to the best Nurse I've ever known." She smiled at Carmen and Lucia. "And to an amazing Lady Capulet." They had just pulled off the show of a lifetime; it was the performance she had always dreamed of. Everyone had seen the talent scouts converging on Rodney afterward, chattering with excitement.

To her relief, she felt Rafe rise to his feet, pulling her up along with him. "We're leaving," he said. "I think Juliet needs some recovery time."

"Yeah sure, Solomon," Chaz said. "We all know what you think Juliet needs."

Although Esti's mouth tightened at the laughter that swept through the cast, Rafe didn't let go of her hand. He led her outside the little café, stopping only when they reached the far edge of the sand.

"You're not doing so good, are you?" he asked. "What's going on?"

She opened her mouth, then closed it again. Her body still ached with the passion of Juliet, and she had no idea how to handle it. Before she could decide what to say, Rafe abruptly leaned over and scooped one arm behind her knees. In a single motion, he picked her up and carried her into the water.

"Rafe, stop." She pushed against him with her fists. Suddenly she realized she was afraid, and it wasn't because she thought she would drown. Rafe's arms felt delicious and perfect, despite everything she knew about him, and she knew she was hovering on the brink of something dangerous.

"Shh. I'm professional, remember?" Rafe stopped only when the water reached the level of his chest. Letting go of her legs, he steadied her against him, holding her gently by the waist. "My mom used to do this whenever I got upset as a little kid. She told me the sea would always give me strength when I need it."

As the warm swells rocked her with their gentle rhythm, Esti took a deep breath, trying to relax.

"My parents' house is on Coqui Beach," Rafe said softly, staring out over the infinite ocean. "I remember having a lot of bad dreams when I was little. Whenever we were back here on vacation, my mom would bring me outside in the middle of the night and carry me into the sea. For some reason, the water always made my nightmares disappear."

To Esti's surprise, she *did* feel better..

"My dad's gotta be racking up a huge phone bill after

what you did tonight." Rafe looked back at her with an awkward grin that reminded her very much of her devoted best friend in grade school, then he slowly shook his head in puzzlement. "You sure don't seem too happy about it. Are you okay?"

"I'm thrilled." Esti forced a wry smile. "Just feeling a little lost. Maybe my soul is pissed off because it can't find me."

"You mean Juliet isn't letting Esti back in?" His teasing eyes caught hers, reflecting the light from the beach bar, and she found herself leaning into him before she could stop herself.

Her lips touched his with a shock that hit her body like a bolt of lightning. As he eagerly returned the kiss, drawing her against him, she wrapped her arms around his neck. The warm sea tickled her skin as she clung to him for a fabulous moment of bliss, and then reality crashed down on her.

She should be with Alan, not Rafe. She *wanted* to be with Alan. Yanking herself away, she stretched her legs through the water, looking for a place to put her feet. Alan should be celebrating her success with her, showing the world their triumph together. How could he hide at a time like this?

Rafe grabbed her as she overbalanced, her head dipping beneath the warm, salty swell for an instant. When he pulled her up, she shoved him away, choking for air.

"Chill," he said, "or you're going to take us both down."

Still gasping, she let him carry her through the water until it became shallow enough for her to walk. Her soul had apparently returned, every bit as soggy and disheveled as the rest of her.

"I'm sorry," she said. She doubted if even Shakespeare could have come up with a more embarrassing first kiss.

To her surprise, he let out a burst of laughter. "Did you just apologize for kissing me?"

A whirlwind of emotions raged through her, sucking any intelligent response out of her mind and throwing it straight into the sea. Although she still tingled from the touch of Rafe's lips, a far more bewildering passion roiled deep beneath the surface. *Juliet has only one Romeo.*

"I'm a little confused," Rafe said. "You got a boyfriend or not?"

You're confused? She couldn't bring herself to look at Rafe as she nodded.

"Is he the reason you're scared?"

At the hint of machismo in his voice, Esti couldn't help wondering if Rafe had known all along it would take less than twenty-four hours before she kissed him. "I'm not afraid of him," she said tightly.

"Where is he?"

"I can't talk about it." She sagged, knowing she sounded utterly ungrateful for everything Rafe had done today. "Thanks for helping me, but I need to go home."

Rafe stared at her for a long time, then finally nodded. "Yeah, mon. Whatever you want."

Act Two. Scene Three.

She was surprised by her strong sense of purpose as she turned on the stage lights. Aurora had been asleep when Rafe dropped her off at the house, and Esti had stayed home only long enough to change out of her wet clothes. Although she'd barely slept during the past forty-eight hours, she felt wired with adrenaline. She quickly made her way to the little basement room and sat in the chair that always waited for her.

"Alan?" Maybe it was because of her overwhelming physical response to Rafe, but the empty darkness seemed creepy tonight.

"Alan." She tapped her fingers on her chair, ready to wait all night if she had to. "I need to talk to you."

"I knew you wouldn't abandon me in our moment of triumph."

She grew rigid at the heavy formality in his voice. She felt as tightly wound as a spring, her body thrumming with anticipation and dread at his words. *He* was the one who had abandoned *her* tonight.

"What a consummate performance," Alan added, his admiration apparent. "One of the best I've ever seen. Yet, I must have done something wrong." His voice grew soft. "Whatever I did, I'm sorry. I wanted so badly to talk to you after each performance. Your father always said you would outshine him someday."

The oddly phrased compliment made her hair stand on end, and she nervously rubbed her arms. "My dad never said that."

Alan was silent for a moment. "Your success is what we've been working toward since I met you."

"Is it?" she asked softly. "I don't know what we've been working toward. All I know is that this—whatever it is—isn't enough anymore."

"Ahh."

"Alan, I need—"

"That explains Rafe Solomon."

She froze.

"He's very handsome. I understand he has an easy way with girls, but I'm surprised to see you fall for that sort of thing."

She felt her cheeks grow warm.

"Does he know about me?"

"I didn't tell him anything."

"I see." Alan's voice tightened.

"We used to be friends. He's nice, that's all."

"Apparently you find him nice indeed."

She swallowed convulsively. "He's *real*," she finally said. "He doesn't hide from me."

Alan was quiet for a long time. "I'm a fool."

"No, you're not."

"You kissed him?"

Esti's heart stopped for an instant. "Yes," she forced out, "but—"

She heard a soft, strangled sound from the darkness.

"Alan, it's *you* who turns me into Juliet." The words burst from her before she could stop them. "You speak in sonnets and fill me with crazy passion, then you say I'm not allowed to see you or touch you. Alan, I can't—"

"That's right." Alan caught his breath, painful and ragged. "You finally understand."

"No, I don't!" She leaped to her feet in agitation. "I can't pretend anymore. And don't act like you don't care. You're all I ever think about, and you must think about me, too. I *need* to see you."

"No." The coldness in his voice raked ice through her veins.

"You're not a jumbee," she cried. "I don't believe that."

"It makes no difference what you believe."

"But Alan—"

"The mistake was mine, not yours." His voice slowly became more controlled. "I knew it the first moment I saw you here. I never should have spoken to you."

"No!" Esti clamped down on her desperation, her chest threatening to explode. "I need you. Before I met you, I wasn't an actress. You pulled me out of my dad's shadow, and you gave me my life back."

"Ah, The Great Legard." Alan's voice had come very close. "I no longer know whether to worship him or damn him."

"What are you talking about?" Unable to stop herself, Esti

reached into the darkness with outstretched fingers. "Alan, please!" Her skin quivered with the certainty of his closeness, but she felt nothing. Where *was* he?

"I am in love with you, Esti." She heard pain and bitterness in his soft laughter.

She fell back into her chair, stunned. "What?"

"I would like to blame it on your father."

"You *love* me?" she whispered.

"Desperately, hopelessly. And if you truly knew me, you would despise me." The pain was gone now from his beautiful voice. All his emotion was gone, replaced by a dead woodenness she'd never heard before. "You don't need me, and I will end this before we destroy each other. I won't be coming back; let Rafe Solomon give you what you need."

"No!" She lunged to her feet, already knowing the attempt was futile. Alan was gone.

Ma Harris discovered her early the next afternoon, deep in exhausted sleep in a corner of the dark basement room. Esti didn't resist as Lucia's mother silently helped her to her feet. She followed her up the stairs and through the tiny passage, coming onstage with eyes swollen and pounding. Once again, she was surrounded by dozens of people and loud voices. She blinked at the brightness, then glanced down at herself, half expecting to see a plastic knife sticking out of her chest.

No, this must be a new drama.

"Where was she?"

Startled, Esti looked into the dark eyes of a policeman.

Ma Harris shook her head with a cryptic look. "She had just appear, Mister Wilmuth. You leave she alone. She shook up bad, an' she don't need no jandam."

"Esti!" Aurora's voice flew across the theater from the main door, high-pitched and scared. "My God, where have you been?"

"Miss Legard—" the policeman began.

"You gon leave she alone, Mister Wilmuth," Ma Harris interrupted. "She shook up right now."

Esti forced herself to look at Officer Wilmuth. He backed off from Lucia's mom, retreating to the front row of the theater, but his eyes didn't leave Esti as he sat down beside another policeman. The balding white cop beside him barked words into a small radio, letting the world know that Esti Legard had reappeared.

"I've been worried sick!" Aurora ran up onstage, flinging her arms around Esti. "You disappeared last night after Rafe brought you home, and people have been talking about this jumbee—"

"I'm sorry." Esti groaned, covering her face with her hands as her midnight memories came flooding back. She'd been so exhausted, she must have fallen asleep in the basement room.

Aurora gave her a frightened look.

"You sure know how to make your entrances and exits." Carmen studied Esti in awe as she came up onstage. "I should start taking notes. Lucia *said* her mom would be able to find you. Were you really kidnapped by the jumbee?"

"Of course not." Breathing hard, Esti swung around to stare at Lucia's mother. The dark face gave nothing away.

"Rafe and his dad are out with the cops, looking for you," Chaz said behind Carmen. "Only the Solomons can get the jandam moving so fast. It usually takes Rafe at least a week to get 'em stirred up, though."

"You're a lot better at publicity than Danielle," Carmen added with a weak smile. "Why *not* play up the jumbee thing while you got so many talent scouts watching you?"

"This isn't a publicity stunt," Aurora said, rounding furiously on them. "Esti doesn't need manufactured drama when she isn't onstage."

"All the world's a stage," Esti blurted out. Aurora had no idea how much drama filled her daughter's life these days.

As everyone looked at Esti again, she began giggling. She couldn't help herself; she felt too bizarre and terrible. She laughed harder as Carmen and Chaz backed away, their faces uncertain. Yeah, she'd finally gone off the deep end. An invisible catapult had taken over her life, gleefully flinging her into chaos. She collapsed against Aurora, guffaws shaking her body. Laughter consumed her, possessing her body like a jumbee might—except that jumbees didn't exist. Maybe Alan never existed at all.

She slid to the floor, still giggling.

Aurora crouched down beside her, her eyes wide with fear. The sight sent Esti into another round of hysterics. Great, now she was scaring her mom. *Hysteria is caused by severe conflict and emotional excess*—the absurd thought popped into her head. Oh yeah, she had plenty of both.

In the front row, Officer Wilmuth exchanged a glance with his partner. As the white cop got up and walked out of the theater, Esti felt her laughter start all over again. Ha— even the jandam were running away!

"Bazadee," she heard someone whisper. Crazy. They all thought she was crazy. Tears squeezed out of her eyes, and she helplessly pressed her hands against her ribs. When Rafe showed up a few minutes later—or was it hours?—her head pounded and her stomach muscles ached so badly she could barely move. Through a fog, she watched Rafe charge up to the stage, his dark eyes wide with concern. His hand reached out, touching hers.

As their fingers twined together, the memory of Alan's last words slammed through her. What if Alan was watching right now, waiting to see how long it took her to replace him? She yanked her hand back, lurching away from Rafe as if she'd been burned.

"Esti?" He stared at her, stunned.

She spun away, unable to meet his eyes. *I'm sorry, I'm sorry,* her thoughts screamed as she rose to her feet and blindly stumbled offstage.

❦

"How now? Who calls?"

Huddled in the wings, Esti watched Danielle walk onto the stage. Relief throbbed down to her toes that Danielle had insisted on taking over Juliet for the closing performance.

"Your mother," Carmen said, indicating Lucia with a flourish.

When Lucia had asked if Esti wanted the role of Juliet's mother back, Esti immediately shook her head. She couldn't play Lady Capulet tonight. Besides, Lucia deserved her full moment in the spotlight.

"Madam, I am here." Danielle gave them a nod, her pretty face drawn and determined beneath the stage makeup.

Esti studied her in dull admiration. Danielle obviously didn't feel well, although she insisted her symptoms were under control. When the others tried to tease her, she had responded with a blistering look that made even Carmen back off.

Danielle was brave, Esti thought. *I, on the other hand, am a coward and a freak.*

Earlier this afternoon, when she could finally speak, Esti had apologized to everyone in sight, mortified by the amount of trouble she'd caused. All she really wanted to do was throw herself into Rafe's arms, adding more sap to this awful melodrama in full view of Alan. Instead, she was stiffly polite, repeating "I'm fine, thank you," until Rafe finally left.

As the audience began laughing at Nurse's monologue onstage, Esti closed her eyes. She had no idea who Alan was, or why he'd spent so much time with her since she moved to Cariba. She only knew that he had brought her back to life. And now that he was gone, she no longer wanted any of it.

Quietly gathering her things, she crept to the deserted back end of the stage and slipped behind the curtain. She didn't bother calling for Alan as she navigated the pitch-black passages to the hidden back door; if he wanted to talk, he would already know she was there. But her exit was solitary, joined only by the coqui frogs as she trudged back up Bayrum Hill.

Act Two. Scene Four.

The jandam came to her house the next afternoon. Esti was lying in bed, studying each crack in the ceiling through aching eyes. The largest crack was a giant question mark. *How could she have screwed up so badly? What would it take to get Alan back?*

In the far corner she could make out a crouching spider, ready to drop on the pretty seashell Rafe had given her, with a venom far nicer than her current misery. *Rafe would never forgive her. She didn't blame him.*

Directly above her head, two eyes stared down at her, forever unblinking. *What if Alan secretly watched her, even if he never spoke to her again?*

And the entire pattern joined together in a ragged spiral, feeding back on itself in an endless, hopeless loop. *What would her dad think, if he could see her now?*

When a familiar voice called "inside," she rolled out of bed and stumbled to her bedroom door to peek into the living room. Officer Wilmuth nodded at Aurora as he walked in the house, followed by the white policeman Esti recognized from the theater. It didn't surprise her to see them, especially after the new uproar she'd caused by disappearing during the play last night.

"Mrs. Legard," the white officer said to Aurora. "My name is George Moore. I think you know Officer Wilmuth."

"Of course." Aurora sounded exhausted. "Please come in and sit down. How can I help you?"

"We ask Miss Legard some question," Officer Wilmuth said. "When she miss school today, 'tis a few more rumor in town."

"Rumors about what?" Aurora's voice grew thin. "Don't tell me jumbees."

Esti leaned against the door frame.

"It may seem unlikely," Officer Moore said, "but word gets around fast on a small island. A lot of people are frightened, and we need to make sure that nobody, including Esti, is in danger."

"She's been sleeping all day." Aurora glared at Officer Moore for a moment, then sighed. "I am very worried about her. I'll go wake her up."

"Do you mind if I ask you a few things first?" He sounded apologetic. "I don't want to upset your daughter any more than necessary. Was she here when you got home last night?"

As Aurora glanced toward her bedroom, Esti shrank away from the doorway. Once again, she'd caused more trouble.

"She was asleep when I came back from the play. She said she snuck out of the theater when no one was looking because she felt sick." Aurora gave the officers a guilty look.

"She even left a message on my cell phone, but I didn't notice it until after I panicked."

Although Officer Wilmuth gave a snort of disgust, George Moore's expression remained calm. "And what exactly did she tell you about the *previous* night?"

Aurora's voice grew even more helpless. "She said she went back to the theater after the cast party and fell asleep backstage."

Officer Wilmuth wrote something in a small notebook. "'Tis where Ma Harris had find Esti, also."

Esti's eyes widened. Ma Harris hadn't found her backstage; she'd found her in the tiny basement room.

"We searched the building a number of times yesterday morning," Officer Moore said gently, "and I don't believe Esti was there."

Aurora sighed. "I'm pretty sure Esti hasn't told me everything. She keeps saying she just wants to sleep."

Officer Wilmuth's face grew stony. "I have ask Rodney Solomon bring his son to talk to us. They's on they way jus' now."

"Rafe?" Aurora frowned. "Why?"

Esti winced at the thought of facing Rafe after the way she'd acted yesterday.

"Although Rafe insists he did nothing wrong," Officer Moore said gently, "we've found some discrepancies. It wouldn't be the first time he's gotten himself in trouble because of a girl."

Esti grew rigid. They were blaming *Rafe?*

"Esti's classmates said they were all at a cast party the night before last. Esti left with Rafe, and he was the last one seen with her before she disappeared. Do you know if he really brought her home after the party?"

"I can't say for sure," Aurora said in a helpless voice. "She's a good girl and has never needed a curfew, so I fell asleep without worrying about her. I didn't find out until yesterday morning that her bed hadn't been slept in. That's when I called Rodney."

"Rafe told us he brought her straight home," Officer Moore said, "but he may not be telling the truth. Does Esti have a boyfriend on Cariba?"

Esti caught her breath.

"No," Aurora said slowly. "She's never had a boyfriend. I think boys are intimidated by her."

"I could believe that." Esti heard a wry smile in Officer Moore's voice. "Her friends also say she hasn't been seeing anyone, so we're confident that part is true. But Rafe insisted she has a boyfriend on Cariba who's been threatening her. He got very angry when Officer Wilmuth accused him of lying."

Esti clutched the doorjamb, trying to stay calm. Hadn't Carmen told her that Rafe once attacked a cop?

"You had see how she react to Rafe when he show up yesterday," Officer Wilmuth said grimly. "I think 'tis only one boy on Cariba threaten she. It don't take Rafe no time to stir thing up when he come home. He gotta realize someday he can't take advantage of girl them, run Cariba any way he want. I think he go to jail this time."

Esti sagged in horror. Rafe had been wonderful to her. He hadn't told the jandam any lies; Esti was the one lying.

"Esti didn't want anything to do with Rafe yesterday," Aurora said with a skeptical look at Officer Wilmuth, "but I didn't get the feeling she was afraid of him. He was a good friend when we knew him in Los Angeles. I'd better wake her up now, before he gets here."

Esti darted back to her bed, burrowing under the covers as Aurora opened her door.

"Esti," Aurora said softly. "Are you awake?"

Esti grunted, trying to slow her breathing.

"Sweetie, the police are here. Are you up for a few questions about yesterday?"

"Sure," Esti managed. She turned to Aurora, blinking and squinting as if she had just awakened. "Let me get some clothes on."

The policemen both stood as she came out of her room a few minutes later. They nodded politely at her, and she nodded back, pasting a tired look on her face. Her mind raced with conflicting ideas about what to say.

"Miss Legard, how are you feeling?"

"Much better, thank you." Esti blinked at Officer Moore, and he returned a cautious smile.

"I've almost recovered from Juliet," she said. "It took me longer than I thought it would." She sat on the edge of the couch beside her mom. "Did Aurora tell you how my dad would go into shock after his best performances too? When you get so deeply into a character, sometimes the character doesn't want to let you take over again. I'm so sorry for the worry I've caused."

Uncertain silence followed her words. "Esti," Aurora began.

"Inside." As Rodney Solomon's voice interrupted Aurora, Esti became exquisitely aware of everyone's eyes on her face. They were waiting for some reaction, seeking proof that they were right about Rafe. She covered her mouth, faking a drawn-out yawn.

"Come," Officer Wilmuth commanded.

Esti felt tension crackling in the air before she even swung around to face the front door. Officer Wilmuth radiated hostility as Rafe walked in, and Rodney gave Esti a stern look of appraisal. Rafe didn't even glance at her, his face hard and closed.

I think he go to jail this time.

She had no choice. She wouldn't let Rafe take the blame for the insanity he'd found when he came back into her life.

"Rafe," she said, feigning surprise. "I'm glad you're here. And I'm sorry about yesterday."

She walked across the room with a not-so-feigned expression of guilt. The hostility in the room warped into disbelief as she threw her arms around Rafe's neck and pressed her cheek into his rigid chest. "You've been great," she said. "Thanks for all your help. I don't deserve it at all."

She *didn't* deserve any of it. She was stuck in a single frame of a bad movie, fumbling desperately for excuses as the other characters watched in eternal rigidity. No one believed a thing she said, not even Rafe.

Shoving thoughts of Alan as far away as she could, she stretched up on her tiptoes, looking into Rafe's cold brown eyes as she touched her lips to his. *My second kiss,* she thought briefly, *even more absurd than my first.* When the ice sculpture of Rafe's body finally gave a tiny hint of thawing, she took his hand and dragged him to the couch. She didn't look up at him as he followed her without a word.

"My mom said you had some questions for me," she said into the silence, drawing Rafe's stiff arm around her shoulders as she leaned into him and turned to meet Officer Wilmuth's eyes. Rodney was the first to break the tension, a flash of amusement crossing his face as he walked across the room to sit on a kitchen chair.

"Yeah, miss," Officer Wilmuth said, his face impassive as he glanced at Rafe. "We need to know what happen to you yesterday. You got a boyfriend have threaten you?"

"I don't have a boyfriend." As Rafe grew rigid once more, she tilted her head back to give him a quick smile. "Not unless Rafe wants to take me out tonight."

Rodney stifled a sudden coughing fit behind his fist.

"Why you act yesterday like Rafe is some badjohn trying to hurt you?" Officer Wilmuth's eyes narrowed.

"I was confused," Esti said, searching for the right words. "I was . . . I wasn't sure where I was, and . . ."

"Was you kidnap?"

"Of course not! I fell asleep backstage."

"Ma Harris say a jumbee had talk to you."

"It's all pretty dumb." She plucked at a long strand of hair draped across her arm, twisting it into a knot around her finger. "I'm embarrassed by how much trouble I caused. Ma Harris kind of saw me talking to myself backstage like a crazy person. *She* thinks it was a jumbee."

The room pulsed back into another surreal fracture in time, all faces contorted into expectant, wide-eyed expressions.

With a deep breath, she forged ahead. "I might have had a couple of hallucinations, because I kept thinking Romeo was talking to Juliet. I was exhausted and then I decided maybe the jumbee really was talking to me. I mean, especially after these rumors, and all my defenses are shot . . ."

The faces remained frozen, no one moving except her mom.

"Esti," Aurora said in concern, "why didn't you tell me?"

"It seemed pointless to talk about some weird Shakespeare voice in my head." Esti gave her mom the most sincere look she could manage. "Do you think Dad would have under-stood about losing himself in a character?"

As her mom's face grew thoughtful, Esti's stomach gave a sickening guilty twist. Her dad had been in complete con-trol. He never would have understood her growing moun-tain of lies.

❧

After the officers left, she and Rafe walked down to Man-chicay Beach in silence. When she finally opened her mouth to explain, he put his finger on her lips.

"Doesn't matter," he said. "I walked in there expecting to be lynched, and you gave me a kiss instead. You want to apologize for it?"

She blushed and shook her head.

"Look," he added, "I got this habit of getting myself in bad situations, so I understand more than you might think. There's some things I won't tell anybody, and you don't have to tell me anything you don't want to. I just need three answers. First, are you in danger?"

He watched her, his eyes locked on hers as she shook her head again.

"I'll buy it," he said, "because I have to. The most important thing is that you're safe. Gotta keep up my reputation as the safest guy on Cariba for a girl to be around." He grinned, then immediately grew serious again.

"Second, you're a lousy liar, and I don't believe in jumbees. So my question is, are you done with that maybe-jumbee Shakespeare guy who isn't your boyfriend?"

Esti cringed, staring blindly out at the calm water. Was she finished with all the secrets seething beneath the surface? Alan had made his exit quite clear. *Let Rafe Solomon give you what you need.* "I think I am," she finally said. "I'm confused."

"He broke up with you yesterday, didn't he?" Rafe's eyes narrowed. "It knocked you on your ass, and you're still hung up on him."

She turned to Rafe in astonishment.

"Been there, done that," Rafe explained. "Pining after someone you can't have and don't want anyone to know about. It's no fun, but . . ." He shrugged. "The third answer I need from you is, do you want me to go away?"

"No." She immediately shook her head.

"Woo-hoo!" He did a sudden victorious dance in the sand, pumping his fists into the air. "That's what I wanted to hear."

"Don't get too excited," Esti said quickly, although she couldn't help smiling. "I'm not promising anything."

"Swimming lessons resume tomorrow," Rafe crowed, then abruptly settled down, his eyes sparkling behind a serious expression. "Completely professional, of course. Hey mon, what pencil have Hamlet use?"

To her amazement, Esti burst into laughter. How could Rafe always make her laugh? "2B or not 2B."

With an answering grin, Rafe began dancing again. Not surprisingly, Esti thought, he was quite good.

Act Two. Scene Five.

"Thanks for inviting me over," Carmen said through a mouthful of coconut and pistachios. "I've missed making cookies with you."

"Me too." Esti smiled. "I've missed you a lot."

"I've been worried. At least now I can tell everyone that Jane Doe is still alive and normal, with crumbs all over her chin."

"Normal? I'd be right at home in a psych ward."

Carmen laughed. "You *are* coming to school for finals, aren't you?"

"I'll be there. I just couldn't handle the gossip this week

while I tried to study. Aurora convinced Headmaster Fleming that I should stay home for a few days."

"What really happened to you?" Carmen stared at her with wide eyes. "You won't believe what people are saying at school."

"You tell me what people are saying," Esti said, "then I'll tell you the truth." *At least I'll tell you what I'm trying to believe.*

She studied her friend in guilty resignation, wondering if Carmen might also be hiding a seething separate life beneath her happy, wide-eyed exterior. Not possible, she decided. Carmen was too eager and open, telling all the details of everything she knew to anyone who would listen.

"First"—Carmen took another bite—"the theater is haunted by Elon Somand. His jumbee has been trying to possess you ever since you got to Cariba. After holding him off all semester, you finally snapped last weekend. That's the one I keep hearing from the locals."

"Oh, I get it." Esti kept her face neutral. Despite Alan's final words to her, she knew he hadn't massacred hundreds of slaves in a past life. "To pay for his sins, Somand is trapped in an eternity of watching high school dramas."

Carmen almost choked on her cookie. "Hee hee, that's good. Okay, here's the next one. A jumbee attacked you after our second performance and did something unspeakable that should have killed you, or at least put you in the hospital."

He said he loved me. Esti forced a smile. "Try again."

"This next one is mostly from Greg. There isn't any jumbee, and Rafe was the one who did something unspeakable to you."

"Rafe is great."

"Fine, fine." Carmen waved her hand in the air. "I still can't imagine you with Rafe Solomon. Anyway, here's Danielle's version of what Greg says. You're trying so hard to butter up Rodney that you slept with Rafe, then it tore you apart because you'd really rather steal Greg away from her."

Esti snorted. "That sounds *very* Danielle. Any more?"

"Those are the main ones." Carmen's eyebrows drew together. "But I want to hear more about Rafe. You *didn't* sleep with him, did you?"

"Of course not."

"Not that I'm barging into your private life, even though I am. Are you dating him?"

"Not really." Esti broke a cookie in half, watching the crumbs scatter across the glass-topped table. She swept them back into a neat pile, wishing she could clean up the mess of her own life so easily. "We've gone swimming a few times. Honestly, Carmen, I've known him for years. He's my friend."

"Okay, I'll lay off." Carmen slowly shook her head. "But you can't say I didn't warn you."

"Besides gossip, what else has been going on at school?" Esti changed the subject. "Tell me you're going to pass your math final."

"If only I can convince them that two plus two really equals five."

Esti laughed. "Do you know how Lucia's doing? Her Lady Capulet was so good."

"Oh!" Carmen almost leaped out of her chair. "I almost

forgot to tell you. A modeling agent wants her photos! I've been *telling* her she's tall and skinny in that cool ethnic way all the magazines love."

"Awesome." Esti grinned. "And what about Carmen's perfect Nurse? Gorgeous Puerto Rican *chicas* are totally in fashion these days too."

"Keep it coming." Carmen snorted. "I'm working on it, Jane Doe. A couple of agents are hanging around until the big Solomon Christmas party, and you can bet I'll be networking right alongside Danielle and Greg. That is,"—she smiled wryly— "if we can pry them away from you."

"Aurora?" Esti dug her toes into the warm sand.

"Yeah?" Although her mom's answering drawl sounded unconcerned, Esti saw Aurora's fingers twitch restlessly beside her. Aurora lay on a big beach towel, soaking up the sun. She acted like she had no worries, yet she studied Esti constantly when she thought Esti wasn't looking.

"I've been missing Dad a lot," she said cautiously, her eyes following the distant movement of Rafe swimming across the bay. In the past, Aurora had always changed the subject, and Esti wasn't sure what her mom would say. "You know how I stopped going to his events the last couple of years before he died. I pulled away from him."

"Oh, sweetie. Do you still worry about that?" The sadness in Aurora's voice masked something else. Surprise, maybe, that Esti would be talking about this now. Perhaps, Esti thought, the fear that they were both losing their minds.

Every night after Aurora thought she was asleep, Esti knew her mom's little laptop was methodically tracking down any website that mentioned jumbees.

And every night, after her mom finally collapsed in exhaustion, Esti had crept back down to the theater for a couple of hours, overcome with guilt. And loneliness. And fear, and anger and grief, and a million other tangled emotions she couldn't figure out. She missed her dad so much, but insanely, the loss of Alan felt even more devastating right now. She often felt almost frantic with the need for Alan's voice.

"It made your father sad, of course," Aurora continued quietly, "but he always understood you better than I did."

Esti nodded, not too surprised by her mom's response.

"He told me it was something you would eventually get through," Aurora said, "so it's just too bad that . . ."

It's just too bad that he died before you got over yourself, Esti.

Esti picked up a handful of sand, watching it trickle out through her fingers. She couldn't hold on to anything, not even sand. She would never forgive herself for screwing up her two most sacred friendships. Her dad had been her best friend until she pushed him away. And Alan . . .

If only she had known more about him. She had thought they were kindred spirits, sharing a lot more than passion for Shakespeare. He seemed to understand her complicated grief. He said he *loved* her!

Get it together, she thought. At least act like you have some control.

"Hey Rafe," Aurora said, relief evident in her voice as he splashed towards them. "Some big waves out there."

"Got a good swell going on. My favorite kind of sea."

Esti struggled up, brushing sand from her arms. Despite all her efforts to keep things cool, a traitorous rush of happiness swept through her body as Rafe sat down beside her and smiled. He took her breath away, muscular and glowing from his swim. As he began explaining to Aurora how distant storms could cause an impressive swell from hundreds of miles away, Esti clenched her fists until her palms stung.

She probably had it all wrong, and Ma Harris was right. Alan was a jumbee, running away with Esti's soul as soon as she let her defenses down. Her feelings for him were no more real than the voice she'd imagined all semester.

On the other hand, Rafe would probably turn out to be as fleeting as the other males in her life. According to Carmen, it was about time for him take advantage of her, or make out with another girl, or attack a cop. Or something. They'd been together—dating? swimming lessons? old friends hanging out?—for less than a week, and Esti already felt much too comfortable around him. Every night she drifted to sleep with his seashell on the nightstand beside her pillow, her anticipation growing with each passing day.

He hadn't tried to kiss her, although she knew by the look in his eyes that he wanted to. It was driving her crazy, and she was certain he knew that. In between swimming lessons, he endured hours of her silence, seeming to enjoy the quiet company as they sat together and watched graceful pelicans or shiny rich tourists. He didn't talk much about his past or his reputation on Cariba, but Esti didn't really mind. Maybe it was because Alan had told her so little about himself, but Rafe seemed amazingly transparent. She knew who he was, who his parents were, where he lived. Once upon a time, she had gone to school with him. So he had some problems; big deal. Who didn't?

As a wave crashed into the sand a few feet away, Esti felt the beach shift beneath her feet. Even if Alan was gone, she didn't want to fall for Rafe so quickly. She could feel the catapult lurking beyond her view, waiting for the perfect moment to shatter her sanity again.

When she returned to school for finals, Esti ignored all the whispers, slogging her way through each exam until she could finally dump her books and escape. To her surprise, Lucia stood patiently beside her locker, looking like she'd been waiting all this time. For a moment, the two girls studied each other in silence.

"You okay?" Lucia finally asked. "Ma, she ask about you."

"I'm fine."

"I have worry, but I am relieve, also." Lucia glanced around, then stepped closer to Esti. "Ma, she say every girl need a warm boyfriend. Otherwise you end up cold and frighten."

"Has your mom talked to him?" Esti whispered before she could help herself, then shook her head. "Never mind; I probably shouldn't know. Rafe is better for me, right?"

"Ma, she say Rafe jus' need a powerful girl get he on the straight and narrow," Lucia said in amusement. "*You* keep Rafe in line, easy."

Esti snorted, then gave Lucia a sincere smile. "Carmen told me you might get an agent for modeling. That's really great."

"Yeah, mon." Lucia's eyes sparkled. "I have hear some melee about Esti Legard, also. I gotta take my last exam now, but I see you at the Christmas party, eh? We maybe all go to Carnival together."

When Esti walked into town an hour later to meet Rafe, she felt unexpectedly relaxed. Carmen and Chaz walked with her, discussing how Carnival traveled from island to island every year. The celebration always reached Cariba after Christmas, but workers were already assembling seahorses and mermaids for a huge carousel at the edge of town.

"The parade is the last weekend of Christmas break," Chaz said, casually grabbing Carmen's hand.

"It's the best time of year," Carmen added, swinging Chaz's hand into the air. "You don't want to miss it."

Esti stared at their hands. "I apparently missed something else last week."

Carmen giggled. "Two little monkeys, sitting in a tree, K-I-S-S—"

Chaz yanked Carmen into a bear hug before she could finish. "Esti, you been to The Boardwalk yet?" He laughed as Carmen struggled to get free. "Carmen promised to buy me dinner there when she gets rich and famous. Rafe's uncle has the most hoppin' place on the island, especially this time of year."

"Not yet." Esti grinned at Carmen's expression. "Rafe says he gets busy. We're going swimming as soon as his shift is over."

Half a dozen Jet Skis raced across the bay, the whine of their engines filling the air like a swarm of giant mosquitoes. As Esti's eyes followed a parasail, hanging in the deep blue sky behind a speedboat, she abruptly swallowed. Two women beside the carousel had turned to stare at her, simultaneously lifting their hands. Esti had seen the motion enough by now to realize that it wasn't a friendly wave.

"The richest tourists spend their vacation getting drunk at The Boardwalk," Chaz added, his eyes still on Carmen. "Rafe's gotta be making serious money."

Forcing herself to ignore the women, Esti quickly followed Chaz and Carmen away from the carousel.

The Boardwalk, true to its name, stretched down a long wooden walkway overlooking Manchicay Bay. Three West Indian men played steel pan drums at the end of the dock, their colorful robes and long dreadlocks swaying in time to the bright calypso music. Crowded tables filled the long boardwalk, and the open-air bar was just as busy, people in chino shorts and designer swimsuits standing three rows deep. Esti heard Rafe's voice before she saw him, laughing and teasing his customers.

Rafe stood behind the bar, deftly mixing drinks as he flirted with three deeply tanned women. When the redhead set a stack of bills on the counter and told Rafe to keep the change, a flicker of jealousy swept through Esti. She studied the women for a moment, then shook her head. They all had to be older than Aurora.

"Serious money," Chaz repeated in awe.

As Rafe flashed his perfect white smile at the redheaded woman, he suddenly caught sight of Esti. "My favorite girl!" he hooted.

To Esti's embarrassment, everyone within hearing distance immediately turned to stare at her as Rafe vaulted over the bar and wove his way through the crowd. Carmen stepped back, rolling her eyes at Chaz.

With a flourish, Rafe scooped Esti into his arms. "I am so ready to see you," he muttered into her ear. "Ten minutes to get rid of the old ladies, and then I can escape."

"The redhead just put that big tip back in her purse," Esti whispered back.

"Get a room," Chaz said loudly.

"There's a reason my mama told me to stay away from guys like you," Carmen added. As laughter flooded the bar, the three women picked up their bags and walked away.

Walking to Manchicay Beach a few minutes later, Esti mused over the easy silence that she and Rafe had already developed. Carmen chattered incessantly with Chaz on one side of her, while Rafe merely held Esti's fingers loosely twined through his. The flirting bartender she'd seen was a completely different person from the peaceful guy holding her hand, yet both sides of him seemed equally real. She wondered what he would say, if she told him his transparency felt like a breath of fresh air.

Dumb as a doornail, she thought wryly.

He glanced down at her with the familiar grin that made her heart beat faster, then came to an abrupt stop. A West Indian man stared at Esti from the ferry dock, his superstitious gesture cut short as Rafe glared at him. Raising his eyebrows, the man dropped his hands back to his sides.

"Rafe," he said awkwardly. "'Sup?"

"Limin' wit' de smartest girl on Cariba," Rafe retorted. "She name Esti Legard. You need some education?"

The man laughed, giving Esti an almost-sincere smile. "You ain't change a bit, Rafe."

Although Rafe's fingers tightened on Esti's, his voice relaxed into an easy banter. "Yeah, mon. You spread de word, eh?"

Astonished, Esti watched the man walk away.

As Rafe continued toward the beach like nothing had happened, Carmen exchanged a gleefully incredulous look with Chaz. With a growing sense of peace, Esti matched Rafe's casual stride. Despite his reputation, she felt safe with him. She hadn't yet learned to swim fast enough to leave thoughts of Alan behind, but it suddenly occurred to her that maybe by the end of Christmas vacation, she would.

Act Two. Scene Six.

Esti collapsed on the beach, giddy with fatigue and relief.

"You did it." Rafe smoothed out a beach towel beside her, but it was too late. Her body had turned into rubber, incapable of movement. Pressing her wet cheek into the sand, she watched him through a comfortable haze.

"I'm tired," she said.

"Over a mile." He grinned. "The whole length of the bay, against a decent tide and a swell. Merry Christmas."

"Christmas isn't until tomorrow." She let out her breath in a long, exhausted sigh. "Unless we missed the party. How many hours did I flail behind you out there?"

"We didn't miss the Christmas party." Rafe laughed. "You know, you're the first girl who ever swam the bay with me."

"I can't move."

"Stay here, and I'll get you something to eat. I know *I'm* starving."

"Mmm," she said. Without lifting her head, she watched him sprint toward the concession stand. She didn't know how he could possibly run after their marathon swim; she wasn't sure she could even stand up.

Closing her eyes as he disappeared, she rolled over on her back, luxuriating in the warmth tickling her skin. Endorphins, she had read somewhere, flooded the body during

strenuous exercise to provide a natural high. She was floating on endorphins right now, drunk with exhaustion and
euphoria.

She replayed the image of Rafe sprinting across the
beach a moment ago, his perfect body dark against the
white sand. It was time to kiss him, she thought languid-
ly. She still missed Alan desperately, but her sorrow held
a growing seed of resignation. She'd been wrong to think
Alan was the answer to all of her problems. Her lonely
imagination had created a ghost in shining armor, when
she really knew nothing at all about him. Washed up on the
beach as a baby? Maybe it was better if she didn't know the
real story.

Now all she had to do was convince herself of that.

When she opened her eyes, Rafe was sitting several feet
away, watching her. His arms were draped over his bent
knees, a can of grapefruit soda hanging loosely from his
hand. She blinked, her body instantly reacting to the hungry
look in his eyes. Yes, it was definitely time. No matter what
Carmen said, Esti wanted those lips touching hers again. She
didn't care about his reputation, and she could think of no
better way to get Alan out of her mind.

As she eagerly sat up, however, her head began to throb.
The endorphins had fled, and she felt like she'd been hit by
a truck. When Rafe reached out to brush dry sand from her
cheek, she winced back from him, pressing her hands against
her temples. "Headache," she muttered in frustration.

Her head was still pounding when she followed him to his

Jeep half an hour later. "Rafe," she said. "I don't think I can go to your dad's Christmas party."

He opened her door for her, waiting until she sat down. "Tired of me?" he asked matter-of-factly.

"Of course not." She met his guarded look with a reassuring smile. "But everyone on the island thinks I was kidnapped by a jumbee, and honestly . . ."

"Yes?"

"I know some talent scouts will be at the party. I'm not sure I can face them yet."

"The hard work's done, babe." Now he sounded amused. "When my dad introduced me around, every one of them asked me about you. All you gotta do is kick back and let 'em come begging."

"It's more complicated than that," she said, trying to feel flattered. After the wonderful days of swimming and no stress, the theater seemed like a threatening former life, loaded with anxiety. "The thought of getting back onstage is overwhelming."

"Because of your Shakespeare jumbee?" Rafe's eyes narrowed. "Should I be worried?"

"Nothing like that." She leaned against the door frame, wondering if Rafe *did* have anything to worry about. "It's a lot of pressure, that's all."

"I bet it is. Well, you don't have to talk to anyone you don't want to." Rafe climbed into the Jeep, flexing his arms. "That's why you got a bodyguard."

She smiled. "I'm lucky."

"Nah, I'm the lucky one. You keep a lot hidden under the surface, don't you?" He studied her face. "You remind me of the sea, beautiful and quiet, and way too easy to take for granted. But there's something dangerous about you that I haven't quite figured out." He gave her a sudden, mischievous grin. "I like that."

❧

When Aurora drove her to Coqui Beach the following evening, Esti tried to act like she was looking forward to it. She couldn't tell her mom that she would much rather be alone with Rafe, throwing all warnings into the wind as she became the next girl on his long list. She couldn't explain how her dreams at night were filled with Alan's voice, drawing her exquisitely close until he hurled her away. She didn't dare say how she ached to sit by the fireplace in Ashland, singing *heigh ho, the holly* with her dad. More than anything, she was tired of pretending to be in control.

Jayna Solomon stood at the door greeting her guests, tall and elegant in a deep blue dress and matching head-wrap that perfectly complemented her dark skin. "How pretty you are tonight," she said warmly to Esti. "I saw your performance at school. You're all Rafe talks about these days, you know."

Esti welcomed Rafe's arm around her shoulder as she and Aurora made their way through the house to the back door, chatting with Carmen and her parents.

"Esti Legard?" An artistic-looking fellow appeared from nowhere, thrusting out his hand. "Darling!"

She cautiously shook his hand.

"I'm sure you know how difficult I am to impress," he said, apparently assuming she recognized him. "After watching your performances, I have to tell you that your remarkable talent reaches a level I rarely see. I take it you studied Shakespeare with your father until his death?"

"He taught me a lot." Esti clutched Rafe's arm, feeling ridiculously intimidated as the man rattled on about Juliet. It was Alan who had given her the magic she needed to perform, she thought, but his disappearance undermined everything. This artistic man expected too much from her.

With a polite excuse about catching the sunset, Rafe finally pulled her outside, past a line of coolers on the big stone porch. She followed him across the crowded beach, leaving Aurora to chat with George Moore, who looked much less imposing in baggy shorts and a gaudy red shirt. The smell of barbequed chicken followed them across the sand, spiked with the scent of rum and coconut.

As they left the crowds behind them, however, Rafe suddenly slowed down. Danielle's sister stood in the sand nearby, watching them. Tight black clothes flattered her petite build, her dark hair pulled into a severe knot on top of her head. She looked nothing like Danielle, Esti thought, but was pretty in an eerie, pixyish kind of way.

"Marielle," Rafe said uncomfortably. "How've you been?"

"Looks like you scored again." As she looked from Rafe to Esti, she raised a single, condemning eyebrow. "Be careful, Esti Legard."

As Marielle turned and walked back toward the house, Esti heard an almost inaudible groan from Rafe.

Esti reached up and put her finger on his lips. "Doesn't matter." At his nonplussed look, she changed the subject. "How long has your family owned Coqui Beach?"

"A hundred years," Rafe said slowly. "More or less. Look, about Marielle—"

"It doesn't matter," Esti repeated. "There's some things I won't tell anybody, and you don't have to tell me anything you don't want to. I want to hear about your family instead."

Rafe was quiet for a minute. "They lived at Manchicay until the massacre. After they moved here, my great-grandfather eventually bought Coqui Beach from his boss. Esti, look—"

"A pretty nice northern swell tonight. Why do you think that is?"

He seemed completely at a loss. "Uh . . . big storm out on the ocean. Hurricane season usually ends in November."

"This seems to be the year for unusual storms." Without saying any more, Esti watched the clouds become pink, then orange. After a moment, Rafe gingerly took her hand and she squeezed his fingers.

As the sky darkened to gray, Ma Harris approached them with purposeful steps. Lucia followed, along with a wiry young West Indian boy wearing thick dreadlocks. Although Lucia gave Esti a smug look, her boyfriend merely stared at Esti as Ma Harris began to talk. Rafe replied in words so fast and deeply accented that Esti didn't even try to understand them. She needed no brains to know what they were talking about. When she heard the word *wicked* followed by *jumbee,* she mumbled an excuse and yanked herself away.

"Hold on, babe," Rafe said in surprise.

She walked faster, back toward the house. Bright lights and cheery calypso music spilled over the porch and onto the warm beach. She could see Aurora, lit up by a bonfire beyond the smoky grills, eating chicken with her fingers and laughing with George Moore.

This was nothing like the snow-dusted Christmas parties Esti's dad had thrown in Oregon. She wanted to be back there, when everything had seemed predictable and normal, her dad tousling her hair as he made his way through the house from one group of friends to another.

She wished with all her heart she was in the dark theater, reciting passages with Alan. Even *that* seemed more normal than this tropically cheerful Christmas party with so many eyes on Esti Legard. A sliver of understanding sliced through her about Alan's obsessive need for privacy.

As Rafe caught up to her, she began to run.

"Wait." He grabbed her arm. "What's the matter, babe?"

"He's not wicked! He's honorable." She clamped her mouth shut at the silly words. A moment ago, as she listened to Ma Harris, she had finally begun to wonder if maybe—the shivers started deep in her stomach—maybe Alan truly *was* a jumbee. It was crazy to believe in ghosts, she thought wildly. He couldn't really be a jumbee, but nothing else made sense.

"He's not," she whispered.

"It's okay." Rafe held both of her hands in his, his dark eyes glued to hers. "All Ma Harris said was that I have to protect you. She said I should take you to Carnival, so you can dance with the moko jumbees."

He smoothed a loose strand of hair behind her ear, a faint sparkle hiding in his eyes. "You's powerful too bad. No matter you all strong and ting, de jumbee he is unpredictable. We gon find moko jumbee dem at Carnival and make sure it have no evil spirit does stalk you."

Esti closed her eyes. "I'm going insane," she muttered.

"No." He wrapped his arms around her shoulders. "But you *are* so damn complicated, I can't even figure out how to make you feel better."

She looked out at the blackness of the sea, beyond the thin white line of crashing waves. "I know how you can make me feel better."

❧

She asked him to drive her to their usual swimming spot on Manchicay Beach, and he willingly complied. Instead of leading her into the warm swell, though, he took a blanket from the back of his Jeep. She followed him to the edge of the sea grape trees where they always found shade during the day. Without a word, Esti helped him spread the blanket over the sand, then sank down beside him, studying his outline in the moonlight.

"Did you know that I've only been kissed twice?" She reached up behind her head, weaving her wind-tangled hair into a braid as she tried to hide her nervousness.

"Twice." He stared at her as if the concept were completely beyond him.

"The first time I almost drowned," she said, "and the second was under hostile circumstances. So they didn't really count."

"You're not serious."

"Onstage doesn't count either, of course. I'm talking in real life."

"*You?* Esti Legard?"

"Darling!" She imitated the flamboyant talent scout. "I'm sure you know how difficult I am to impress."

Rafe didn't laugh. "That's not possible. Don't tell me your honorable jumbee never kissed you."

"I don't want to talk about him." Esti met Rafe's eyes, her body roiling with emptiness and fury and desire. "I just want to know what a real kiss feels like."

Rafe stared at her with an inscrutable expression.

"What?" Esti looked at him defiantly. "Don't you *want* to kiss me?"

His chest rose in a fierce breath, but he didn't speak. Esti forced herself to meet his gaze, trying to ignore a sudden panic that she had somehow alienated him too. After what seemed like forever, he finally came closer. Although she wished she knew what he was thinking, the desire on his face was unmistakable. As the sand shifted beneath his knees, she choked back a fleeting sense of hysteria. *Would* this make her feel better?

But Rafe didn't kiss her. He reached out with his hand instead, touching her cheek. His fingertips lightly followed the line of her jaw, then her nose and the ridge of her eyebrows, exploring the shape of her face. His eyes not leaving hers, he let his fingers move to her mouth, tracing the curve of her lips. His touch felt like fire on her skin, glorious and frightening and wonderful.

Abruptly he leaned forward. His fingers twisted into her hair, cupping the back of her head and tipping her face up to meet his. His mouth took over where his hand had begun. Esti melted into him, heat exploding through her body as his tongue traced the tip of her tongue, the line of her teeth. Slowly, his lips discovered the rest of her face, returning to her mouth every now and then as they brushed against her closed eyes, her cheekbones, the lobes of her ears. When he finally straightened, still cupping her head in his hand, she sagged and stared up at him.

"Did that kiss feel real enough?" he whispered.

Instead of answering, Esti reached up to his face. She let her hands make their way across his smooth dark skin, caressing his lips, his nose, his soft eyebrows. She ran her fingers along his cornrows, like knobby silk beneath her fingertips, then brought his head down to hers again.

She was barely aware of him pulling her onto his lap, their lips locked together. His hands felt warm and delicious as they stroked her face, her shoulders, her arms. Her body arched against him hungrily. She was awkwardly unfastening the shoulder straps of her dress, when he abruptly pulled away. Gasping for breath, she stopped, embarrassed.

"I can't be the only guy you ever kissed," he said.

"Three times now," she managed. "You just made up for all those years of wondering."

"Oh." He closed his eyes.

"What?" she asked. "What's the matter?"

"You've never done anything else then either."

"No." She looked away, hating the sudden thickness in her throat. She didn't want to think about what she was doing right now. She just wanted to let go and stop worrying, like he'd suggested so long ago.

"Does it matter?" She tried to touch his face again. "I want to do it now. All of it."

"Crap." He backed away, dropping to the sand just beyond her reach. "Yeah, it does matter. *He's* in your head tonight, isn't he? Even though he left you alone in a dark corner, all you can say is that he's honorable."

"Rafe . . ."

"I don't think I've ever wanted a girl so bad." He slumped over, panting. "I've been waiting for this since the minute I laid eyes on you. If you were any other girl, it would have been a week after we met, but I don't want you just one time." His voice rose angrily. "I've been with enough girls to know how girls are, and I ain't making the biggest mistake of my life tonight just because you're not done pining over *him* yet. I got more honor than a dumb-ass jumbee."

"Rafe, please."

"Don't look at me like that," he snapped.

She ran her hand along his arm. "It's not a mistake."

With a groan, he turned his eyes up to the sky. Suddenly pounding his fist into the sand, he leaped to his feet and crossed the sand in a few long strides. As water churned up around his feet, Esti rolled over and covered her face with her hands.

By the time he returned, dripping with salty water, her raging emotions had subsided into an annoying string of hiccups. She watched his moonlit outline in embarrassment, noticing how he carefully sat down on the edge of the blanket so he wouldn't get her wet.

"I'm sorry," he said.

"No." Esti couldn't look at his face. "*I'm* sorry."

"If I'd stayed here one more second, I would have ripped your dress off."

"Aurora would have been pissed." Rubbing her eyes, Esti rested her chin on her updrawn knees. "It was a Christmas present. Probably a bad idea for me to leave it in shreds on the beach."

"I made you cry." His voice was glum.

"Rafe, why do you put up with me?"

He snorted. "*That* is a weird question."

"I mean it. I'm not the most stable girl you've ever met."

"Do you want the truth? You might not like it."

"I want the truth." Esti sat up straight.

He looked out at Manchineel Cay, dark against the starry sky. "Okay, truth. I've always been the guy who can get girls. Girls are predictable and needy, and basically good for one thing. The minute I saw you after all those years, I had

one thing on my mind. Definitely not honorable, and I figured it would take me a week, tops." He gave her a sideways
glance.

"I already knew all that."

"You did?" He seemed stunned.

"Well, duh." Esti half smiled. "Carmen told me about your
reputation months ago. But it's been three weeks now, and
you just turned me down."

"I'm an idiot." He shook his head, looking back out at the
sea. "Every time I think I've got you figured out, you knock
my feet out from under me. The first night when you told
me why you changed your name, that threw me. I watched
you blow everyone away with your power onstage, then
land shivering on the beach, totally vulnerable. You kissed
me, then set me up to get busted, then bailed me out, then
said you're having some kind of affair, then practically killed
yourself to swim the bay with me. Your head seems wrapped
around this other jerk, except I really do think I'm the only
guy you've ever kissed. And now I'm all worried about a stupid thing like honor." He slowly shook his head. "I never met
a girl like you before."

"How many times have you used that line?"

"Esti . . ."

"That wasn't fair." She sighed. "Sorry. Everything I know
about love, I learned from Shakespeare. Boy wants sex; girl
wants boy. If boy gets sex too easily, he doesn't want girl anymore. If boy has to work for sex and prove himself to girl,
that's a much more interesting story."

"Huh." Rafe looked at her suspiciously. "Is that why *he* left you? I thought you never—"

"I never," she said dryly.

"So, why . . . ?"

"Why am I throwing myself at you?" She dug her fingers into the sand, letting the grains spill out between her fingers. "I'm trying to be careful, but maybe that doesn't mean what Marielle thinks it means. I don't want to fall in love with you."

Rafe scowled. "Because I'm a jerk."

"No, you're not," Esti said. "But that's the thing. I don't want you to be honorable right now."

He shook his head, baffled. "What do you want?"

"I don't know what I want." Esti lifted a handful of sand into the air. Would it be possible to actually *keep* Rafe Solomon in her life? "Look, Rafe. You're cute. Your dad is rich and famous. You know how to kiss."

His eyes narrowed.

"I'm predictable and needy, and good for one thing."

As his expression turned stony, she gave him a rueful smile.

"And maybe you want the truth."

"Yeah," he said. "Truth."

"The truth is, I trust you." A gust of whispery wind blew her disheveled hair into her face. "You're my friend. You let me be myself, and you don't freak out when I occasionally lose my mind. When I'm with you"—she closed her fingers around the sand—"I know I won't drown."

He slowly shook his head. "You're knocking my feet out from under me again."

"You do happen to be gorgeous, which is a bonus," Esti said softly. "And your kiss is killer. The problem is, I am completely messed up right now."

"You're irresistible right now."

She closed her eyes. "I don't want to fall in love with you because I'm afraid of hurting you. But part of me wants you to hurt me first, so I can blame being messed up on you." Anger flared through her as she realized her words to Rafe seemed eerily like Alan's words to her. "That's a dumb way to go through life, isn't it?"

"Dumb as a doornail." Rafe's arms went around her, strong and solid as he pulled her close.

As seawater soaked through her dress, she leaned into him.

"I'm tough," he said. "You're not going to hurt me, and I'll make sure I don't hurt you."

"I'll stop worrying, then." She nuzzled into him, pressing her ear against his chest to hear his heartbeat. "I *am* falling, even though I told myself I wouldn't."

"For me?"

"For you."

"I got a real chance then, long as I don't blow it."

She felt his fingers on her skin again, deliciously following the outline of her face.

"I'll work on my honor," he said, "even if it kills me. Nothing more than this; not yet." He traced his lips along her hairline, breathing in the scent of her hair. "And speaking of that killer kiss . . ."

As Esti eagerly tipped her face up to meet his, she became aware of Alan's necklace against her throat. Unexpected grief broke into her bliss, followed by a rush of anger that she still even cared. How dare Alan intrude right now? Hoping Rafe wouldn't notice, she unfastened the clasp with one hand. She held the chain in her fist for a single, aching moment, then flung it into the sea grape trees behind them.

It wasn't hard to lose herself in the blissful touch of Rafe's lips. She could forget about theater for a while, forget the necklace and the entire fantasy named Alan. And when she went to Carnival next weekend, maybe Ma Harris really would find some magical spell to banish him from Esti's thoughts. Esti didn't know if she would ever impress the talent scouts again, but she did know one thing. Her days of being cold and frightened were over.

Act Two. Scene Seven.

"It's so loud, I can hear it from here."

"Wear earplugs, then," Rafe countered Aurora's complaint. "I guarantee it's gonna be too much for your tender Continental ears. Some of the bands have been going nonstop since they got here last weekend."

"I know," Aurora said. "I haven't slept in two days. You'd think the rain would slow them down."

From the safety of her bedroom, Esti made herself smile. Carnival held no appeal for her today, not after the tangled logic that now amounted to her own private jumbee hunt. Esti could not make herself believe that any type of silly dancing might have some effect on Alan's existence, but she knew that the disturbing gestures on the street might be the tip of a more threatening iceberg. If she watched the moko jumbees today, maybe the locals would think she was cured.

Looking one last time in the mirror, she smoothed the purple sundress against her skin, then walked into the living room.

"Ooh, baby!"

She laughed as Rafe leaped from the couch. He'd been very funny and sweet since Christmas night, making sure that everyone on the island knew that Rafe Solomon had finally been caught. Esti didn't have to pretend she enjoyed herself with him, and she instantly melted whenever Rafe kissed her at The Boardwalk or on the beach, or in the deep water of Manchicay Bay.

But yesterday evening her mom had asked if she knew whether Mr. Niles was doing Shakespeare again next semester. Esti had jolted upright in the middle of the night, Alan's voice filling her with longing before she came fully awake. *Desperately, hopelessly in love . . .*

Fiercely shoving the memory down, Esti flung her arms around Rafe's neck. She pressed herself against him as his warm lips touched hers, but he immediately pulled away to smile at Aurora.

"I'm glad to see your manners," Aurora said. "I've been a little worried by the gossip, but Esti assures me that you're good for her."

"The safest guy on Cariba," Esti said firmly, ignoring Rafe's smirk.

"Her father always liked you, Rafe." Aurora chuckled. "Your dads both joked about the two of you getting together someday, although Jayna said it wouldn't be easy. *The course of true love never did run smooth.*"

Esti's eyes widened. She hadn't heard a Shakespeare quote from her mom since the diagnosis.

"For true," Rafe said. "Esti isn't easy."

"But Rafe sure is smooth," Esti countered automatically.

When Rafe winked, Aurora burst into laughter. "Sweetie, do you happen to have any earplugs?"

Esti was happily surprised by her mom's lighthearted mood. Aurora seemed more relaxed today than she'd been in months. Maybe it had something to do with Rafe's charm, or the fact that he was an old friend. Or maybe, Esti thought guiltily, it was because this was the first time she had really invited Aurora to come with her on a social outing.

By the time they walked downtown, Esti wondered if she should have brought something for her own ears. Dozens of semi trucks had arrived on the island, pulling huge flatbed trailers piled with giant speakers and live bands.

Deafening soca filled the air with incessant percussion

threaded through lyrical songs of political satire and sexual double entendre. Reggae and calypso poured from the other trucks, each group trying to drown out the others with lilting refrains of love and lust. Costumed dancers followed every trailer, wearing masks and feathers, and giant colorful wings of wire and gauze.

Some of the dancers walked on stilts high above the crowds, moving with as much vigor and grace as everyone on the ground. Esti thought their shimmering costumes looked particularly bright against the cloudy morning sky. These moko jumbees danced between heaven and earth on their stilts, Rafe had explained, protecting the crowds from evil spirits. Although they looked impressive, Esti seriously doubted that a costumed stilt walker could ever scare a real ghost.

With a shiver, she forced herself to ignore the moko jumbees. She just wanted to go home. Alan would never show up at a giant public gathering like this, even if he *was* some kind of jumbee. Esti knew him too well to believe she could possibly summon him in full daylight.

Rafe held her hand, waving at Aurora to get her attention. "Follow me," he shouted.

Esti barely heard him over the noise, but she grabbed Aurora with her other hand when Rafe began pulling her through the crowds. As he led them down a side street, she turned away from a woman crossing her fingers in a hostile gesture, almost tripping over a masked dancer dressed in black. The dancer ducked his head, his pale eyes brushing uncomfortably past hers. The black-garbed dancer was followed by a colorful stilt walker, who laughingly maneuvered his stilts over them all.

Black-wrapped dancers seemed to be everywhere, and Rafe shouted that these were the local jumbee dancers, inspired by the real black-clothed jumbee that haunted Manchineel Cay. "They only perform during Cariba's parade, dancing between the stilts of the moko jumbees," he yelled over the music. "People come from all over, especially to see them."

The parade had already wound partway through town, and music from the giant pounding speakers vibrated through Esti's body each time they passed a truck. She began wondering if she would ever hear properly again. The volume level hadn't gotten any better by the time they ended up by the harbor. As they got closer to the picnic tables, Esti saw Carmen and Chaz at a table with Ma Harris and Rafe's parents.

With a grin, Rodney held up a daiquiri for Aurora. "Rum is on special this week!" he shouted. "Help yourself."

Lucia and her boyfriend danced at the edge of the parade nearby, Lucia tucking a stray dreadlock beneath Quintin's bandanna with a deliberate, teasing look.

"Did you see Steve?" Carmen shouted into Esti's ear. "I thought he'd left the island when he got kicked out of school, but I just saw him with one of the bands. He looked high as a kite."

Esti couldn't help a growing sense of unease as she looked around. She had no desire to see Steve, and she'd never experienced anything like the strange, uninhibited energy surrounding her. The occasional burst of rain wasn't stopping anyone.

Perhaps Ma Harris was right. Maybe ghosts *did* appear at times like this, safely hidden in the throngs of costumed revelers. When several more jumbee dancers ran past them, Rafe pulled Esti behind him again.

"Let's walk around," he shouted into her ear.

The pulsating music was impossible to resist, and Esti felt herself moving in rhythm to it as she followed Rafe along the street. Everywhere she looked, she saw shaking hips and strutting feet and dark arms waving in the air. She watched a procession of solemn little West Indian girls dressed in matching silver leotards and twirling batons in perfect time. Although several small faces anxiously studied Esti and Rafe as they marched past, their batons didn't miss a beat.

Another black-masked dancer walked by them, blue eyes staring at Esti slightly too long. Esti watched him walk away, wondering if he would make a sign warding off evil now that he had recognized her. Rafe wasn't shy about returning the suspicious looks from all sides, and Esti was grateful for his protective arms, his strong body moving in perfect rhythm beside her.

"You de one talk to jumbee dem?"

A West Indian man stopped so close in front of her that she smelled the rum on his breath. Another man stood beside him, holding a beer. They both grinned as Rafe pulled her away from them.

"What you want, mon?" Rafe glared at the man with the beer.

"We hear dis white gyal does talk to a jumbee." The man with rum on his breath gave Esti a look that made her skin crawl.

"Leave she be," Rafe said.

"She limin' wit Rafe Solomon," the man drawled. "Sweet ting like fun-fun, eh?"

Rafe stiffened and edged toward the man. Esti's heart began to pound. She grabbed Rafe's shirt, pulling him to a stop.

"You go drink you rum," Rafe said tightly. "An' I don't teach you a lesson today."

The man shrugged and turned. As the other man walked by, however, he reached out to touch Esti's face. "Jumbee gyal," he cooed. "I show you some nice spirit, if you come wit'—"

Rafe slammed the man's hand down, shoving him back so hard he stumbled against the people behind him. Shrieks and cursing rose above the blasting music as the man straightened. The crowd around him began muttering, several hands flashing into the air as they caught sight of Esti. Her heart sinking, she desperately yanked on Rafe's shirt again to stop him, then stifled a scream as the drunk West Indian lunged at her.

A jumbee dancer darted between them, his foot gracefully snaking out to trip the man before he could reach Esti. As the drunk man fell, Rafe leaped furiously at him. The dancer grabbed Rafe, safely spinning him out of the way before he could start a fight. Esti caught sight of blue eyes again as the dancer glanced at her. Suddenly a policeman appeared, glaring at the restless crowd.

"You causin' trouble, Rafe?" he demanded

"Dey have harass my girl!" Rafe exploded. The rum-breath man lurched to his feet, fleeing into the crowd with his friend. Esti felt her skin crawl as she realized the blue-eyed dancer had disappeared into the shifting horde of jumbee dancers.

"She mind she own business," Rafe raged, "and I don't let no one—"

"Keep you cool, Rafe." The cop patted a nightstick attached to his belt, glancing at Esti. "You might see the inside of my police van today. I ain't forget about last summer."

Esti pulled Rafe close as he looked around for the two men. She couldn't imagine what might happen if the police dragged Rafe away, leaving her alone here. The officer watched them without speaking, and Rafe finally looked back at him.

"You keep de badjohn away from my girl," he said stiffly, "and I's cool. Just do you job, mon."

Esti felt the cop's eyes on them as Rafe sauntered away, dragging her along behind him. She couldn't help a shaky feeling that she had narrowly escaped disaster. If the jumbee dancer hadn't tripped the drunk man; if he hadn't stopped Rafe from getting into a big fight . . . She suddenly knew the dancer had been following her since she got here. Fragments of hope and fear began darting through her mind.

When they got back to the park, Rafe's mom was pulling sandwiches from a cooler.

Esti stopped at the edge of the table, Rafe spinning her around in an expert move to the music. She grabbed his shoulders in surprise, just as she recognized a familiar curry smell. As she saw the wrapped roti chicken, she jerked away, tension churning inside of her.

"Babe, are you okay?" Rafe asked.

She nodded toward a group of moko jumbees passing by. "I'm not hungry yet. I'd rather watch them."

Rafe grabbed a sandwich, grinning at the others. "Hey," he yelled over the music. "She wants to dance with the moko jumbees!"

"Good," she heard Ma Harris say.

With a chaotic surge of emotion, Esti pulled Rafe away and continued toward the street, ignoring the light mist of rain that had started again. She didn't want to dance; she wanted to find the blue-eyed dancer and demand to know his name. What did his voice sound like?

The stilt walkers in front of them were some of the most graceful she'd seen, kicking their long, colorful legs high in the air and leaning back in impossible shimmies to the steel pan drums. On the ground, jumbee dancers darted between their stilts, somehow avoiding danger.

Esti walked past the pounding speakers, her eyes searching the shifting black dancers as she lead Rafe away from Ma

Harris's intense gaze, away from Aurora and everyone else. She wasn't going to dance; she was going to ask Rafe about the guy who had helped him. Had the dancer said anything when he yanked Rafe out of the way?

Rafe followed without protest until she finally stopped. When he held up his food, she nodded. She would try to calm down while he finished eating. She pressed her hands against her temples as Rafe looked up at the high stilts, her skin twitching with anxiety.

Suddenly a breath of air brushed her neck, like a long, slow sigh. The scent of frangipani enveloped her, just as a white blossom dropped to the ground at her feet.

"I miss you." Goose bumps crawled down her spine at the familiar deep voice in her ear. "I could teach you how to choose right, but then I am forsworn. So will I never be."

She slowly turned her head. Rafe was eating his roti chicken, fully absorbed by the amazing stilt walkers beside them. The jumbee dancer had stopped on Esti's other side, so close that she could see the turquoise shimmer in his blue eyes.

"So may you miss me," he continued, his words more beautiful than music. "But if you do, you'll make me wish a sin: that I had been forsworn."

She almost couldn't hear him over the pounding beat, but she knew the quote so well that he seemed to speak directly to her mind. His eyes blazed into her, burning themselves into her consciousness. Fifty years from now she knew she would remember every detail of those sea-colored eyes. Without thinking, she reached out with her free hand, her heart racing. As her fingers closed around his black-gloved fist, she almost grew light-headed.

She was not insane.

He seemed to stagger at her touch, and she tightened her fingers, terrified that he would disappear. "Beshrew your eyes," he forced out. "They have overlooked me and divided me. One half of me is yours, the other half"—his expression softened, the look he gave her helpless—"yours. Mine own, I would say; but if mine, then yours. And so all yours."

"Alan . . ."

"You talking to me, babe?"

She glanced up as Rafe turned to her, his eyes lingering on the stilt dancers. Although it took only a second, it was long enough for Alan to pull away before Rafe saw him. When she looked back, Alan was gone, lost in a swirl of black.

"No!" She shook off Rafe's grasp and darted among the dancers, catching hold of the first black-garbed man she came to. Startled brown eyes looked at her, and she flung him away. She seized another man, barely avoiding the stilts beside her.

"She possess, for true," someone yelled.

"Esti, come here." Strong hands grabbed her, dragging her away from the dancers.

"No." She yanked herself away from Rafe. "Alan's here. I saw him."

Rafe grabbed her again, then picked her up and walked back toward the curb. His arms tightened around her as she struggled to get away from him.

Although she felt the growing fear and suspicion from the people nearby, she couldn't help herself. "Let me go! I have to find him."

Rafe put her down, firmly holding her shoulders. "You're gonna get hurt."

"She hornin' you, Rafe," someone taunted. "She chase a jumbee dancer, mon."

Rafe spun around. "Who said that?"

Esti looked frantically at the blur of motion beside them. "He was there."

"His name is Alan?" Rafe demanded, forcing Esti to look up at him.

"Yes." She tried to hide her exploding joy, but Rafe's growing anger made it clear that she still wasn't any good at lying.

"He doesn't even have the guts to face me," Rafe snapped.

Esti recoiled at Rafe's fury. "He did! He kept you from getting in a fight."

"What the hell are you talking about?"

"He's been following us ever since we got here." As people edged closer, Esti tried to stay calm. "Didn't you see him? He tripped that drunk guy, and then he—"

"That *crappo* has been hanging around you all morning?" Rafe stared at her like she was crazy. "And you didn't bother telling me?"

"I didn't know it was him until after he helped you." She felt herself panicking at the anger in Rafe's eyes, searching for words. "Look, he's known about you from the beginning.

He told me I should go to you, because he couldn't—"

Rafe grew rigid in disbelief. "*That's* the reason you're dating me? Because Alan gave you permission?"

"No!"

"What does he look like?"

Through a brief pause in the music, she heard growing mutters from the crowd. "He was wearing a mask," she said.

Rafe leaned closer, his eyes narrowing. "Don't tell me you don't know what your boyfriend looked like."

"He wasn't my boyfriend."

"Stop lying to me!" Rafe grabbed her shoulders so tightly, she winced.

"I am not lying," she said through clenched teeth. "And you're hurting me."

As he flung her away, he seemed to become aware of the restless mob around them. He instantly drew her back, but for once, the embrace wasn't a loving gesture. "If you talk to him," he snapped, "I'm going with you. I'll make him apologize."

"He already did," Esti said stiffly, fear pulsing at the edges of her mind along with the crowd closing in.

Rafe glared at her. "When?"

"Just now. He quoted Shakespeare."

"That's a bunch of bull." Rafe's fingers tightened again, bruising her arms. "Why didn't I see him?"

"Rafe, stop!"

His grip relaxed, but he didn't let go of her. "What did he say?"

As his face came closer, she really began to struggle. She had never realized how intimidating Rafe could be. "Portia's words, from *The Merchant of Venice*," she whispered fearfully.

Hostility swirled through the air like a growing fog. "Tell me."

"He said, 'I could teach you how to choose right . . .'" She trailed off.

"He tells you who to choose," Rafe said bitterly. "You went out with me because he told you to, and now you're running back when he calls."

"That's not true."

As Esti tried again to pull away from him, Lucia's low voice cut in. "Leave she be, Rafe."

Esti almost fell when Rafe instantly let go of her. Lucia stood in front of them, her arms folded sternly across her chest. Given that she was only a skinny fourteen-year-old, Esti thought in a daze, Lucia was easily the most imposing girl Esti had ever met. Behind her, Quintin hovered silently, his cold eyes on Rafe.

"She hornin' me." Rafe glared at Quintin, as if he thought Lucia's boyfriend might somehow understand.

"You should be shame," Lucia snapped. "Crawl home now, an' leave we be."

Slamming his fist into a nearby booth piled with tourist gifts, Rafe flung the table on its side, scattering cheap, colorful masks everywhere. He strode away without looking at Esti or anyone else. His departure was followed by a few gleeful expressions, but mostly uneasy faces turned back to look at Esti.

"Esti, come." The crowd left them alone as Lucia calmly pulled Esti into the street, Quintin close on her other side.

She never could have guessed that Lucia—of all people—would end up rescuing her from Rafe. Matching her footsteps to the incessant percussion, Esti felt herself hovering on the edge of hysteria once again. *Bazadee, for true;* flung by the catapult out of Rafe's life as quickly as they'd been thrown together.

Act Two. Scene Eight.

Esti lived through the eternity of a day and a half, before she was finally able to sneak back to the theater building. *Yes Aurora, Rafe and I had a fight. No, he didn't try to take advantage of me. Yes, he got jealous of a jumbee dancer who flirted with me. No, I don't know if we'll get back together. Yes, I'm just fine. Perfectly fine.*

Esti had no idea how to explain Lucia's involvement, but Aurora had eventually stopped pushing for details. When Esti said she was going to Carmen's after dinner, her mom quickly retreated into a bottle of wine. Esti watched helplessly, aware that she'd become a truly impossible daughter. By the time she slipped into the familiar darkness of the theater, she was ready to scream from the effort of once again pretending to everyone that she was in control.

She turned on a single stage light with a determined flick of her fingers. She was done with the dark, and done with hiding in the basement. A trickle of sweat crawled from the back of her knee to her ankle as she walked calmly down the aisle, her flip-flops slapping quietly against the carpet. She sat on the edge of the stage beside the bright floor light.

"And so," she said, continuing Portia's quote as though Alan had spoken a mere moment ago, "though yours, not yours. Prove it so."

"I thought you would never talk to me again." Alan sounded nervous. "You're not wearing my necklace."

"I lost it. I'm sorry." Esti closed her eyes, trying to forget the details of Christmas night. "I've wanted to talk to you every minute of every day since you told me to get out of your life."

"Forgive me," he whispered.

"Who are you? What are you?" She opened her eyes again and looked around the empty stage. "*Where* are you?"

Her question was followed by a deep silence.

"You have no reason to fear me," Alan said quietly. "I would never hurt you."

"That wasn't my question." She tightened her jaw, thinking about the suspicion she encountered everywhere she went. "Why is everyone on Cariba afraid of you?"

When he didn't answer, she swung her feet off the edge of the stage. "I'm leaving."

"Don't go." Tension filled his words. "Please. I want you to stay."

"Prove it so." She stretched her cold fingers over the warm halogen bulb beside her, throwing eerie shadows across the stage. "Don't hide from me anymore."

"Esti . . ."

"Maybe you're running from the law." Focusing all her effort on keeping her voice steady, she resorted to the speech she'd prepared last night. This time she was ready for his evasions. "I've heard that criminals sometimes come to the islands to hide. Do you live in the theater basement because you have nowhere else to go? I wouldn't have come back here if I didn't trust you, but you have to tell me the truth."

"I'm not running from the law," Alan said softly. "And, as much as I enjoy this theater for the escape it provides me, I don't live in the basement."

"Where do you live, then?" She studied the glow of light around her fingers.

"Manchineel Cay."

A chill crept down Esti's spine. "No one lives on Manchineel Cay. Anyone setting foot on the island is never seen again."

He snorted. "Who has seen me?"

"I saw you."

"Did you? What do I look like?"

"Your eyes are as blue as the sea." Esti would never forget how deeply they had burned into her. Her breathing grew more rapid. "I held your hand."

"You're the only one who ever has." She heard his answering breath, deep and uneven.

The chill in her spine grew, spreading goose bumps along her arms and legs. "So, you're telling me you *are* a jumbee."

"I'm telling you what you demand to hear."

"I need the truth. Show me your face." After another long silence, she rose to her feet. "Good-bye, Alan."

"Don't!" The desperation in his voice stopped her. "Please don't, Esti. Ask me for anything else."

"No." She shook with growing anger. "I won't share the stage with empty shadows anymore. I want you to hold my hand again. And if you really live on Manchineel Cay, show me your house, too. Prove to me that I'm not obsessed by a figment of my own imagination."

When a long, predictable silence followed her words, she kicked her foot against the stage light in sudden fury.

"I am so sick of—*ouch!*" Darkness blanketed the stage as the halogen lamp burned out with a soft pop. "Ow, ow, ow. That really hurt."

"Esti," Alan said in a panicked voice, "are you okay? Did you break the glass?"

"No." With a painful groan, she sank back down to the dark stage, gingerly cradling her foot. "I hit the inside of my foot on the light box."

"Is it bad?"

"I can't tell." With a disgusted grimace, she pulled off her flip-flop and touched the cut. "I think I'm bleeding. You don't happen to have a Band-Aid," she added sarcastically.

Almost before the words were out of her mouth, a firm hand gently pulled her fingers away from her foot, lightly tracing the painful bare skin of her instep. She couldn't move, paralyzed by the shock of the unexpected, sensual touch in the darkness. A soft cloth brushed the sole of her foot, quickly wrapping up and over her arch to bind the wound. Before she could reach out to him, he grasped both of her hands. He pressed her fingers down and tight around the bandage, his hands solidly on top of hers.

"I'll take you to Manchineel Cay," he said in defeat.

Esti's body quivered with the overwhelming sensation of his hands holding her hands hostage, his breath tickling her cheek. Although the afterglow of the halogen lamp blurred her eyes, she could almost make out his dark shape crouched in front of her.

"It will be a mistake, of course," he said "But such is my love, to thee I so belong, that for thy right, myself will bear all wrong."

"Is it dangerous?" Esti could barely whisper the words.

"The island is mine." His fingers tightened on hers, seeming to tremble with the effort. "You'll be quite safe, as long as you're with me. The danger is only to me."

"Why is the cay dangerous to you?"

"It's not the cay that frightens me."

She forced out a tiny laugh. "Are you worried that I'll find out your real name is Elon Somand?"

He moved so quickly that she couldn't keep him from pulling away again. "When you come to my house, perhaps you will finally know who I am."

❧

"You're here!"

The moment Esti walked into the theater the next day, Carmen leaped out of her chair in the back row.

"I *said* you'd be back today," Carmen cried, flinging her arms around Esti. "I knew the new rumors weren't true."

Esti returned Carmen's hug, feeling confused and a little silly as everyone turned around to look at them. "More rumors? Fancy that."

"I guess the jumbee didn't possess you during Carnival."

Esti twitched her toes, aware of the soft cloth wrapped around her foot beneath her sneaker and secured with a rubber band that Alan had found on the stage before she left. She had studied the bandage in detail after she got home last night. A jumbee wouldn't carry around a fine linen handkerchief, she quickly decided. Of course, she wasn't sure a normal twenty-five-year-old guy would have one either.

"Do you know," Carmen added, "you're the strangest girl I've ever known?"

Esti snorted. "*That* I believe."

Carmen pulled Esti down to the seat beside her, leaning close so no one else could hear. "Rafe asked me out last night. He was pretty insistent about it."

Esti caught her breath.

"I finally met him at the park, even though Chaz would kill me if he found out."

Esti felt a stab of jealousy, tinged with dismay. Was Rafe going after Carmen in revenge? Would Carmen do that to

Chaz—or to Esti? Not that Esti had any right to judge what either one of them did.

"Carmen, look . . ."

"All he wanted was to talk about you. He said you dumped him for a jumbee dancer."

Esti scowled. She had warned Rafe that he might get hurt. She'd *tried* to be truthful with him.

"He kept asking if I knew what was wrong with you," Carmen continued. "I finally managed to dig out of him that you were dating this other guy all last semester, even though you never told me a thing. Why are you keeping all these secrets from me? I swear, Rafe was seriously bummed. I never thought in a million years you were really his type, but he's totally into you. Honestly, Jane Doe, what else do you have going on behind my back?"

Esti's head spun in sickening loops as she tried to think how to answer Carmen. She didn't know what was going on. She'd been doing all she could to get over Rafe, spending hours in her bedroom studying Manchineel Cay with binoculars. She knew the cay wasn't visible from Coqui Beach, but it was within shouting distance from The Boardwalk. Would Rafe shout at her, if he knew she would soon be there with Alan? If Rafe pulled her into his arms, would she melt into his kiss without a second thought?

"I have some things going on right now," she finally said. It sounded pathetic, even to her.

Carmen's eyes narrowed. "Like fooling around with a jumbee?"

"I've never fooled around with anyone but Rafe." Esti's cheeks grew warm as the words blurted from her mouth. She couldn't believe she'd just said that to Carmen. Now the whole school would know.

"I knew it," Carmen crowed. "Rafe's always gotten every girl he ever wanted. But you dumped *him* before he could dump you. Jane Doe has out-Rafed the infamous Rafe Solomon!"

"Carmen." Esti closed her eyes. "I'm never telling you anything again."

"You never tell me anything in the first place. All I can say is, I can't wait until your name really is as big as your dad's. You're gonna give the paparazzi a field day."

"You don't know what you're talking about."

"*Now* what's going on?" Carmen abruptly raised her voice. "Lance, stop messing with the lights."

As Esti opened her eyes again, she was half blinded by the brilliance surrounding her. Every light in the house had come on. Over the excited voices of the others, she heard a muffled shout from center stage. She raised her hand against the floodlights in time to catch a movement followed by a pained cry. Frowning, she rose to her feet.

"Mr. Niles." Danielle's strong voice pierced the air. "Oh, my God!"

Fear shot through Esti as she ran down the aisle behind Carmen, trying not to limp from the pain in her right in-step. The theater had become so bright it almost seemed on fire, light blazing from every corner. The rest of the class was gathering in front of the stage, where Mr. Niles huddled on the floor beneath the lights. He clutched his leg, swearing in a harsh, steady stream of unintelligible West Indian dialect. Danielle crouched beside him, glancing up at Greg with frightened eyes.

"What happened?" Carmen asked Chaz.

"No idea."

Esti strained to hear Chaz over Niles's cursing.

"The lights came on," Chaz said, "and then Niles charged out from backstage. I didn't see him fall, but Danielle says he went off the edge of the stage like a jumbee pushed him." Chaz shook his head, his eyes wide. "This place *is* haunted."

The swearing stopped in time for Chaz's last words to be clearly heard.

"It's because of you," Mr. Niles said. "Everyone on Cariba knows it."

Chaz turned deep red, but Esti felt a profound apprehension as she met the theater teacher's frightened eyes. Mr. Niles wasn't talking to Chaz.

"Esti was with me," Carmen said into the silence. "We were talking in the last row when the lights . . ." She trailed off uncertainly.

As Mr. Niles lifted both hands in a deliberate warding gesture, Chaz stood up. He glanced uneasily at Esti before running toward the main door with a mutter about getting some help.

"You have hear the news?" Lucia stopped beside the court-yard bench, her expression even more somber than usual. "Mr. Niles he quit."

"Great." Carmen stared morosely out at Manchineel Cay. "Esti, are the talent scouts not coming, then?"

"I told you, I don't know what's going on," Esti said. She hadn't seen Lucia since Carnival, and they exchanged a cautious glance. Carmen instantly sensed the new energy in the air, her eyes darting back and forth between Esti and Lucia.

"I hear the melee," Lucia said darkly.

"More gossip?" Carmen briefly grinned.

Esti glanced at the theater building. Alan couldn't have caused Mr. Niles's accident. Danielle had seen it happen with every house light on; a bunch of them had watched Niles leap from the stage, pursued by nothing and no one.

"It have melee the jumbee he is a talent scout." Lucia stared at Carmen with narrowed eyes. "Or the jumbee had curse talent scout them. Could be that Rafe save Esti from the jumbee or"—she gave Esti a somber look—"maybe Esti have curse Rafe."

Esti's stomach turned at the thought that Lucia might really believe that.

"It have melee also"—Lucia's eyes turned back to Carmen—"Carmen had curse Esti. Carmen want Rafe come to she instead."

"Stop it, Lucia." Now Carmen looked shaken. "What is up with you?"

"It have melee the jumbee he curse Mr. Niles," Lucia said. She caught Esti in her piercing gaze, then shrugged. "When melee does convince a West Indian he got a jumbee after him, he ain't so stupid to stick around, nah."

"There she is!"

Esti shrank against her bench as Greg burst from the theater building, followed by the others.

"Danielle just called Mr. Niles on his cell phone," Greg said as they approached. "He's at the hospital. He canceled auditions. Theater class is over." Greg threw his hands up into the air. "Manchicay's theater department is history, my career is shot—" He looked at Esti in angry confusion. "What did you *do?*"

"Get off her case, you moron." To Esti's huge relief, Carmen instantly jumped to her defense. "If Niles quit because he's so clumsy, it's not Esti's fault."

"Theater class isn't canceled." They all swung around as Headmaster Fleming approached them. He was followed by the thin, artistic-looking man who'd fawned over Esti at the Christmas party.

"I would like to introduce all of you to Frederick McKenzie, an agent from one of New York's prime talent agencies," Mr. Fleming continued.

Everyone grew wide-eyed at the name. Esti studied the man in wonder as Mr. Fleming talked. At the party she'd had no idea who he was, but even her father had mentioned *the* Frederick McKenzie from time to time.

"You probably all know that his background is in theater.

Mr. McKenzie saw your Christmas performance. He was dropping by to talk to Mr. Niles when all the excitement happened this afternoon. To make a long story short, he signed a contract as your temporary teacher for a few weeks, until I can find someone for the rest of the semester."

When the new man beamed at Esti, she could only stare back at him in disbelief.

"I've assured Mr. McKenzie he won't have any problems, particularly with superstitious students." Headmaster Fleming glanced around the class, turning last to Esti. His eyes locked on her for a long moment before he raised his eyebrows and smiled.

"Isn't that correct, Miss Legard?"

Act Two. Scene Nine.

"Did you talk to Frederick at the Christmas party?" Esti still hadn't gotten over Mr. Fleming's bombshell announcement this afternoon.

Aurora sat down beside Esti on the balcony, her expression solemn. "Of course. We were introduced last year at one of your father's ceremonies."

"Oh." Esti couldn't help feeling deflated. "Frederick was one of dad's friends, then."

"A business acquaintance. I'm sure you never met him."

"Because I stopped going to dad's events?"

Aurora shrugged. "You obviously need to have your own life."

Esti picked at the label on her soda bottle, worried about the edginess in her mom's voice. Esti had always thought of Aurora as so independent, but she was clearly miserable these days. Maybe she had secretly needed the credentials of The Great Legard to be happy.

"I mean," Aurora added, "look how busy you were with Rafe at the Christmas party. I was surprised to see you disappear right after Frederick McKenzie gave you an extremely rare compliment. Then again, I'm beginning to wonder if I ever really understood you."

"I talked to Frederick this afternoon." Esti yanked the soda label off with a jerk. "He insists we all call him Frederick instead of Mr. McKenzie, and he calls everyone 'Darling,' even the boys. Carmen loves him."

Aurora raised her eyebrows. "When will he hold auditions?"

"We're not doing a new play yet." Despite her lingering pain—and guilt—Esti couldn't keep her enthusiasm from growing. "He wants us to do *Romeo and Juliet* again, two weeks from now. It will be a special showcase for Manchicay School. He's got a couple of Broadway producers coming from New York to see us. He talked the art teacher into loaning him her best students to help with sets, because he's already redesigned the entire stage. This guy is good."

"Two weeks?" Aurora's voice remained distant. "He certainly set that up fast."

"He started making phone calls before Christmas. He told us he doesn't know a single New Yorker—even a busy one—who hasn't scrambled to rearrange their schedule for a free January weekend on a Caribbean island."

A haven for shiny scouts wanting a paid vacation in the tropics. With a smile, Esti twitched her foot against the handkerchief again, thinking of Alan's healing touch in the darkness. "Rodney is making all the local arrangements. I guess we impressed everyone."

"You mean *you* impressed them." Aurora's cool expression didn't match her words at all. "I've been very proud of you lately, thinking that maybe your hard work was finally paying off."

"All of us, not just me." Esti studied her mom, trying to figure out what was going on with her today. "Frederick made that very clear."

"Who's playing Juliet?"

"We're doing two shows and taking turns. One night I'll play Juliet and the other night I'll do Lady Capulet."

Aurora took a sip of wine, staring out at Manchineel Cay.

"It's a good idea, anyway, don't you think?" Esti uneasily followed her mom's gaze to Manchineel Cay, wreathed in dark clouds. Maybe it would be a good idea to finally mention the drinking. She wondered if Alan was at home right now, enveloped in the gloomy fog and thinking about her. A sharp edge of white rode the top of each wave, the air heavy with the smell of rain.

Esti glanced at her mom's wineglass. "Frederick knows

what he's doing," she said slowly. "He had everyone get on-stage for a few minutes before class was over and work on some quick focus exercises, like Dad used to always do."

"Hopefully he'll be immune from jumbee curses." Aurora didn't smile.

"He's not superstitious. He's tons better than Mr. Niles."

"I'm sure he is." Aurora finally met Esti's eyes. "Will you be sneaking off with Alan again this semester?"

Cold shock crept through Esti's body and into her finger-tips. She should have known it was only a matter of time.

"I understand Alan is quite the Shakespeare expert," Aurora added darkly. "Rafe told me what happened at Carni-val. I'm astonished—no Esti, I'm incensed—that you would treat Rafe like that."

Esti put down her soda bottle, trying not to panic at the condemnation in Aurora's eyes. "When did you see Rafe?"

"Last night after you told me you were going to Carmen's. He spent a couple of hours talking to her at the park, then he came over here. You apparently *weren't* at Carmen's. How many other lies have you told lately?"

Esti couldn't make herself look up. "Aurora, I—"

"Were you with this . . . this Alan last night? I'm warning you, Esti: If you lie to me now, I will buy plane tickets and take you back to Ashland tomorrow."

"Yes." Esti stared at the table, her temples pounding with guilt. "I was with Alan."

"I am trying very hard not to lose it," Aurora continued in a steely voice. "You never lied to me before we came to

Cariba, but apparently you've been doing it since we got here. Tell me why this is the first time I've ever heard of a guy named Alan."

"Weren't you married to one?"

The silence instantly grew brittle.

"I'm sorry," Esti said miserably, "I tried. A couple of months ago, I started telling you about a tutor who works behind the scenes at Manchicay."

Aurora drew her brows together, then took a sip of wine. "That sounds a bit familiar."

Esti's eyes fixed on her mom's wineglass. "You finished a whole bottle of wine that night before I got home."

Aurora guiltily looked away.

Esti knew she was using her mom's problems to climb out of her own mess, but she couldn't help herself. "You started crying before I could finish, so I ended up not telling you. You've been having such a hard time since we got here that I didn't want to worry you."

"Thank you, Esti," Aurora said stiffly, "but if this is a guy I need to worry about, why are you seeing him?"

"You don't need to worry about him, it's just that . . ." Esti glanced out at the approaching rain column, taking a deep breath of the rapidly cooling air.

"Just that *what?*" Aurora stared at her wineglass for a moment. "Why have you been lying to me? Is he using you?"

"Using me for what?"

"Don't be naive," her mom snapped. "Talent scouts love pretty young things like you."

"No." Esti tried not to get angry. "He is not using me."

"How old is he?"

"Twenty-five."

"I've never met a major talent scout that young."

"He's not a talent scout; he's an actor. We study Shakespeare together."

Aurora took a small, deliberate sip of wine. "Are you sleeping with him?"

"Aurora!"

"I do not believe that your breakdown before Christmas was due to a bad study session." Aurora locked eyes with Esti. "Have you had sex with him?"

"No." *We've held hands. Almost twice.*

"What happened, then? What did he do that hurt you?"

"He didn't hurt me." Esti cast around for a believable excuse. "He said he didn't want to tutor me anymore, and I overreacted."

"I think you're lying again." Aurora hesitated, her mouth tightening. "Rafe says you don't know what Alan looks like."

"I'm not lying, and Rafe is jealous, that's all." Esti dodged the question. "Alan has blue eyes. He's a little taller than I am."

"Then he's not a jumbee, despite what you told the jandam. Alan is your boyfriend."

"No. He's just an actor I've been studying with." Esti hesitated, frustrated that she had never been able to shout to the world, *ALAN IS MY BOYFRIEND!* "At Carnival," she said slowly, "he did finally ask me if I would go out with him."

It was true. In a way.

"In front of Rafe?" Aurora's eyes narrowed. "How incredibly tacky of both of you. Did you plan to date Alan, then, without ever telling me?"

"No, but—" Before Esti could finish, rain hit the balcony roof in an explosion of noise. They both jumped in fright, Aurora tipping over her wineglass as she reached out to the table. Esti didn't even hear the glass shatter as it hit the floor.

For a moment she stared at her mom in the deafening thunder of the downpour, Aurora's uneasy expression echoing Esti's rapid heartbeat. Then a gust of wind blew rain into the balcony. Aurora shrieked as they both leaped to their feet and dashed for the door. Before they'd gone two steps, however, the rain stopped as abruptly as it had started. The first tentative frogs were already starting their rain song.

"Well," Aurora finally said into the silence. She looked like she'd stepped halfway into a shower, her flowing skirt plastered against her right side and her hair flattened over one eye. Red wine had splattered across the floor like drops of spilled blood, surrounded by broken glass.

Esti studied a jagged shard sticking out from the sole of her sneaker beneath the wound Alan had tended. Despite her guilt at deceiving Aurora, she felt strangely lighthearted after practically admitting that she was now

Alan's girlfriend, even if it wasn't entirely true. As she cautiously reached down to pluck the sparkling dagger free, a hysterical giggle tried to push up from beneath the churning surface of her thoughts.

❧

Frederick was—as Carmen put it that evening—fabulous. He sat everyone in a circle on the stage, discussing body and voice control.

"Stanislavsky said there's only one way to connect deeply and truthfully with each other, and that's to bring your own personality with you onstage." He waved his hand expansively. "The truth of your character has to be believed by your audience. To reach this believable truth, you must let your own emotional memory control your actions. Now, what's the best way to prepare for a role that involves fear?"

"Remember something frightening," Greg said.

"Absolutely right, darling."

Carmen poked Esti, barely able to hold back her laughter.

"Then you can act your part in the emotional space of that fear you already know." Frederick gave Esti an oblique glance. "Of course, Legard took the notion of control and believability one step further. He said that if *you* believe you're in control, people will believe you. You can control people's belief in you, by believing in your control."

Carmen nudged her again, but this time Esti barely noticed. A familiar sweet scent tickled her nose, just as she saw the white blossom on the stage beside her.

"Our goal is to convince the audience that our characters

have an interior life," Frederick continued, his enthusiasm growing.

Esti casually picked up the flower, trying to pay attention to Frederick as she touched each of the five white petals. *Rosemary was for remembrance,* she knew from Hamlet, *and pansies for thoughts.* She'd also discovered that seashells represented fertility, which had sent her into a fit of giggles . . . how ironically perfect for the surely unsuspecting Rafe.

When she'd looked up the meaning of frangipani, however, she'd found that it stood for a confusing array of things, including devotion, surrender, and protection from evil. Such tangled meaning was perfect for Alan, of course. Briefly lifting the sweet flower to her nose, she tucked it behind her ear, pushing away thoughts of seashells.

"You don't want a stereotyped villain or heroine," Frederick said, "but rather a complex human with contradictory feelings and desires."

Contradictory, Esti thought. That would be me.

"You become that character, and you let that character become you, plumbing the depths of your soul with the hope of going just a little bit deeper each time."

After rehearsal, Esti could barely stand still as she waited in the darkness on the other side of the courtyard. Aurora had flatly stated that she expected to meet Alan before Esti spent any more time with him, and Esti had promised to come home immediately after rehearsal. Even so, she wouldn't leave Alan waiting without a quick explanation. Besides, she wanted to thank him for the flower.

Carmen and Lucia glanced around as they walked out together, and Esti wondered if they were looking for her. They didn't linger, though, and Frederick shortly followed them out. To her surprise, he pulled the theater doors firmly shut behind him, patting his pocket as he walked away. As soon as he was gone, Esti raced back over to try the doors. They were locked.

Of course, she thought. Someone from New York City wouldn't believe that locals on Cariba never locked their doors. She shook her head in irritation. People here only barred their windows against jumbees.

She hurried to the corner of the building and peered down the hill toward the back door. Frowning, she started down the pitch-black slope, trying not to trip over rocks. She was pretty sure she could find the narrow path through the wild tamarind, but she wished she had a flashlight.

Within a minute of entering the tamarind grove, however, she was lost. She kept turning downhill, and she realized almost immediately she had missed the trail. Whenever she tried to change direction, she was dragged back by tiny hook-tipped branches. She could already feel trickles of blood on her hands. When her shirt ripped as she pulled away from yet another one of the grasping branches, she finally sat down in defeat.

"Damn, damn, damn," she whispered. "Aurora's going to kill me." She would deserve it too, but she *had* to talk to Alan tonight. Were a few short minutes with him too much to ask?

The night air was warm and humid, and very dark. Although she knew the theater sat right in front of her, Esti couldn't see enough to escape from the tangle of thorns. She imagined the new flurries of gossip when she was found in the morning, exhausted, mosquito-eaten, torn, and bleeding. She would be back in Oregon before she had a chance to open her mouth.

"I'm an idiot," she muttered.

"Esti?"

"Alan!" She leaped to her feet, ignoring a new slash of pain across her arm.

"What are you doing here?" His voice had never been so welcome.

"Frederick locked me out," she said stiffly. "I was trying to get in the back door, but I got lost in the dark. Now the thorns are holding me prisoner."

Alan laughed.

"Don't laugh at me." Her cheeks felt like they were on fire. "I'm going to be in so much trouble."

"I'm sorry, I'm sorry. If you can get yourself loose from the ketch-n-keep, the path is over here."

He kept talking and she slowly followed his voice, wincing as needle-sharp thorns yanked at her hair and arms, ripping her blouse further. After a few minutes she was able to see his dark shape in front of her. He turned away just before she got close enough to touch him.

"Follow me," he said, "and I'll take you back up to the theater."

When she emerged from the dressing room a few minutes later, hastily cleaned and safety-pinned, she headed for the hidden passage. As soon as she reached the basement, her heart leaped hopefully to her throat. Flickering light played on the floor outside the tiny practice room.

Holding her breath, she stopped just before the doorway and peeked inside. Several candles illuminated the room this time, and she recognized the rough wooden table. But everything else faded to insignificance beside the black-masked figure in the other chair. Esti couldn't tear her eyes away from him as she walked into the room.

"Hello, Esti," he said softly. His voice soaked through the pores of her skin, into every cell of her body.

It took enormous effort to move normally as she sat down, a million confused questions crowding her brain. He was still wrapped in black, a dark hood covering his hair. His hands were hidden by black leather gloves so fine that she might not have noticed them last night when he held her hands. She longed to ask why he wore a mask even now, but she was positive he would somehow disappear if she pushed too much.

His blue eyes searched her, resting briefly on the scratches that covered her arms. After a moment, he leaned back, his expression concerned. Wiry and graceful, he moved with the same powerful elegance as he spoke. "Well, here I am."

"Here you are," Esti said.

When he laughed, she couldn't help laughing with him. In the candlelight, his eyes seemed to glow from within, as bizarre and beautiful as a ninja. She wanted to crawl across the table before he disappeared again, wrapping herself in his rich voice, his healing touch, his sea-colored eyes.

"Does this mean I'm allowed to ask questions?"

He laughed again. "Have I ever been able to stop you?"

"Every time I've tried." The question that came out of her mouth, however, wasn't the one she'd planned. "What happened with Mr. Niles this afternoon?"

As a flash of irritation crossed his eyes, she studied him uncomfortably. She hadn't realized until now how much Mr. Niles's accusation bothered her.

"Niles is afraid of his own shadow," Alan said calmly. "He spooked himself right off the stage."

"Did you have anything to do with it?" She held her breath as the words left her mouth. What if Alan's answer was yes? Would it make any difference?

"I didn't touch him, Esti." Alan looked at her with a steady gaze. "I was nowhere near him when he fell."

"Why did he say it was my fault?"

"Niles is a superstitious fool. Despite his intelligence, he is deeply West Indian, and he fears the thought of jumbees. He also fears anyone"—Alan smiled ruefully—"associated with jumbees."

She slowly nodded.

"Did you happen to notice that Frederick McKenzie is superior?" Alan asked.

"Of course." As she studied his gloved fingers on the table, Esti couldn't help wishing he would reach for her. "Did you watch us this evening?"

"I did." Now Alan sounded pleased.

Esti returned another tentative smile, glad that Alan didn't seem jealous. As his eyes smiled back at her, she let herself be engulfed by a sense of peace she had rarely known around him. His eyes met hers, as deep and mysterious as the ocean, and without thinking, she reached across the small table. He took her hands in his, their palms pressing together for a single searing moment.

As she leaned toward him, yearning for more, he winced as if in pain. He yanked himself away, his chair screeching across the floor. Outlined in the flickering light, his body pressed against the wall behind him, as far from her as he could manage in the tiny room. Although she should have known by now what to expect, Esti almost cried out with the shock of it. The silence in the room was broken only by the sounds of their ragged breathing.

"Not even a palmers' kiss?" she asked as soon as she could speak.

He wouldn't look at her. "You have no idea what you're asking for."

"Apparently not." Trembling with frustration and desire, and a little bit of fear, she forced herself to relax. "Maybe you should tell me."

"Meet me here at five o'clock Sunday morning." He turned to her, his eyes glowing fiercely in the candlelight. "Before the day grows light, I will take you to Manchineel Cay."

Act Two. Scene Ten.

Esti kicked her feet against the bench in the courtyard, restlessly glancing at her watch. She heard Lucia behind her, discussing sets with another girl. The school campus was usually deserted on Saturday afternoons, although Frederick's morning rehearsals left a few stragglers.

She studied Manchineel Cay, certain she had memorized every one of its white beaches on this side, all the crags in the rocky cliff, each emerald hill defined by the changing shadows of the sun. She had some ideas where Alan's house might be hidden, remembering the path of the lonely light she'd watched from her bedroom window. Even so, she couldn't relax. Melee had it, Carmen had informed her this morning, that Rafe was demoted to washing dishes after getting in a fight with a customer who said Esti put a curse on him.

Picking at the frayed edge of her shorts, Esti tried to ignore the nice tan she'd gotten during Christmas break. She didn't want to think about those delicious days in the sun with Rafe. Rehearsals were going beautifully, and Frederick loved her. She was achieving everything she ever wanted, and she could feel her dad's approval deep inside.

Alan's dreamy voice constantly filled her mind, and she saw his startling eyes every time she looked at the sea. Although she hadn't dared get together with him again, she often found stray blossoms hidden in odd places around the theater. *Devotion, surrender, and protection from evil.* Catching the deeply sweet fragrance of a flower she'd tucked behind her ear, she was surprised all over again by the joy she felt at Alan's surrender and devotion.

Then, out of the blue, she would find her stomach churning with uncertainty. Lucia remained as inscrutable as ever, and Esti's friendship with Carmen had developed an unpleasant edge. Although they still sat together during practice, they rarely saw each other outside of the theater. Although Esti knew it was her own fault, she didn't know how to change things.

She couldn't wait for the upcoming showcase next weekend, but she missed Rafe a lot more than she wanted to admit. She needed to apologize; to know that he didn't hate her. She wanted him to understand why she had gone back to Alan. And . . . she kicked the bench harder. She hated herself for being so fickle. What she really wanted was to throw herself at Rafe, feeling the warmth of his arms around her, his lips on hers, his hands in her hair. She'd gone to sleep last night with her arms wrapped tightly around herself, pretending that Rafe held her.

Leaping to her feet in agitation, she walked back toward the theater. Tomorrow she would see Alan's house. She hadn't thought of a good alibi for Aurora yet, but something would surely come to her. She didn't want to go home and spend this afternoon avoiding conversation with her mom. Maybe she could sneak down to the basement for a couple of hours. If Alan was there, he could help her come up with an excuse that wouldn't result in Aurora buying plane tickets back to Oregon. If Esti got lucky, he might even let her hold his hand.

As she neared the theater building, she came to a sudden stop. Danielle's sister stood beside Lucia, intently watching Esti through a curtain of dark hair.

"Esti," Lucia said, "Frederick, he tell me and Marielle how to make a perfect Capulet orchard with three sheet of plywood."

"That's great," Esti said sincerely to Lucia, then made herself meet Marielle's piercing eyes.

A tiny, triumphant smile played around Marielle's mouth. "You broke up with him, didn't you?"

"Yes," Esti said, abruptly changing her mind about the theater. The last thing she wanted right now was to be trapped into a girlish rant against Rafe. She was wearing her swimsuit beneath her shorts. Maybe the sea would give her the strength she needed.

"I'm going for a swim." She forced a smile at the two girls. "Have fun with your orchard."

Before they could reply, she turned and sprinted to the parking lot. It felt good to run, and she moved even faster as she headed down the road, not stopping until she got to the beach. Heaving for breath, she paused on the sand just long enough to kick off her shoes and drape her sweaty clothes on a tree branch. She ran into the water with a gasp, the sea closing around her.

By the time she finally dragged herself back out of the water, the sun was getting low in the sky. Carrying her things to the low-walled shower area by the parking lot, she rinsed the sand from her feet, then pulled her clothes back on over her wet swimsuit. She would be sweaty again anyway by the time she walked up Bayrum Hill.

As she sat down to put on her socks, however, she was startled to see a piece of paper sticking out of one of her shoes. She pulled it free, staring at the letters scribbled across the front.

S.T.

Holding her breath, she unfolded the note. *Pretty impressive for someone who's afraid of the water. I blew it, huh? Don't know what Shakespeare would say, but this boy wants girl. Is that enough for an apology?*

Esti looked around hopefully, but the parking lot was deserted except for safari taxis and tourists waiting for the sunset. Smiling, she held the note against her cheek. It was more than enough. If anything, she owed Rafe an apology. And a kiss. . . .

She shook her head, looking out at Manchineel Cay. Nothing made her happier than those rare moments when Alan opened up to her. She had chosen him long before Rafe came back, and she had no regrets. When she went to Manchineel Cay tomorrow, she would finally know the truth.

❧

She almost made it out of the house without any mishaps. As she carefully closed the screen door, however, she tripped over the rosemary that Aurora had planted to repel jumbees. The small ceramic pot shattered loudly as her foot kicked it across the porch. *Rosemary for remembrance,* she thought in disgust. *Or hindrance.*

Sure enough, light suddenly glowed from the window of Aurora's bedroom. As quietly as she could, Esti fled down the road. She had left an honest note explaining where she was going today. Aurora would be furious, of course, but Esti could tell her everything when she got back home. Forgiveness was easier than permission.

Although the theater was locked again, Alan had given her a key to the front door. As Esti fumbled for the key under the weak yellow security light, however, a graceful shadow detached itself from the wall nearby.

"Are you ready to brave the ketch-n-keep?"

She stuffed the key back in her pocket with a smile. "I'm counting on you to keep me out of it this time."

"You'll be perfectly safe, as long as you stay with me."

"Safety tip number twenty-three," she intoned, "always trust the jumbee when he lures you to his haunted island."

"Am I luring you there?" he asked softly.

"No." She gave him a rueful smile. "It's the other way around. But you can trust me, honest."

He let out a quiet burst of laughter. "If you hold my hand, I'll show you the way."

As she studied the proffered black-wrapped arm, she hesitated. Would it matter, she thought, if he somehow proved that he *was* a jumbee? Did she care? With a burst of impatience at herself, she reached for his leather glove, supple and warm beneath her fingertips. None of it mattered. She ignored the flash of headlights from Bayrum Hill as they started down the path

Alan led her along the slope into the trees, slowing frequently to warn her of rocks or an exposed root that might trip her. He moved with effortless grace, like a lion slipping through the forest, and Esti reveled in his sure guidance. She had always imagined Alan's physical side matching the power of his voice. The journey reminded her of a blindfold game she used to play at summer camp, her trust building with each guiding step of her partner.

When her feet finally came down on sand, she recognized the familiar scent of the sea grape trees behind Manchicay Beach. With a touch of guilt, she shoved away her memories of Christmas night with Rafe.

"The water will reach no deeper than your knees," Alan murmured. "Follow me closely to avoid the mangle." Tightly grasping her hand, he splashed ahead of her.

Warm water swirled around them both, soaking the bottom of Esti's jeans and filling her shoes. She had no idea what mangle was, but she didn't like the sound of it, or the thick, swampy smell that made the air difficult to breathe. The ground beneath the water was uneven and silty, sucking at her feet with each step. As they moved forward, Esti felt branches closing in around her, a strangling canopy so dense, she panted for breath in the swamp-smelling air.

Alan finally came to a stop, steadying her with his hand.

"Reach up here." He lifted her hand to a branch, solid and hard above her head. "Hold tight with both hands, and bring your legs up out of the water."

She grabbed the branch without asking why. As Alan let go, she heard something big moving in the water nearby. With a gasp, she curled her body as far out of the water as she could.

"Good," Alan said, his voice calm. "Now bring your feet back down."

Her feet came down into a boat. She sank to the bottom as it rocked with her weight, terrified it might tip over.

"The barge she sat in," Alan said, easily swinging himself aboard, "like a burnished throne . . ."

Esti gripped the sides, laughing helplessly as he compared her to Cleopatra and Venus, sitting on a yacht made of gold.

Within moments they were free of the suffocating trees. As a breeze swept across her cheeks, Esti looked around in awe. After the deep darkness of the forest, the stars had never seemed so brilliant. She recognized the bright swath of the Milky Way on the horizon ahead, broken by the familiar outline of Manchineel Cay. To her relief, the sea was calm, captured in a brief lull between late-season storms.

Behind her, the lights of Cariba blended into the starry sky. If Aurora wasn't out in the car somewhere, Esti guessed she would be sitting on the balcony, stewing over Esti's note as she looked out at the dark water. She couldn't possibly see the little rowboat from up there, but it wouldn't matter if she could. Everyone knew the jandam would never go to the haunted cay to rescue fruitcake Esti Legard.

Esti, the jumbee girl. *Bazadee child.*

"Are you afraid?" Alan's voice startled her before she could start feeling guilty about Aurora. He rowed the small boat silently, save for the rhythmic splash and creak of the oars.

"Should I be?"

"Of course not. I've looked forward to spending an entire day with you." He sounded so shy that Esti couldn't help smiling. "I think you'll like my place."

"Typical bachelor's pad?" Esti teased.

"Yes." He laughed softly. "But I did sweep the floor and gather enough food together so you won't starve to death while you're here."

"Potato chips and cheap beer? My dad's friends had a lot of bachelor stories."

"I'm sure your father never drank cheap beer."

"He liked potato chips."

"The food of life." Alan laughed again. "So are you to my thoughts as food to life, or as sweet-season'd showers are to the ground."

With a happy sigh, Esti leaned back against her seat.

"And for the peace of you," he continued, "I hold such strife as 'twixt a miser and his wealth is found."

This was *right,* she thought in contentment. It had taken an entire semester, but she was finally in paradise.

As they approached the cay, however, she began to hear a whispery moan and a drumming deep in her bones. The black silhouette of the island's cliff blotted out the Milky Way like a jagged hole in the sky. She watched silently as Alan brought them close to the looming cliff.

Waves crashed into the island with unexpected violence, and she grabbed the side of the boat. Her stomach lurched as they rose to meet the rocks. Just in time to avoid a crash, Alan yanked on the oars. The boat spun around the side of the cliff, and the sky disappeared.

Manchineel Cay had swallowed them.

Act Two. Scene Eleven.

Esti clutched the edge of the boat, straining to see something. Heavy booming filled the blackness, vibrating her body with the island's erratic heartbeat. The water lifted and lowered them to the pulse of the sea, beating into the niches of the cave with deceiving power. A salty breeze breathed past, whispering uneasy secrets. As the boat scraped against rock, she felt Alan place the oars beside her feet. A shiny-smooth wall of rock slipped past her fingers, and after a moment, Alan got out of the boat, dragging it onto something solid.

"We're here," he said, his deep voice multiplied by the hard surfaces around them. "I hope you're not afraid."

"Of course not." As he helped her out of the boat, she tried not to grab his hands too desperately. "Safety tip number twenty-three."

"Come, then." Although he didn't laugh, she heard his amusement as he drew her after him. "The path through the cave is steep."

The breath of the sea came from behind them now, smelling of salt and fish. Strands of her hair tickled across Esti's face.

"The cay has opened her heart to you—a rare occurrence indeed." Alan's voice echoed in the blackness around them. Although Esti was already breathing hard, he didn't seem to notice the climb as he led her up the rough slope.

"Your island is alive?" She tried to sound amused.

"Very much so." He seemed utterly serious. "Our lives are closely intertwined, my lady cay and I. I'm taking you through her body now, to my home. I live in a fold of her skin, guarded against curious eyes and prying fools. Her breath cools me and empowers me; her sweat feeds my thirst and my hunger. She protects me, and I, in turn, treat her with the utmost respect."

Esti opened her mouth, then closed it again, suppressing an odd stab of jealousy at the near worship in his voice. She had learned to expect his weirdly formal speech whenever his emotions grew strong, but she never knew what might set it off. She certainly hadn't thought he would take her question about the cay seriously.

Above them, the wailing breath grew more plaintive as the pounding heartbeat faded below. The breeze on the back of her neck made her shiver, the steep path rough beneath her feet. As she clutched Alan's hand in the darkness, he drew her forward, almost lifting her in places as he helped her along. She tried to ignore the jeans clinging to her clammy ankles and the absurd squelching of her wet shoes.

The moaning ahead became even louder. Although the breeze still felt mild, the sound soon rose to a shriek. If an island could truly be alive, this one cried out fiercely against its new intruder. After a moment, Alan pulled Esti behind him to the right. To her relief, the path leveled out, and they drew away from the unearthly screaming. She soon heard nothing more than a distant groan.

"What happened?" she gasped. "What was that?"

"My lady protests at the power I take from her," Alan said with a smile in his voice. "She is generous in meeting my needs, although the payment can be harsh."

Esti began to shiver again. What kind of power would someone get from an island—and at what cost?

As they emerged from the deep cave, she could see the beginnings of light in the sky to the east. Alan pulled her along behind him even more rapidly. He didn't speak as they plunged onto a dim trail through the trees. When they finally came to a stop beside a steep rock wall, he let go of her hand so abruptly she almost fell against the wall.

He stood silently for a moment, breathing hard. The climb through the cave had seemed much more difficult to Esti than the level forest trail, so she was surprised by the effort he took now to control his breath. She didn't see the door in the wall beside them, until he slowly pushed it open, heavy and so perfectly camouflaged that it might have belonged in a fairy tale.

Open sesame, she thought absurdly.

"Welcome to my home," he said. "Take off your shoes, if you like. I imagine they're wet."

As his eyes slid away from hers, she suddenly giggled. "You're as nervous as I am."

"Well." He shrugged. "I haven't had many guests."

"Am I the first?" She held her breath.

"Actually, no. You're the second."

The answer startled her almost as much as it filled her with relief. "Who was the first one? Some chick you met in a bar?"

Even though he didn't answer her question, at least he laughed. Leaning against the wall, Esti peeled off her soggy shoes and socks, then rolled up the wet cuffs of her jeans. She fully intended to get some real answers from him before the day was over.

"Come out to the porch," he said when she straightened. "The sunrise is beautiful from there."

Esti glanced around the dim room, relieved to see that it wasn't a cave at all. Although it was difficult to make out any details other than large openings and the bulky shadows of furniture, it was deeply reassuring to see evidence of a real human who lived in a real house.

"Now will you tell me who you are?"

"Soon." He sighed. "But first, would you like some tea?"

Esti studied him uncertainly. She was tempted to joke that

tea must be what he offered all the girls he brought home, but something in his eyes held her back. Briefly imagining Rafe in the same situation, she bit down on another giggle. Rafe would be offering something vastly different right about now.

"I'd love tea," she said firmly.

She sat on a hand-carved wooden chair to wait, happily listening to roosters in the distance as the sun appeared over the horizon. Beneath the vine-wreathed porch she saw several chickens scratching around what might be an odd-shaped vegetable garden making its way down the hillside. When Alan returned with two steaming mugs, one for her and one for himself, she almost laughed.

Ha! she thought. Jumbees don't drink tea, or raise chickens and vegetables.

She smiled as he sat down, touching her wooden mug to his. Black tea, she thought, with milk. Taking a contented sip, she looked back out at the pretty view. The stone-paved porch overlooked a valley of verdant trees, punctuated by bursts of flamboyant red blossoms and bright yellow cedar. The scent of frangipani hung heavily in the air.

From the corner of her eye she saw Alan watching her, occasionally turning away so that she couldn't see him drink his tea.

"Tell me how you built your house," she said, "if no one knows you live here."

His eyes smiled at her. "The house has been here for a very long time."

As the rich morning sun lit up his eyes, Esti slowly forgot everything else. She had never seen eyes so like the Caribbean sea, brilliantly blue with green sparkling in their depths. She wanted to dive into them and never come back up for air.

When she lifted her hand to touch his mask, his reaction was explosive. He lunged back from her, leaping to his feet so abruptly that his chair fell over and his mug crashed to the floor, tea splashing everywhere.

"I'm sorry!" she said, her heart thudding in fear. "Alan, I didn't mean—"

"You did nothing wrong," he muttered. He closed his eyes for a moment, then turned and straightened his chair.

"Alan, I'm sorry. Does it hurt when I touch you?"

"No." He barely seemed in control as he glanced at her. "I'm a bit jumpy, that's all."

Esti took a deep breath. "That's an understatement."

"I am going inside to make breakfast," he said stiffly. "When you're done with your tea, feel free to look around the house. At that point, I imagine you will be ready to discuss a few things." Picking up his empty mug from the floor, he fled inside.

Breakfast? Esti had heard jokes about the morning after, but everything with Alan seemed to happen in reverse. His voice and his personality, his appearance—his very existence—were all a mass of contradictions. Maybe he would finally kiss her after tea and toast.

Holding her mug in both hands, she stood and walked to the edge of the porch, still wound up from his intense reaction. She wondered what he planned to discuss after she looked around. It sounded more like a homework assignment than a guy inviting a girl to check out his place.

As she studied his valley, she realized that he had concealed his home thoroughly, even from overhead eyes. The house was completely hidden, built into a fold of the hill and sheltered by a rocky overhang. An irregular, vine-wrapped trellis covered the stone porch. The vegetable garden sprawled among bushes on the hillside, difficult to make out from any distance. She saw no flat spots anywhere, no place for even a helicopter to land.

When he agreed to bring her here, he'd said the only danger would be to himself. Would he somehow be required to pay retribution to his jealous lady cay in return for Esti's visit? She couldn't help thinking about the awful shrieks surrounding her when they got here. The breeze alone couldn't make that much noise, and the possibilities that came to mind were unsettling. An angry cay, furious at being violated by a stranger. Souls of the people taken by the island.

What price would a vengeful island demand, she wondered, if Shakespeare had written this play? As visions of *The Tempest* flitted through her head, she quickly stood up. Even if it was merely unease that made her feel like the island watched her, she no longer wanted to stay outside.

When she reached the doorway, she was startled by the beauty of the room in full daylight. The house nestled directly into the side of the cliff. Large boulders and living ferns made up the interior vertical wall, interspersed with framed posters of Shakespeare festivals and plays. Vents between the boulders blew air into the room, a whispery moan behind the cool breath.

Rough steps made their way up the rock wall to a small kitchen loft, an open window dominating one end of the airy space. She heard Alan moving around the loft above her as she walked in, clattering dishes in an absurdly domestic way as he fixed breakfast. Beneath the kitchen steps, a second stairway led down into a cave-like darkness she assumed was the bedroom.

A row of tall wooden doors to the porch stood open along the entire exterior wall, and bookcases stood at either end, crowded with books, and—she smiled in satisfaction—a very normal laptop computer. Her smile slowly faded, however, as she began studying the Shakespeare images resting on the boulders. In disbelief, she forced her eyes to make their way across the wall of rocks.

Every single frame held a print of her father.

In the center of the rock wall sat the largest poster, Legard playing Caliban in London ten years ago. *Alan,* the signature read, *you are impressive, and I'm glad I met you. Best wishes, Alan Legard.* Esti felt a chill at seeing her dad's unmistakable handwriting.

Next to the poster, she saw a smaller print of her dad as Macbeth in New York several years later. *Alan,* he had written, *it was great to see you once again! Thanks for the help with Banquo.* The rocks were covered with pictures of her dad over the past ten years, each one lovingly signed to Alan.

In a daze, Esti made her way across the room, reading each inscription.

She stopped at the famous photo of herself beside her dad when she was fifteen; her only television performance with The Great Legard immortalized in a nation-wide advertisement. He had praised her performance as he signed that one, and she read it three times, incredulous, before she could move on. *Esti will outshine me someday,* he said, *if she lets herself believe it. Thank you, Alan, for helping me through the most challenging performance of my life. You have a remarkable ability to give me strength when I need it.*

She had to be dreaming.

The last poster she found was her dad as Richard III at the Ashland festival, three months before his death. *Alan, your extraordinary intelligence is one of the greatest gifts I've ever been given. You've been through tremendous adversity; I can only hope that someday you make your peace.* She looked up from the signature, abruptly aware that Alan no longer moved around in the kitchen. He stood at the top of the stairs, watching her.

"Why didn't I know this?" she said. "You never said he was your friend."

"Legard was the best friend I ever had." Alan stared at her, his eyes filled with yearning. "I too was grieving when you and I met, and I didn't know what I should say. I didn't want to upset you."

Esti walked to the couch and sat down, shaken.

"I knew he hadn't told you about me," he continued, "and

it seemed best to keep things that way. I had no idea that you would . . . That I would end up. . . ."

She studied him, trying not to tremble. His mask suddenly seemed frightening, his voice too surreal. "You're not my half brother, or something weird like that."

"No." His expression softened. "Legard wasn't my father by blood, only by his actions. He was the only family I truly had, but my blood is very different than yours."

"But . . ." Esti floundered. "Why didn't he ever talk about you? Did he tell my mom?"

"No," Alan said flatly. "He was good at keeping my secrets."

The Great Legard trumps his daughter once again. Esti felt her hysteria circling beneath the surface. "How did you know him? Where did you meet?"

"He was my mentor."

"Your mentor." Her eyes narrowed in sudden understanding. "At your boarding school, during one of his seasons in London."

"He taught me Shakespeare. He gave me hope when I had none."

"You already knew everything about me, then. The first time you talked to me at Manchicay."

"No." Alan walked down the stairs and sat on the bottom step, placing his gloved hand against the rocky wall as if to reassure his lady cay. "Not everything. I had watched you perform Juliet with him. I sat in the audience during the filming, disguised with your father's help by some complicated tricks of movie make-believe. I didn't completely fall in love with you then. The dream was pointless, and it wasn't until you came here . . ."

The dream? Esti pressed her fingers into her temples to keep her head from spinning. She wasn't sure what she should feel, either toward Alan or her dad. Anger? Fear? Love? "What did he mean about his most challenging performance?" she said.

"Legard wasn't sure about acting with you."

"He wasn't sure?" Her heart stopped.

"He was afraid that Juliet would be too much for you, as his daughter. He tried to temper his performance, but in the end, the actor was stronger than the father. He never fully forgave himself when he lost your trust."

"He never forgave . . ." Esti leaned back into the couch, reeling from a second bombshell, equally as unexpected as the first. She couldn't meet Alan's intense blue eyes. "Why didn't he ever tell me that?" she said hollowly.

"It wasn't his fault, Esti. He didn't doubt your acting, not for a minute. I convinced him that he would have done you a disservice to treat you as anything other than a profession-al."

"*You* convinced him?" She wrapped her arms around herself, trying to make sense of her frightened, churning thoughts. Her voice began to rise. "I thought you were my kindred spirit, but you were his friend all along, not mine."

"Esti, it's not—"

"You said you had only one other visitor here," she added slowly. "Was it him?"

Alan slowly nodded.

"So what am *I* doing here?" She tried not to shake as shock and anger made her voice quiver. "What do you want from *me?*"

"You are here," Alan said in a defeated voice, "because you insisted on it."

As Esti buried her face in her hands, the crowing rooster outside fell silent. She rubbed her forehead, trying to erase the noise in her head, but the roaring slowly grew louder. When the house began to shake, she grabbed the couch in fear, looking at Alan, but he merely stared at her until the shaking went past them and disappeared.

"My lady shivers," he whispered. He caressed the wooden stair rail with a gloved hand. "Perhaps the rooster has been warning me all morning."

Esti shuddered. It didn't help to know the Caribbean often had earthquakes; the timing of this one was outright sinister. "Warning you of what?"

"I am as mad as the Prince of Denmark."

"Hamlet wasn't real," Esti said fiercely.

"Amleth was." Alan sounded bitter. "Shakespeare's source for *that* tragedy."

"Don't hide behind Shakespeare. All you ever do is hide."

"I've spent my life haunted by my blood," he snapped. "I shouldn't have brought you here."

"Take me home, then."

"If it were dark outside, I would."

Esti didn't reply as she glared at the poster-covered wall.

She couldn't believe that her father, with his mighty control, had been telling lies for years. She was stunned to find Alan's paranoid secrecy reaching deep back into her family, before she'd even moved to Oregon.

"You're not in love with me." She tried to control her breathing. "This is some kind of twisted hero worship."

Alan abruptly rose to his feet. Crossing the room with the deadly grace of a panther, he crouched in front of Esti. He grabbed her hands before she could move, his eyes burning into hers. Terror crawled up her spine as she realized that no one would even hear her scream.

"One half of me is yours," he whispered, "the other half, yours." Before she could move, he rose again and moved away, silently disappearing through the porch doors.

Act Two. Scene Twelve.

Esti spent the morning fuming on the couch. She glowered at her dad's posters for what seemed like hours, then finally turned her furious gaze to Alan's nearby bookshelves. Even his collection of books aggravated her. She saw endless volumes of Shakespeare, and classic literature as timeless as Straparalo and Leroux. How could Alan be so scholarly and romantic and *perfect* for her, and yet so . . . so mind-bogglingly creepy? He'd devoted entire shelves to everything The Great Legard had ever written.

Despite her very strongest evil eye, however, not one volume burst into flames.

It was the call of nature that finally drove her from the couch. Tiptoeing nervously to the tall wooden doors, she peered outside. Alan sat at the far edge of the porch, slumped in the shade of the trellis with his head in his hands. Esti studied his black silhouette for a moment, then slowly turned back inside, confused and angry again. He didn't look like a psychopathic stalker; he looked like a guy with a broken heart. *One half of me is yours . . .*

Tentatively testing a light switch at the top of the basement stairs, she was relieved to see what was clearly a bathroom at the bottom. She raced down the steps, her feet heavy with anxiety, even though she knew her fear was idiotic. She had spent countless hours alone with Alan; his bathroom was no more dangerous than any other part of this freakish house.

When she returned upstairs, she forced herself back to the rock-covered wall. She read each inscription again as calmly as she could, trying to put herself in her father's shoes. It was a strange, uncomfortable feeling to discover this side of her dad. She had never imagined him keeping an enormous secret like this from her or Aurora.

She wondered if her mom had ever feared the distant side of The Great Legard, the pure actor whom the world held in awe. Had Aurora known that he kept secrets from her? Or was it enough that the world loved him, and he loved her? Maybe all that mattered was that he danced with Aurora and treated her like a queen.

Wiping her hand across her nose, Esti turned away from the posters. Her dad was no different than she was; in fact, Esti was much worse. She had treated her mom like dirt lately, avoiding her and ignoring her grief, as well as keeping secrets and lying to her. Could she blame that on Alan? Could she blame her father's secrecy on Alan?

She trailed her fingers over her dad's rows of books, then pulled out one of his earliest works to read another heartfelt inscription to Alan on the cover page. As she slid the book back into place, she noticed a slim paperback volume beside it, its spine notched at the top in an unusual way. Before she could look at it, however, a noise from the porch made her spin around.

Alan stood rigidly in the doorway. "I'm sure it doesn't help for me to say I'm sorry. I had hoped . . ." He sagged. "I don't know what I hoped."

"You hoped we might be friends?"

As his eyes widened, she decided that Alan's feelings for her could no longer be tied to her dad, at least not completely. Alan had rescued her from The Great Legard's shadow. He had given her . . . *her*. And now he'd offered her an enormous new insight into the man she had also spent her own life worshipping.

"I want to see you," she said. "Have I already mentioned that?"

He looked at her like she'd spoken in Greek.

"Alan," she said, "take off your mask for me."

"No." The whispered answer didn't surprise her.

"Why not?" she asked.

He looked away.

She kept her voice as casual as if she were asking him the time "Is it because you're deformed? I don't care, you know."

"But I do."

"Alan, unless I know what you—"

"That is the one thing I cannot give you." He strode across the room, his wiry body taut and powerful. "Please don't ask me again."

"Then tell me why people think this island is haunted," she said in frustration. "Tell me how the jumbee stories started."

"Jumbee stories." He leaned against the wall, his eyes guarded. "Once upon a time in West Africa, the word *jumbee* meant evil spirit. But there are many kinds of spirits, each with their own way of haunting. For example, a baby who died before being named will move things around in the house where he died."

"That's not what I mean." Despite her frustration, she almost smiled.

"Or you might find the spirit of a woman who died in childbirth, leaving her baby alive. She roams the island at night, crying mournfully."

"Alan . . ."

She saw a flash of amusement in his eyes. "Now, if the moon-gazer catches you outside at night, he'll suck out your brain through the palm of his hand, while the lady vampire sucks the blood of unsuspecting victims as they sleep."

She couldn't hold back a reluctant laugh. "Would you quit?"

"Fortunately, blood-suckers are relatively easy to catch. Leave a large pile of rice on the floor before you go to bed. As she enters your house, this jumbee is compelled to count every rice grain. Since her hands can't hold much, it's only a matter of time before the grains begin to fall back to the ground, and she has to start over. In the morning you will find a tired and very distressed vampire counting rice. Before she can run away, you quickly beat her to death with a special anti-jumbee broom."

Still laughing, Esti shook her head. "And what about the jumbee of Manchineel Cay?"

"Now there's a goblin damned." Alan's voice grew quiet again. "I don't think the African legends cover that one."

"Oh, but they do." Esti studied his eyes. "He walks between heaven and earth to protect the girl he loves from evil spirits. I'm not sure if he uses rice, but I want to know if he's as *moko* as he is *loco*."

He gave an unwilling chuckle. "Moko was an African god. A tall one, apparently. The moko jumbee foresees evil from his high vantage point, striking terror into the hearts of those who plan any wrongdoing. But you see, Esti, I'm no taller than you are."

"I'm sure I'll find your stilts hidden somewhere on the island. How about a hike after lunch?"

"You don't hate me, then?" His voice was almost inaudible.

"You infuriate me." Esti scowled at him, then sighed. "I'm so confused right now, I don't know how I feel. But no, I don't hate you, and since our lives seem to be tied together, I should probably get to know your lady cay. You brought me here to meet *your* family, right?"

❧

When they returned from their trek into the island, she was sorry she'd asked. The manchineel trees were the icing on a deadly cake of stinging nettle and caustic milktree, needle-sharp ketch-n-keep and razor grass. In addition to dozens of new scratches, Esti had twisted her foot in a hidden rocky crevice, then finally been stung by a wasp.

"Your cay does *not* like me." She leaned against the couch, rubbing her aching ankle and wincing as Alan smeared a paste of baking soda and vinegar over the fiery sting on her forearm. "I'm not usually so clumsy."

"I'm sorry," he said softly. "My lady is very jealous." As before, Esti was taken aback by the utter sincerity of his response.

"Set foot on the island, and you're never seen again," she quipped with a shiver. "No wonder people are afraid to come here. How do *you* get through that gauntlet without breaking your neck?"

"I paid my dues long ago." As he covered her sting with an adhesive bandage, his hands began to tremble. Smoothing the bandage flat, he lightly ran his forefinger down her arm to the small bones of her wrist, his finger just barely stroking her. Esti's skin twitched along the path of his touch, the sensation both eerie and delightful.

He glanced up with a fearful expression, waiting for her to pull away. When she didn't, he looked back down with a sharp breath. Still trembling, he lifted her hand in both of his. Esti watched his eyes in fascination as he reverently touched her skin with his gloved fingers, studying the fine hairs of her forearm, the wrinkles around each knuckle, and her unpainted fingernails. It was like he had never seen the hand of a girl before.

When his butterfly touch raised goose bumps on her skin, he looked so surprised that Esti giggled. After an embarrassed moment, he turned her arm to study the underside of her hand. She felt like a priceless work of art as he traced his finger along the life lines of her palm and the webbing between her fingers, memorizing the whorl of each fingerprint. It was a long time before he finally placed her hand gently back in her lap.

❧

They spent the afternoon talking about her father. Esti had never met anyone—not even her mom—who knew The Great Legard's work so intimately. She couldn't have imagined the deep uncertainties that forced her dad along as he strove to conquer the theater. And, as the sun dropped lower in the sky, Alan finally mentioned her dad's difficulty with fatherhood.

"I think you intimidated him," Alan said frankly. "He told me that someday the tables would turn and he would be known as Esti Legard's father."

"Yeah, right." She burst into laughter, looking at the long

line of Legard's writing on Alan's bookshelves. "No one intimidated my dad. What he told *me* was that I needed better control of myself, if I ever wanted people to notice me. My character depended too much on the attitude of everyone else on stage. He said I was shallow." She swallowed as the words came out of her mouth. She had managed to forget the painful conversation she'd had with him when the cameras finally stopped. She had never told anyone how he had chastised her performance even after it was all over, destroying her last shreds of confidence.

"Proving his control." Alan nodded. "Control was so important to him that he couldn't be completely honest."

"That's it." Esti gave Alan a flabbergasted look as he opened yet another window into her dad. "Was he that way with you too?"

"Yes." Alan led Esti upstairs to begin dinner. "He considered me a prodigy, but I hated the spotlight. My attraction to Shakespeare had far different roots than his."

"What was your attraction?" Esti asked curiously.

"My family has always claimed ancestry from Amleth."

"Ah-hah." Esti laughed. "*To be or not to be.* Your insanity goes way back, then."

"Precisely." Smiling, he pulled a chair away from the small kitchen table so she could sit down. The length of the kitchen overlooked the living room below; her chair beside the open window looked out at the valley.

Shadows played against the beautiful hills outside from the late-afternoon sun, and Esti felt a sudden, strong twinge of guilt. Was Aurora watching the same shadows from her balcony, drinking wine as she worried and waited?

"Do you ever try to help people when they get into trouble on your island?" she asked Alan. "Have people really died here?"

To her surprise, Alan merely shrugged. "It's not my business."

"What's not your business? Saving lives?"

"You've met her." He handed Esti a glass of water. "You know how she is. There are signs posted everywhere, warning of the danger. If someone is foolish enough to disturb her, who am I to save them?"

Esti took a sip, thinking about the distant, angry shriek. The cay wasn't *really* alive; it couldn't be. "Suppose someone lands here by accident. Do they deserve to die for that?"

"I learned long ago not to question my lady. Those who face her judgment are paying for the sins of their past. I don't interfere."

Esti studied the shadows outside, taken aback by the stiffness in Alan's voice.

"You interfered with me," she finally said. "Won't I have to pay?"

The silence following her words lasted so long that Esti felt a shiver of apprehension.

"If a price must be paid for today," Alan finally said, "it will not be you who pays it."

He refused to talk about Manchineel Cay any further,

instead showing Esti how to make calalloo soup. It was almost dark by the time Alan covered the table with candles while she ladled the soup, rich with seafood and spinach, herbs and coconut milk. A thrill shot through her when he reached for her hand at the end of dinner, his eyes glowing in the candlelight.

"Thank you," she said, "for finally trusting me."

"This has been the best day of my life," Alan replied softly. "But my mind misgives some consequence, yet hanging in the stars . . ." He trailed off at her wide-eyed stare. "It's time for me to take you home."

Esti silently followed him down the steps and put her shoes on. Romeo's suicidal quote about the stars disturbed her deeply, and she wished Alan hadn't said it.

When she stood up, he had disappeared. She walked around the living room one last time, waiting for him. As she passed his books, the slim paperback again caught her eye, sandwiched between her father's earliest works. Esti stared at the notched spine for a moment, then carefully pulled the paperback out of the bookcase.

Before she could open it, however, she heard Alan coming up the steps from the bathroom. Almost without thinking, she stuffed the book into the back of her jeans waistband. When he reached the top of the stairs, she was tucking her shirt back in, aware of her breathing and her pounding heart.

They made the dark trip back down to the boat in silence, the cay moaning in rancorous protest as Alan led

Esti to the boat. As they floated back out into the calm sea, Esti was intensely relieved to be away from the forbidding presence of Manchineel Cay. As she heard the oars move in the darkness, however, she couldn't relax. She strained to see Alan rowing the tiny boat in his black clothes, random thoughts churning through her mind. She had more questions now, she thought in confusion, than ever.

What deformity could keep Alan in this lonely, awful place? It seemed that he had always lived this life of bizarre secrets, even as her dad's close friend. What sort of relationship could Esti have with him, if he never allowed her to see him?

Listening to the splash and squeak of the oars, Esti quelled a traitorous longing for Rafe. Rafe strode fearlessly through life, straightforward to the point of getting himself in trouble. He had nothing to hide, no complicated emotions to untangle. Esti couldn't deny she missed his killer kiss and his easy smile. He kept her warm and safe without even trying. Most of all, she missed his honesty.

She twitched, aware of the book she smuggled in her jeans. She felt terrible for the way she'd left Aurora this morning, and she totally deserved the trouble she would be in when she got home. No matter what Alan had done, Esti was in no position to judge him, or anyone else.

The suffocating trees where Alan moored his boat didn't seem nearly as frightening now, after the implicit anger she had felt from his jealous lady. She clutched his gloved fingers as they made their way through the watery mangle, and when they reached the glow of lights outside the theater building, she didn't let go of his hand. She hadn't planned to do it, but her body seemed to act on its own, intent on resolving the most difficult issue between them.

As Alan turned to give her a questioning look in the pale yellow light, her other hand darted up to his face. Before he could protest, she gently pulled off his mask.

Act Three

Act Three. Scene One.

"NO!"

The word exploded from Alan with such force that Esti reeled back. Nothing could have prepared her for the sight of him. The mottled skin on his face was deeply furrowed and cracked, alternately shiny and covered with thick, dark scales. His mouth twisted in rage, his eyes stabbing into her with horror at what she'd done. In the sickly yellow light he looked like he could have crawled out of a grave. He was terrifying.

"This." His voice became an inhuman croak. "This is the payment my lady demands."

Esti couldn't help the scream that burst from her as he grabbed her arm. He yanked her close to him, his furious eyes piercing hers.

"Then go ahead and look."

Icy fear crawled through her body. Wrenching her arm loose, she scrambled back in terror as he followed her across the grass.

"Get away from her!" A familiar voice broke the darkness, and someone hit Alan with such force, he ended up several feet away.

Aghast, Esti watched the two shadows struggle in the dim light. With one part of her mind, she understood that somehow Rafe had appeared. With another part, she realized he didn't stand a chance. Alan attacked with unearthly rage until Rafe staggered back. Alan followed him, as deadly and wicked as a phantom.

"No," Esti cried, leaping at them. "Alan, don't."

She was too late. Alan's fist landed on Rafe, and he crumpled. Esti threw herself against Alan to stop his other fist. When a glancing blow caught her, she lurched backward, holding her jaw.

"Esti!" Alan's voice filled with panic. "Beloved Esti, I didn't mean to."

She stumbled and fell to the grass, scrabbling back as he came after her. Several feet away she heard a dull groan, but Rafe didn't move. She couldn't hold back another scream as Alan's hideous face loomed above her.

He became deathly still as she shrank from him. After a moment, he slumped to the grass, panting. "Oh, my lady is harsh."

Esti pressed her hands against her ears, but it didn't help. His tormented breath shredded her heart.

He looked back at Rafe, hatred growing in his eyes. As he began to rise, Esti grabbed his arm.

"No, please," she whimpered. "Leave him alone."

He sank to the grass again, and Esti made herself stare into his awful face. He slowly pulled away until she let go of him, his eyes never leaving hers.

"Gentle Esti," he said woodenly, reaching into his pocket. "The queen of betrayal."

Her eyes widened in horror when she saw the delicate chain sparkling in the dim light. She couldn't move as he clasped it around her neck, the tiny frangipani pendant resting against her throat.

"If you remove this again," he said, "I will know you despise me." Picking up his mask from the ground, he silently stood and walked into the darkness.

Esti watched him, frozen, until he disappeared around the edge of the theater building. She wanted to curl up against the wall and die, but Rafe lay motionless in the grass, his dark face shiny with blood.

"Rafe. Oh my God." She dropped down beside him, trying to soak up some of the blood with her shirt. "Are you okay?"

He opened one eye, then groaned and shut it again. His nose was bleeding, and his other eye had already swollen shut. Blood welled from a deep cut across his forehead, and more from a split in his lower lip.

"You're bleeding." Her voice broke in disbelief. "He hurt you."

Rafe's eye opened again. After a moment he sat up, breathing deeply and holding his head. "I heard you scream."

Esti clenched her teeth, wincing at the ache in her jaw. She wouldn't let herself cry. "What are you *doing* here?"

"Aurora called me at the restaurant a while ago." Rafe spoke the words carefully, grimacing as he touched his fingers to his bleeding mouth. "She said the jumbee had smashed her rosemary and kidnapped you. She sounded drunk and nearly hysterical." He stared at Esti, squinting against blood that dripped into his eyes from the gash in his forehead. "I saw it attack you."

"No." Her shirt was already soggy with sweat and blood, so she pulled the front of his T-shirt up and wiped his eyes as gently as she could. She could never explain. "I'm taking you to the emergency room."

"Forget it. I'm not going there." He pulled his shirt up to wipe more blood away. "I barely saw that thing before it decked me, but I can tell you right now, it wasn't human. Where did it go?"

Esti shuddered in fear. "You're bleeding really bad, and I think you need stitches. Where's the hospital?"

"Not a chance." Rafe grimaced. "I'm not going near that place."

She couldn't argue, and she had no idea where the hospital was. She'd take Rafe home. Aurora would know what to do. "Okay, we're going to my house. We should hurry."

"I can't see anything. I think I got blood in my eyes."

"I'll help you to the car. Why don't you let me drive?"

She hadn't driven since she moved here, but Rafe didn't argue. Her hands shook as she helped him get in the Jeep. She found a dirty beach towel he'd thrown on the floor, and gave it to him to staunch the blood. Somehow, she managed to make it up Bayrum Hill without stalling or driving on the wrong side of the road. She was trembling as she parked in the weeds past the driveway.

"Come on," she said, helping him to the front door. When they stumbled in, however, her heart sank. Two empty wine bottles stood on the counter, and from the corner of her eye she could make out Aurora's prone body on the couch. Esti closed her eyes for a desperate second, then led Rafe across the living room to her bedroom.

"In here," she said. "I'll get some ice for you."

As soon as she helped him lie down, she rushed back out to the kitchen, pausing to kick off her wet shoes and yank the paperback book from the back of her jeans. The pages had warped, soggy with sweat and blood. Barely glancing at it, she tossed it on the kitchen table.

Her hands began shaking again as she piled ice cubes into a bag and wrapped it all in a wet towel. She hurried back to her room. Kneeling beside the bed, she pulled the bloody beach towel from Rafe's forehead and dropped it on the floor. As she replaced it with the icepack, his hand came up to cover hers.

"Thanks, babe."

Pressure burned behind her eyes, but she refused to cry. She couldn't fall apart. Instead, she tried to clean his face with a washcloth. Blood seemed to be everywhere.

His fingers tightened on hers. "What happened down there? I always thought jumbees were a bunch of bull, but I just changed my mind."

"No." Esti closed her eyes, trying to forget Alan's horrible face. She had no idea what to do now. She wanted someone to take care of her, but she'd done a thorough job of losing everyone who might be able to help her. Her dad was dead, Aurora was drunk, Rafe was bleeding, and Alan . . . God only knew.

She wiped her nose with the back of her hand. "I can't remember your parents' phone number."

Even after Rafe told her, she had to dial it twice, and when she heard a voice on the other end, she almost dropped the phone.

"Rodney?" She cleared her throat. "It's Esti."

"Esti, of course." He sounded very interested, rather than surprised she would be calling late on a Sunday night.

She took a deep breath. "Rafe is at my place," she said. "He's been hurt."

"What happened?" He became all business.

"He—someone beat him up."

"He got in another fight?" Rodney's voice hardened. "*Chupse.* Have you called the jandam?"

"I haven't. Something cut his head open, though, and he's bleeding pretty bad. I think he should go to the hospital, but—"

"No," Rafe protested.

"No," his dad said simultaneously. "I'll be there in twenty minutes, and I'll bring a doctor with me. Can he make it until we get there?"

"Yes," she said, weak with relief. "Thank you."

She closed her eyes as she hung up. After a moment, she felt Rafe's hand on hers again.

"You're great," he said.

"No, I'm not." She abruptly stood. "I'm horrible. This is all my fault—you and Alan and Aurora, and everything." She hurried out before Rafe could reply. She didn't want Rodney to see Aurora drunk in the living room.

Her mom opened her eyes as Esti pulled her up from the couch. "Esti," she said blearily, trying to focus. "You're here."

"Yes, I'm home."

"You're a mess." Aurora frowned at her, then closed her eyes and sagged into Esti's arms. "A mess."

"You have no idea," Esti muttered, walking Aurora toward her bedroom. "Just sleep now, and we'll talk in the morning."

As soon as Esti got back out to the kitchen, she tucked the empty wine bottles deep in the trash can, piling plastic bags on top to hide them. When she heard a noise behind her, she spun around to see Rafe leaning against the doorway of her bedroom. He looked terrible, the ice pack he held against his forehead stained crimson.

"Why are you cleaning the kitchen?"

She blushed. "You need to stay in bed until your dad gets here. You lost a lot of blood."

He squinted at her. "I always wanted a girlfriend who would put me in her bed and order me to stay there."

Her blush deepened, and he shook his head.

"Yeah, just because your jumbee beat me up doesn't mean you want me in your life." He made his way to the couch and sat down.

Esti began to shiver again, and she followed Rafe across

the living room. "I'm scared," she whispered, sitting beside him. "I didn't know he would hurt you like this. And I want . . ." She touched his swollen face, then helplessly leaned her head on his shoulder. "I do want you in my life."

"Aw, babe." As he pulled her against him, they both heard a noise at the front door.

"Inside! It's Rodney Solomon."

Rodney's eyes widened in shock as she opened the door. Esti knew she must look awful, but she just waved him in. His eyes widened further when he saw Rafe. A very tall West Indian man followed Rafe's dad, carrying a large black briefcase.

"Esti, this is Dr. Leroy Tyler."

The doctor gave her a withering look that made her want to shrink into the floor, then crossed the room to kneel in front of Rafe.

A disgusted hiss burst from Dr. Tyler as he sucked his breath in through his teeth. "*Chupse*. When you gon grow up, Rafe?" He had a very deep voice, and Rafe grimaced as the doctor pulled the icepack away from his head. "Still fightin' over girl dem."

"Jumbee have attack her, mon."

Dr. Tyler paused and gave Esti another look. "Jumbee? Bull nonsense you chat."

"I ain't chat no bull. No human have hit me."

The doctor studied Esti thoroughly. He finally turned back to Rafe, and she leaned against the wall, light-headed. She sank to the floor, wrapping her arms around her knees.

"You okay?" Rodney crouched beside her, staring at her.

"I'm all right."

"Any of that blood yours?"

"Excuse me?"

He gestured at her. "Is the blood on you all from my son, or are you hurt?"

Esti closed her eyes. "I'm not hurt. Rafe got hit pretty hard."

"If Esti hadn't—" Rafe broke off. "Ouch! What you doin'?"

"Hold still, boy," Dr. Tyler said. "You all mash up. You gon need a shot of anesthetic before I stitch you."

Rafe's dad was still staring at Esti when she opened her eyes, and she forced herself to her feet. "I'd better get cleaned up. I'll be back in a few minutes."

Esti caught a glimpse of herself in the mirror as she closed the bathroom door. Dirt and blood streaked her arms and face. Her hair was matted and sticky, with bits of grass in it. She dropped her filthy clothes on the floor and stepped into the shower before she could see any more. It seemed to take forever to rinse the blood from her skin and hair.

Rafe's blood.

She closed her eyes and plunged beneath the pouring water. She knew she was taking a heavy toll on the rainwater cistern, but she couldn't help it. By the time she walked back out in a clean tank top and jeans, Rafe had a large bandage on his forehead. His eye was swollen shut, his face puffy and discolored even through the darkness of his skin. He was deep in a heavily accented discussion with his dad and Dr. Tyler, but they broke off as she came into the living room.

She hesitated, then held out a T-shirt to Rafe. "This belonged to my dad," she said. "I thought you might want something clean."

He nodded and stood up, carefully peeling off his bloody shirt and dropping it on the floor. Esti watched him put on her dad's T-shirt, then she turned away again. "I'll let you guys talk."

"We're done." Rafe caught her hand and sat back on the couch, drawing her against him. She winced as her jaw pressed on his shoulder.

Dr. Tyler's eyes narrowed. "You have a bruise on your face. Were you involved in the fight?" His dialect disappeared as he addressed her directly.

"I fell and hit my chin," she whispered.

Rafe stared at her chin for a moment, then tightened his arm around her as he looked back at the two older men. "I'm staying here tonight. Esti needs the company."

His dad frowned. "You come home. You're in bad shape."

Rafe looked at Dr. Tyler. "Am I gonna die?"

"Not now." The doctor laughed. "Long as you stay away from jumbee dem."

"'Tis why I stay here."

Rodney sighed. "Esti's in high school, Rafe. You know what happened last time."

"I sleep on de couch, mon." Rafe glared at his dad.

Dr. Tyler laughed again. "It have no difference. De painkiller I had give he does come in ten minute; he out like a baby."

"Where's Aurora?" Rodney looked around. "I don't think she'll like it."

Esti cringed. "My mom's in bed. She has the flu."

Dr. Tyler raised his eyebrows. "She's so sick she could sleep through all this? Do you want me to take a look at her?"

"No! She'll be fine by tomorrow." Esti felt her cheeks redden as Dr. Tyler exchanged a knowing glance with Rafe's dad.

"Okay." Rodney stood up. He thrust his fist at Rafe, shaking his head. "You sleep on the couch, Rafe."

Rafe reached up with his own fist and bumped knuckles with his dad, then with Dr. Tyler. "Thanks, Dr. Tyler. Thanks, Dad. I'll call you."

Esti shut the door behind them, then turned around.

Rafe looked exhausted. "You're a lousy liar, babe."

She closed her eyes and leaned against the wall, nodding.

"He nailed you, didn't he? That's how you bruised your jaw."

"It was my fault," she said dully. "I got in his way so he would stop hitting you."

After a moment she heard Rafe get up from the couch, then his arms were around her. "He is one serious badjohn. Should we call Ma Harris, since she's the—"

"No!"

"Why not?" Rafe said in surprise.

Esti shook her head. "Not Ma Harris. I'll tell you everything tomorrow. It's a long story, and de painkiller does come in ten minute."

"I fire coffee quick before you change your mind. Dr. Tyler gave me some good stuff. I feel great."

"You're not drinking coffee right now." She hesitated, too embarrassed to look up at him. "And you're not sleeping on this awful couch. Aurora's already mad at me anyway."

Rafe smoothed Esti's hair back from her face. "She's drunk, isn't she?"

"That's my fault too," Esti whispered miserably. "What was that hissing sound Dr. Tyler made when he was disgusted and sucked on his teeth? That's how I feel right now."

Rafe chuckled. *"Chupse."*

"Yeah. *Chupse.*" She leaned her head against his chest. "Come on, you need to go to bed."

Five minutes later, Rafe was asleep on top of the covers, fully clothed. Esti sat on her bed watching him for a long time. Whenever a shudder went through her, she touched his hand, reassuring herself that he was real. She finally leaned over and kissed him gently on the lips, then stood and went out to the kitchen table. For a moment she stared down at the bedraggled paperback book she had stolen from Manchineel Cay.

Bringing Shakespeare into the American Audience. The last treatise her dad published before his death. It was only logical that Esti would find it on Alan's bookshelves, of course, along with all the other books her dad had given him. She caressed the peculiar little notch at the top of the spine, aching inside and wondering if it was possible for two copies of a book to have the same defect.

She tried to smooth the book flat, but it had warped beyond repair. A large dark smear ruined the cover. Rafe's blood. With a growing sense of fear, she finally sat down and opened it. Little doubt remained in her mind where Alan had gotten this copy of her dad's book, but she still hoped she wouldn't see the beloved inscription on the first page.

Sweet Esti, her father began. *You've come so far. I've seen you hold an audience with your voice and with your passion, clothing your characters in the words Shakespeare has written . . .* Although the ink had blurred in a couple of places, the words were still legible.

Closing the book with shaking hands, she held it against her chest. With slow deep breaths, she forced down the terror trickling in from the darkest corners of her mind. She hadn't seen this book since the airlines lost her luggage. The day she and her mom moved to Cariba.

Act Three. Scene Two.

Esti saw her mom leaning against the bedroom door as soon as she opened her eyes. Aurora looked awful, her bloodshot eyes studying Rafe through a curtain of tangled hair. She glanced at the filthy towels on the floor, then turned away without a word. Cringing, Esti rolled out of bed and staggered out to the kitchen, stunned to realize it was almost noon.

Aurora slumped at the table, grimly staring into her coffee. "Why is there blood all over our house?"

"Rafe was at the school last night when Alan brought me back." Esti cautiously sat down across from her mom. "They got in a fight."

"And Rafe won. Is that why he's in bed with you?"

Esti winced. "He got hurt pretty bad. He lost a lot of blood, and the whole thing was my fault. When Rafe's dad came over here with Dr. Tyler—"

"Here?" Aurora finally looked up. "Last night?"

Esti nodded.

"Great." Aurora leaned her forehead against her hand. "That's wonderful, Esti."

"I'm sorry," Esti muttered. "I know that's my fault too. I threw away the wine bottles, and you were in your room by the time everyone got here. They didn't see you."

Aurora just groaned.

"You both sound pathetic." Rafe came out of the bedroom, gingerly touching his mouth. "Damn, that hurts." He looked almost worse than he had last night. Blood stained through the white bandage taped to his forehead. His eye was still swollen shut, his lower lip puffy beyond recognition.

Aurora stared at him in disbelief, then turned to Esti. "You let Alan beat up Rafe—"

"Wait a minute," Rafe interrupted, putting his hands on Esti's shoulders as he stood behind her. "Let's see if I get this straight, babe. Last night you said it was all your fault the jumbee scared you and made you scream. Then you forced him to hit you. Your mom thinks you're the reason I'm such a wimp he was able to beat the crap out of me. And I just heard you take credit for Aurora being a lush."

"Rafe, you are a jerk." Aurora closed her eyes. "Please tell me you didn't say that Alan *hit* Esti last night."

"It's not what you think," Esti began, but Rafe interrupted her.

"Hey, mon, I say it like it is."

"I am so . . . upset about all this," Aurora said. "*Upset* is the wrong word. It doesn't begin to come close to how I'm feeling. Thank you, Rafe, for rescuing my daughter, and I'm truly sorry you got beat up."

She opened one bloodshot eye to glare balefully at Esti. "I need more coffee and Rafe needs a shower. He looks even worse than I feel." She propped her elbows on the table, covering her face with her hands.

"And then," she muttered, "Esti has a lot of explaining to do."

❧

It was late afternoon by the time Esti finished. She tried to be as honest as she could, describing the first time she ever heard Alan's voice, his withdrawn nature, and his extensive knowledge of Shakespeare. She managed a calmly detached explanation of her breakdown when he decided the tutoring must end, then his apology during Carnival.

Aurora listened with very few interruptions, although she

grew frighteningly pale at the descriptions of Manchineel Cay. When Esti began explaining the Shakespeare posters and the boarding school near London, however, Aurora slammed her hand down on the kitchen table.

"Your father never knew this guy. I would have known."

"He said Dad was like a father to him. And Dad's inscriptions were—"

"He lied," Aurora ground out. "He forged the posters to make you believe him."

Esti slowly shook her head. "What about the boarding school?"

"If your father had tutored a boy like Alan," Aurora snapped, "he would have told me. He did *not* keep secrets from me."

Esti couldn't bring herself to mention that she had never kept secrets from Aurora either, not until she met Alan. She felt a surge of pity for her mom, followed by an even greater burst of pity for her dad. She knew the posters weren't forged, even if her dad had regarded Alan merely as a prodigal student, rather than some kind of adopted son. Until yesterday, Esti had never dreamed that her dad might have had cracks behind the façade. *You have the remarkable ability to give me strength when I doubt myself,* he wrote to Alan. If Esti hadn't experienced the same thing from Alan, she wouldn't believe it either.

Despite her resolve to be neutral, she finally broke down when she tried to explain about removing Alan's mask. Her throat grew so thick she couldn't talk, and after the third try, she gave up and stared out at Manchineel Cay.

"Rafe," Aurora asked in a steely voice, "did you see Alan?"

"Yeah, mon," Rafe said. He hadn't uttered a word all afternoon, merely holding an ice pack against his face as he sat on the couch and listened. "I saw a monster, anyway. I guess that was Alan."

"Esti?" Aurora said.

Esti could only close her eyes and nod.

Her mom was quiet for a long time. When Esti finally looked back at her, Aurora picked up the stolen Shakespeare treatise with a fierce, questioning look. Staring at the bloodstains, Esti forced herself to tell the truth.

"We're moving back to Oregon tomorrow," her mom said when she finished. Aurora no longer looked angry, merely exhausted.

"But I want to finish the showcase," Esti protested.

When her mom stared at her in disbelief, Esti felt a growing sense of determination. She wasn't sure why, but it suddenly felt like the most important thing in her life.

"I need to do it, for Dad's sake." *And for Alan's sake.*

"For your father's sake," Aurora ground out, "we are getting out of here the minute I can get you on an airplane."

"Alan's afraid of me now," Esti said, unable to stop her fingers from reaching up to touch the necklace.

"He's afraid of you?" Aurora let out a burst of incredulous laughter.

"He is," Esti said calmly, not allowing the slightest hint of her desperation to show. "He didn't want to take me to

Manchineel Cay, but I talked him into it. I'm the one who let things get to this point, even though he warned me."

"Warned you of what?"

Esti slowly tucked the necklace beneath her blouse. "He said all along that it was a mistake, but I didn't listen. This whole mess is my fault."

Aurora stared at her in disbelief. "He almost killed you."

"No," Esti said softly. "He never hurt me."

"Look what he did to Rafe!"

Esti abruptly covered her face with trembling hands. She didn't know what to say. After a moment, she heard Aurora's chair screech on the floor tiles, followed by the slam of the cupboard and the familiar rasp of the balcony door as her mom stomped outside.

"What's up, babe?" Rafe's voice was flat. "You're still not over the monster?"

Esti stood up, aware of the catapult trembling in anticipation. "I'm over him." Walking to the couch, she gently settled herself on Rafe's lap. She reached up to his swollen face, trying not to cry. "He almost killed you, and I can't forgive him for that. Ma Harris always told me he was too dangerous, but I didn't believe her."

"You're not serious about wanting to finish the showcase, then."

"I am serious. If I leave him alone, he'll leave me alone." She leaned against Rafe, resting her aching forehead on his chest. "Manchicay School has a lot riding on this, and Frederick isn't the only one who'll hate me if I quit now."

"For true." Rafe's arms tightened around her. "You wouldn't believe the industry heavies Frederick convinced to come next weekend. Some of them are already here, and he's set up a bunch of yacht tours and parties."

"I know." Esti felt Rafe's hands moving, absently stroking her hair. "I can't run away now."

"What if Alan comes after you?"

"He won't."

"And if he quotes Shakespeare at you?"

"I'm done with him." She placed her hand on top of Rafe's. "I won't let him hurt you again."

At his skeptical expression, she twined her fingers through his, gently bringing his hand up to her lips. "I promise."

Although he still looked unconvinced, he slowly nodded. "I guess that means you're *my* bodyguard now. I've never gotten whipped that fast."

Esti couldn't even smile.

"My dad's gonna throw a fit when he finds out Aurora wants to leave." Rafe glanced out at the balcony. "He ain't no cop, but he's hugely respected on Cariba, and the jandam does whatever he wants. Everyone knows how important this is for the school."

Esti nodded bleakly, watching Aurora through the screen door. Her mom didn't even bother with a wineglass this time. Taking a swig straight from the bottle, she stared out at Manchineel Cay.

"*That's* not your fault, you know," Rafe said softly.

"Maybe." Esti looked up at Rafe again, his beautiful face

barely recognizable through the swollen mess. "All I do is cause trouble. It's your mom who's going to throw a fit when she sees what happened to you. Your parents must hate me."

"They would figure something was wrong with me if I wasn't getting in trouble. My mom says I got testosterone poisoning, and she gives you all the credit for keeping me out of jail this time. They love you, believe me."

"I almost got you *into* jail." Esti stretched up and touched her lips to his. "I'm still not sure why you put up with me."

"Because you're irresistible." Smiling crookedly, he slipped his hand beneath her necklace to caress her shoulder blade. "Does this hurt?"

She stiffened. "Does what hurt?"

"You didn't even notice. You got a couple blisters on your shoulder that had to come from Manchineel Cay."

Esti relaxed. Rafe wasn't talking about the necklace.

"Spots this big will leave permanent scars," he said. "Manchineel sap does that. Keep 'em covered up as much as you can. You don't want people to know you went to the haunted cay. Superstition runs deep on Cariba."

"What would people do to me?"

"Nobody's gonna do anything to you. It's just that I'm not in the best shape after last night, and I'm tired of washing dishes."

"Oh." She winced. "I'm sorry."

He gave her a lopsided smile. "You know, when I left Los Angeles, I thought I would get bored here."

Aurora hadn't moved from the balcony by the time Rafe

drove away. Esti went into the bathroom, craning her neck to see in the mirror. She studied the two blisters on the back of her shoulder, each as large as a nickel. Damaged skin trailed beneath them, where the sap had dripped before coming to a stop. As awful as they looked, she was surprised they weren't painful.

She sagged against the sink, then straightened and methodically washed her face. When she finally went back to the living room, Aurora still hadn't moved. Taking a deep breath, Esti walked outside.

"Okay, Esti." Aurora didn't look at her. "I heard you and Rafe talking. I won't let Alan destroy Manchicay School. If the police promise to protect you, we'll stay until Frederick's showcase is over. Next week, though, we're out of here. I'll call Ashland High and make arrangements for the rest of the semester."

"That's fine." Esti stared out at Manchineel Cay.

"Esti, I want you to promise me you're through with him."

She leaned numbly against the doorway. "Yeah."

"Swear you'll never talk to him again. I want to hear the words."

"I swear I'll never talk to Alan again." Esti tightened her jaw and looked back at her mom. "Now it's your turn. I want you to stop drinking."

"I'm not an alcoholic." Aurora's voice grew thin.

"I didn't say you were."

The balcony was silent for a minute, tempered by the chirps of distant frogs.

Finally Aurora sighed. "You'll give up your addiction if I give up mine." She picked up the bottle and held it over the rail, pouring the last of her wine into a bougainvillea bush. "If you stay away from Alan, I won't drink another drop until you're out of high school. Now I'm going to call Rodney. If he gets a couple of policemen down to the school, I'll let you go to rehearsal tonight."

For a moment, they stared at each other, then Esti leaned forward into her mom's arms. She closed her eyes, trying to remember the time, not too long ago, when Aurora had been her friend. Although the hug was awkward, it was nice to feel her mom's arms around her.

By the time her mom dropped her off at the theater, Esti was late. Carmen glanced pointedly at her watch as Esti approached, but Lucia greeted her with an expression so somber that Esti winced.

"We gotta talk," Lucia said. She folded her arms across her chest and glared at Carmen. "'Tis not for melee, what I say to Esti now."

Carmen's eyes grew wide. She instantly nodded, for once not saying a word.

Lucia looked around to make sure no one else was listening, then leaned against the building. "Ma say something happen to the jumbee last night. Something bad."

Although Esti met Lucia's piercing gaze, she couldn't make herself speak.

"You have scare him away." Lucia's eyes narrowed. "Ma

she want you to bring him back. She say 'tis a bad thing you do."

"I can't bring him back," Esti whispered.

"Ma vex that you got more power than she."

"I don't have any power," Esti said, shaken. "Your mom has known him a lot longer than I have. He'll talk to her again, even if he never talks to me."

"Ohmigod," Carmen breathed. To Esti's surprise, Carmen wasn't looking at her, but across the grassy courtyard. "What happened to him?"

Rafe stood at the edge of the parking lot, watching them. His battered face looked serious as he approached with a hardcover book in his hand.

"I gotta talk to Esti alone," he said.

Lucia studied his split lip and swollen eye, and the bandage on his forehead. After a moment, she turned and silently walked inside the theater. Carmen lingered for another moment, her expression desperate to know more, then reluctantly followed Lucia.

"What is it?" Esti asked in apprehension.

"Let me read you something about Elon Somand."

Esti glanced at Manchineel Cay. "He isn't Elon Somand," she said stiffly.

Rafe opened his book. "My dad showed me this when I got home."

He flipped through the pages until he came to a bookmark. "Elon Somand was a Danish slave owner, known from a very young age as the 'monster of the islands.' His reputation came from his notorious cruelty, as well as his revolting appearance. Historians now believe he suffered from a rare skin disorder."

Esti grew numb.

"He massacred most of his slaves before vanishing from Cariba Island in 1848, on the day that Denmark abolished slavery in the West Indies. Although it's believed that Somand met his fate at the hands of his few remaining slaves, his body was never found. He was in his mid-twenties."

Rafe looked back up at her. For a moment they stared at each other in silence, then his eyes flicked down to her fingers, nervously twisting the necklace Alan had given her. Without thinking, she jerked her hand away.

Rafe's eyes widened. "Did he give that to you?"

Esti swallowed. "It's not what you think."

"What is *wrong* with you? I thought you were done with him."

"I am done with him." She began to shake.

"Why are you wearing his damn necklace?"

"It's my way of proving I don't hate him." She stared at Rafe with pleading eyes. "I can't despise him for what he looks like."

"You're not over him," Rafe said furiously. "He's holding your soul with that thing."

"Oh, yoo hoo, Esti." Frederick peered out of the theater doors, his voice a bit testy. "We're waiting for your fabulous Lady Capulet this evening."

"I have to go." She gave Rafe a helpless look. "I'm late."

"Yeah, Alan taught you how to choose right, for true." Slamming the book shut, Rafe reached out before Esti could move. With a twist of his fingers, he pulled the delicate chain from her neck.

"Rafe! Give it back."

He shook his head. "Listen, babe," he said grimly.

Alan's despairing words stabbed into Esti's heart. *I will know you despise me.*

"No," she said.

"Esti, darling?" Frederick's eyes had widened at the sight of Rafe's face. "We can't start the next scene without you."

"Give me my necklace," she demanded. "Right now."

When Rafe silently held out the chain, Esti snatched it from his hand. He turned away without a word.

"Darling," Frederick said to Esti as Rafe stomped away, "I won't ask about your lovers' spat, because I don't want to know. I do not approve of my students being late, however. Not even my shining stars like you."

"I'm sorry," she muttered. "It won't happen again."

After her scene, Esti sat by herself several rows back to work on the delicate link that Rafe had broken. She could see Officer Wilmuth slowly pacing in the wings, his hands clasped behind him as he made his way back and forth behind the stage. She didn't expect the relief that swept through her when she finally clasped the chain around her neck during Danielle's bedroom scene. And she certainly didn't expect the quiet voice that immediately tickled her ear.

"Danielle has gotten better in the past two weeks, hasn't she?"

Esti closed her eyes in shock.

"It's because of you," Alan murmured. "Frederick makes her study your techniques whenever you're onstage. The difference in her acting is already noticeable."

She shouldn't be listening to him. She should leap to her feet and run away as fast as she could. Alan could have killed Rafe last night. He had shown a horrifying ruthlessness that she still couldn't believe.

But he had never once tried to hurt her, she thought miserably. How could he still sound so good?

"I've been watching Frederick McKenzie since he got here," Alan said gently. "He searches for ways to improve your Juliet and your Lady Capulet, but he finds nothing to criticize. You can do nothing wrong."

Esti shook her head as a tear slipped from beneath her eyelid. She'd done it all wrong from the beginning. Gentle Esti, the queen of betrayal.

"Don't cry," he said, his voice stroking her. "Oh please, don't cry."

"Esti, you okay?" Lucia called down from the stage.

Esti realized she had missed her cue. She couldn't bear to go up onstage now, knowing Alan was watching her. Knowing she couldn't talk to him.

Her tears started in earnest.

"I've hurt you again." Alan sounded like a bewildered child. "What did I say?"

No. She shook her head again. *I'm hurting you. That's all I've done since we met.* She couldn't tell him that, of course. She had promised Aurora she would never talk to him again. She had betrayed her mom so deeply this year; she couldn't do it anymore.

"Forgive me." His voice became soft and pleading. "Whatever I said, I'm sorry."

She put her hands over her face. There was no answer.

"Esti?" Lucia's hand touched her shoulder. "I have watch you since you sit down. I think the jumbee he talk to you."

Esti's eyes flew open, and she swiped her fist across her nose. Officer Wilmuth was rapidly approaching with Frederick; the other cast members stared curiously from the stage.

"Listen to me," she hissed to Lucia. Alan must still be listening. He would have to hear her.

"I can't keep hurting him. I would tell him if I could, but I swore I'd never speak to him again. If I stay here, I'll"—her voice broke—"I'll be forsworn before the night is over. I'm quitting the play. I hope he can forgive me."

"No," Alan whispered.

"You're joking, darling." Frederick had drawn close enough to hear her last words. "I'll never forgive you if you quit."

She wiped her nose again, then rose to her feet. She couldn't sit here and ignore Alan, when all she wanted to do was talk to him again. Despite her love for Rafe, despite Alan's terrifying face and fury, and his endless disturbing secrets, she couldn't make herself let go.

"I have to leave."

"No!" Alan protested, more loudly.

Frederick hesitated at the sound, and Officer Wilmuth's eyes widened.

"I'm sorry," Esti gasped. Without waiting to hear any more, she turned and fled.

❧

When Aurora and Officer Moore burst through the front door half an hour later, she was ready for them.

"Esti," her mom began urgently, then trailed off in confusion. Esti had forced herself to calm down as soon as she got home, surrounding herself with classical music and sandalwood incense. She'd dialed the number for Rafe's restaurant half a dozen times, hanging up each time before it rang.

Now she looked up from her cup of tea and smiled. "Hi," she said.

"What in the world happened?" Aurora studied her. "I almost had a heart attack when Officer Wilmuth called us. Frederick told us you ran off in tears, swearing to quit. I just knew that Alan had come back for you. Thank God I was wrong."

"No, you were right."

Aurora sank down beside her on the couch, her eyes wide.

"I heard his voice," Esti continued, "but I kept my promise. I didn't say a word to him, and then I left." She raised her eyebrows at Officer Moore. "I hope you don't mind melodrama."

He briefly gripped her shoulder. "I'm worried about you, is all."

"What did Alan say?" Aurora demanded.

"Nothing much, really. A few things about Frederick's teaching. I left before he was finished, and he didn't follow me. I knew he wouldn't."

"This terrifies me, Esti."

"It shouldn't," Esti said softly. "I quit the showcase."

"You did what?" Aurora stared at her, stunned.

"I quit." As Esti repeated the words, Officer Moore's cell phone began to ring.

"It's Rodney," he said, glancing at the phone. "I think we all know why he's calling."

Taking a deep breath, Esti looked out the open window as he answered the phone. She couldn't see Manchineel Cay in the darkness, but she definitely heard a wail in the trade winds. She imagined Rafe's dad was probably on his way to her house again, accompanied this time by Frederick. She wondered when Rodney would finally throw his hands up in the air and decide that even The Great Legard's daughter wasn't worth this much trouble.

"Esti," Aurora said, "look at me."

Esti turned to her without protesting.

"Is Alan a jumbee, or is he some crazy stalker?"

"I don't know." Esti met her mom's frightened gaze. "Honestly Aurora, I really don't know. All I know is that he's never tried to hurt me, and I'm not afraid of him."

Aurora shook her head in disbelief. "Then why did you quit the play just now?"

"So I wouldn't have to lie to you. I want to talk to him,

just like you probably want a glass of wine right now, but I promised you I wouldn't."

Aurora sighed. "You sound twenty years older than you are. I feel so guilty for bringing you to Cariba."

"It was my idea." Esti leaned her head on her mom's shoulder.

"Do you really want to quit?"

"No."

She heard Frederick's excited voice coming through the phone now. We'll surround her by cops; make sure the jumbee doesn't come near enough to talk to her; ensure he never touches her again. We have to convince her to stay. She wondered how many minutes until Rodney walked in the door.

With a sigh, she stroked the tangled chain in her pocket. No matter who Alan was or what she decided to do now, she would never again throw it away.

Act Three. Scene Three.

She had just shoved her math book in her locker the next day when Lucia walked up behind her.

"You heard?"

Esti turned around. "Heard what?"

"The heavens are vex mad."

Esti stared at the sky, gloomy and gray with clouds. She looked back at Lucia in confusion.

"Ma she got fired," Lucia said. "I'm quitting school."

"What! You can't do that."

"I can," Lucia said, her eyes flashing in anger. "The jumbee he is vex; all the new sets are tip over and tore apart."

"No," Esti breathed.

"Frederick he yell at Ma this morning when he see it. They had a big fight, and Mr. Fleming had fire her after lunch. He say 'tis her fault."

"Oh, no." Esti slumped against her locker.

"I go home now," Lucia added, her voice soft, "and I put a curse on Frederick. He don't believe in jumbee them. When a Continental don't even try to understand, he will pay for it. Mr. Fleming, he been here five year. He should respect we belief, mon. Is time they both learn a lesson, for true."

"Lucia, wait."

But Lucia was already walking away.

Esti sagged against the wall. She didn't know what to believe anymore. Maybe Alan really was a hideous monster, wreaking havoc as he haunted his old sugar plantation. Maybe he had never studied Shakespeare with her dad, never providing strength and advice as The Great Legard faced the world from his mighty stage. Maybe Alan made it all up, faking the posters and the books and his disturbingly deep knowledge of everything in Esti's past.

Or maybe her dad had known Alan was a jumbee. Perhaps he knew that no one would ever believe him if he tried to explain. That was why he never told Aurora, or anyone else.

Esti shoved her fists against her eyes with a groan. If her dad were alive, he would make everything clear. He could take over, the way he'd always done. He would tell her the truth about Alan, so she wouldn't have to do this by herself. He would . . .

He would tell her to handle it. *You're in control, Esti.*

Alan had been so nervous when he first showed her his house. His hands had gently guided her through the dark; he'd shown her how to make calalloo soup. He raised chickens and vegetables, for heaven's sake. A centuries-old monster couldn't be so human. So vulnerable. Could he?

She slammed her locker shut, glancing at the gray sky. She would spend the rest of the afternoon in the library.

"How do I love thee? Let me count the ways."

Esti's mouth went dry. She dropped the book of land ownership she was holding and clutched the library table.

"I love thee to the, um, to the depth and breadth and height my soul can reach, uh . . ."

Although her heart still pounded, she began to smile.

"I love thee to the level of every day's most quiet need, by sun and candlelight."

As she heard a soft rattle of paper behind her, she glanced around to see Rafe peer at something in his hand. When he saw her move, he immediately looked up at her, his eyes solemn. He looked much better today, if not yet back to his gorgeous self.

"I love thee freely, as men strive for right. I love thee . . .

I love thee . . . oh, crap. Something about passion in my childhood. And, if God choose, I shall but love thee better after death."

Esti pressed her hand against her mouth to keep from laughing.

"I figured I better learn some Shakespeare," he said, abashed. "Maybe you'll forgive me for being such a *crappo* last night."

Esti bit her lip. "That isn't Shakespeare."

He stared at her in dismay. "What is it?"

"Browning, I think. Elizabeth—"

"Chupse." He crumpled the paper in disgust. "My dad said it was Shakespeare."

"It worked, anyway."

"It did?" He looked hopefully at her.

Esti couldn't hold back a giggle. As the librarian cleared her throat at the front desk, Esti gave Rafe a quick kiss. She pulled him over to the table where she'd been stacking books.

"You're not wearing the necklace," he said softly. "Is it because I broke it?"

"No, I fixed it." Esti hesitated, then shook her head. "I'm just not wearing it anymore."

Rafe stared at her for a minute, then kissed her again. When the librarian cleared her throat even louder, he pulled away and looked at the table.

"Historical Origins of Shakespeare. Mythology of the Danish Vikings. Hmm. *Land Titles and Island Ownership.* You study way too much.

My dad said you walked out on the jumbee last night after he tried to talk to you. Just like you did to me when I was being a jerk before rehearsal. You're smarter than both of us."

Esti shook her head.

"Everyone's talking about you again," Rafe said. "Like usual. I had to educate a couple customers at lunch today, but they took it well. I even got a tip from one of them." He smiled. "I think it's because I'm so beautiful right now."

"You are." Esti couldn't help smiling back. "And you'll end up in huge trouble because of me. Again."

"I'd be in trouble anyway. Look, I gotta get back in time for the dinner rush, but I wanted to come and apologize."

"It was a beautiful apology."

He gave her a more thorough kiss this time, grinning at the librarian as he sauntered out the door. It seemed like only a few minutes before the librarian told her the doors were closing. Esti stretched and glanced at her watch.

"Ahh," she groaned. Frederick and Rodney had talked her into coming back to rehearsal—surrounded by cops and all—but she was late again. Frederick was going to kill her.

As she raced across campus through a light rain, she shook her head in disgust. She couldn't even read most of the complicated Danish names. The property titles only covered parcels on Cariba. How was anyone supposed to find out who owned the other islands?

To her surprise, Carmen sat on the ground outside the theater building, slumped against the wet doors.

"You okay?" Esti asked.

"Why should you care?"

She took a step back. "What?"

"Everything's messed up, you idiot. You hadn't noticed? After your little drama queen scene last night, someone destroyed all the sets. I'm sure you heard about Lucia and her mom. Frederick yelled at *me* because the sets are wrecked and you can't play Juliet because Lucia won't play Lady Capulet, so you might as well not even show up now."

Carmen heaved herself to her feet. "Then Frederick yelled at me again because you're late tonight, like I'm your babysitter. He's making everyone work on sets tonight. Everyone hates me, and the place is crawling with jandam, and the play's a disaster. It's all your fault."

Esti blinked. "Carmen—"

"You need all the attention, don't you? Never enough drama without adding a little more. You're a fantastic actress, and everyone except Danielle would love to be your friend, but you're so secretive and intimidating. I give up. You probably don't even care if you ruin this chance for everyone else. I mean, you're The Great Legard's daughter. What else do you need?" Without waiting for a reply, Carmen stomped back into the theater and slammed the door behind her.

Esti stared at the closed doors, stunned. After a minute, she slowly turned and began the trudge up Bayrum Hill. No matter how mad Frederick might be, no matter how many jandam were waiting for her, she couldn't do it. She wanted to go home and feel Aurora's comforting arms around her, telling her a bedtime story that ended with *happily ever after*.

"What are you doing here?" Aurora said in a startled voice. "I thought you were going straight to rehearsal from the library." Her expression grew concerned. "What happened?"

Esti closed the front door, surprised to see George Moore sitting casually on the couch beside her mom. She wondered if she had interrupted something.

"They're—uh—we're all working on sets tonight," she said. "Everyone's mad at me because I ran out last night."

"Sweetie—"

The phone rang. Glancing at the caller ID, Esti grabbed it before her mom could stand up.

"Hi, Frederick."

"We're *waiting* for you," he said testily.

"I know I'm late." She shot a guilty look at her mom. If something nice was starting between Aurora and Officer Moore, Esti wouldn't let her own selfishness get in their way. She had screwed things up enough. "I'll be right there."

"I've worked with a lot of divas, darling, but you are trying my patience."

"I'm sorry, Frederick. Ten minutes, I promise." She hung up before he could say anything else, then abruptly forgot about rehearsal as she glanced at George Moore's uniform. "*You* probably know how to find out about property ownership."

"Whose property?" he asked, unfazed.

She took a deep breath, her scalp tight with tension.

"Manchineel Cay," she said. "I want to know who owns it."

Aurora's eyes narrowed. "Why?"

"So I can learn who Alan really is."

"Listen, Esti—"

"Why not?" Officer Moore shrugged at Aurora, then leaned back, pulling his cell phone from his belt. "Let me make a couple of calls, then I'll drive you down to the school."

Esti watched in astonishment as he dialed a number. Could it be that easy?

"Rodney, it's me . . . Yeah, everything's okay. Look, I'm trying to find the legal owner of Manchineel Cay. Who can help me here?" He paused, then let out a burst of laughter. "Your jokes are getting stale. I heard that one months ago. Okay, I'm ready to write . . . Celestine Samuel from the tax assessor's office. I know that name. Doesn't she have those nine-inch fingernails, and she started in on—ha, I thought so. She won't mind if I call her at home?"

He hesitated, then winked at Esti. "She's standing right in front of me. I'm doing this for her, actually." He paused again. "Sure, Rodney, I will. Thanks."

"Esti, can you help me set the table while George makes his phone calls?" Aurora said stiffly. "He's having dinner with us."

"Good evening, Miss Samuel?" He was already talking again. "Rodney Solomon gave me your number."

"Why don't you have a quick bite of chicken, Esti, before you go back down to the school?"

Esti shook her head, trying to hear Officer Moore over

her mom's chatter. *George,* she thought. Aurora had used his first name.

"Five years ago?" His voice dropped in surprise. "I didn't know that . . . Yes, of course I believe you. If the taxes are always paid up, there's not much you can do. And that assessor was never seen again? . . . Well, if that doesn't beat the band. I know the jandam won't go near the island anymore—"

Aurora started filling water glasses, and Esti turned the faucet off, begging with her eyes to be quiet and listen.

"I suppose the government can't just condemn the whole place," George continued. "Oh, it went to court? No kidding. I imagine it *would* become a big liability. What else can you do? . . . Yes, she is an interesting girl, and we're not about to let anything happen to her. . . . Don't worry, we'll keep the jumbees away. . . . That's right, and thank you, Miss Samuel, I do appreciate it. I'll let Mr. Solomon know. Have a good evening."

Esti stared at him with a sinking feeling.

"Well, *this* isn't a typical thing." He sat back against the couch.

"Why?" Aurora asked. "What did you find out?"

He shook his head. "The title of the cay is controversial. The government tried taking it over about five years ago, but a guy disappeared while surveying the island. Never found another trace of him. Then some attorneys showed up and slammed the government with illegal trespass and confiscation of private property. No one ever discovered who hired the lawyers, but these guys knew what they were doing.

Local officials settled out of court, put danger signs all over the place, and washed their hands of it. Now they refuse to have anything to do with the island."

He paused, giving Esti a look of exasperation. He clearly enjoyed the anticipation.

"So, who owns it?" she asked wearily. "There's got to be a name on the title. Did Miss Samuel actually tell you, or what?"

"Esti," Aurora said. "Don't be rude."

"The name on the title of Manchineel Cay . . ." George hesitated for a long moment, then finally gave in. "Well, I guess it's not a big surprise. Elon Somand, just like it's been for over two hundred years."

Act Three. Scene Four.

Esti felt dozens of eyes on her as she stopped in front of Lucia's apartment house the next afternoon. Lightning flashed somewhere nearby, but she barely heard the thunder over the rain pouring down on the metal roof. *Alpha*, they were calling the storm growing in the Atlantic east of Cariba. Hurricanes never hit in January, of course, although a few people were making halfhearted preparations.

She might be imagining the eyes, Esti thought. Only idiots would brave this kind of weather, looking for a two-hundred-year-old jumbee.

"Inside." The word came out barely louder than a whisper.

Nothing happened. She tried again, louder, then finally gave up and knocked on the door. It swung open almost immediately.

"Come," Lucia said.

Esti's heart went into her throat. She took off her shoes and her dripping raincoat, then followed Lucia into the living room. The smell of fried johnnycakes and sugar filled the air. Ma Harris and her brother, Domino, sat on overstuffed chairs in front of the noisy television, Quintin sprawled on the couch beside them. Their eyes didn't leave Esti as Lucia turned off the TV and dragged two hard-backed chairs in from the kitchen.

"Esti," she said. "You sit here."

Esti wondered if anyone could hear her heart pounding over the thundering rain on the roof. She sat on the edge of one chair, acutely aware of the jumbee masks and tribal statues glaring at her from all sides of the room. Gathering all her courage, she finally looked at Ma Harris.

"I want to talk about Alan."

Ma Harris narrowed her eyes.

"Do you know who he really is?"

Ma Harris didn't answer. Lucia perched rigidly on the edge of the other kitchen chair, glancing from her mother to Esti. Quintin alone seemed relaxed, staring at Esti with open curiosity.

Esti tried again. "I think you help him somehow. I hoped you might know his real name."

As the silence got thicker, Esti finally gave Lucia a pleading look.

"Why you want to know?" Lucia asked, although her expression seemed sympathetic. "You cause many problem."

"I know," Esti whispered, defeated. "But—"

"Too many problem," Ma Harris muttered.

Esti didn't have the energy to defend herself. "Never mind. I'm sorry."

No one stopped her as she walked back to the door and slipped her coat and shoes on. She was dragging herself up Bayrum Hill half an hour later when an unfamiliar voice behind her made her jump.

"Hey, Esti!"

She swung around to see Quintin vigorously splashing through puddles, his dreadlocks trailing behind him as he ran.

"Lucia she want me tell you someting," he panted, coming to a stop. "Her ma she got de vex from being fired an' ting. She upset what de jumbee did. She fear you, an' you fear she, an' Lucia fear she, an' everyone fear de jumbee." He gave her a quick grin. "I ain't fear nobody."

Esti stared at him. She had never heard Quintin speak a word before.

"I help Lucia curse Frederick," he said, "but she say I first show you dis. Her ma keep it secret forever, but Lucia have find it. She say 'tis an omen."

He opened an umbrella, then handed Esti a scrap of paper. Holding the umbrella closely over their heads, he waited for her to read. It was an old newspaper article, faded and yellow.

Hurricane Death Toll Rises.

Esti frowned and glanced through the article. Partway through the list of casualties, two sentences had been underlined. A baby, discovered by two local teenagers on a beach beside his parents' grounded sailboat, suffered dehydration and severe manchineel burns over most of his body. Authorities say his parents were killed in the storm.

She read the words again. Alan had told her he was found as a baby in the wreckage of his parents' sailboat. When he said he'd paid his dues long ago to his lady cay, did he mean manchineel burns? Ma Harris had kept the article for twenty-five years, according to the date at the top.

"Twenty-five years," Esti whispered.

Quintin peeled the article from her numb fingers. "I gotta take it back to Lucia before her ma she miss it."

"Quintin?"

He paused.

"Lucia must be furious," Esti whispered. "Why do you guys keep helping me?"

"Lucia she got de gift. She maybe learn a lot from Esti Legard." Quintin carefully tucked the article into his pocket, then grinned again. "For true."

Snapping the umbrella shut, he jogged back down the hill, his dreadlocks flying as his feet sought out the biggest puddles. Esti watched him for a moment through the rain. She started walking again, then came to another abrupt stop.

The article hadn't mentioned any names.

"Queen's Manor Preparatory School."

Esti rubbed her forehead, trying to push the headache away. She'd been making phone calls to England since she got home from Lucia's house. Aurora wasn't going to like the phone bill.

"I'm looking for information about one of your former teachers," she said. "It would have been about ten years ago."

"I'm terribly sorry, madam. Queen's Manor didn't exist ten years ago. We are a fairly new school, specializing in—"

"That's okay. Thank you for your time."

Esti glanced at the clock, hoping she would be done before Aurora got home. Queen's Manor must have been one of the last schools her dad worked at. It frustrated her not to know more about her dad's time at his boarding schools, but somehow that knowledge had been lost along with everything else Esti shoved away.

Resolutely moving to the next school she'd found in her mom's address book, Esti dialed the number.

"Boothsby Hall." A clipped voice came through the phone so strongly, she winced.

"Yes," she began. "Can you tell me when Boothsby Hall first opened?"

"Founded in fifteen hundred and fifty-one," the voice said proudly, "by Sir Alexander Boothsby under Letters Patent of King Edward the Sixth."

"I'm looking for information on one of your faculty members from about ten years ago."

"Hmm. Hold one moment, if you might."

After a long pause, an elderly man came on the line. "Edward Thornton here. How may I help you?"

"Please," Esti said. "I need to find out about a man who may have taught about ten years ago. He was my father."

"I've been here for over fifty years." Mr. Thornton's voice quavered with amusement. "What is your father's name, my dear? I would have known him if he taught here."

"Alan Legard. He was a theater teacher from the United States who—"

"Of course I remember Mr. Legard. He worked with the Royal Shakespeare Company now and again. He has always been quite famous in America, I understand. You're his daughter?"

"Yes." Esti took a deep, shuddering breath and leaned her elbows on the table. "He died last year, and I've been trying to find out—"

"I heard about that. I'm so sorry, my dear."

"Thank you. I've been trying to find out—"

"What did you say your name was?"

"Serene Terra Legard." She closed her eyes, concentrating on keeping her breathing under control. "I need to find out about one of his students while he was there."

She hoped Aurora wouldn't walk in and catch her in the middle of another lie. "Before he died," she said, "my father told me about an unusual student of his who was very good at Shakespeare. The boy had a terrible skin problem."

"Ah yes, the skin problem," Mr. Thornton said. He no

longer sounded amused. "I've never forgotten that one."

"Could you tell me about him?" Esti said tightly, trying to keep her voice professional. "I'm researching my dad's past for a—for a school project I'm working on. This boy had a pretty strong influence on my father."

"Did he, indeed? A good influence, I hope."

Esti swallowed. "Yes."

"Well, I'm glad to hear it," Mr. Thornton said. "Who would have ever thought? As I recall, the boy had a ghastly case of inherited ichthyosis. Mendicosta disease, or some such. He always denied it, declaring that a madwoman had burned him with acid. He was one of the most delusional children I ever encountered. He insisted he was the great-great-grandson of Shakespeare's Hamlet." Mr. Thornton sighed sadly. "I believe the other boys called him Caliban. Fishface, you know, from *The Tempest*."

Esti felt like Mr. Thornton had punched her in the stomach.

"I did try to pity the child, since the others picked on him so. He spent most of his time acting out his Shakespearean fantasies, or else fighting. We eventually had to keep him in solitary confinement for his own protection. Since his uncle made large donations to the school during the years he was with us, the trustees wouldn't let us expel him. Of course, I shouldn't be telling you all this." Mr. Thornton sounded chagrined. "Mr. Legard certainly had a way of calming him. He was fascinated by the boy in every regard: his origins on a tropical island, his intelligence, his obsession with Shakespeare. He tutored the boy privately."

"Can you tell me his name?" Esti whispered.

"I beg your pardon?"

"The boy's name," she said more loudly.

"Oh, dear." Mr. Thornton hesitated. "If you don't already know his name, I don't think I should divulge that information." The elderly voice quavered. "I've said far too much already, with all these new rules about privacy. It's just that I made such an effort to put the boy out of my mind when he left. Are you telling me you don't even know his name?"

"His first name was Alan."

"Well . . ." Mr. Thornton hesitated again. "He insisted we call him Alan after he met your father. He told us his name meant Alan in Danish, but I doubt that was true. It wasn't his real name, at any rate."

Esti closed her eyes. "Not his real name."

"Beg pardon?" A touch of impatience now colored Mr. Thornton's voice.

"Elon," Esti forced out. "His real name was Elon Somand."

"Of course." Mr. Thornton sounded relieved. "You do know, then. Thank the Lord his accursed disease was hereditary, and not contagious. Elon was a clever boy, beneath his unfortunate exterior. Your father certainly had more patience with him than the rest of us did, even helping the poor boy after he dropped out of school. From what I remember, I believe it was your father who took him back home."

As Esti reached the soggy campus, she felt her footsteps slowing. She was late once again, and Frederick wasn't going to be happy. She couldn't blame him, of course. Last night he had chewed her out in front of the cast, Officer Wilmuth glaring at her throughout his lecture. The jandam hadn't left her side all evening, except when she was on the stage. The rest of the cast thought she was a total freak by now. Worst of all, she hated what this must be doing to Alan.

Staring at the theater building, she cringed at the sight of the policemen waiting for her in their cars. She slowly pulled the necklace from the pocket of her raincoat. As she fastened it around her neck, however, she saw Quintin running toward her in the rain, his eyes wide.

"Come," he called.

"What's the matter?"

"Gotta stop you jumbee, quick-quick."

She looked at him in alarm. "What's he doing?"

"Danielle she make fun of you."

"Danielle always makes fun of me."

"De curse have backfire. You jumbee he rage at she. You's de only one can stop de jumbee. Come quick!"

Esti ran across the courtyard behind him. From the corner of her eye, she could see policemen jumping out of their cars in concern. In front of her, Quintin yanked at the doors, almost falling backward when they didn't open.

"He lock de door dem," he cried. "Dey all trap inside!"

Esti fumbled for the key that Alan had given her after

Christmas. As she flung open the door, she heard a loud crash. Frederick and the others lunged back from the stage as a newly painted plywood set landed on the stage between Danielle and Greg. The theater was dark except for a brilliant spotlight aimed at Danielle.

"Stop!" Danielle pressed her fingers to her ears, wildly looking around. "Stop saying that."

"Stop," Esti echoed in disbelief.

Danielle began to move, but another set toppled in front of her. Greg flung himself forward to catch it, and Danielle sank to the floor. "Leave me alone," she whimpered, curling up with her hands over her head.

The only reply was the sharp crack of splintering wood. The little wooden table flew across the stage, missing Greg and Danielle by inches before coming to a crash against the painted plywood orchard. As another set began to wobble, Esti stumbled through the door.

"Leave her alone," she cried out, her voice thick with fear. "How dare you!"

Her cry echoed through the theater, followed by deathly silence. All eyes watched Esti lunge into the room, her wet raincoat plastered to her legs. The theater seats disappeared as she ran through her nightmare. Panic crawled throughout her body, her legs working harder and harder as they barely moved her toward the stage.

Instead of her pounding footsteps, she heard only breathing from the floors and walls of the silent room. No one moved, frozen in another twisted frame of the horror movie that had become Esti's reality. When she finally reached the stage, after a lifetime of running through Alan's tortured breathing, she almost threw up.

Gulping for air, she took the steps two at a time and flung herself at Danielle in center stage. "Are you okay?" She put a shaking hand on Danielle's arm, desperately willing her churning stomach to calm down.

Danielle shivered, nodding as Greg pulled her close to him.

Esti rose to her feet again, her emotions twisting with terror and rage as she saw a furtive movement in the darkness of the wings. Alan was lurking back there, invisible in his black clothes as he vented his hopeless rage against Danielle.

She could hear Officer Wilmuth charging up the aisle, barking orders to the cops behind him. Despite her fury, Esti found herself flinging up her hand to stop them. To her surprise, they skidded to a halt, their eyes wide with suspicion and fear.

Caliban, Edward Thornton had called him. *Fishface.* Kept in solitary confinement so the other boys wouldn't beat him up. Alone.

Esti studied the jandam for a moment, then shook her head. "Only a coward enjoys other people's fear," she forced into the silence, knowing that Alan listened, "and it isn't hard to despise cowardice." She wrapped shaking fingers over her necklace. From the edge of her eye she caught sight of the narrow catwalk above, and an unbidden image of Paul Wilmuth came into her mind.

Paul had been making fun of her before he died. She had whispered that she wanted him to fall. Oh, God.

Her throat tightened in a convulsive swallow. Alan hadn't actually hurt Danielle. She couldn't accuse him of murdering Paul in front of the entire cast. She might be wrong.

"This will not happen again," she said, her voice sounding husky and strange. "No more temper tantrums. No guilt trips or manipulation. If you want me to finish the play, you must stop."

She twined her fingers into his necklace. "Leave everyone alone. Please leave me . . . alone."

"Yes." The cracked whisper barely brushed her ears, then was gone.

She looked out at Officer Wilmuth. "The jumbee is gone," she forced out. "He won't bother us anymore."

He stared speechlessly at her, his dark face as rigid as stone.

She gestured the jandam forward. "Do whatever you need to," she muttered. *You won't find him. Please don't find him.*

As they fearfully made their way up to the stage, she turned to Frederick. His eyes were huge beneath a jaunty black beret.

"Can you get Ma Harris her job back?" she asked woodenly. "I need her help."

The beret bobbed in a quick, jerky nod.

"She's innocent," Esti added.

"Of course, of course." Despite the terror on his face, he nodded even more vigorously. Esti knew he would be able to talk Mr. Fleming into it.

"Quintin," she said. "Do you think Lucia will come back?"

"I tell she," Quintin said calmly. "She come back."

"Danielle, I'm sorry." Esti's shaky legs finally gave out, and she sank down on the stage beside Danielle. "I'm so sorry."

Two drama queens, she thought, both reduced to a quivering mess by the jumbee of Manchicay. For once, Danielle's blue eyes held no hostility as she looked at Esti. Everyone else just stared in shock; even Carmen huddled fearfully into her seat.

"I'm finished with today's drama queen scene." Esti couldn't meet Carmen's eyes. "If we work all night, we should be able to fix the sets in time for tomorrow. I'm ready to get this showcase over with."

"Of course, darling," Frederick said weakly. He glanced nervously around the theater, then sighed and covered his eyes with pale, expressive hands. "I was about to say the same thing."

Act Three. Scene Five.

It was two in the morning when cell phones started ringing again. Esti barely heard Rodney's phone over the pounding of hammers on plywood. Dazed with exhaustion and paint fumes, Esti leaned against Rafe for a minute. Aurora wearily chatted with other parents in the rows of seats, her tense eyes never leaving Esti for more than a minute or two. Everyone was doing what they could to fix the damage, while a dozen jandam patrolled the theater. The sets were almost repaired.

Nearly every parent had shown up last night, after Esti suggested that Rodney call them all. If anyone could keep people from panicking right now, Rodney Solomon could do it.

She had made a point of deliberately tucking the necklace beneath her T-shirt while she hoped Alan watched. She couldn't let Rafe know she wore it, but Alan needed to see that she hadn't taken it off. The policemen were pointless, though, and the absurdity of the situation didn't help her headache.

"What do you mean, a hurricane?" Rodney's voice rose into a brief lull between hammering.

"Hurricane Alpha," he said a few minutes later. The activity fell silent while everyone listened to him. "My wife said they're calling it *Hurricane Impossible* on the weather station. It's tripled in size since yesterday, and is headed toward Cariba."

"When does it hit land?" Officer Wilmuth demanded.

"If it stays on this course, landfall tonight. Worst case, sometime around sunset."

"That *is* impossible." Frederick anxiously tapped his foot. "Hurricane season is long over."

"Except this year," Rafe said in amusement. "Ocean's too warm, atmosphere too unsettled."

"Too many jumbees around," Carmen added, staring coolly at Esti. "They should call it Hurricane Elon."

Esti forced a smile. She knew Carmen was still mad at her, but she didn't know what to say. She deserved Carmen's anger. She deserved everyone's anger.

"We got sixteen hours before it hit," Officer Wilmuth said flatly. "The play is now cancel. Everyone go home, be safe from the storm."

"Absolutely not!" Frederick folded his arms across his chest. "I have too many friends who rearranged their busy schedules for this showcase. They don't have the time for a tempest. The show will go on."

"Don't need no backchat from you, Mr. McKenzie," Officer Wilmuth said. "'Tis God's will, no matter if you, and you Yankee friends, don't understand the danger."

"Lester, I have live here long as you." Rodney's voice rose over Officer Wilmuth, his accent thick for once as he argued with the jandam. "De theater it have de best shelter on Cariba, have stood hurricane dem for two hundred fifty year, so don't you go tell me we ain't safe here." He paused. "Long as you ain't afraid of jumbee dem."

Rafe grinned at his dad, then pulled Esti close to him. "Check this out," he whispered, pointing at the ceiling. "I just noticed that round black thing up there."

When she looked at the catwalk, he gently nudged her chin farther to the right. She tried to ignore the growing arguments around them, swirling like mini hurricanes across the stage.

"Looks like a satellite dish," Rafe muttered into her ear, "painted black to blend into the ceiling."

She squinted at the black ceiling, gradually making out a matte black circle among the black-painted pipes and wires and framing.

"It's a parabolic reflector. We used those things in science class to make reflecting telescopes, parabolic microphones, car headlights, and . . ." Rafe paused with a grin. "Focusing a voice onto a precise location. Your jumbee's pretty smart. He probably even controls the direction, aiming his voice anywhere onstage he wants to."

Esti studied the thing in weary astonishment. Of course Alan would be capable of that.

"Yeah, mon, the building is safe," Officer Wilmuth continued, "but—"

"Once it hit," Rodney interrupted, "God Almighty know when de island does recover. You know how long it had take last time, Lester. Me and Frederick we got a lot does ride on this, mon."

"I'm going up there right now to destroy that thing," Rafe whispered. "If it *is* his, I ain't about to let him use it on you again. I bet there's speakers somewhere up there, too."

Esti slowly nodded.

"Frederick have one show dis afternoon," Rodney said. "We show off Esti Legard, and we all home safe before it hit. If it catch we early, we throw a big fête until it pass by. I bring party food and rum to stash under de desk."

"I have a suggestion." Everyone fell silent at Esti's unexpected interruption.

Danielle had slumped against a plywood tree when Rodney said Esti's name, and Esti couldn't stand it. It was all so wrong.

"We're *all* counting on this," Esti said tiredly, ignoring Rafe as he made his way to the catwalk's ladder. "We need two shows, just like we always planned. One this morning, and one this afternoon."

"Excuse me, miss?" Officer Wilmuth glowered at her.

"Two shows." Esti glanced at Frederick. "If Danielle doesn't get a chance to prove herself in front of your friends, I won't do it either."

"Yes, my darling. Of course." Frederick clasped his hands together, his eyes shiny with stress and exhaustion. "Two shows it is."

At Danielle's stunned look, Esti could only shrug. "Would you rather go first, or second?" she asked.

Danielle just stared at her. "Why?" she finally said.

"Because." Esti shook her head, then glanced at Carmen. "It's not all about my name."

Carmen gave her a half smile. "Go, Jane Doe, go."

"You're brave," Esti added sincerely to Danielle. "And you're a good actress."

To her surprise, Danielle shuddered. "I'm sorry," she said. "I didn't . . ." After a moment, she straightened and shook out her blond hair. "You're an impossible act to follow. I'd better go first."

"Brilliant," Frederick said briskly. "It's settled, then. The sets are good enough. You all go home and get five hours of beauty sleep. Everyone back here at eight o'clock sharp. First performance starts at ten. I'll get the word around."

"Wait jus' a minute," Officer Wilmuth snapped. "Hurricane does take preparation, and the kids need to help they family board up they house and—"

"No problem, mon," Rodney said smoothly. "I think of no better job for de jandam dis morning."

Officer Wilmuth slowly shook his head as he studied his friend. "You gon owe me big-time after this one."

❧

When the flawless first performance came to an end, Esti was impressed. For the first time, Danielle had allowed Greg's Romeo to mold Juliet in subtle ways that made them both shine. Even if Esti matched her own Christmas performance, which was unlikely, she knew a couple of Broadway producers who wouldn't easily forget Danielle.

As Frederick's friends sampled rum in the courtyard during lunch, Rafe snuck into the dressing room.

"The bigwigs like it," he said, with only a slightly lopsided grin. "My dad says their appetites are whetted."

"Meaning they'll eat Esti for lunch?" Carmen asked.

Rafe laughed. "She always makes *me* hungry."

Esti winced, wondering if Alan was listening. When Rafe leered at her, she whacked him with Juliet's cap, pretending to be more lighthearted than she felt. "What about the hurricane?"

"On course," he said, growing serious. "The rain quit, but the clouds are looking scary." He shrugged. "My dad was

right, though. We're in the safest shelter on Cariba. Standing room only, and it's not just for the show. Word's gotten
around about our hurricane fête."

Pushing back her exhaustion, Esti stared into the mirror.
She just hoped Alan wouldn't be stuck in the theater during
her celebration party, brooding alone in his eternal solitary
confinement

❧

"If I profane with my unworthiest hand this holy shrine, the
gentle sin is this: My lips, two blushing pilgrims ready stand,
to smooth that rough touch with a tender kiss."

Esti stared at Romeo in wonder as his fingertips lightly
brushed hers. Although his performance with Danielle had
been perfect, Greg spoke even more beautifully now. She felt
the magic growing, as it had during the Christmas shows. Despite herself, her Juliet automatically responded in delight.

"Good pilgrim, you do wrong your hand too much, which
mannerly devotion shows in this." She shyly turned away.
"For saints have hands that pilgrims' hands do touch, and
palm to palm is holy palmers' kiss."

"Have not saints lips, and holy palmers too?" he asked softly.

"Ay, pilgrim." Esti felt her body warming as she looked at
him again. "Lips that they must use in prayer."

"O then, dear saint, let lips do what hands do."

The warmth in her body grew stronger, and she smiled in
astonishment. Greg was beautifully controlling her mood,
drawing her along with him.

He leaned forward, blue eyes gentle with love behind the

masquerade disguise. "They pray, grant thou, lest faith turn to despair."

"Saints do not move, though grant . . ." Esti trailed off as her eyes flicked down to his gloved fingers, then back up again. Romeo's mask was different this time, subtly covering his entire face. And Greg's eyes weren't blue.

She stepped back. The audience waited in silent anticipation, but the eyes had become wary. Alan knew she had recognized him. The show had to go on, she thought desperately. They were counting on Esti Legard to bring magic to the stage. *You're in control, Esti.*

". . . though grant for prayer's sake," she whispered. Her throat closed around the words.

"Then move not," Alan murmured, "while my prayer's effect I take."

His voice twined around her like the web of an exquisite spider, trapping her with a longing that wasn't his alone. Juliet wanted to kiss Romeo, no matter who he was, how he looked, what his name might be. She had so often dreamed of playing Juliet to Alan's Romeo. She couldn't stop him now; she didn't want to stop him.

As he stepped forward, she licked her dry lips, trying not to panic. How would he kiss her through the mask? What would he do when this scene was over?

She heard an uncomfortable cough from Frederick.

Alan couldn't play Romeo without a mask. Greg would have to do it, but . . . Reality slammed down on Esti, crushing the breath out of her.

"Where is Greg?" she whispered.

Alan backed away from her now, and Esti heard cast members stirring restlessly in the wings. No, she thought numbly, gasping for breath. She had dreamed of playing Juliet to Alan, but not like this.

"What did you do to Greg?" Her voice rose.

"Madam!" Carmen ran out onstage, trying to save the scene. "Your mother craves a word with you." She took Esti's arm.

"Did you kill him too?" Hot fear blazed through Esti as Alan spun away from her. She wrenched her arm free from Carmen, reaching out to grab him. He ducked, and her hand swept across his head. With a crash of plastic hitting the floor beside a rustling wig, Romeo was unmasked. Alan froze, fear and disbelief on his hideous face.

"The jumbee." Rafe's stunned voice rang across the silent stage.

Alan moved before anyone else could react. Grabbing Esti's arm, he yanked her behind him into the wings. She was too shocked to struggle.

Aurora's scream and Rafe's enraged shout were instantly followed by Danielle's shriek from the audience. "The jumbee killed Greg?"

Alan dragged Esti to the electrical box on the wall. With a vicious swipe, he flipped the main breaker. The theater plunged into darkness. More screams rang in the air as he pulled Esti behind him again.

"Let go of me," she cried. "Let me *go!*" She tried to pull free, but Alan's strong fingers tightened on her wrist. She heard a door click shut, then she swung around to look behind her at diffuse light coming through a grille-covered vent. Alan had brought her into a new passageway, one she'd never seen before.

Small video screens surrounded her, detailing every aspect of the theater. In one screen, Esti saw people running up onto the stage. A terrified jolt rocked her as she saw Greg, crumpled lifelessly on the floor in another. A familiar shape raced through a third screen, briefly darkening the vent opening beside her.

"Rafe!"

As Rafe spun around, trying to find her voice, Esti felt a gloved hand clamp across her mouth.

"If he finds us," Alan murmured, his breath tickling her ear, "I will do whatever it takes to stop him."

Icy fear swept through her, starting at her scalp and crawling down her spine. Alan let go of her, stripping off the masquerade costume that covered his black clothes. As he grabbed her wrist again, she looked back at the stage. Several police officers had their guns drawn, sharply ordering people off the stage. Someone called out in horror as they discovered Greg. Aurora's voice cried Esti's name.

Esti opened her mouth, then closed it again, light-headed. She was no longer Juliet, so what was the reality of Esti? If Alan was kidnapping her, her life had become a nightmare straight out of Leroux. But she would never brutally expose Alan to the world with a cruel sweep of her hand. He would never threaten her. George couldn't be brandishing a gun on Manchicay's crowded stage. Greg wasn't really dead.

None of this was happening.

Rafe yelled in vain for everyone in the noisy theater to shut up so he could hear. Then Alan dragged Esti around a corner, and they all disappeared.

"Please," Esti gasped, "you don't have to do this."

"You've no idea what I have to do," he snapped.

The light disappeared behind them as they reached the back stairway, but Esti needed no light for the familiar steep steps. Alan dragged her across the musty basement, then shoved open the tiny back door and drew her outside.

The sullen afternoon light shocked her. Although it no longer rained, warm air draped across her skin, silent and muggy. Holding her wrist in a steely grip, Alan locked the door with his other hand, then turned and pulled her down the narrow trail behind him.

"Alan, wait." As she twisted her arm in an attempt to free herself, she tripped over her gown. Without slowing, he yanked her back to her feet. Still stumbling, she frenziedly gathered red velvet up into her free hand. "Where are you taking me?"

He ignored her, but Esti knew it was a pointless question. They were going to the cay. No one could follow them there, not even Rafe. Especially not with the hurricane coming.

"How could you—"Her voice broke in fear. "How could you kill Greg?"

Alan spun around so fast she ran into him, his awful face

inches from hers. She stiffened at the sight of his scaly, tortured skin in full daylight.

"I did not kill Greg." He immediately turned around again, pulling her forward with wiry strength.

"Please." She couldn't let her terror overwhelm her. "You've sworn you won't hurt me. Will you be forsworn?"

"So will I never be." She heard his muttered words, but he didn't slow down, nor did his grip lessen on her wrist.

"Is this how you repay my dad's compassion, then?" Her voice sounded shrill and unfamiliar to her.

"Compassion!" Alan tossed the word over his shoulder. "Yes, Legard showed me compassion. I don't doubt that he respected me. He acknowledged the mind and feelings behind my face when no one else would. Did you know that I was the one who convinced him that darkness was the best way to control his voice? I told him that practicing in the dark would keep his acting honest."

Esti gasped as Alan continued, his voice bitter.

"He told me to get involved with the theater department at Manchicay School, but again, the actor was stronger than the friend. He didn't wish for you to come here." Alan dragged in a deep, painful breath. "The thought of *you* becoming friends with me frightened him. His compassion was limited, Esti."

She stumbled again, and again he smoothly kept her from falling. She knew her dad had told Rodney that Manchicay School wasn't the best place for her, but she had never dreamed the true reason.

Alan barely seemed to notice her frantic struggles as he

pulled her into the water, plunging through a swampy thicket of red mangroves. The sea was very different now. Rhythmic swells brought the water from Esti's knees to her shoulders, Juliet's gown floating absurdly around her.

Her fingers involuntarily tightened on Alan's hand as she saw the tiny boat in front of them. He waited until the swell subsided, then turned and lifted her, depositing her in the boat. As the water began rising again, he grabbed the branches of a mangrove tree and swung himself in after her.

"Alan," she tried one last, desperate time. "Please let me go."

"The sea is rough with the approaching storm," he replied flatly. He sat down, then planted his feet wide in the boat and picked up the oars. "When we emerge from the mangle, I recommend you stay as low as you can."

The sea wasn't rough, it was terrifying.

The boat dipped and swayed in a macabre drunken dance as Alan pulled on the oars. They rode to the top of each ten-foot swell, hovering at the crest before plunging into the troughs between. Esti clung to the bottom, cringing with each new wave.

Alan watched without expression as Cariba Island retreated behind them. He automatically shifted his weight with the motion of the boat, but Esti saw the tightness in his scaly jaw as they approached Manchineel Cay. Huge waves crashed against the northern cliff, jets of seawater spraying them as they drew near.

Esti didn't know how they could possibly maneuver

through the crashing water into the cave, but Alan didn't hesitate. He glanced over his shoulder, timing the waves and using the oars to keep them moving. A swell caught them, and he pulled with all his might. Esti swallowed a scream as they hurtled toward the face of the cliff. As the wave washed under and past them, the boat fell into the deep trough just in time for Alan to turn them around and slide between the narrow slot in the rocks.

The cave echoed with familiar deep booms that shook Esti's bones. In the dim light, she saw a rocky ledge in front of them. The sea rose again as they reached the ledge. Alan leaped from the boat and pulled it over the lip of rock, then dragged it as far as he could until the water began subsiding.

"Get out," he ordered. "Quickly."

Her heart in her throat, Esti scrambled out, gathering her skirt into her arms and running several feet up the path. The tunnel quickly narrowed, becoming pitch dark. Although she listened for the eerie wailing, the cave ahead was quiet this time except for the gathering wind. She sagged against the wall, waiting for Alan to lead the way. Whether she liked it or not, her life was in his hands.

Act Three. Scene Six.

By the time they reached the forest trail, Esti's fear had turned into anger. She'd wrenched her hand from Alan's the minute they left the darkness of the cave. He didn't protest. Grimly following him along the path as the clouds grew darker overhead, she shivered as a breeze gusted through her drenched gown.

She came to a determined stop just inside the house. Alan bolted the door without a word, then turned on a light and disappeared down the steps to his bedroom. Esti stood rigidly against the door, studying his living room with narrowed eyes. His beautiful, organic house had become a prison. Waterproof plastic containers stood in stacks before empty bookshelves and the bare rock wall; the enormous wooden doors to the porch were barred shut.

When Alan reappeared several minutes later, he wore dry clothes and carried a large cardboard box. He hadn't bothered with a mask. He gave Esti a grim look as he crossed the room to drop the box beside her. Her last name and Manchicay's address were written in large letters on the top, next to an airline tag.

"You may find some clothes in here," Alan said. "I haven't gone through it, so I'm not sure what it contains."

"You're lying." Esti clenched her fists. "You found my dad's book in there."

"I have never lied to you," he said coldly. "The book was on top. When Ma Harris delivered the box last summer, neither of us knew you had arrived on Cariba. I had received many packages from Legard, and in my wildest dreams, I never guessed you would come here. Ma Harris assumed the box was for me when her brother brought it home from the airport."

Of course. Domino worked in the freight area of the airport.

"Legard's death was a devastating blow. I couldn't bring myself to open the box until after I met you, and I immediately closed it when I realized it was yours. But . . ."

He turned away. "By then I couldn't bear to part with it. I thought it might be the only piece of you I would ever have."

He climbed the steps to the kitchen, leaving Esti alone with her box. She had forgotten what she packed, but she finally found a pair of old shorts and a T-shirt. Alan remained silent above her as she tucked everything else back into the box and trudged down to the bathroom cave.

She took her time, dumping her Juliet costume in a soggy pile on the stone floor. Faint pounding from the distant sea cave echoed in the quiet room as she changed into dry clothes. She ignored the bone-deep sounds, concentrating on scrubbing her face with soap and water until she felt no more traces of greasy makeup.

Removing Juliet's cap, she untangled her hair as well as she could with her fingers, then resolutely made her way back up to the living room. As she climbed the stairs, she smelled rain against the stone walls of the house. The storm had grown outside, gusting now against the big porch doors and the high shuttered window in the kitchen. Rafe had told her a hurricane could whip up hundred-mile-an-hour winds within a few minutes when the storm finally hit.

Alan leaned against the wall of boulders, watching her and waiting. She studied his terrible face for a long time before she finally spoke.

"So," she said. "You've given me back my belongings. Does this mean you no longer need just a piece of me, since you've stolen all of me?"

He cringed and closed his eyes.

"Are you going to kill me now?" Her breathing sped up as she finally voiced her fear. "You killed Paul, didn't you?"

Alan flinched, but he didn't deny it.

"Did his death make your unhappy life better? Or Greg? What about Mr. Niles! Tell me, Alan," she said in a shaky voice, "did you do something to make Danielle sick before the Christmas show? What about Steve's locker?"

He still didn't reply.

"Don't you realize how much you hurt me," she whispered, "how much you terrify me, when you hurt other people?"

He opened his eyes again, staring at her with an expression she couldn't read.

She forced her breathing back under control. "I don't

understand why you brought me here," she said. "Tell me what our story will be. Are we finished with Shakespeare?"

She took a step toward him as wind rattled the shutters. "Maybe you were hoping for a fairy tale. Beauty, trapped by the Beast with no hope of escape. But you've shown me how to sneak past your cay's vicious traps, and Rafe taught me how to swim. You can't hold me here forever. I truly believed you were honorable, but what I see is a coward."

"A coward!" he finally snapped. "Yes, perhaps I am a coward."

Esti stumbled back in fear as he shoved himself away from the wall, breathing hard.

"You were right, it's not difficult to despise cowardice." His voice rang flat over the storm. "So teach me, dear creature, how to think and speak. Tell me what I'm to do when people shrink from me in loathing. Teach me how I'm supposed to feel, when the only gift I have to offer is fear. No one will touch me, not even Legard, who gave me so much."

His breathing filled the room, harsh and painful. "Only you, Esti, ever sought out my company for no other reason than to be with me. You're the only one who has ever held my hand. Shall I tell you how Niles hid backstage in the dark, trying to catch me by surprise? I was scattering frangipani blossoms for you to find onstage, when he turned on the lights from the wings. Every light in the house, to keep me from hiding in the darkness. I merely looked at him. I didn't even move before he fled across the stage and broke his own leg."

Esti slowly nodded.

"Steve brought about his own end. Perhaps I hastened it into the light with an anonymous note to the headmaster, but I did nothing wrong. I took thorough steps to ensure that Danielle's discomfort would be far less than the suffering she caused you over the semester. And then there's Paul Wilmuth." Alan slowly approached her. "Shall I tell you how I killed Paul Wilmuth?"

She couldn't even swallow, her throat paralyzed with fear.

"I saw you practicing that morning. Your first day at Manchicay School. An unexpected miracle from the only man I ever respected; the fulfillment of a dream I didn't even know I had. For twenty minutes I watched you play Juliet to my empty theater, and I fell in love. And then Paul interrupted you."

The blue eyes had pinned her, and she couldn't look away.

"When you left the stage, I came out of hiding and stared at him as he crawled up to the catwalk. I couldn't comprehend why he would stop you, how he could laugh at you. I *looked* at him, Esti. And when he saw me looking at him, the sight sent him plunging from the catwalk in fear. That's how I killed him."

Alan took a deep, controlled breath. "Even you, my beloved Esti, screamed when you saw my face. So please tell me how to enjoy other people's happiness, when all I am allowed to give is terror."

Esti couldn't talk. She felt like he'd punched her in the stomach, like she felt when Mr. Thornton called him

Fishface on the telephone. For a moment only the howling wind laughed at Alan's words, then she heard a sound at the front door.

"Esti, you in there?"

"Rafe!"

Alan grabbed her arm as she lunged toward the door. "My lady allowed him here?" he said in disbelief.

The pounding changed over the wind. Rafe must have heard her, and he threw his body against the bolted door in an attempt to break it down. Alan's fingers tightened as Esti struggled to pull away.

"Let him in," she cried. "The storm will kill him."

"So it will." Alan's eyes became expressionless again. "She protects me after all. He won't find his way back to the caves now. The hurricane is on us."

"You can't leave him out there." Esti was horrified.

"If he's foolish enough to challenge my lady, he deserves his fate."

"He's here to save me."

"Rafe Solomon is not my responsibility," Alan said quietly, "even if he finds it necessary to save you from me."

Esti glared at him. "If he dies, I'll never forgive you. Never."

He was still gripping her arm, and as the roar of the wind rose to a new pitch, she grabbed his free hand.

"Open the door," she begged. "Whatever you want from me, I'll give it to you."

For a moment Alan didn't answer.

"Please!"

He clenched his jaw. "Marry me."

She felt her heart stop. His obsession shouldn't have surprised her by now, yet the shock reached all the way through her core.

Marry you?

She looked at his face. Surely she would get used to the sight of him; she would someday be able to look at him without flinching. She had sworn his appearance didn't matter to her; she'd dreamed of kissing him, before she pulled off his mask. Now his blue eyes dared her to fulfill her rash promises.

The thrashing outside the door had already weakened against the fury of the storm. Esti felt any control she'd ever had over her life yanked away from her and tossed by the catapult into the violent winds. Control meant nothing. She controlled nothing. Life and tragedy were random, their victims chosen on a whim.

Her heart thumped again, slowly and painfully. "Okay," she said. "I will."

Alan didn't hesitate. Pulling away, he strode across the room. He braced himself, holding the door in both hands to unbolt it. Despite his caution, the door ripped away from him, slamming against the wall. Rafe landed on his hands and knees inside the house, his flashlight skittering across the stone floor.

Esti staggered back against the couch from the force of the wind. Alan fought to close the door, and she scrambled forward again to help him. The instant the wind let up, she pushed against the heavy door with all her strength. Alan managed to bolt it again, just as a new gust battered the side of the house with renewed fury.

Esti turned to see Rafe rising to his feet, soaked and exhausted. His filthy clothes trailed leaves and thorny vines. As she took a terrified step toward him, however, Alan stopped her with his hand.

"Don't touch him," he commanded. She shrank back against the door.

"You would dare—" Rafe began furiously.

"You're covered with manchineel."

Esti stared at Rafe with new fear as Alan reached down with gloved fingers to pick up a small oval leaf from the floor, a single pale vein splitting its length in perfect symmetry.

"I see you got lost after you left the caves," he said. "If Esti touches you, the toxic sap will be on her as well. Is that what you want?"

Rafe's face, still swollen from the fight, contorted with anger. "I'll deal with you, then," he said. "You've earned some manchineel sap."

"Perhaps I have." Alan's bitter laugh knifed into Esti. "Believe me, you can do nothing that my lady hasn't accomplished a thousandfold. For Esti's sake, I will spare you the same fate. At the bottom of the stairs"—he pointed—"is a shower. I recommend you wash yourself quickly, before you begin to blister. Esti doesn't need a second monster vying for her attention."

He laughed again at Rafe's expression. "No doubt you didn't envision your heroic rescue ending like this."

Rafe turned to Esti in disbelief, and she met his gaze as steadily as she could.

"Go," she said. "Hurry."

But he didn't move. "Has he hurt you?" he demanded. He glanced at Alan again, his eyes narrowing. "Did he *touch* you?"

"Of course not." The words dropped woodenly from her mouth. If she allowed a single emotion to slip through, she would shatter. "Please wash off the manchineel before it scars you."

Rafe studied Alan's scarred, scaly face. "Your skin disease has nothing to do with manchineel," he finally said. "Esti told me you inherited it." Without waiting for an answer, he turned and walked across the living room. He slammed his fist against the wall as he started down the steps.

Esti forced herself to look at Alan. Part of her wanted to throw herself at his feet in gratitude for saving Rafe and sparing him from the manchineel. Another part wanted to lash out at Alan for trapping her into a promise she couldn't believe she'd made. But she was taken aback by the intense gleam in his eyes.

"Exactly what do you know about my skin disease being inherited?" His voice held a strange note she'd never heard before.

She took a shaky breath. "I think it was made worse by manchineel burns you got as a baby. But you told me you were haunted by your own blood, and Edward Thornton said—"

"Edward Thornton?" His voice became brittle.

The expression in his eyes frightened her and she involuntarily stepped back. "When I called Boothsby Hall—"

"How dare you!" He grabbed her arm, his words wrapping around her like a whip. "You have no right to dig up my past. What else did you find out about me?"

"No, how dare *you*." Esti wrenched away from him, overcome with sudden fury. As she spun back, her arm hit a stack of waterproof boxes. The highest one toppled, Shakespeare posters spilling from the container and crashing against the stone floor. She ignored them, flinging her words at Alan. "You want my future, but you won't even give me your past. You're so wrapped up in your selfish misery, you can't believe anyone might actually care about you."

She took a furious step toward him. "I'll tell you the horrible things I found out about you. I discovered that two local teenagers rescued you when your parents died. Ma Harris, I would guess, and her brother, Domino. Twenty-five years ago she gave you your life. She must know you're not a jumbee, but she lives to protect you. She does everything she can to make sure people stay away from you, everything she can to keep you safe and be your friend."

Alan stared at her in silence.

"I know my dad tutored you," she continued, her rage growing again. "My dad gave you hope, you told me, and friendship." She stabbed her finger at the posters on the floor, and Alan took a step back. "His inscriptions to you are as heartfelt and sincere as anything he ever wrote to me. He respected you, and it's possible he also feared you; I can only guess. But he brought you back here, to your home. He clearly loved you."

Alan shook his head, and Esti moved closer to him.

"I discovered other things," she said. "I know Manchineel Cay marked you as her own when you were a baby. I don't know if she fears you, but if an island is capable of vengeance, then why not fear? Why not love? Your lady cay must love you desperately, Alan. She long ago guaranteed you would come back to live your life with her, alone."

Esti narrowed her eyes. "And I found out one last horrible thing. I realized I'm capable of doing almost anything for you. I've learned to lie and steal and sneak around in the dark, keeping secrets and breaking promises and feeling guilty for everything I do. My love for you has driven me to hurt everyone I know." She ticked them off on her fingers. "Aurora and Rafe. Carmen, Lucia and her mom. Even Rodney and Frederick have suffered because of me. Because of you."

She followed him as he shrank away from her.

"You've destroyed people for me," she continued in a softer voice, "so yes, I am afraid of you. It's not because of your face, Alan. You've caused me pain I could never have imagined. But you've also given me beauty like I never dreamed of, and I would do anything in my power to make your life happy."

She studied the terrible face in front of her. Alan had backed into the wall of boulders, his expression close to panic. This is it, she thought. The most challenging role I'll ever play. Forgive me, Rafe.

"If this were a fairy tale," she said, "and I could turn the jumbee into a handsome prince with a kiss, don't you know I would do it?"

She leaned forward and kissed him, her heart pounding with anger and fear as her lips met his. An unnamed longing swept through her, aching for something that could never be. He didn't respond, still frozen against the wall as she pulled away.

"Unfortunately," she continued, her voice shaking, "it's not that easy. The people you allowed near have all respected you, yet you look for rejection. That's all you want, even from me. Your threats might earn you pity and a desperate promise, but they destroy everything else. I will always be your friend, but I can't heal your misery for you."

The wind roared past the house like a fighter jet close overhead. Alan stared at her with haunted eyes that widened at a sudden violent banging from the kitchen upstairs. He hesitated, his desperation evident. As the banging became more urgent, he turned toward the stairs, swearing bitterly under his breath.

Act Three. Scene Seven.

Esti shoved her dad's Shakespeare posters back in their waterproof box, then raced up the steps behind Alan. One of the big shutters had come loose, banging against the side of the house. As Alan tried to grab it, it ripped free and disappeared into the grasp of the storm. A dishtowel on the table followed, sucked out the window by the careening wind.

Swearing, Alan pushed past Esti and leaped back down the steps. She huddled against the far wall, peering out through the window. The wind shifted for an instant. Rain blasted through the opening almost horizontally, spraying Esti with water and leaves. Her ears popped with the change in pressure. She lunged against the counter, but the wind abruptly turned and pulled the debris back out.

Alan reappeared, carrying a toolbox and a piece of plywood larger than the window. He dropped the toolbox on the floor and yanked out a hammer. With a grimace, he lifted the plywood to cover the opening, wincing as it pinned his gloved fingers against the frame with the suction of the wind. Esti reached up to hold the wood in place for him, and he glanced at her, startled. He obviously hadn't expected help. They both staggered back as the wind changed again for an instant, then Esti braced herself against the table.

Alan began nailing the plywood to the window frame as quickly as he could. Another gust of wind battered it, and Esti suppressed a shriek as her feet slipped.

The plywood steadied as Rafe appeared beside her, his clothes dripping clean water on the floor. As they forced the wood back against the opening, Alan gave him a blank look. Rafe just glared and Alan started again, moving with desperate efficiency. They didn't relax until the plywood was firmly in place with a dozen nails.

"These nails won't hold for long if the wind—" Rafe began, but Alan was already nodding.

Without a word, he disappeared down the steps.

Rafe finally looked at Esti, and she forced herself to meet his eyes. Before she could protest, his arms were around her. He felt wonderful—so strong and loving and protective— and she nestled hopelessly against him, gasping as he pressed his lips to her tangled hair. By the time the hurricane passed, either her betrayal of Alan would be complete, or Rafe would discover she'd promised . . .

She couldn't let herself think about it.

"Are you okay?" He spoke into her ear.

She nodded, holding her breath. "What happened to Greg?"

"He woke up with a headache. Your jumbee was a lot nicer to him than he was to me."

She sagged in relief. "How did you get here?"

"Everyone told me I'd have to wait until after the storm passed. I said to hell with 'em all and swam here with my scuba gear."

"You're crazy," she said, holding him more tightly.

They heard a crash against the stairs. Esti pulled away from Rafe and leaned over the railing to look. Alan had moved one of the empty bookcases to the base of the steps and was starting up, pushing it ahead of him.

"Christ!" Rafe exploded. Esti huddled against the wall as he swept past her, reaching down to grab the upper end. Together he and Alan maneuvered the bookcase into the kitchen loft. Esti tried to stay out of their way as they placed it on its side on the table and pushed it against the plywood window cover.

As soon as it was in place, Alan glanced at Rafe, then silently went back down the stairs. This time Rafe was ready. They wedged the second bookcase solidly between the first one and the refrigerator.

"That will hold." Esti barely heard Alan above the wind. He looked at her, then quickly looked away. "Come downstairs. It's the safest part of the house." He brushed past her, cringing as their arms accidentally touched. Rafe's eyebrows drew together in a frown as he watched Alan start down the steps.

To Esti's surprise, Alan continued down the second staircase as soon as they reached the living room. Esti looked around as she walked into his bedroom. Compared to the chaos upstairs, calm permeated the cave-like room. Irregular rocky walls framed a stone-paved floor. A wooden wardrobe sat in the corner, its doors neatly closed; a tidy cot rested against one wall. The bedside table held piles of books, along with an old-fashioned wind-up clock showing the time to be after seven.

Alan planted himself against the opposite wall, his stance rigid and embarrassed. Rafe remained in the doorway, every bit as uncomfortable as Alan. Esti studied them both, completely at a loss. She didn't know what to say to either of them, and exhaustion began creeping along her skin, reaching through her blood and deep into her bones. The pounding of the sea echoed faintly in the caves and rocks of the cay beneath them.

With a shrug, she leaned on the wall between them, nervously shaking her head as Rafe took a step toward her.

"What? I'm not allowed to touch you in front of him?" He stopped as something else caught his eye. "It's the necklace," he said in shock. "You're wearing his necklace again."

Esti winced. She'd forgotten about the necklace.

Before she could move, Rafe launched himself at Alan. "You put a curse on it, didn't you? You *are* holding her soul with the thing."

"Rafe," she yelled, "stop!"

She heard the thud as they hit the wall.

"Stop it, stop it, stop it!" Flinging herself at them, Esti burrowed between their struggling bodies. "I won't let you fight again," she cried. "This is insane."

Alan seemed stunned by the impact of the stone wall behind him, but Rafe was still moving. Esti saw the flash of a dark fist, and Alan grunted. With the hopeless knowledge of having done all this before, Esti forced herself in the way of Rafe's other fist. Pain exploded in her head.

"Esti!"

She stumbled away and sank to the floor, holding her nose. She could see them pulling back from each other, staring down at her, freezing in horror. She didn't know who had called her name.

Glancing at her bloody nose, Alan took a furious step toward Rafe.

"Fine!" Esti struggled to her feet again. "Go ahead and kill each other. I don't care anymore." She half ran to the bedroom door, sobbing and wiping her nose on her shirt. "I'll be outside with the storm."

"Esti—"

"No—"

"Shut up, both of you." Sniffing blood, she turned around and glared at them from the doorway. "The Three Stooges," she said bitterly. "Let's take turns hurting each other to see who's the best at it. Isn't there anything else around here we can do for fun?"

For a moment no one spoke, and then Alan cleared his throat.

"The necklace," he replied, his voice almost as bitter as hers.

Esti looked at him in confusion, holding the hem of her shirt against her face.

"Huh?" Rafe said.

"Give me the necklace," Alan demanded. He held a gloved hand out toward Esti.

Recoiling at the fierce look in his eyes, she quickly unfastened it.

Although he barely sounded in control, his eyes softened as she looked at him. "Please throw it to me," he said. "If I come over and take it from you, the testosterone level in the room will probably rise."

Rafe gave an involuntary snort.

Esti hesitated, then tossed the little chain toward Alan. It snaked across the room to land, sparkling, in his hand.

"Rafe thinks I hold your soul with this, but he's wrong. You hold my soul with it." Holding the necklace in front of him, Alan began pulling it apart, each tiny piece falling to the floor at his feet. "I release you from a burden you never asked for."

Esti watched in silence, until the chain was nothing but a small pile of golden sparkles.

"All that glitters is not gold," Alan whispered.

His words tugged at her heart. Was he releasing her from her unholy promise?

"That's gotta be Shakespeare," Rafe said. He also sounded subdued. "I don't get this at all. I don't know what I thought I'd find here, but it sure wasn't a hot shower and some home repair, followed by me beating up my girlfriend, and then a bit of Shakespeare."

Esti heard a faint huff from Alan, and she almost smiled.

"I figured you'd be trying to kill her," Rafe said, "or some fate worse than death. But you're acting like the gentleman while I'm the frickin' bad guy. I'm really sorry, Esti."

She gave him a tight smile. "If you and Alan can treat each other with a little respect, I might forgive both of you."

"Respect, huh?" Rafe slowly shook his head, then turned to Alan. "I really don't get any of this. You've been screwing with her head since before Christmas, and all she does is defend you. I don't get how you can beat the crap out of me like you did last week, then save my skin as soon as I get here. I would have killed you twice already since you let me in, but my damsel in distress is busy fixing your broken windows and defending you as stupidly as she defends me. Your whole island is a freak show. I mean—where does your electricity even come from, since you disabled the wind generators? I totally don't get it."

"Wind generators?" Esti said, startled. "What wind generators?"

"The ones I saw on my way in here. I never thought of hiding one in a cave," Rafe said, glaring at Alan, "but it's even more brilliant than the parabolic reflector above the stage. The caves funnel the trade winds, and he convinces people the place is haunted by the noise. Even though he took the blades off for the storm, I've heard lots of 'em in southern California. They sound like they're screaming when they run."

Esti stared at Alan in shock. *My lady protests at the power I take from her,* he'd said about the horrible wailing. Wind power.

"Batteries store the power," Alan replied softly. "Those are also in the cave. Unfortunately they're not large, so I imagine the electricity will be out before midnight."

"That whole cave thing is wild," Rafe said, looking interested despite himself. "Esti told me how you brought her in last time, but if I hadn't had my scuba gear, I never would have made it. I don't know how you work past those rocks, even in calm seas. How did you get in through that storm swell? It couldn't have been in the little rowboat I saw."

Alan's mouth twitched. "I've had some practice."

"You're insane, mon." Rafe shook his head, but Esti heard a note of reluctant admiration in his voice. "I really want to hate you, but you're not what I expected." He glanced at Esti, then shrugged. "Well, you sure got all the wrong people pissed off at you now. You're in big trouble, once the hurricane is over."

Alan was silent for a minute, then he also glanced at Esti. When he spoke again, his voice was subdued. "You're not what I expected either."

Esti rested her head against her knees again, completely exhausted. Rafe and Alan had somehow reached an uneasy truce; she just hoped it would last until the hurricane was over.

It was the calm that woke her up—an absence of wind, and the murmur of soft voices in the room. She lay on her side, the stone paving hard and cold under her. The room thrummed in rhythm with the violent sea pounding deep in the heart of the island. For a moment she didn't open her eyes, pretending it was all a bad dream.

Curling into a ball on the cold floor, she fought an overwhelming longing for her mom. She would give anything right now for Aurora's chirpy voice and the familiar smell of sandalwood. She wondered what Aurora was doing at this very moment. Hopefully not drowning her fears in a bottle of wine. Esti prayed she was at the theater, comforted by George and surrounded by concerned people.

Bracing herself, Esti opened her eyes. A blanket lay over her, another tucked beneath her head. Instead of the light, a hurricane lamp now flickered in the dim room. Rafe sat on the floor beside the door; Alan leaned against the far wall. They both looked tense and tired, despite their conversation, and she glanced at the wind-up clock on the bedside table. Long after midnight.

"You inherited your skin thing from him," Rafe was saying in a tight voice, "but I thought he didn't have any family. He got killed by my ancestors."

"Elon Somand was not killed by your ancestors," Alan retorted. "His slaves did not know how to swim, and they didn't realize he could. He dragged one of his females with him when he escaped to Manchineel Cay, and she eventually bore him a son."

Esti's eyes widened.

"He built the foundations of this house," Alan continued, "subsisting on the land, and happy to hide from a world that hated him."

"I'd hide too," Rafe said, then added suspiciously, "But that doesn't explain *you*."

"I don't owe you an explanation, Rafe Solomon."

"Alan." Esti struggled to sit up. "I want to know about your family."

Alan's expression instantly softened as he looked at her.

"I think you owe it to *me*." She kept her voice steady.

He sighed. "When my family came to claim Manchineel Cay, they did not expect to find Elon here. They took him back to Denmark with them, where he took great pleasure in excluding them from his will. He left the family fortune to his mulatto child of rape. So much for my noble heritage."

Alan chuckled, bitterness deep in the soft sound. "The firstborn son has always inherited the fortune and the family name intact, defying Danish tradition. My father also inherited the family curse, and he rebuilt our ancient home on Manchineel Cay. My ruthless lady seems to have an affinity for the Somands."

He was silent for a moment. "After my parents died, my uncle took me to Denmark for a few years, sucking away what money he could for himself until I was old enough for school. He took great delight in telling me that his brother was able to marry only after finding a woman as ugly as himself. He despised the fact that I was the sole heir to the Somand fortune, and used Boothsby Hall to justify wasting enormous amounts of my inheritance. The moment I was old enough to make my own legal decisions, Legard helped me come back here."

The sadness in Alan's expression was almost too much for Esti to bear.

"Needless to say," he added, "my parents had nothing to do with anyone on Cariba. They found that the jumbee legends served them well, just as I have. It's a compelling argument for people to stay away."

Esti heard a strong, solitary gust of wind upstairs. "Is the hurricane over?" she asked weakly, wishing she knew something profound to say.

Alan's expression was gentle. "The eye is upon us, but the wind is starting again. You slept for several hours."

As Rafe abruptly scrambled to his feet, Esti shook her head in warning. She didn't want to upset their fragile truce.

"What?" Glaring at her, he came to a stop. "I'm getting sick of this."

Esti winced, wishing she hadn't sat up.

"The necklace is gone," Rafe said, "so what else is going on here? You're hiding something from me."

"Nothing is going on." Her voice broke at the thought of her desperate, ridiculous promise.

"You're still a lousy liar." Rafe shoved himself away from the wall, his eyes on Alan. "And you're still scared of him, aren't you? He's got a hold on you, even without the damn necklace."

The wind upstairs was already rising to a distant roar, echoing the growing tension in the room.

"You swore you haven't messed around with him; okay, I can believe that part. You say he's your friend and he'll never hurt you, and I think you actually buy that. But you're wrong, babe, he's got you fooled. You've been hurting because of him since the night I saw you doing Juliet."

Rafe's body was taut, his fists clenched so tightly that his dark knuckles paled. "Has it ever occurred to you that a guy doesn't kidnap a woman with friendship in mind?"

Esti swallowed, trying not to whimper.

"He inherited a lot more from the monster of the islands than bad skin," Rafe continued roughly. "He's not the first in his family to take whatever he wants."

Esti buried her face in her hands, violently shaking her head as Rafe's arms went around her. He just held her more tightly when she tried to pull away. A sound from across the room made her look up. Alan had risen to his feet, his ugly face expressionless as he stared at her. Without a word, he tightened his jaw and strode out the door.

Act Three. Scene Eight.

Esti wasn't sure how long Rafe held her. He didn't ask her to talk, he just sat with his arms around her, gently rocking her. He wrapped a blanket around them both and leaned against the wall, pulling her close to him. They listened to the furious wind and the distant pounding of the sea while he stroked her hair.

Eventually his hand dropped to his side, and Esti knew he had fallen into an unsettled sleep. For a long time she sat without moving, without thinking, without feeling. She was threadbare and wrung-out, like a tired old washcloth. Other than the storm, she hadn't heard any sounds from upstairs, but she knew Alan must be in the living room, silent and alone. With a sigh, she looked at the clock.

Four in the morning. Aurora would be frantic.

Rafe was right about one thing: Alan had a hold on her. It wasn't the promise he had forced from her to save Rafe's life. No matter that she honestly loved Rafe, Alan had trapped her the first time he spoke. She remembered the exact timbre of his unexpected words. The thought of it still brought goose bumps to her arms.

Even now—even after being brought here against her will—Esti trusted Alan not to hurt her. He wouldn't force her to stay, not if she insisted on leaving. For all the pain she'd felt since she met him, she couldn't point to a single instance of deliberate malice against *her*. Although no one else would ever understand, Esti couldn't even blame him for kidnapping her. It was the only possibility she'd left him, if he wanted to talk to her again.

From the very beginning, their relationship had been doomed to a series of terrible misunderstandings. As devastating as the finest Shakespeare tragedy, she thought humorlessly. But Alan's lonely suffering had been much worse than her own, and she felt her heart twist. He wouldn't make her stay, but if she broke her promise, she might destroy him for good.

She rubbed her temples, trying to suppress an urge to go upstairs and talk to him. As she caught sight of the second blanket on the floor, however, the urge grew stronger. She could picture him brooding on the couch, cold and alone, unwilling to come back down and see her in Rafe's arms.

She wondered if she could possibly sneak up the stairs just long enough to give him a blanket, without waking Rafe. Leaning forward, she slowly moved away. Rafe stirred restlessly, but he didn't open his eyes. She finally turned and touched her lips to his forehead. Wrapping the blanket around him again, she grabbed the second blanket from the floor and stood up. Her heart pounded almost as loud as the wind against the shutters upstairs.

By the time she reached the top of the stairs, she was poised to flee back to the safe bedroom. The living room vibrated with the storm's fury, and she couldn't see Alan anywhere. A flickering hurricane lamp lit the room with dim light, reflecting against a pool of water covering the floor. Deeper puddles formed in a few places, reaching back almost to the stairs. The smell of wet stone and damp earth filled the room, and as Esti watched, a noisy gust of wind rattled the big porch doors, threatening to tear the house apart. Rain flooded in through all the cracks, although the doors held tight.

Holding her breath, Esti cautiously made her way around the puddles and glanced up at the kitchen. The bookcases still braced the broken window opening, filling the small kitchen with their bulk. When she turned, she noticed that Alan had wrapped her cardboard box in a tarp to protect it from water.

And she finally saw him. Her pent-up breath burst out in an explosion of relief. Alan lay on the couch, leaning against the armrest with his eyes closed. Clutching the blanket against her chest, she crept closer to study his face. The flickering light of the hurricane lamp smoothed his scaly skin, showing off a strong jaw and proud bearing, even in sleep. If it weren't for the curse of his ancestors, she realized, he might have been attractive.

As she watched, his mouth curved in a wistful smile. His eyes flickered open, then widened as he saw her in front of him.

"I dreamed of waking up to you," he said, "and here you are."

The wonder in his voice broke through the fury of the storm like a ray of sunlight. His eyes remained guarded, however, as he glanced toward the bedroom stairs.

Esti shoved the blanket at him, embarrassed. "I didn't want you to be cold."

"Thank you." His wonder grew even stronger. "For the blanket, and for the thought. And thank you for . . ." He trailed off, searching her face.

Esti couldn't help blushing.

He sat up and took the blanket from her. "I apologize for frightening you yesterday. I truly wasn't planning to—to steal all of you, when I took over the role of Romeo. I can't deny I enjoyed being onstage, though, even if only for a moment. It's something I've always wanted to do."

She thought about the terrible way it had ended. "I didn't

mean to knock off your mask in front of everyone."

"It wasn't your fault. I shouldn't have hurt Greg. I shouldn't have destroyed the theater sets. Things got out of hand."

"Don't they always?" Esti tried to smile.

Alan wearily shook his head. "I'm so sorry. At least I had a chance to perform with you for a moment."

"I ruined it."

"No. You did nothing wrong." Alan stared at her, his eyes sad, then glanced at the bedroom stairs once more. "You have made my life better than I ever thought possible. I know the reverse is not true."

Before she could ask about her promise to him, he looked back at her. "Shall I compare thee to a summer's day?" His eyes softened as he put aside his despair to give her the only gift he could. "Thou art more lovely and more temperate."

Esti sank down on the other end of the couch, unable to tear herself away. This was the hold he had on her, then: his ability to weave Shakespeare's magic into her soul. It was something she couldn't explain to anyone, not even Rafe or Aurora. No one would understand the exquisite beauty Alan invoked to life, except maybe—Esti felt her throat grow tight—maybe her dad had understood. She closed her eyes, and the storm outside disappeared as Alan brought her under the spell of the most perfect sonnet ever written.

"But thy eternal summer shall not fade, nor lose possession of that fair thou owest," he finished. "Nor shall Death brag thou wander'st in his shade, when in eternal lines to time thou growest. So long as men can breathe or eyes can see; so long lives this and this gives life to thee."

She reached across the couch to take his hand.

"Esti." His gloved fingers tightened on hers. "It's almost sunrise. I think the hurricane is finally moving away."

* * *

She woke Rafe just as the sun was coming up. For a moment, he stared at her in confusion.

"What's going on?" he finally said.

"The hurricane's gone."

"Where's Somand?"

"Alan is outside, checking the damage."

"Quick." Rafe scrambled to his feet. "We gotta leave before he comes back."

"We can't get out of the sea cave without his help. The water is dangerous." Esti put her hands on his shoulders. "Listen."

The pounding of the storm-churned sea deep within the heart of Manchineel Cay seemed especially loud in the absence of the storm.

Rafe's expression tightened. "We'll find another way off the island. Once we make it to water, I can help you swim. The sea will be rough for hours, but it's not that far to Manchicay Beach."

"There is no other way off. The cay is as treacherous as the sea, believe me. And Alan's already been outside. He said manchineel is everywhere this morning, tossed around by the storm. The caves are the only way we can go, and I don't think either of us knows the path well enough to get there without him."

"Bull." Rafe clenched his fists. "He's trying to scare you. I'm getting you out of here."

"He promised to lead the way as soon as he comes back. It won't be long."

"And you *believe* him?"

"He's never lied to me." She suddenly frowned, listening hard. Through the deep pounding beneath them, she heard something new, a sharper, chopping sound.

"Helicopter," Rafe whooped, leaping for the stairs. "They're looking for us."

"No!" Esti raced after him, dragging him to a stop on the top step. "We can't let them see us."

He stared at her in disbelief. "What?"

"His house is secret." She desperately hoped it was still camouflaged from above, after the storm damage.

"What is wrong with you?" Rafe exploded. "They're trying to *rescue* you." He pulled away from her and headed across the living room. Alan had already opened the big porch doors, a tangled mass of fallen trees and vines obscuring the irregular porch outside.

"Rafe, stop." Esti grabbed his arm.

"Are you saying you don't want to be rescued?"

"I'm saying I can't ruin the rest of Alan's life."

"He kidnapped you!"

"He won't keep me here against my will."

"I don't know what he's doing to your head, but he's fooled—"

"He won't hurt me, Rafe. Please don't force me to do something I know is wrong."

"This is all his own fault," Rafe snapped, turning to the door. "That's what it's about."

"No, it's about compassion." Determination gave her sudden strength, and she pulled Rafe from the doorway. As the helicopter chopped loudly above, her heart caught in her throat. "If you go outside now, you'll hurt him more than you can imagine. Think what the jandam will do when they see him, under the circumstances. They'll destroy him."

The shadow of the helicopter passed overhead, and she instinctively ducked, holding her breath as it went by. "Please, please trust me."

Although Rafe's eyebrows drew together, he didn't move. "I know I'll regret this," he finally said, "but you can call the shots. I think I understand why you always protect him, but I don't trust him at all. He gets one chance to prove himself."

Weak with relief, Esti wrapped her arms around him. She felt his fingers twine fiercely through her hair.

"You sure don't make it easy, babe."

Alan returned a couple of minutes later, gasping for breath. He studied them from the front doorway, his mottled face expressionless. Rafe kept his arms around Esti, and she didn't try to pull away.

"Get your shoes on," Alan finally said, turning to wait for them on the path.

Esti didn't look back as she followed Alan away from the house. The morning sun had already burned through the high cirrus clouds, oblivious to the destruction wrought just hours before. Thick humidity weighed down the air, nearly as heavy as the water dripping from the trees. She could practically smell the coming decay from the dead animals and vegetation Rafe said always followed a hurricane.

The trip to the cave no longer meant a smooth trail through the forest. Torrents of rain had slicked the dirt into a slippery soup of mud and red clay; broken trees and branches crisscrossed in front of them. Esti followed numbly, climbing over fallen trees and catching herself when her feet slid out from under her. Although Alan frequently pointed at manchineel or ketch-n-keep to avoid, he didn't speak.

The chop of the helicopter approached again before they had gone very far. Alan spun around with a tight expression, but Esti had already grabbed Rafe's hand, dragging him under the cover of a bay rum tree that still had a few leaves left after the storm. Alan quickly joined them, his blue eyes uneasy as he met Rafe's grim stare. The helicopter roared past, police markings stark against its side. After a moment Alan started forward again.

By the time they reached the end of the trail, Esti was drenched with sweat and red mud, grateful for the cool darkness of the cave. The pounding sea vibrated through the rocks. Alan surprised her by picking up a powerful flashlight just inside the cave opening, and she studied the tunnel as they descended into the cay. Irregular walls followed an oddly smooth arc over her head, occasionally dipping low enough that Rafe had to duck.

"Flattened lava tube," he muttered, antagonism warring with his natural curiosity. As Alan led them into another branching cave, Rafe pointed to a disabled wind generator spanning the breezy space.

They came upon the sea with a suddenness that startled Esti. She should have known by the drum of water inside the cavern, but the tunnel had seemed much longer in the dark. Several shafts of sunlight pierced the large space from above, and Alan placed his flashlight on a rocky ledge.

A shiver of apprehension swept through Esti as she watched the water level rise nearly to the boat at their feet, beating fiercely into the rocks and niches of smaller adjacent caves. Then the sea dropped away, gradually exposing a narrow, sunlit sliver in the rocks in front of them. *That* tiny opening was the only way out of the cay?

"Come on," Rafe said as the water began rising again. He pointed to the scuba gear he'd stowed inside the little rowboat. "You're wearing the vest, babe. It'll help you float while we swim home."

Esti looked at him, beautiful and full of energy, impatient and eager to get out of this eerie place and move on with life. Beside him, Alan studied her impassively, his blue eyes resigned to his lonely fate. He'd known all along that she would break her promise, and he wasn't going to challenge her.

As the catapult grabbed her one last time, she knew it

wasn't merely about compassion; it was about friendship and honor and betrayal. No matter what she did now, the choice was wrong. Romeo's dagger had found its sheath in the hearts of everyone she loved.

She stepped forward and wrapped her arms around Rafe, pulling his head down to hers for a last, fierce kiss. Then she pushed him away.

"You go ahead, Rafe. I'm staying here."

Act Three. Scene Nine.

"I made her promise to stay." Alan's sharp reply followed her words so quickly that Esti lurched back. He didn't even glance at her as he cut off Rafe's furious protest. "I agreed to save your life, Rafe Solomon, only after Esti promised to give me her life in return." His words echoed in the cavern.

Esti pressed her hands against her face, unable to meet Rafe's disbelieving stare.

"But Esti taught me something after I snatched you from the hurricane," Alan continued, the power of his voice seemingly all that kept Rafe from attacking him. "Even if she gives me her life, she can't heal me. If I keep Esti against her will, my misery will consume me until I am destroyed. Perhaps, as Legard would say, I have more control over my life than that."

Rafe scowled.

Alan turned back to Esti, his expression strangely joyful. "It's enough for me to know that you would do it, Esti. Now, I'll take you far enough away from my lady to make sure you're safe."

"Alan—"

"You have to share your talent with the world, as Legard did."

"I don't know if I can." She ached so deeply, she could barely speak.

"Esti." Alan's expression became severe. "The actress lives in every fiber of your being. You would have spent your life longing for the stage, even had Legard been a garbage collector, and I"—he glanced at Rafe—"a bartender."

Rafe's eyes narrowed.

"You will be happier with Rafe." Alan's mouth twisted in a painful smile. "I love you, Esti, but your life is not better with me in it. You need someone who can shine with you, and that person is not me. I would not survive your spotlight."

"But onstage you could—"

"All the world is not a stage."

The painful truth of his words made it hard for Esti to speak. "What will you do?"

He shook his head. "I will never forget you. Now get in the boat, both of you."

Still scowling, Rafe quickly detached the life vest from the rest of his scuba gear. Numb, Esti let him slip the vest over her shoulders, trying to stay calm as Alan dragged the rowboat partway down the slope. As soon as they settled inside, Alan shoved the boat free, plunging the oars into the water.

"*Chupse,*" Rafe hissed.

She reluctantly looked up. The exit was barely visible beneath the high water. Alan watched over his shoulder, waiting for the sea to recede. As the water level began going down, he pulled at the oars. The little boat shot toward the rock wall. Rafe's hand tightened painfully around Esti's as they slid through the narrow slot.

The moment they emerged, the boat rose up along the side of a tremendous wave. Esti clamped her lips together to keep from crying out, as the sea pushed them back toward the side of the cliff. The tendons in Alan's neck stood out as he rowed with all his strength, pulling them over the crest of the wave and away from the cay.

Esti barely heard the sharp crack of wood over the crashing water, but the sudden look on Alan's face sent a chill of terror through her. She met his eyes as he held up the broken oar.

"Jump!" he ordered.

Before Esti could move, Rafe was dragging her over the side of the boat with him. As water closed over her head, she felt Rafe grabbing the shoulder strap of her life vest. It seemed like forever before the vest brought her back to the surface. Gasping, she tried to kick in the direction Rafe pulled her.

By the time he stopped long enough for Esti to look around, she was already exhausted. They hadn't gotten very far. When the next wave lifted them high in the air, she cried out in horror. Pieces of the rowboat churned in the spray against the cliff, breaking up even as she watched.

Alan had disappeared.

"Alan!" she screamed, frantically searching the water with her eyes before she and Rafe slid into the oncoming trough. Rafe grabbed her vest with both hands as she tried to pull away from him.

"You can't do anything!" he yelled over the crashing waves. "We gotta get out of here."

She knew he was right. Her mind wailed in protest as she turned and followed him. Torn seaweed and leaves, and entire uprooted trees floated on the surface with them. They swam forever through the flotsam-strewn swells.

She vaguely heard Rafe tell her the current was helping them, but the words meant nothing. Eventually she heard the police helicopter overhead and saw Rodney above, speaking urgently into a radio.

She didn't realize they had made it to shore until her bare feet scraped against sand. Somewhere she had lost her shoes. Rafe dragged her through the rolling surf, and they both lunged forward as a large wave pushed them onto the beach. Rafe stumbled and went down, and she tripped over him before she could stop herself, gagging on the salt water that filled her mouth and nose.

Then someone helped them up, pulling both of them past the high water mark. Carmen and Chaz, she realized, soaking wet and looking more frightened than Esti had ever seen either one of them. As she collapsed on the sand beside

Rafe, choking for air, Aurora flung her arms around them both.

"Esti," she sobbed in relief. "Oh God, I knew Rafe had to somehow save you. We all spent the night in the theater, and the storm was horrible, and I was so terrified . . ."

Esti leaned against her mom, crying with her. She felt Rafe's hand, and she tightened her fingers on his, clutching him like a lifeline. After a few moments, she looked at the blurry crowd held at bay beyond George Moore. On Rafe's other side, his mom merely shook her head, tears streaming down her face.

The helicopter landed down the beach from where they sat. Esti's mouth dropped open as she looked around. The hurricane had destroyed Manchicay Beach, stripping much of the sand down to bare rock and leaving trash and dead trees in its wake.

Every bit as startling were the crowds of people Esti hadn't noticed when she stumbled out of the water. Frederick studied her with tired, red-rimmed eyes. The cast huddled behind him, most of them standing with their parents. Around them, a vast throng of dark faces stared at Esti. The entire island had gathered on the beach, it seemed, to see if Rafe would rescue her from the jumbee.

Rodney climbed down from the helicopter, followed by Officer Wilmuth. Rafe's dad looked exhausted as he walked toward them. "You okay?" he asked, coming to a stop.

"Yeah, mon," Rafe replied calmly. "Matter fix."

"*Chupse.*" His dad shook his head. "I have always know you

give me a heart attack, Rafe. But you girlfriend she does steal the show."

"Like I always say, the paparazzi are going to love her," Carmen added from beside her.

Esti almost smiled.

Rodney's expression softened as he studied Esti. "The jandam are headed back over to Manchineel Cay now, and they need—"

"No," Rafe said. He picked up Esti's hand again, very gently this time. "The jumbee is dead."

A small sound reached Esti's ears, practically inaudible over Aurora's cry of relief and the murmuring of the crowd. The voice matched the ache in Esti's heart, and she looked around in time to see Ma Harris sag against Domino.

"What you mean?" Officer Wilmuth stepped forward.

"He drowned." Rafe looked up at the policeman. "That's what I mean."

"You saw he?" the officer insisted.

"Yeah mon, I saw he."

"Jumbee them can die, for true?"

"What you think?" Rafe snapped. "I ain't no jumbee expert."

Lucia's mom straightened as everyone turned to her. Her face showed no emotion, but the ache inside Esti grew stronger at the look in Ma Harris's dark eyes.

"Manchineel Cay is danger," the woman said. "It have death for anyone set dey foot on it. Leave it be." She turned and walked toward the parking lot.

Lucia gave Esti a sympathetic glance, then followed her mom, holding Quintin's hand.

Esti looked back at Manchineel Cay. It took a moment for the movement at the top of the barren cliff to register in her mind, and then the dark silhouette disappeared. Rafe's fingers tightened convulsively on hers. He'd seen it too.

Alan was alive.

Esti's mind raced. He must have climbed up to the exposed cliff to watch them swim to Cariba. He had risked discovery by the helicopter to make sure they made it home.

"Rafe and Esti had survive," Officer Wilmuth pointed out in a determined voice. "If the jumbee he dead, the cay—"

"Is haunted," Rafe interrupted. "You don't want to go there, believe me."

In surprise, Esti realized what Rafe was trying to do. He wanted to protect Alan.

For her.

As his hand caressed hers, she felt a rush of love for him. Taking a deep breath, she forced herself to stand, pulling Rafe up with her. Aurora scrambled to her feet beside them.

"Rafe convinced the jumbee to let me go," Esti said to Officer Wilmuth. The people around them stared at Rafe in awe.

Esti heard Frederick's voice telling his New York friends how Esti's real-life drama added to the emotional depth she was capable of. They should have *seen* how Esti took on the ghost, he exclaimed softly, when it tried to destroy the theater the other night. Not even a jumbee could possibly touch a fabulous talent like Esti Legard.

She didn't have to fake the tremor in her voice as she continued. "The jumbee paid for what he did," she said. "He'll never bother me again."

Officer Wilmuth still studied her with troubled eyes, and she remembered the afternoon he politely sat beside her to ask for Paul's last words. Sadness swept through her as she realized he could never know the truth about his nephew's death. She almost reached out to touch his hand, then thought better of it.

"Just leave it be," she whispered.

She turned to Frederick, surrounded by the cast and his cadre of friends whose plans had been destroyed. With a deep breath, she met his eyes. *You're the one in control, Esti. No one else.*

"Shall we try one more time?" she said. "If the rest of the cast is up to it, give me a call after I've had a chance to recover. What about tomorrow?"

"Are you serious?" Frederick lit up like a little boy in a candy shop. "Yes, darling, I'll make it happen! Somehow I'll make it happen."

"Mr. Mackenzie . . ." Officer Wilmuth trailed off in disgust. He turned and walked back toward the helicopter.

No one tried to stop Esti as she turned away from Manchicay Beach. She heard voices behind her, sensed Rafe and Aurora following while George held the crowd back. As she passed the open shower area, she saw a Jeep parked within its low walls, left there by Rafe in his frenzy to follow her. Beyond the showers, a rusty blue pickup made its slow way across the crowded parking lot, Lucia and Quintin looking solemnly at her from the open bed.

With a start, Esti suddenly knew what she had to do. Exploding with a burst of determined energy, she sprinted across the wet gravel as fast as she could in her bare feet.

Domino sped up as their eyes met through the windshield, but she reached the exit first, gasping for breath. He braked hard, skidding on the gravel and coming to a stop inches away from her. Grabbing the edge of the truck so Domino wouldn't drive past, Esti strode to the open passenger window.

Lucia's mom stared straight ahead.

"He's alive." Esti leaned in the window. "But he's without a boat now. The cay destroyed his old one."

She recoiled at the fierce look Ma Harris gave her, her numb fingers slipping from the rusty door.

"He needs you," Esti said. She closed her aching eyes and pressed her forehead to the door frame for a moment. "He's so lonely out there. Please take care of him."

When she stepped back, she almost expected to be hit by gravel from spinning tires. Ma Harris still didn't look at her, but the truck pulled away more soberly than it had approached.

"What are you doing?" Aurora caught up to Esti, her voice tired and helpless. "I thought this was finally over. Why are you talking to Ma Harris?"

"It's over." Esti met her mom's eyes. "I just wanted her to hear it from me."

They both turned and watched the truck until it reached a bend in the road. Quintin and Lucia glanced back at them as the truck disappeared from sight.

"Okay, Esti." Aurora sighed. "Okay. But we're going to Ashland as soon as the airport opens."

"Why?"

Her mom stared at her.

"Why do we have to leave?" Alan had released her from her promise, and she wouldn't run away now. "I told Frederick I would play Juliet tomorrow. As much as I love the land of eternal Shakespeare, you know what will happen in Ashland. I'll fall back into Dad's shadow, where no one can see *me*."

"People have always seen you, sweetie," Aurora said, but her eyes slowly softened. "Was it really that bad?"

Esti nodded.

"You should stay," Rafe said, wrapping his arms around Esti's waist from behind. "My dad says Esti needs to graduate from here. It's important for Manchicay School."

Aurora's eyes flashed in anger. "I will do what's safest for Esti, not what's best for your dad."

"Why isn't it safe?" Esti leaned her head against Rafe's soggy T-shirt. "Alan isn't a problem anymore."

Aurora hesitated, then looked at Rafe, her face hard and unforgiving. "Rafe Solomon."

His arms tightened in surprise. "Yeah?"

"After everything you've done for Esti," Aurora said steadily, "I don't doubt that you'll risk your life for her. But I'm not staying here unless you swear you're not lying. Is Alan dead? Tell me the truth."

Esti squeezed her eyes shut.

"He was in a boat, Aurora," Rafe said. "Esti and I were swimming when we saw the boat crash against the cliffs and break apart, then a little while later I saw his body. Esti, did you see it?"

Without opening her eyes, she slowly nodded.

"Nobody could survive a boat crash like that." Rafe gently kissed the top of Esti's head. "And I swear I'm not lying. My life is going to get a lot more boring now. Maybe I'll learn some Shakespeare, so Esti doesn't get tired of me."

Esti pressed her fists into her aching eyes, overwhelmed by Rafe's trust in her—and in Alan. Turning to him, she pulled his head down to hers.

"You've proven your honor," she finally whispered. "I'll make sure your life isn't boring." As she cupped his face with her hands, kissing him again and again, she felt him smile against her lips.

"Esti," Aurora finally said, relief evident in her tired voice. "Back off. Didn't your mother ever teach you any manners?"

Epilogue

The old stone building buzzed with anticipation. A corner of the roof had peeled away, as if mangled by a giant can opener, and water still soaked all the chairs in the back rows. Generators growled outside, providing the theater with mostly steady lighting and a faint reek of burning fuel. Several of Frederick's friends had joined the cleanup, good-naturedly moving enough debris from the parking lot to accommodate at least half the usual amount of cars.

From the humid dressing room, Esti occasionally heard Rafe's voice, laughing and chatting in the front row as the theater filled. She sat at her table, staring into the mirror as she pulled back her hair. Although the entire cast was packed into the small room, they were subdued as they each put the final touches on their makeup. Esti couldn't miss the surreptitious looks thrown at her from the moment she walked in.

"You sure you're okay?" Carmen said for the third time in as many minutes. "Do you want another triple chocolate coconut cookie?"

"I'm good."

"I know you're *good*," Carmen said, rolling her eyes, "but no stage fright this time?" She pinned Juliet's cap on Esti's hair, smoothing a few stray brown wisps under the hairpin.

"A little." Esti reached up to squeeze Carmen's hand. "Have I ever told you what a great friend you are?"

Dropping into the chair beside her, Carmen grinned. "Dang, Jane—no. Esti Legard. It's about time." And then she began to sniffle.

"Esti," Danielle said unexpectedly from the door. "I'm glad you're safe."

. As Esti looked over in surprise, she became aware of the deathly silence in the room, broken only by Carmen's muffled breaths. Everyone had frozen, staring at Esti. They all looked frightened.

"We were all so worried." Danielle was the first to break the silence, her voice clear even over the buzz from the other room. She sank down in a chair beside Greg. "I'm sorry. I don't know how you . . ." She trailed off, her determined blue eyes telling Esti all the things she couldn't put into words. "Did the jumbee really take you to Manchineel Cay?"

Esti glanced around the room, and slowly nodded. "Yes, he took me to Manchineel Cay."

She could swear that all the breathing in the room had stopped. Lucia pulled back the curtain of the girls' changing area, sticking her head out to listen.

"But you know what?" Esti added firmly. "He never hurt me, not once. And he let me go."

"Because of Rafe," Carmen said, wiping her eyes. "Rafe Solomon actually swam through a hurricane to rescue you."

"Yes." Warmth spread through Esti's body at the thought. "Rafe is amazing."

"You've changed Cariba's bad boy into a respectable boy-friend." Somehow Carmen turned her hiccups into an exaggerated gesture of awe. "You *do* have supernatural powers."

Esti heard Lucia's faint chuckle as the changing area curtain dropped back into place. The sound seemed to break the spell, and suddenly everyone wanted details about the hideous monster and the haunted cay.

"Stop!" Esti jumped to her feet. The overwhelming chatter stopped as instantly as it had begun. "I'm Juliet now. I'm going onstage for a minute to get in the mood. When I come back, I need to be in Verona, surrounded by Capulets and Montagues."

She took a deep, shuddering breath and looked around the room. "Please?"

As every head in the cramped dressing room began nodding, she decided she would rewrite her dad's famous mantra. *If you pretend you're in control, people will believe you.*

She walked to the door, hesitating as she reached Greg. "Art thou not Romeo," she asked, "and a Montague?"

He raised his eyebrows. "Neither, fair maid, if either thee dislike."

"How's your head?"

"I'm fine, Leg-guard." He shrugged in embarrassment. "What about *your* head?"

"I'm fine," she said. "Ten more minutes, then look out, Romeo."

He grinned.

She didn't smell any frangipani when she stopped in the

middle of the darkened stage, merely diesel fumes drifting in from the generators outside. On the other side of the heavy stage curtain, she heard Rafe proclaim over the murmuring crowd that Esti was the bravest girl he'd ever met. Aurora's voice merged with that of George, both of them sounding hopeful and upbeat.

Despite herself, Esti grinned.

She tilted her head to look up at the darkened ceiling, toward the high area that had once hidden a parabolic sound reflector. After a moment, she forced her eyes to move to the catwalk.

"Paul Wilmuth," she whispered, "I finally got my chance at Juliet. In Alan's name, I dedicate this performance to you."

Alan deserved everything she could do for him without forcing him into the spotlight. She had seen a hint of grudging respect between him and Rafe. If she could fan that spark into friendship, Rafe would never again be bored. Ma Harris might truly be Alan's friend now, and Lucia seemed ready for the challenge, not to mention Quintin, who didn't fear anyone. Maybe even Aurora would come around eventually. Alan didn't have to spend his life alone; Esti would make sure of it. Her father would be proud of her.

Now she knew what Alan had meant when he said the actor was stronger than the father—and the friend. The actor controlled every breath her dad took, every decision he made. Perhaps it was the core of his magnificence, but it was also his greatest weakness. His compassion was limited.

And compassion was the only way Esti would truly escape

his shadow. Alan had forced her to see the beauty of the beast, the courage behind fear, the truth within lies. Those gifts would always guide her when she searched for the complex character in her script. Compassion, not control, would be the mantra of Esti Legard. Compassion and honesty.

With a smile, she focused her emotions into those of a naive girl. Slowly the chattering audience on the other side of the curtain became vendors hawking their wares on the streets of Verona. As she smiled at the delicious thought of Romeo in cornrows, the warmth inside her body began to grow. With a wondering smile, she headed back to the dressing room.

Juliet was ready to get onstage.

The End